MIDNIGHT

at the

WANDERING

VINEYARD

Also available from
Jamie Raintree
and Graydon House Books

Perfectly Undone

Jamie Raintree

MIDNIGHT

at the

WANDERING

VINEYARD

GRAYDON
HOUSE

GRAYDON
HOUSE

Recycling programs
for this product may
not exist in your area.

ISBN-13: 978-1-525-80600-1

Midnight at the Wandering Vineyard

Copyright © 2019 by Jamie Raintree

GraydonHouseBooks.com
BookClubbish.com

Printed in U.S.A.

To the sisters I'm raising.

May you always be best friends.

MIDNIGHT

at the

WANDERING

VINEYARD

ONE

*T*he summer before I left for college, I lost everything. I lost my best friend, I lost my heart, and I lost my grasp on all the plans I had for my future.

I lost who I was.

Some goodbyes were inevitable. Like leaving my parents to move to New York, where I would attend Columbia University. That alone would have been difficult enough. Half my heart never left the family vineyard, with all the memories that were made there, all the people I loved. The other half of me was tentatively stepping out into the world on the wobbly legs of a fawn, ready to run.

There were also unexpected goodbyes. A lost love. My first. He walked into my life that summer, seemingly with the sole purpose to make me question everything I believed about life, relationships, and myself. By the time I got on the plane, I'd been shaken, broken down to the core, ready for a fresh start if there ever was one.

Then there was the devastating goodbye. After one too

many bad decisions, my best friend—the person I considered a sister—walked away from our ten years of friendship with one final, ultimate blow: the declaration that she didn't know who I was anymore. The implication that she didn't want to. I couldn't blame her. That summer I did things I didn't know I was capable of, and I hurt her. But after everything we'd been through, I was sure there was nothing that could ever break us apart. I was wrong.

But despite the years that have passed and my many heartbreaks our small wine town has witnessed, it calls me back, pulling at my heartstrings. I sense it now—its unique gravity—at eleven minutes before midnight as I take the final right turn onto the dirt road that leads to The Wandering Vineyard.

My home.

I snap the radio off in the little four-door rental car and sit up straighter in my seat. With a knee on the steering wheel, I twist the elastic out of my thick hair and shake it out in preparation for the greeting I've looked forward to all day, and every day that's passed since my last visit. Then, so I don't disturb anyone, I switch off my headlights, drowning the car and the expansive property in darkness. The car continues to jostle down the long drive, the moonlight guiding my way, and I wait for the house to come into view. It's been almost ten years since I left Paso Robles and moved to New York but the scents, the sounds, the feeling that washes over me is the same. Home never changes.

That's what I love most about it, but also why I couldn't stay.

I roll down the windows to let in the warm spring night as I drive beneath the arching welcome sign, and past the refurbished barn turned tasting room, the paint still as fresh looking as the day I helped roll it on. Though the dozens of acres of land that surround me are shrouded in darkness, I can picture it in my mind's eye. The rolling hills, the trails I've trodden a thousand times, the smell of the dry earth, the bitterness of unripened grapes on my tongue. I know the song every tree sings when the wind blows, calling me out into the hills… farther, farther.

When I reach the top of the hill, the house finally appears— a dark ghost, looming in the distance. It's the house I grew up in, the porch light on like a beacon. Farther up, the outbuildings come into view. The stables. *The guest house.* I think of him still.

I swallow back the memories and creep my way up the parking lot, dust and gravel betraying my arrival, and park next to my dad's new pickup. When I turn off the engine, it's deathly silent. So silent I feel the pressure on my eardrums. The kind of silence that doesn't exist in New York City.

I tiptoe down the path to the stables. The barn door clicks as I lift the hatch and pull it open. I leave the lights off. I can walk the path to Midnight's stall with my eyes closed, but enough moonlight shines through the high windows that I don't have to. It's a full moon. A sign, maybe.

"Midnight," I call into the open space. The only sound is the rustle of live animals.

I call again and when her nose pokes into the breezeway, I let loose a laugh, no longer caring about waking anyone. I close the space between us and open my palm to her silky lips.

"Hey, girl," I coo. "I've missed you so much."

Between earning my degree at Columbia, working random, low-earning jobs to pay for it, and then landing my first position at a respected marketing firm, my visits home have been few and far between. The last time I was back here was two long years ago, and the love of my horse—that fierce, accepting, unwavering kind of love—is what I've missed the most. I rub my fingers over the length of her nose and rest my cheek against hers.

When she grows antsy, I grab Midnight's halter from the wall and lift the stall door latch. With the quick motion of a choreographed routine, I slide the halter over her muzzle and lead her out of the stall. Her dark color blends into the night, aside from her white haunches, which practically glow. Her coat shimmers with every subtle shift of her hooves.

"Want to go for a run, girl?" I ask.

"Not even gonna say hi first, are you?" a rough voice responds.

I start, my hair whipping over my shoulder as I look behind me. The light in the stable office flicks on, and my dad stands in the doorway. He leans against the frame with his hands in the pockets of his jeans, holes in the knees, because all his jeans have holes in the knees. But his jaw is smooth and his plaid button-down is one of the two he saves for holidays. He dressed up for my homecoming.

"Dad," I say, breathless. I run to him and throw my arms around his neck, allow myself to be enveloped in his earthy scent, his subtle strength, and his love.

"You are in big trouble, Mallory Victoria," he says, his voice watery. "You are not allowed to leave your room for the next twenty years. No, make that thirty."

"I missed you, too," I whisper in his ear, grinning.

"Could've fooled me." He gives a gruff laugh and nods toward Midnight.

I shrug, unabashed. Anyone who knows me would expect nothing less.

Dad takes my shoulders and holds me at a distance. He looks me over and shakes his head, tears brimming in his eyes.

"How did you get so grown-up?" he asks. "You were still a little girl when you left."

"I saw you last Christmas," I laugh.

"Is that what you call handing each other gifts over the

salt and pepper shakers at a restaurant I can't even remember the name of?"

"Sorry, Dad. But any apartment this girl can afford isn't big enough for houseguests. I don't even have a full set of dishes." I laugh. "I appreciated you coming, though. And I love the necklace."

I dig the pendant out from beneath my shirt—an abstract outline of a horse, its mane blowing in the wind of my breath.

Dad rubs his calloused thumb across the white gold surface and his smile saddens.

"Hey, none of that," I say, nudging his shoulder. "Save that for when I leave."

"You just got here and you're already talking about leaving?" He groans and feigns stabbing himself in the heart.

I have a flight booked for a week from now, the day after the planting party I've returned home for. At least that's the excuse I've given my boss and myself. Subconsciously, I rub the dark symbol inside my right wrist. When I catch myself, I drop my hands.

"Dad, don't be dramatic."

"Oh, go on," he says, shooing me toward Midnight.

"Are you sure?" I ask, even as I'm stepping toward her.

"Go on."

I smile, plant a kiss on Dad's cheek, then grab hold of Midnight's mane. I throw my leg over her bare back, send one last glance toward the only man I could ever really depend on, and then with the quick hitch of my heel, Midnight trots out of the stables into the night.

When I wake in the morning, the sun is high in the sky, lighting up my childhood room in a soft orange glow. Just behind my eyelids are memories of the night before—the pounding of Midnight's hooves against the earth, my hair in the wind, the moon chasing after us. The images flash in my mind like the highlights of a lover's tryst. I tried to find a substitute for this feeling in New York but nothing else has come close—not praise from my boss, not presenting a successful pitch, not a first kiss, not getting lost on an endless beach. The closest I get are these dreams. But when I open my eyes this time, I'm actually here.

Not all of my reasons for coming home are so sweet, though. And if the good memories come back so easily, the bad ones can't be far behind. I groan and pull a pillow over my eyes.

Half an hour later, I finally drag myself out of bed and rummage through my suitcase for running clothes, the only casual attire I own. I catch a glimpse of my old riding boots sitting in the corner of my room where I left them, worn in and dusty. I pause, reminiscing on a time when they were practically part of my body, and then lace up my tennis shoes.

Outside, the weather is cool but the undercurrent of warmth that seeps up from the dry ground promises that summer will be here soon. I never have gotten used to the penetratingly cold New York winters, and the sun on my skin warms me to the core. There's a hint of moisture in the air, which we only get in Southern California when the heavens are smiling down on us. I send a prayer to the sky—the new vines we'll be sowing at the planting party will need a healthy amount of water to acclimate to the new soil.

When I reach the stables, Tiramisu's stall is open and I hear the clanking of a bucket on the horse feeder. I already know who it is. I stop at the entrance and say, "Hey, cowboy."

The bucket clatters to the ground and I cover my ears with my hands, laughing. When Tyler peers around the corner, his eyes light up and his jaw hangs open.

"No way," he says. I laugh as he jogs toward me, wraps his arms around my waist and spins me. "Your dad told me you were coming back and I didn't believe him. But shit, you're actually here."

His mouth is still slack as he looks me over, gauging how much I've changed. I haven't seen him since my last summer here, after which, according to Dad, Tyler also went in search of greener pastures. And yet, here we both are again.

"Look at you," he says. "You're, like, a woman." He stumbles on the last word like it's explicit. Tyler and I have always had a sibling-like relationship, especially since neither one of us have any of our own. But we haven't seen each other since I was eighteen and he was twenty-two. I *am* a woman now.

"Look at you," I counter. He's changed, too. His face isn't as soft as it used to be, having grown into its angles. His cheeks are scruffy with strawberry stubble where it was once as smooth as a freshly polished saddle. He's still got the stocky muscle of a working man, though.

I swipe his baseball cap and run my fingers through his cropped red hair. It's darker. "You've grown up yourself."

"And still no cowboy hat," he says, snatching his cap back from me and pulling it onto his head.

"I'll get you one for your birthday."

"You wouldn't dare."

I shrug. "Part of being a woman. I'm more stubborn than ever."

"As if that's possible."

I smack him on the arm playfully and he laughs. Something foreign stirs inside me at the exchange. I clear my throat.

"Want to go for a ride?" he asks. "I was just about to saddle up Rocket."

"Like you have to ask."

A few minutes later, as we ride out between the vines, Tyler says, "Ten years, Mal. Jeez."

He draws out the words as he sits atop Rocket, a large

American Warmblood who stands two hands above Midnight and me. Rocket's coat is a splotched dark brown and white, like chocolate milk not fully mixed together. He is technically Dad's horse, though my parents rarely ride, trusting Tyler to manage the vineyard trail rides. Rocket's affection for Tyler is obvious and understandable, being the only person who can handle his unruly nature.

Midnight and Rocket saunter side by side through the rows of grapevines that spread as far as the eye can see. Looking out to the east, I see the plot of land that has been prepared for the new vines, the trellises currently standing empty, waiting. Having been gone for so long, I appreciate its growth anew. Dad moved us here twenty-one years ago when the Paso Robles wine country was just *up*, not so much *coming*.

"Has it gotten quieter since I was here last?" I ask.

Tyler laughs. "No. You just have a lower tolerance for it."

"I couldn't even sleep last night. I swear, I could feel it pressing in on me."

"You went and turned into a city girl on us, didn't you?"

I narrow my eyes at him, assaulting him with a long glare. "Never."

He laughs. "When was the last time you even rode a horse?"

I hesitate. "Yesterday? Well, how many stables do you think there are in New York City?"

"Fair enough," he says.

Tyler and I point the horses up the trail that leads to the top of the hill overlooking the vineyard. Tyler lets me lead, and I breathe in the fresh air. Midnight rocks side to side beneath me with every step and the sensation is so familiar, I could be a teenager again, full of hope and confusion…love and a broken heart.

"So your boss finally let you take a vacation?" he asks.

"Something like that," I say.

"What's it actually like?"

I smile. Tyler hasn't changed at all—always a straight-to-the-point kind of guy—and I adore that more than I probably should. People are supposed to change. Life is supposed to march on. But it's been nice to imagine that home has been frozen in time, here waiting for me when I was ready to come back. With Tyler, at least, that seems to have proven true.

"I'm up for promotion," I say. "Which isn't necessarily the best time for a vacation but once I get it, I'll be even busier. I don't know when I'll get another chance. My boss can be pretty demanding—it's just the norm in the marketing industry. She really didn't want to let me come but... I had to."

Tyler nods but doesn't push. "Assistant marketing manager, your dad said? What exactly does an assistant marketing manager do?" Tyler asks, unabashed by his own ignorance. He has little interest in the corporate world and makes no apologies for it.

"I would be working more directly with clients of the firm and helping oversee the project teams. Coming up with strategies to promote client products and services. Basically, we make sure their messaging is clear, concise, and catchy." When Tyler gives me a blank stare, I add, "You know, product names, slogans, web content, ad content..."

I trail off when Tyler shows no signs of catching on. A nervous laugh slips through my lips. I assumed coming home would be awkward, but it's as if I'm speaking a different language.

"I'm sure you're very good at it," he offers.

I shrug. "I suppose. My boss kind of took me under her wing during my internship there. I'm not entirely sure what she saw in me, but I'm glad she did."

"I know what she saw," Tyler says, a twinkle in his eye. I glance away, uncomfortable with his flattery.

"Well, I learned my diligence from the best."

I learned from Kelly.

At the thought of my best friend—I refuse to think of our friendship in the past tense—my smile falters.

We climb the final incline, focusing on avoiding the sharp, dry tree limbs overhead. I used to be able to maneuver around every branch that jutted out, thirsty for blood. Now there are too many, the path less trodden.

We reach the top and Tyler brings Rocket to a trot next to me. We lead the horses to the break in the trees, stopping at the edge where we can see the entire property. Straight ahead is the house, on top of the bare hill, the other buildings snuggled around it. The grapevines spray out in every direction like the sun's rays. I used to sit here and memorize the horizon for hours.

"Why did you have to come home?"

Tyler asks the question I've asked myself a thousand times over the last few weeks.

"Why now? Really?"

I take a deep breath, letting it out slowly. Why now, indeed? I'm building a life in New York. I have an amazing job at a top marketing firm. I have an apartment that isn't much, but it's mine. I've been there for a decade, which seems impossible. And yet, it never quite feels like home. There's something here I can't let go of.

Not something. *Someone.*

Kelly.

I hoped that if I could talk to my best friend, explain why I made the choices I did our last summer together, she might forgive me and I could stop carrying around the guilt for the mistakes I made. I could stop holding on to the past and fully step into my future.

The problem is, she hasn't spoken a word to me since I left.

"When I take this promotion," I finally say, "I want to feel settled. I want to be all in."

Tyler's expression is curious as he tries to apply this new information to the Mallory he used to know. The old Mallory didn't think through decisions like this. She made one and let the cards fall where they may. But the stakes are so much higher now. I don't trust myself anymore.

"What?" I ask.

"I don't know. It's just...you usually run headlong into any opportunity that presents itself. That's kind of your thing."

I find a loose leaf of leather on Midnight's saddle and pick at it. "Well, I'm not a teenager anymore. Everyone is a little reckless when they're teenagers."

"Some things don't change."

"Some things do."

"Maybe. Maybe not." He winks, taking some of the pressure off the conversation.

"You know," I say, "you talk a lot for a cowboy."

"I'm not a cowboy."

Tyler moves Rocket sideways until he's close enough to hook his arm around my neck, pulling me into a rough hug.

"It's good to have you back," he says.

I slip my arm around his waist. The way his T-shirt sticks to his back hints at the sheen of sweat beneath and reminds me of many summer days spent washing horses and polishing saddles with him.

"It's good to be here," I say.

"You see Kelly yet?" he asks, reading my mind.

I let my arm fall away from him.

"No. I haven't."

TWO

My last summer at home with Kelly started off with long, hot days and an innocent ease—horseback rides and binge-watching our favorite TV shows in my bedroom, an attempt to escape the dry summer heat that seeped into our bones, leaving us languid and drunk on freedom. That first week, Kelly almost never left my house and that was how it was supposed to be for the next three months. We were set to leave for Columbia together in the fall, but we planned to have one last adventure at home, knowing that adulthood would change us, that once we left Paso, nothing would ever be the same.

But things began to change sooner than either one of us expected, the day I started my summer job with my dad.

Just that morning, Kelly had made me promise for the third time that my summer job wouldn't get in the way of our plans. She would be working at the coffee shop but her ability to clock out ensured we could have our grand adventures around her schedule. After eleven years of running and living on a vineyard, my dad no longer had any use for clocks—a trait I may have inherited from him, not that I would ever admit to it. Dad lived by the sun, and in the summer the sun hardly sets before it's up again.

But when Kelly and I were on our ride that day, I laughed at her need for reassurance. With Midnight's sure feet beneath me, I settled into the saddle and my hips rocked along with her natural rhythm. I reached my hand toward the sky and felt the warm, early sun press against my eyelids. Who needed reassurances when the summer itself seemed to be promising us everything?

"Cross my heart," I told her anyway. "Don't worry. I would never stand in the way of you and a to-do list."

"It's not a to-do list," Kelly called out, riding Tiramisu—Mom's horse, a beautiful bay quarter horse that looked golden in the sunlight. Kelly's red braid had a golden quality to it, too, and it trailed behind her, horselike in itself. "It's a bucket list. A summer bucket list. And will you ever slow down enough that I can keep up?"

The hooves of the horses pounded out a steady beat beneath us, barely more than a walk, through the vines, up the hill.

The Summer Bucket List had been Kelly's idea. Determined to make the most of our last few months at home, she decided we'd make a list of all the things we wanted to experience together during our final days between childhood and adulthood. We'd been adding to the list for the last month.

"It's a to-do list," I teased, but while Kelly was known for her penchant for planning, this one seemed especially important to her. So instead of asking her if she'd ever stop letting Tiramisu boss her around, I said, "Road trip."

She huffed. "In my beater or yours?"

I shrugged. "Mine. Yours. My dad's."

"Uh-uh, Mal. Committing a felony is not on the list."

"Please. My dad wouldn't call the cops."

"Your dad would call the cops. On principle."

I relented. "Fine. Mine."

We made it to the top of the hill and looked out over the land, the vines still in their infancy for the year. For the briefest moment, I felt ungrateful that I wanted to leave this place, with the endless blue sky and the feeling that to step off the porch could take you away from the world. Or closer to it, depending on how you looked at it. But then I closed my eyes and wondered what it would feel like to roam free, with no one expecting anything from me. Where no one knew me and I could be whoever I wanted to be.

Kelly already knew what she wanted to be when she grew up, had pretty much always known. Most of the time, I envied that in her, but sometimes she needed to be shaken out of her careful planning.

"Do something spontaneous," I said.

"You want me to plan not to plan?"

"Isn't that the only way you'll do it?"

I grinned and after a skeptical moment, she laughed.

"Fine," she said. "Added."

Before the sun fully rose in the sky, our list was finalized and Kelly's worries seemed to be assuaged. We rode the horses back and Kelly left me to my dad.

I dreaded the idea of working, my first act of adulthood. I would need money, my dad assured me, for living expenses in New York. He wasn't as convinced as I was that I would be perfectly content with two feet below me, a blue sky above me, and the occasional protein bar or two. So I waited in his office for the first sign of him and the business consultant he'd hired to help him rebrand and market the vineyard.

Up until now, Dad had been focused on maintaining the

vines he'd inherited from the previous owners and, in his free time, refining the flavors that would become his own unique signature. Finally, he felt it was time to break away from the vineyard's established reputation and create his own.

The night before, when my mom had asked what exactly the consultant would do, Dad had said, "He's going to assess the company's blah, blah, and create a strategic blah, blah, blah, and then charge me out the ass for it." My job was to do all the menial labor to allow the consultant to do his job most efficiently. Personally, it was an attempt to put some of Dad's money in my own pocket. For protein bars.

Waiting for the consultant's arrival, I sat with my feet propped up on Dad's desk in his barn office, twisting and untwisting a paper clip. I heard their voices first, as they entered the breezeway, my dad speaking.

"The previous owners used to do trail rides and I've been meaning to get back to it."

This was the first I was hearing of this plan. Usually Dad just complained about the feed costs.

"I think that's a great idea."

The stranger's voice was different than I expected. There was a melody to it, a finesse.

I set the paper clip down and inched my way toward the door. I peeked my head out so I could get a look at him before he saw me—to assess the man whose right hand I'd be for the next few months, ready to talk Dad into letting me run trail rides instead. I'd expected one of the older schmoozing types he'd previously worked with—their receding hairlines, their guts hanging over their belts, their *little ladys*. That was not who was standing next to my dad.

He was young—in his midtwenties, I thought, though I'd been bad at calculating age before I'd seen enough of life to know how it affected the lines of a person's face. He was dressed in slacks and a button-up shirt, his sleeves rolled up to reveal his smooth forearms. His dark curls were a little long for business, but styled to perfection. Everything about him was perfect, in fact, like he'd been sculpted by an artist exactly the way he appeared now, not born and grown into the man who turned to me and smiled.

Brown eyes.

Soft lips.

"There she is," Dad said and motioned for the consultant to shake my hand. I swallowed hard and wiped my hand on the front of my jeans as they walked closer.

"Mal, this is Sam. Sam, this is my daughter, Mallory."

They stopped in front of me and Sam lifted his hand with the grace and experience of a man who'd shaken the hands of diplomats and queens.

"Nice to meet you, Mallory," he said in a deep, strong voice.

I searched my mind for something clever to say, but all that came out was, "Nice to meet you, too."

I slipped my hand into his smooth fingers, and in that moment, I knew all the things I'd planned to focus on that summer had converged and narrowed down to one thing.

Him.

THREE

*W*hen I get back to the house after my ride with Tyler, Mom is humming in the kitchen, flipping pancakes and frying bacon. She's in sweatpants and a tank, her dark hair messy down her back, no bra. This is her small rebellion against the nine-to-five life. Dad's rebellion was to give up a job in construction, move us halfway across the country, and deplete my parents' entire savings to follow his hasty ambition to run a vineyard. My mom forgoes bras on the weekend.

"Hey, Mom," I say. She squeals when she sees me and her bare feet dance across the Mexican tile as she rushes over to wrap me in a hug. She kisses me all over my face like I'm still four years old and I laugh, allowing her this indulgence. In the time I've been gone, we've only seen each other on a handful of occasions and it's been as painful for me as it has, no doubt, been for her.

"I made everything," she says and motions toward the

breakfast bar on the kitchen island. I tie my hair back into a ponytail and pull up a stool.

"Dad out *loving on* the vines?" I ask with finger quotes. I didn't see him out there but Mom's smirk says it all. She sets a plate in front of me, stacked high with pancakes, bacon, scrambled eggs, half a grapefruit, and some strawberries.

"What time did you get in last night?" she asks.

"Midnight," I say between bites of egg, realizing I haven't eaten anything since the pretzels I had on the plane.

She grins, shaking her head. "Your dad was out there waiting for you at six. I couldn't even get him to eat dinner."

Her words are laced with affection, but it doesn't ease the guilt I feel about being away from home for so long, for making excuses to stay away even though I've wanted to be here as much as they've wanted me to be.

But the more time that passed without seeing, speaking to, or more important, apologizing to Kelly, the more insurmountable the task felt. It was one thing to allow a few days for us to cool off, but as the weeks passed, I realized I was angry at her, too. What I did that summer was selfish and inexcusable, but she wasn't faultless either.

Eventually, I convinced myself that Kelly had forgotten about me, moved on. I never stopped thinking about her, though. Not for one day.

"How's work been?" Mom asks. She still eats standing up at the island, I see. She sits for so many long hours at the office that if she isn't in front of the computer, she's moving. Mom has worked at the same small legal firm since we moved here, the only paralegal to two family lawyers. She's almost always in front of the computer. I have more sympathy for her plight than I did as a teenager.

"Good." I sip my coffee. "Fine."

"Looks like more than fine," she says. "The portfolio on

the company website has been growing quickly these last couple of years."

"You're stalking the company's website?" I ask with an exasperated laugh.

"Just occasionally. On my lunch breaks."

I roll my eyes, but her support warms my cheeks with pride.

"It seems like they really value you there."

She could only be basing this assumption on the fact that I never leave. I haven't told my parents about my promotion yet. Mostly because it won't be official until I get back. A lifetime of changing my focus with every shift in the breeze has taught me to keep my mouth shut until I'm sure.

Besides, this trip isn't about me.

"They seem to," I say vaguely.

My tone and the way I pick at my eggs with my fork must be less than convincing.

Mom comes around the kitchen island and wraps her arm around my shoulders. I lean my head against her collarbone.

"I hope…" she says, the sound of it vibrating through her rib cage. "Well, I hope you feel good about the direction your life has taken. I hope you don't regret going to New York."

New York had been the plan for years but I think Mom always knew it was because I'd taken Kelly's lead. She commented once, a long time ago, how much it surprised her since I'd never had the tendency to follow anyone. But that was how my friendship with Kelly was right off the bat and I think my parents were just grateful I'd chosen a worthy role model.

A lot changed in those final weeks and though I never spoke with Mom about my fallout with Kelly—I was too ashamed and afraid of disappointing her—her probing questions and sideways glances proved she wasn't entirely ignorant.

In light of everything that happened, I could have chosen to stay.

I could have gone anywhere.

I look up at my mom. "Things are good," I say. "I'm good."

Her expression softens and she plants a kiss on the top of my head.

The back door slides opens and Mom turns to greet our visitor. I expect to see Dad standing there, but Kelly appears in the doorway, and the sight of her sets the hair on the back of my neck on end.

I was planning to see her in the next couple days but I thought I would be more settled by then. I thought I would have time to mentally prepare myself. I didn't expect her to show up in my kitchen unannounced. Is she still as comfortable dropping by as she was when I lived here? If she has a reason for being here, my parents never mentioned it on the phone. Then again, they probably got the message loud and clear that Kelly was a sore topic after my many changes of subject. Now that I think about it, they haven't brought her name up in conversation in years.

Kelly halts, too, her mouth falling agape. She had to have known I would come home for the party, but maybe like me, nothing could prepare her for being face-to-face again. I cling to that explanation rather than the possibility that she believed I would miss this important milestone with my family. Not that I could blame her if she did. I've already missed so much.

She looks strikingly the same as when I saw her last. Her red hair is even twisted together in the braid I was accustomed to seeing her wear. Her fair skin is as bright and flawless as it was when she was seventeen, or even seven, splotched with orange freckles. Her petite frame is adorned in the simple jeans and T-shirt she's always worn, out of preference or necessity it's hard to say.

For a long moment, we stare at each other. My last memory of her is her yelling at me, accusing me of lying to her and of breaking all the promises we'd made each other that summer. Never mind that she was breaking promises of her own. Standing in front of me now, she's the collected, put-together person I've always known her to be, my presence the only crack in her armor.

I wait for her to speak first, to see if the silent treatment between us still holds.

"Hi," she finally says but her eyes don't warm a single degree.

"Hi," I say.

After another long pause, Mom says, "Oh, come on. It's been ten years. The past is the past, right?"

Her bold confrontation of our cold-shouldering does the trick. A nervous laugh escapes Kelly's lips and she looks away.

But could forgiveness be that easy? I certainly don't deserve to be off the hook without a fair amount of groveling but that doesn't stop me from hoping. Maybe it's cowardly of me to be willing to release Kelly of her sins so easily but to know she didn't hate me would be a load off my heart. Maybe it would stop me from questioning every choice I make in every area of my life. Maybe it would allow me to open up to relationships again.

To my surprise, Kelly breezes through the dining room and with only a slight hesitation, wraps her arms around me. She smells like sun and dirt and home.

At first, I'm taken aback, but then I wrap my arms around her. I don't know if there's meaning behind the gesture or if she's only doing it to appease my mom, but I revel in it anyway. There have been so many times in these years without her that I would have given anything to feel her support and love again. Growing up together, Kelly had become a part of me. I didn't realize how much until that part was removed.

Too quickly, she pulls away.

"It's good to see you, Mallory."

She uses my full name, which she hasn't done since the day we met, clarifying where we stand. My stomach sinks.

"It's good to see you, too," I say softly.

"Well," Mom says, patting us on the shoulders, "that's more like it. Want some breakfast, Kel?"

"Oh," she says quickly, "I already ate. Thank you. I'm just going to get to work."

I don't know what I expected when I spoke to Kelly for the first time, but this dry, polite greeting and empty dismissal wasn't it. I would have taken anger, sadness, even hatred over this. But as they say, the opposite of love isn't hate. It's indifference.

"Okay," Mom says. "Help yourself if you get hungry later."

Kelly nods and lets herself out the way she came, not glancing at me as she goes, and leaving without whatever she came in for. Maybe for Kelly the past *is* in the past, any love she once had for me gone along with it.

Kelly and I met on our first day of second grade. My parents and I had moved from Chicago earlier that summer and until school started, I hadn't met anyone my age. Kids didn't come to the vineyard and I never left, following Dad around as he learned everything there was to know about winemaking. I loved being outside, free to wander in a way I never had been in the city. But it was a relief when the first day of the school year arrived.

I spotted Kelly before she noticed me. She sat two rows over and was distracted by the boy sitting behind her who kept pulling on her ponytail. The way she bit her bottom lip and tried to pretend she didn't notice his existence made my stomach clench in a way I hadn't felt before.

By the time we made it to lunch, I'd gotten the distinct impression that this wasn't an uncommon occurrence for her. I'd seen her be teased in the lunch line and denied a seat at one of the cafeteria tables. These were long-standing prejudices. She'd clearly grown up with these kids and even at my young age, I pondered over the unfairness of it all. I couldn't see how Kelly was any different than the rest of us. In fact, she was quite pretty, but the way she kept her head down and avoided making eye contact with anyone proved she didn't know it.

It must have been because I wanted to know what was in store for me once I caught my new classmates' attention that I followed Kelly at recess. I watched her pass the swing set and the slide and take shelter under a tree with a trunk three times as wide as she was. She picked up a stick, crouched close to the ground, and began to draw figures in the mud. From my angle, hidden behind a nearby tree, I couldn't see what the pictures were, but I watched her. She dug the stick into the ground with increasing fervor and it struck me that she was taking out her anger at those kids who teased her and bullied her.

And then, the worst thing that could happen to a seven-year-old made time slow as I watched Kelly lose her balance and land butt-first into the mud.

A gasp escaped my lips. I waited to see what she would do. For a long moment, she was in shock, her delicate pink mouth gaping open. And then she began to cry. Not a sob, but a silent, contained mourning. Because she knew what I knew—once the kids saw the stain on the seat of her pants, that would be the undoing of her. She would spend the rest of her life in this small town, growing up with the same kids, and they would never let her forget this day.

I looked down at my own clothes. I wore a pair of leggings underneath my skirt. I quickly slipped the skirt down over my hips and stepped out of it, then I bundled it up and hid it behind my back. With no one looking, I hustled over to her and crouched beside her.

She was still crying but when I held out my offering, her sniffles abruptly stopped. She looked up at me with watery eyes, a puffed-out bottom lip, and a question. I nodded to her once and with that, she pushed herself up to standing, hid behind the tree, and quickly yanked the skirt up over her own pants.

I left her in privacy and we didn't so much as glance at each other for the rest of the day. I didn't want anything from her in return. I only wanted to ease the uncomfortable churning I felt in the pit of my stomach whenever someone teased her.

The next day she came to me outside the classroom before the bell rang and handed the skirt to me. It was freshly cleaned and folded. I wondered if she'd recounted the story to her parents, or if she'd sneaked it into the washer and dryer herself. (I found out months later that it was likely the latter, since her dad had abandoned her before she was born and her mom was... well, not doing Kelly's laundry anymore.) I stared at it and then at her, and when she smiled, I smiled back at her.

As the years passed, not much changed between us. Maybe it was that I didn't have any siblings of my own, but I took on the role of Kelly's protector, especially the more I found out about her home situation. I didn't become a target for bullying like Kelly was. The boys found me pretty enough to be nice to me and the girls found me not pretty enough to be a threat. I didn't much care what anyone thought of me, but my status kept Kelly safe from hair pulling and the names of spices being murmured under kids' breaths.

In return, she protected me in her own way. I would never have been accepted to Columbia without her making sure I finished my homework and turned it in on time. The concept of deadlines had always escaped me, and my parents were too busy trying to keep our lives afloat to hover. I'd never given them any reason to believe I needed them to. Every report card I brought home proved I was doing fine without their supervision, but it wasn't my own studiousness that ensured my success, it was Kelly's.

She was also the one who pushed me to apply to Columbia, who combed through my application over and over again, and sent it out for me. My parents were as shocked as I was when I received my acceptance.

Kelly and I have always brought out the best in each other and while she seems to have forgotten that, I'm not ready to let it go.

After I shower the morning's dust and sweat off me and respond to emails from the office, I find myself alone, with nothing but Kelly's words to keep me company—both her coldness this morning and her accusations years ago.

I've come to accept responsibility for my deceit but what even I don't understand is what came over me in the first place. I'd never purposely hurt Kelly before. I'd never purposely hurt anyone. Being three thousand miles away from this place made it easy to forget, but being back, there are reminders around every corner.

I amble outside and stand at the edge of the porch, gripping the wooden rail in my hands. The dry heat simultaneously suffocates and grounds me. I glance at the guest house, nestled behind a few shady trees next to the barn. It calls to me, luring me to it with the promise of explanations and of memories— bad ones, yes, but good ones, too. As a girl, it used to be one of my favorite places to hide away from my parents—my own little home away from home. The few times I've come back to visit, I haven't been brave enough to go inside, but I've avoided it—all of this—for too long.

The guest house is a small, one-room cottage with a queen-size bed, a bathroom, and a kitchenette with a mini-fridge and coffeepot. My last summer here it was a minefield of questions, uncertainty, and the overwhelming emotions of first love. It sits there unobtrusively, among the dust and sunlight like a faded photograph, but it holds my secrets.

I approach the door and reach for the key, dependably on top of the doorjamb. I wiggle it into one of the French doors, the billowing white curtains inside guarding the windows from prying eyes, and push it open.

The sunlight flows in behind me, lighting up the room and the dust motes floating in the air like glitter. My breath hitches as my gaze lands on the bed with its fluffy white comforter. In the corner sits the white wicker chair I used to curl up in when I talked to Sam in the early-morning hours. There's a nightstand with a table lamp, a wobbly standing fan, neatly folded towels on the foot of the bed. Two chairs and a small table for eating to my left, the kitchenette on the right. There's no room for much else, but it was everything we needed that summer.

I take a tentative step in and drop the key on the counter. It all looks exactly the same, like he never left. My mind flashes back to those hot summer mornings and I wait for him to emerge from the bathroom rubbing his eyes and smiling shyly. But it's just me and the stillness. Was it always so still or did I not realize then how his electricity charged the air?

I walk to the bed and perch at the end, waiting to jump up if anyone catches me here. When I don't hear Dad's truck tires on the dirt road, I sink back into it, my arms stretched out in either direction and my hair splayed out around my head. The comforter wraps itself around me the way I always wished Sam would…the way he did. I swear I catch the scent of his cologne, and then I remember. I remember why I almost gave up everything.

★ ★ ★

That night, I help Mom throw together some spaghetti before she retreats to her home office to spend the evening typing up contracts for work. I dish up two plates and turn off the lights in the house, leaving only the dim glow from beneath the microwave and the sunset sneaking in through the blinds.

As I carry the plates to the patio, I catch sight of Dad performing his evening ritual—sitting at the patio table as he watches the darkness of night swallow his vines whole. The remnants of daylight dance over the tops of their leaves and glint off his glass of white wine. His feet are crossed and perched on the seat of the chair in front of him.

The scene is so familiar, déjà vu overwhelms me. I almost expect to see Sam sitting out there, too, next to Dad, the way he did so many nights. I expect to see his velvety curls, the sleeves of his dress shirt rolled up, the way he cupped a wineglass delicately with the tips of his fingers. I close my eyes and the echo of his laugh haunts me.

But when I open my eyes, he's not there.

The sliding door chews on the dust in its track as I nimbly pull it open and close it again.

"There's my girl," Dad says without looking up.

I set his plate on the table in front of him, exchanging it for his glass of wine. I sit in the chair next to him and bring it to my nose, breathe in the citrus, and in a way that makes my dad cringe, take a large swallow.

"I take it back," he says. "You're not my Mallory. Someone has replaced you with a Mallory who drinks wine."

I laugh. "I like wine now, Dad. No one gets through four years of college and a job in marketing without developing a penchant for alcohol. And beer...?"

I shudder at the single memory of its bitterness on my

tongue. I tried it at a frat party, then turned around and left as quickly as I arrived.

"Well, at least you haven't forgotten everything I've taught you."

"I haven't forgotten *anything* you've taught me."

I take another swallow of wine and hand the glass back to him. Dad, sucking noodles into his mouth, takes it in his weatherworn fingers. I reach beneath the flop of hair that hangs over his forehead and rub my thumb against the strands above his ear that have gone gray. He smiles in a way that reminds me of Midnight when I rub my palm between her eyes.

"How's the season going?" I ask, because if I don't talk about grapes, Dad has little else to discuss. I want to talk about grapes and weather and bugs. They say you can't go back to your childhood, but listening to my dad talk about the vineyard is close.

"Really good, honey. Really good. I think it's going to be a good year."

"They usually are."

Some years have been harder than others, but Dad has an understanding of the land that seems to transcend the ups and downs. Still, Mother Nature cannot be predicted and the lines on my dad's face prove that he never forgets it. He gives a coy smile, then raises his glass to the heavens—a prayer.

"So... Mom said you picked a red?"

Dad clears his throat and gives me a sheepish grin.

"Cabernet."

"Wild man," I tease.

The Wandering Vineyard is known for our white wines—chardonnay, zinfandel, and Riesling specifically. Though Dad would be the first to stress that there is no such thing as perfecting a wine with the yearly variations in weather, precipitation, and temperature, those who travel far and wide each year to taste them straight from the source might beg to differ.

Dad takes a sip of his wine. "Well, the whites are the ones that got us here, it's true. But..."

"But doing something new is what keeps it interesting."

Dad chuckles. "Exactly. And keeping things exciting is what life is all about, right?"

I nod but can't help thinking about my life in New York. Once I left for college, I committed to that path. Checking off one accomplishment after the other was easy because the plan had already been laid out for me. I focused on my classes, my schoolwork, and then on my internship. I got hired at the same firm and set my sights on climbing the corporate ladder—I had no reason not to, no other prospects. I couldn't imagine simply changing trajectory for the sake of keeping things interesting. Not after doing so much work. But maybe when I'm my dad's age, I'll see things differently.

"Congratulations, by the way," I say. "On your new wine, and how well the vineyard's doing. I'm really happy for you. I know how hard you've worked to get here."

"Thank you, honey. That means a lot to me. And you've made a lot of sacrifices over the years to support me in this. I appreciate it."

Dad doesn't quite meet my eyes when he says this, always grateful but apologetic about the concessions Mom and I have made so he could follow his dreams.

I never explicitly told my parents I planned to pay for my college tuition, but when I entered my second semester and they hadn't seen a bill, they figured it out. That was the last time they nagged me about not coming home to visit and I suppose I held tighter to that responsibility than I meant to. Initially I stayed away to pay my bills, but eventually my workload around the office became too demanding to unload onto anyone else. It was easy to ignore my other reasons for avoiding coming home.

"I'm proud as hell of you," Dad adds, seeming to follow my thoughts. He laughs but tears swim in his eyes. He reaches across the table and places his hand on top of mine, enveloping it completely. Its warmth is a balm to my heart after all the exhausting days and lonely nights spent on the other side of the country.

It's worth it. It's what I've chosen. But sometimes I wonder how I've gotten so far from the girl I used to be.

"Thank you," I whisper, unable to manage more. I would never tell them this, but most of the decisions I've made in my adult life have been to make my parents happy—so they don't feel like they have to worry about me, and to make them proud of me. I have a habit of ruining every other relationship that's important to me. I won't ruin this one.

The sliding door opens, breaking the moment, and Mom pokes her head out.

"Rich, did you get the guest house ready for tomorrow?" she asks.

Dad curses under his breath, and I laugh. Why would Mom ever expect Dad to remember something unrelated to grapes? Then again, with me gone, I suppose there's no one else to do it.

"I'll take care of it," I offer.

Thank you, Dad mouths to me so Mom can't see. He refills his wineglass and slides it over to me in repayment.

"Who's visiting?" I ask Mom, sipping on Dad's drink. It feels so natural, this familial intimacy that I've missed so much. It isn't the same with my coworkers, could never be. We may have an open floor plan but our separate cubicles ensure that there's always a wall between us, the lines drawn.

"Sam," Mom says with a grin. "Isn't that nice?"

I choke on the wine halfway down my throat.

"Sam?" I gasp. "Like... Sam?"

Mom laughs. "Um, yes?"

"Why is Sam coming to visit?"

I didn't realize my parents were still in contact with him since he'd disappeared all those years ago without a word. Did they still talk? Had he come to visit before? How much was I missing in my temperature-controlled corner of New York?

"We invited him to the planting party," Dad says. "He played a big role in the success of the vineyard. He should be here to celebrate with us, don't you think?"

"Sure," I mutter. "Of course."

Outside of shock, I can't decide how I feel. My anger at Sam has mostly subsided over the years, more because I had no productive use for it than because I've forgiven him. During those first few months, I used to fantasize about all the things I would say to him if I ever got the chance, but I never thought that day would actually arrive. I tried to put it behind me. But Sam and I face-to-face again? My heart didn't survive it the last time.

"Does he know I'm here?" I ask.

"It never came up," Dad says, returning to his food.

Of course it didn't. I was never a factor in any of Sam's decisions. And Dad wouldn't think to mention it. My parents, as far as I knew, were blissfully ignorant about what happened between Sam and me that summer. Most of our time together was spent after Dad went to bed and Mom was hidden away in her office. Sam was an expert at withdrawing from me whenever anyone was around.

The way Mom's eyes narrow at my reaction to the news, though, makes me wonder just how clueless she is. She was obviously more in the know about what happened with Kelly than I realized.

"I'm sure he'll be thrilled to see you," she says.

I doubt it, I think, but don't say. Instead, I chew a bite of spaghetti, the noodles and my words becoming mush in my mouth.

"I can take care of the guest house," Mom offers, letting me off the hook.

"No, it's fine," I say. I swallow the spaghetti down and it sits heavy in my stomach. "I can handle it."

FOUR

*T*he next morning, I stand on the back porch, watching the vineyard hands walking up and down among the trellises, examining the newly budding grapevines. Dad walks alongside them. The grape-growing process is closely monitored all throughout the year but the start of growing season sets Dad in a particular frenzy after long winters when the vines are dormant and Dad's work is inside, going over the year's production numbers and watching his barrels age in the basement cellar. Mom always says she doesn't know which season is worse— summer, when she hardly sees him at all, or winter, when she sees him entirely too much.

I sip my coffee and listen to the distant chirping of the birds. The breeze settles into a hush over the land, but there is no peace inside me. The news of Sam's return had me tossing and turning in bed as I asked myself why I cared. So much time has passed. That's what Sam is, the past. But as long ago as it was, something fundamental shifted inside me that summer and I haven't been the same since. That's what I can't let go of. I may have used my heartbreak and shame to fuel my ambition at work, but I also haven't allowed myself to get close to another person since. I haven't felt able to trust a man, or a friend, and after the way the lies slipped so easily off my tongue to Kelly's ears, I certainly don't trust myself.

I came back for the planting party, and for my parents, but more so, I came back for Kelly and if she and I have any chance of reconnecting, how can I convince her to forgive me when the very reason for our falling-out will be laying his perfect curls against the pillow in the guest house tonight?

Then again, maybe Sam's presence is a blessing. We may be in the same place, with the same balmy air luring us into impulsivity, and the same romance of wine at sunset. But none of us are the same people. What better way to prove to Kelly that I've changed than to be placed in a similar situation and make different choices?

With that in mind, I return my coffee mug to the house, grab the keys to my rental car, and head into town.

Driving through my hometown for the first time in a decade is a surreal experience, akin to seeing your doctor out of scrubs and drinking with her girlfriends at the bar. The familiar features are the same, but out of context everything feels shifted and disjointed, like a dream. Fast-food chains have popped up between familiar buildings that look dilapidated in comparison. Overpriced restaurants and shops have been added to Paso Robles's thriving tourist hub. Locals often complain there are two faces of Paso Robles—the one you see when passing through, flashy and beckoning the money out of visitors' pockets, and the Paso Robles locals live and breathe, where one turn off downtown lands you in neighborhoods full of honest people struggling to make a living.

One night, a few years after I left, Dad got on the phone with heartbreak in his voice. "They're breaking ground on a

Walmart," he said, and our little town hasn't been quite the same since.

Monet's Mug is tucked a few blocks off Highway 101, a common meeting place for the people who live here and the occasional visitor who wanders off the beaten path. I pull into the parking lot and turn off the engine in the space next to Kelly's car. I sit for a long, silent moment with my hands on the steering wheel, unsure of how Kelly might be feeling now that she's had time to process my presence here. I shift in my seat to check for the folded pink paper in my back pocket, though I know it's there. It's always there.

"All you can do is try," I tell myself in the rearview mirror. I sigh and get out of the car.

When I step through the front door, the bell jingles and a few of the patrons look up at me, no recognition in their eyes before they go back to their conversations. I used to know everyone who lived here.

This place, at least, looks exactly as I remember it. Six small round tables speckle the sitting area and a purple booth lines the side wall. Acoustic music plays over the speakers and like before, the paintings and photographs of local artists cover nearly every inch of the brightly colored wallpaper. The artwork is new, of course.

Kelly is alone behind the counter, steaming milk with a high-pitched whistle. Willpower and the bitter aroma of coffee beckon me farther inside.

When she places the last customer's coffee on the pickup counter, Kelly sees me. She must have expected I'd drop by because her expression doesn't change. In her maroon apron, she returns to the espresso machine and wipes down the steam wand like I've seen her do hundreds of times. If it weren't for her inhospitable greeting, I could have stepped back in time.

"The usual?" she asks as I approach the counter. I haven't

had anything so sweet since she used to make me the white chocolate raspberry mochas she got me hooked on that summer, but I nod.

As she levels off the coffee grounds, I ask her how she's doing. I'm not sure I've ever asked her that question before—I've never had to. Growing up, there was nothing we didn't know about each other. I was as surprised as she was to discover that had changed.

"Shorthanded," she says, "but the morning rush is over."

"Are you still working four shifts a week?" I ask.

"Six," she says, pursing her lips at me, like I've caused that, too. Seeming to recognize her unfairness, her voice is softer when she adds, "Mom's medications keep getting more expensive."

"Is there anything I can do to help?" I ask, more out of reflex than having any real capability. She needs more help than I can offer in a one-week visit or with my New York budget. Knowing this as well as I do, she ignores the question.

Instead she asks, "Did your dad mention if he got that supply order in? I'd planned to swing by this morning and do it myself but I had to come in early to cover Elinor's shift."

"No…" I draw out the word. Why would Kelly know or care about Dad's supply inventory? Is that what she came looking for yesterday?

I piece the puzzle together—her extra shifts here, her unannounced visits to the vineyard.

"So you're working at the vineyard?" I ask.

Dad had said something about needing more help in the office.

"Part-time," she says. "When I'm not at the coffee shop. I needed more income to pay for my student loans and Rich was nice enough to offer me a job filing paperwork and making phone calls."

My old summer job. I'm grateful and not at all shocked that

Dad would support Kelly in whatever way she needs. She's been like a daughter to them since the first time I brought her home. Still, I can't help the slithering in my stomach that whispers I'm being replaced in my own home.

"That's great," I say. "Have you finished your courses?"

The week after I got settled at Columbia, my parents told me Kelly had been accepted to get her degree through distance courses. She would be able to stay in Paso to take care of her mom while also earning her bachelor's degree in psychology.

Kelly stares at me for a long moment, as if deciding whether or not she wants to open the door to a real conversation with me. In the end, her manners win out.

"I did," she says, pouring milk into a steaming pitcher. "It took me a couple of extra years but I graduated four years ago."

"Did you walk?" I ask.

If she came all the way to New York to accept her diploma with her graduating class and didn't reach out to me, our friendship is likely already beyond saving. We may have missed each other the couple of times I've returned home to visit—the first time, because I was still too scared to face her, and the second because she was taking her mom to doctor's appointments in LA—but if she'd come to New York, she would have needed a place to stay. She would have needed someone to show her around.

"No," she says, looking into the milk.

Another thing she's missed to remain here, to be her mother's sole caregiver.

"Oh," I say. "I'm sorry."

Kelly turns on the steamer, interrupting our conversation. I drum my fingers on the counter, anxious for her to give me a lifeline, anxious to run away. The guilt I feel for living the life she wanted for herself is like a monster inside me, trying to eat its way out.

I reach for the pink paper in my pocket, the ace up my sleeve, but let my hand fall. It's a gift, not an act of desperation.

When the milk is done steaming, Kelly pours it into a paper cup, presses a lid onto it, and passes it to me. Her eyes meet mine. A decade's worth of disappointments and struggle have dulled them.

"How is your mom?" I ask.

It's the wrong question, I quickly realize, when Kelly turns away from me. She grabs a wet rag and wipes down the counter.

"Really?" she says.

I've lost the right to know, apparently. The right to even ask.

As she vigorously rubs at a spot of dried syrup, I catch sight of the dark ink on the inside of her wrist. She notices me looking and drops the rag, a rosiness rising to her cheeks.

"Okay." I hold my hands up in surrender. "I'm sorry."

"Listen, I have to catch up from the rush. The coffee is on the house."

I wait for her to offer a better time to catch up, to give even the slightest indication that she'd be willing.

She offers up nothing.

It pains me to put more distance between us when there's already so much. I wish we could go back. I wish I could have made different choices that summer. I wish I could be the friend she needs.

"Okay." I step toward the door. I lift my coffee toward her. "Thanks."

If she works at the vineyard, she can't avoid me all week. So for now, I lower my head in temporary defeat, shoving a few dollars in the tip jar as I go.

That afternoon, I return to the guest house to fulfill my promise to my mom—the one I made before I fully realized what I was volunteering for. The idea of Sam being here is still surreal, abstract. The reality of it will no doubt be awkward on both sides. There are so many things I wish I'd said the last time we were here, and I'm sure he expects there will be things I want to hear, if he expects me at all. The real question is whether or not I actually do want Sam's explanations, or whether it matters anymore.

I reach for the key above the door frame, muscle memory taking over. When I open the door, the sunlight bleaches the space, and this time, I see no magic here. It's just an empty, lifeless room that holds a thousand reminders of all the times Sam proved to me that he never loved me and I was a fool for ever wishing he could.

Of course Sam will be staying in the guest house. The place practically has his name on it. He spent two months living in it the last time. It has his imprint on it, for sure. The memories of Sam are overlaid on every inch of the vineyard. With him here, flesh and blood, I don't know how to continue to think of him in the past. He will be very much present.

I'm nervous. It takes me a moment to name the feeling. Before I decided to come back to face Kelly, it had been a long time since I cared about the outcome of a situation enough that it felt like I had anything to lose. The last time I remember feeling this way was the day I interviewed for my internship. These past few weeks, the tightness in my chest has been a constant companion.

It isn't the silence that's been bearing down on me, I realize. It's the fear that I'm incapable of being in a relationship. And now, unexpectedly, the last—and truly only—man I've seen a future with is returning with all our baggage.

It's not that I haven't dated. There were a couple guys in college; they're so vague in my mind that they're hardly worth mentioning. I lost my virginity in my dorm room bed a few months into my freshman year to a football player in my study group—something Kelly would be horrified to know. In high school, we avoided the jocks particularly avidly with their arrogance and smooth lines. My Romeo didn't have any lines. In fact, the only thing I remember about the experience was the uncomfortable silence. I'd given in to his dry, openmouthed kisses to get the act over with and cried afterward because I'd felt nothing and feared I never would again.

Since then, I've gone out for drinks with a few guys I've worked with, colleagues from visiting firms or men I've met at conferences. Work is the only place I would have the opportunity to meet someone. Jack, the analyst who sits three cubicles over, had flowers delivered to the office under a code name to keep our few dinner dates a secret. In return, I slept with him out of sheer boredom. It didn't help and only complicated my work life so I vowed never to do anything like that again.

Only one man has ever made me feel like my skin was made of stardust. And when he left, my light all but burned out.

But I'd be stupid to delude myself into thinking Sam could fix me now. And his presence certainly won't help me fix my relationship with Kelly.

I cross the room and begin to tear the blanket off the bed, sweat forming on the back of my neck. As I toss the blanket haphazardly on the floor, a knock on the open door startles me. A shiver runs up my spine. Before I turn around, I already know who will be standing there. I can feel him, my body responding to his presence in a way it never has with anyone else.

When I look up, I see him. Nothing about him has changed—he looks like he stepped right out of my memory. He still has the same flawless skin, the same warm brown eyes I used to melt into, the same sense of style. His hair is shorter and his face is clean-shaven, but otherwise, he looks exactly like the Sam I never really knew.

I expect all my nervous energy to reach a combustion point, but instead a cool calm floods through me. Is it relief at seeing that all the reasons I fell for him weren't all in my mind, or is it shock?

"Hey, Mallory," he says like it's the most natural thing in the world to be standing in front of each other again.

Not entirely. There's an underlying sheepishness. He should be anxious. One of the last times I saw him, he was twisting my hair between his fingers and smiling at me like nothing else in the world mattered. That was right before he disappeared without a word. No explanations. No apologies.

But uncertainty is an emotion I've never seen on him, and I admit to some satisfaction at being the cause. I'm glad I'm not out on this limb alone.

I swallow hard and force a smile.

"Samuel B. Ryder," I say, inadvertently resurrecting one of our inside jokes. His smile widens.

"How are you?" he asks.

"I'm good," I say. "It's…good to be home."

"Yeah. It is."

He laughs nervously, rubbing the back of his neck.

Sam never did know how to small talk—didn't believe in it.

"You don't have to do that," he says softly, pointing toward the bed. It ratchets up my agitation again, the way he talks to me with the level of intimacy that only two people who spoke under the cover of the stars can share.

"It's fine," I say, not allowing myself to get caught up in my emotions. I can't allow myself to fall back into old patterns with him.

I get the sheets off the bed and balled up with the comforter. I pick them up and hold them tight to me to provide a barrier

from Sam's gaze. He hasn't stepped inside the room and I want
to keep it that way. I once promised myself I would never be
under this roof with him again—a promise much easier kept
when we were on opposite sides of the country.

"Okay. Thanks," he says. But he doesn't move.

A thick pause bubbles in the space between us and its discomfort urges me to fill it.

"You look…" I start, but I realize there are no words to describe the way he has always looked to me. Still otherworldly.
Still so…perfect, which was our problem from the start.

"And you look…" He looks me up and down and seems to
struggle for adjectives, as well. I shrink ever so slightly under
his stare. "Mature," he finally settles on, vaguely.

I clench my jaw and look away. Pain and embarrassment are
heavy on my shoulders, anger biting at my heels. How many
times did he call me *kiddo*?

"I suppose ten years will do that to a person," I say.

Sam opens his mouth, his eyebrows lifting like he wants to
say something important. But nothing comes out.

I almost ask him. Why he left. Why he came back. If I mis-
read every word he said, every touch, every kiss. I realize I
have the unexpected opportunity to get the answers to those
questions, to set my feelings for Sam at rest, too. Maybe it
would ease the emptiness I've felt since the day he disappeared.

But I can't begin to think about resolving issues with Sam
until I've resolved my problems with Kelly.

"We'd better not be late for lunch," I say, moving toward
the door.

He smirks knowingly. "I wouldn't want to offend your
mom."

"I don't think there's anything you could possibly do to
offend her."

It pains me to admit that my mom adores him, that my parents could have such a different perspective of Sam. It makes me question my own judgment. Did Sam really lead me on? Or was I blind and naive?

"You can grab your luggage," I say. "I'll bring these back when they're done."

He watches me for another long moment, and then he steps backward out of the doorway. I squeeze through the space to avoid being close to him, but I can smell his skin and feel his breath and I wonder if I will be strong enough to avoid Sam this time.

FIVE

*I*t started innocently. The crush. Looking back now, I think it was only natural. I didn't have many crushes in high school. Never dated boys, though I'd been asked. Because to me, that was exactly what they were: boys. They played practical jokes on each other in the halls and thought it was funny to make faces at the teachers behind their backs. They bragged about whose prom date was hottest. As if any of that mattered. Rumor around school was that I would have made one of them a good trophy but I asked Kelly to prom instead and we had more fun than all the girls whose dates ditched them half an hour in.

And then Sam walked into my life.

Not a boy at all. There was something immediately worldly about him. He was calm, cool, not easily ruffled. There was a confidence in the way his shoulders were always rolled back and the way he stood as if he was rooted to the center of the earth.

His first week at the vineyard, he followed Dad around with a leather portfolio and I followed him. That was my official job and I tried to keep my eagerness in check. Truly, I reveled in the opportunity to spend so much time in his orbit, watching him, soaking him in. I held my breath every time he looked over his shoulder at me and smiled like we had a shared secret. I ran down the stairs each morning hoping today would be the day I'd find out what it was.

That first Friday was a surprisingly cool day. The clouds had settled over the hills, threatening a rainy night. The wind swirled the dust around our feet but as we walked the vines, Dad, Sam, and I welcomed the relief after a long, hot week.

At the end of the day, Dad turned to Sam and said, "Well, I think that's about as much as you need to know to get started. Except for one last thing."

Sam smiled, amused by Dad. Despite their twenty-plus-year age difference, they'd clicked immediately. Dad had always wanted a son. Luckily for him, I was tomboy enough to, in a way, be both to him. But having Sam around was different—he had an interest in what Dad did in a way I never would.

"What's that?" Sam asked.

"You couldn't possibly sell my wine without having a few glasses, right?"

Sam's smile grew. "Makes sense to me."

"Join us for dinner?"

"Sure. Sounds perfect."

I remember that dinner well. Mom came home from the office late but she wanted to impress our guest anyway. We sat on bar stools at the kitchen island and Mom asked Sam about his family while she cooked.

He told us he grew up in Washington, was an only child, and that he graduated from the University of Washington with a bachelor's degree in business two years ago. He had been consulting for small businesses since and he listed off the names of a few. We wouldn't have recognized their names until recently, but we'd seen commercials for one or two after Sam helped them create national marketing campaigns.

Dad knew this already, of course, but Mom looked at Sam in a different light after that, clearly impressed and hopeful that Dad's passion project might finally start making money. For me, it only reinforced what I knew to be true: Sam was not a boy. I couldn't ignore him if I tried.

After Mom finished making dinner, she took her plate to her office, like she did most nights. Dad, Sam, and I carried our plates out to the back porch, where two bottles of wine shone in the light of the sunset like a jeweler's offering.

As we took out seats, Dad introduced our most popular wines.

"We've got a five-year sauvignon blanc and a three-year chardonnay," he said.

"Don't undercut it, Dad. It's not *a* sauvignon blanc, it's *the* sauvignon blanc." When I realized Sam was staring at me intently, waiting to hear more, I blushed. With a shrug, I added, "You want to know everything about the vineyard, right? This wine is the vineyard. It's what Dad is known for."

Sam grinned. At me. "Good to know," he said.

Dad, his chest puffed out, set his plate down and reached for the older bottle.

"This one was my first as the owner. I managed the vineyard for the first five years while the owner called the shots from Florida. A nice enough guy, but he was all business. He never had a passion for the grapes. He thought owning a vineyard would make him a quick buck." Dad laughed at this idea. He had yet to see a buck of any kind. "At the first sign he was tired of running a business he couldn't see, I offered him all the money I had and begged him to carry the note for the rest."

Dad filled a glass one-quarter full, watching the liquid stream down the side of the U-shaped bowl. Then he filled his own glass. Dad had stopped offering me taste tests after repeatedly offending him with my mock-gagging motions.

Sam picked up his glass and took a sip. Both Dad and I cringed.

"What?" he asked. "It's good."

"Not if you drink it like that."

Sam looked to me for help. I shrugged and laughed behind my hand.

"I forgive you for defiling my wine," Dad said, "but let's teach you how to drink it right."

And for the next hour, that's what Dad did. He taught Sam the proper technique for swirling the wine in the glass, how to smell it to capture the body and subtle nuances of it, how to assess the color—especially beautiful against the sunset— and finally, how to swish it around his mouth to catch every shade of flavor from the moment it touched his lips to the moments after it slid down his throat, revealing its final flourish.

I listened with my chin resting on my hand, entranced anew by Dad's instructions and explanations. I'd known it all by heart since before I started middle school, and I'd listened to the same lesson dozens of times, but there was something about the way Sam took it in with his whole body—eyes narrowed, upper body leaned forward, mouth slightly agape—that made the subject enthralling. As the wine touched his lips and left glistening bubbles behind, which he promptly caught with his tongue, I felt things I'd never experienced before…things I didn't know how to corral.

Once conversation turned to business, I sat back in my chair and zoned out, looking out at the vines, but I watched Sam's every move from the corner of my eye.

We sat like that for another hour or two before Dad offered to get another bottle of wine from the cellar.

"No, I shouldn't," Sam said. "I have to get myself back to the hotel."

"Are you sure?" Dad asked. "We've got a guest house if you want to stay."

My heart leaped as I waited for Sam's response, too surprised by the possibility to decide which way I hoped he would answer.

"I appreciate it, but I've got plans in the morning." Sam rose from his chair and shook my dad's hand. "You're right, though," he said. "Your wine is great. Amazing, actually. Thanks for the lesson."

Dad glowed at Sam's remark, and I knew no matter what happened from there, Sam was in.

SIX

I wake the next morning to the sound of tapping on my window and darkness on the other side of my eyelids. My head aches. Most people who visit the vineyard report never having slept better in their lives. Most people who visit, though, aren't surrounded by emotional minefields.

I hear another tap on the window and blink my eyes open. The clock on the nightstand reads 5:31 a.m.

I spent yesterday afternoon helping Tyler muck stalls, which most people wouldn't consider relaxing but was helpful in keeping my mind off all the ways this trip has already gone wrong. Sam and Dad ate dinner on the back porch, the way they used to, and I kept Mom company in her office, then went to bed early.

When a third tap pings through the room, I pull myself out of bed, tripping over my suitcase on my way to yank open the blinds. Tyler's smiling face stares up at me from below. He gives me an exaggerated wave of his arm, motioning me toward the stables. Not that he has to. I know why he's here.

I grin and shake my head at the familiar sight. I hold up a finger.

Stumbling into the bathroom, I brush my teeth and hair, then meet him outside in a pair of old jean shorts I found in my dresser.

"Hey," I say, cutting through the still predawn air. The morning, for now, is cool and rushes over my skin like water.

Tyler waits with his hand outstretched, offering it to me.

"We're not too old for this, are we?" he asks.

"Never."

"I've got the horses saddled up."

He leads me to the barn. Already my mind feels clearer.

In the dim light of the stables, we hoist ourselves onto Midnight and Rocket, and before our butts hit the saddles, we urge them forward—first at a walk, then a trot, then we take off at a full run. As we ride toward the rising sun, I can almost hear the horses' laughter—their thrill at the closest they get to freedom—as Tyler and I encourage them on, faster, out of breath. Weaving around each other with sideways glances. Kicking up dust, our grins wild. The pounding of hooves reverberating against our eardrums.

We come over the hill just as the first rays of sunshine break over the mountains, dancing and twinkling across the pond that sits at the edge of the vineyard property line. Before we reach the water, we pull the horses to a skidding stop, laughing.

"I don't think I've done that since you left," Tyler says a few minutes later as we sit along the shoreline.

The pond is small, only waist deep, but it was my most frequent escape from home when I needed time to think. The horses drink from the warm water on either side of us. I dig my toes into the sandy mud and shift my weight, leaning off one hand and back onto the other as the pebbles bite into my palms.

"Why not?" I ask, baffled.

His only response is a lazy shrug.

"It's so much prettier here than in the city. I've missed this place. I'd forgotten just how beautiful it is in real life compared to my memories."

"You didn't have to stay away so long, you know."

"I know. It's just…complicated." It's the first time I've admitted to anyone that my motives for staying in New York haven't been entirely work related. "What else have you been doing while I was gone?"

"Just breathing. That's all I could manage," he says. "I've been completely lost without you. Sobbing into my pillow and everything."

"Shut up," I say, and he laughs.

"Nah, mostly the usual. I went to LA for a few years to try to make more money installing satellite TV, but wearing a uniform and calling people by their last names wasn't worth it."

I giggle at the picture of an elderly woman opening the door to Tyler, hair disheveled and searching for the nearest window to climb out of. No doubt he looked adorable in his uniform but it could never suit him.

"Thanks for that," he teases. "Otherwise, just working here. Then my second job at the bar a few nights a week. It's good tips and I've been saving up to get the heck out of here."

"Out of here?" I ask, my laughter stopping abruptly.

I shouldn't be stunned. I left first and unless you want a career in wine, there isn't much reason to stay in Paso Robles. But I've never really believed there would come a time when Tyler wouldn't be here. He's as much a part of this place to me as Midnight, as this pond where we've shared so many heartfelt conversations.

"Where are you going? When?"

Tyler dips his fingers into the water and flicks it at me, making me cringe.

"Nothing is set in stone. I still don't have as much money as I'd like. But hopefully in the next couple months. My uncle's starting up a horse ranch in Montana. Said he'd let me run it, but I'll have to cover my expenses while I build up a boarding clientele."

"Your dad's brother or your mom's?"

Tyler doesn't like to talk about his alcoholic father back in New Mexico but he still talks to his mom, who, though she loves the man too much herself, understood Tyler's need to leave.

"Mom's," he says.

I shake my head. So much has changed, and is changing, around here. I've been romanticizing the idea that I could come home and pick right back up where I left off, the way it was before things fell apart with Kelly, before Sam, before I wore pumps instead of riding boots.

"Montana. Wow. I've heard it's beautiful there. I've always wanted to go."

"Lots of air," he says with a grin, referencing a conversation we shared once. "Well, you'll come visit me, then. I'd be happy to have you."

I let his offer hang in the air, too overcome with emotions to speak. It took me years to get back home, and with my promotion, what are the chances I'll ever see Tyler again?

"I saw Sam," he says, his whole demeanor changing. He tosses a pebble into the pond. It hits the water with a small splash and sinks straight to the bottom. The water is so clear I can watch its journey as it beelines for the dirt bottom and crashes into it. "I can't believe he has the nerve to show his face here."

MIDNIGHT *at the* WANDERING VINEYARD

"Yeah. My parents invited him back for the planting party. They don't know what happened between us."

No one does. I told Tyler more than I told anyone else about that summer, but not even he knows everything.

"And you're okay with this?"

I shrug, feigning more resolve than I feel. "I don't have much choice. He's here, and I can't leave now. I owe my parents this. I owe Kelly more effort than I've given an apology so far. I don't know how she'll react when she finds out he's here, though."

I sigh and run my hands through my hair. I feel Tyler's fingers rub the space between my shoulder blades.

"Are you okay?" he asks.

"It's stupid, right? To be holding on to the heartbreak still?"

"Yes," he says, concise as ever.

I laugh. "Well, don't be sensitive about my feelings or anything."

Tyler deflates, his anger at Sam visibly seeping out of every muscle in his body. He's always restrained himself when it comes to Sam, for my sake.

"He lured you in, Mallory. He knew what he was doing. He had to have known he'd only hurt you."

"It's not just the feelings I had for Sam. I'm…embarrassed. I'm ashamed. Being on the other side of the country, working, focusing on my day-to-day life, I could almost forget I was ever that girl. But I was, and being here, especially all of us together…it's like going right back to that place. I don't want to feel that insecure again. I don't want Kelly to be right about me."

"I think you're being too hard on yourself," Tyler says.

I scoff. "Kelly would beg to differ."

Tyler turns his body so he can face me. It's painful to meet his eyes but I do.

"You don't get it, Mal. Your argument with Kelly was never about Sam. It was about who you became when you were around him. Be the Mallory we all know and love, and him being here won't matter."

"It's been a long time, Tyler. I am different now."

"Not in here," he says, pressing the tip of his finger to my chest. "People don't change in here."

His sincerity is so genuine, I could cry. I bite my bottom lip, afraid to say the words on the tip of my tongue. "But what if I forgot who that Mallory is?"

Tyler frowns and pulls me into a hug. With his mouth right next to my ear, he says, "Then we'll remind you. That's what friends are for."

When I first moved to New York, sometimes I would sneak past employees at the stables near Central Park and sit with the horses until someone found me and kicked me out. I would never ride them—I couldn't afford it—but just being near them reminded me of home and comforted me when the fast pace of the city became too much, when missing my parents and Kelly and Tyler became too much. It brought me back to center when I felt like I was losing sight of who I was. It happened so frequently that eventually the staff just ignored me until I left.

When that stopped working, I would walk out to the ocean on a Saturday morning and traipse along the shoreline until I didn't know how much time had passed, where I was, or where I was supposed to be. I would stumble to the nearest road, hail a cab, and pay the ten-mile fare.

My conversation with Tyler, though helpful, doesn't ease that familiar desire to walk away and forget all my worries, to get lost on a beach or a hiking trail that leads to nowhere. As I stand in my bedroom, drying my hair with a towel, I force myself to feel my feet on the carpet. I recall Tyler's words, and the possibility of Kelly's friendship, and I ground myself here, now. I came home to face my life and all the things I've been running from. I won't let fear make me run again.

My phone chimes on the nightstand and I grab it. It's a text from my boss, Denise.

Are you bored yet? she asks. Don't forget to swing by the office when you get in so we can catch up!

The smile on my face is involuntary. Denise is New York born and raised, and she never misses the opportunity to remind me how different our personalities and lifestyles are. When I told her I was coming home for a week, she curled her lip and asked, *But what will you do?*

I text her back. Was in bed by ten. Jealous?

With as much time as Denise and I have spent together over the last six years, her mentorship has grown into something resembling friendship, for which I'm grateful. Keeping her happy has given me a sense of purpose in New York.

Her message is a not-so-subtle reminder, though, that my clock here is ticking.

Once I'm dressed, I head down to the kitchen. When I reach the bottom of the stairs, Sam is standing at the coffeepot alone. I stop with my hand still on the railing. I still haven't decided how I want to handle his presence here. He looks up at me and smiles so I pull my lips into a polite acknowledgment the way my mom taught me.

"Morning," Sam says. His hair is slightly damp, his curls all but gone. He wears a suit, like he always did. Suits never go out of style. Today his shirt is violet with light gray slacks to match. He's skipped ahead to his evening habit of unbuttoning the top button and rolling his sleeves back. Maybe that's his usual now.

"Morning," I say back.

"Coffee?" he asks.

"Sure."

I take a deep breath and join him at the coffeepot. My pulse quickens as I draw closer to him and the emotion doesn't feel as much like anger as I wish it did.

He fishes a mug out of the cabinet and hands it to me. There's something both comforting and unsettling about how at home he is in my kitchen. But then, why shouldn't he be? Nothing has changed since he was here last, when my dad welcomed him like the son he never had.

"Did you sleep well?" I ask.

"I did," he says. "I've always slept well in that bed. All this fresh air."

Or maybe the wine, I want to say. Every time he slept in that bed, it had been after a few too many glasses.

He clears his throat as if the words are written on my face.

"Is something wrong with the coffee maker in the guest house?" I ask.

I reach around him to grab the coffeepot and he stays infuriatingly still, making the close quarters tighter. I'm careful not to brush against him.

"The carafe is cracked," he says behind his mug.

"Oh."

There's an awkward silence as I fill my mug.

"So…what have you been up to?" I ask. "Still in Washington?"

"Yep," he says, nodding. "I bought a house a few years ago. In Port Orchard. It's a bit of a drive for work, but it's worth it. I have a beautiful view of the mountains from my kitchen window as I drink my coffee each morning."

The mountains. I can't believe he would bring that up. I clench my jaw to hold back a biting retort.

"You must be missing that this morning," I say as I place the carafe back on the burner. Sam finally takes a step back.

"The views here are just as beautiful," he says. "I didn't realize how much I missed them until I walked out on my little porch this morning."

I nod, genuinely agreeing with him, but his presumption of ownership over any part of the vineyard, however small, gets under my skin.

"Do you hike them much?" I ask, unable to stop myself. I turn away from him, to grab the creamer from the fridge. I don't want to make eye contact and risk giving away what a sensitive subject this is for me.

There's a brief pause and I listen for the feeling behind it. Without analyzing his expression, I can't make it out.

"Not as much as I'd like," he says. But that's probably why he moved there. That was one of the "life hacks" he always tried to teach me—keep your goals in front of you and the goal will come to you.

I suppose it worked for me. I've kept work in front of me every waking hour and I will soon have a new title to show for it.

"You must be doing well, though, to have waterfront property. Sounds like you've gotten what you always wanted."

He shrugs. Uncertainty again? This time, I can't bite my tongue.

"It's not everything you've wanted?"

Sam clears his throat and pulls the sugar to him. He stirs in a couple of teaspoons.

"I've been working with my dad, actually. Turns out, it's a lot of work to get new medical practices established so my dad has been sending me clients when his students graduate."

"Students?"

"Oh, he's teaching at the University of Washington now. Medical program."

"Wow," I say. I pour creamer into my coffee until it's the color of a palomino. "Your dad, huh?"

When Sam was here last, I got the distinct impression he and his dad were hardly on talking terms, but Sam would never elaborate.

He pushes the sugar in my direction but I shake my head.

"You don't take sugar in your coffee anymore?"

I could laugh at the question. I can't blame him for assuming. I let him believe it because sitting on the back patio in the early mornings with him, sharing a single cup of coffee, was one of the greatest thrills of our time together. The morning after our first kiss, he seemed to take so much pleasure in teaching me what he called the perfect cup of coffee and then handing me the same mug that had touched his lips—the way I had only hours before—and urged me to take a sip. When I did, it wasn't the sugar that woke me up, it was the way he revealed something about himself to me—one of the few things he ever had. And because of my infatuation with him, I drank it up, the coffee and this small piece of him.

I place my spoon on the counter with a sharp clink. "I never did."

He furrows his brow, like this information is life altering, like he's never met me before.

"Listen," he says. "I can see this is uncomfortable for you and I'm sorry. When your dad called, I was honored that your parents would still think of me after all this time. Your parents' kindness has always meant the world to me. And honestly, I figured you'd be long gone by now."

"Long gone?"

"You had that itch to get out there, see the world. And I know how all-consuming that can be."

I huff a laugh. "Yeah, well, reality is more consuming. I've been in New York all this time, actually."

"Right. Columbia."

"Yep."

Any other viable option disappeared with him. But this time, I'm the one who doesn't elaborate. I don't want Sam to know that I haven't done any of the things I told him I wanted to do. Or that he might have been the reason.

"That's great," he says.

The back door opens and Kelly steps into the open kitchen. When she sees me standing next to Sam—too closely, I realize— her jaw tightens. I straighten.

"Sam," she says in greeting, not even pretending to be glad to see him.

He takes a step away from me and nods in her direction. "Kelly. You look well."

"Is your mom around?" she asks me, ignoring Sam altogether.

"She's at work," I say. "Can I get something for you?"

Kelly shakes her head. "I just needed her help with something in the cellar."

"I'll help," I offer as she turns away. I'm already crossing the kitchen before she has the chance to refuse. I ignore her sigh, shuffling out the door behind her.

I sneak a glance at Sam. He raises his mug to me, his provocative smile promising we'll have more time to catch up.

I trail Kelly to the wine cellar. The entrance is around the back of the house where two doors open into an underground room like an old storm cellar in the Midwest. It's been this way since it was built in the 1980s and is in desperate need of updating but the vineyard's lack of money means it sits untouched, a portal into a different time.

Kelly graciously motions for me to enter first, both of us ducking our heads as we descend the creaky wooden stairs. The cellar is dank and humid and extends the length of the house. Thankfully, Dad updated the lighting shortly after we moved in, brightening the space and showcasing the wooden barrels stacked two high along each wall.

"So…what exactly are we doing down here?" I ask Kelly. She uses the rusty old key to unlock the storage room at the far end of the cellar.

"All the event supplies are down here and your mom wants me to sort through it so she can see what else she needs for the planting party. I'm not sure exactly what she wants but we'll just grab anything that looks useful."

Dad has had planting parties before—gatherings of friends and neighbors who come together to sow a new crop of grape-vines on Dad's land. We eat, laugh, and drink wine. But this planting party means much more than a few acres of new grapes. It's an expansion and a celebration. Most people ro-manticize the life of a vintner as all affluence and glamour, but in reality, my dad is a farmer through and through. He has struggled to make the vineyard a success for nearly two decades.

Kelly yanks open the swollen storage room door.

I step inside and flip on the lights to find thirty years' worth of lost things. Rickety tables are stacked against the left wall. Dusty boxes are piled nearly to the ceiling. String lights are wound up like wreaths and stuck anywhere they would fit. I run my fingers over one of them. One night ten years ago, I thought these lights looked like stars, like magic. In this crowded storage room, they look forgotten.

"I'll take the left, you take the right?" I suggest.

"Sure." Kelly wedges her body between the boxes.

Once I clear a space to sit, I open the first box, finding an ancient set of CorningWare. I close it back up and set it aside. The second box is full of clothes I grew out of when I was twelve. Eventually I find some tablecloths, serving dishes, and signs to direct visitors, but my focus is always on Kelly, waiting for her to say something about Sam's reappearance. She was never short on opinions about him.

When I open a box in the corner, I immediately recognize the centerpieces Mom made for my sweet sixteen party—two horseshoes glued together with pink silk flowers woven into the nail holes. I run my fingers over them, loving memories filling me up like warm milk. That day was arguably the best of my life. It was the day my parents gave me Midnight, the horse I had been longing for since we'd moved West. And it was the day of my surprise party, which was entirely coordinated by Kelly because she wanted the day to be a memorable one. It had been.

When I realize the sound of shuffling on the other side of the room has ceased, I look up and find Kelly staring at me.

"That was a long time ago, wasn't it?" she asks.

I set the centerpiece back inside the box and brush the dust off on my pants. I don't know if she means temporally or emotionally but either way, it feels like a lifetime ago.

"Yeah, it was. How did that happen?" I ask with a soft laugh, knowing there's no answer.

Kelly looks down at her lap. "Your parents are happy you're here," she says. "They've missed you."

"I'm happy to be here. I've missed them, too. And you," I add.

She lifts her face but doesn't respond. When I can't take her empty stare any longer, I grab the next box and open it up. I hear the groan of her pulling one across the dirt floor, and the cardboard screeches as she opens the folded flaps.

"How have they been?" I ask, staying on a neutral subject, one she's deemed safe.

"Good," she says. "Your dad has been really excited about the new vines. He scoured the internet for months, calling people from all over Europe. And then, of course, he had many long talks with the shipping company to make sure nothing would happen to his babies on the way over."

As she says it, I see the first hint of a smile.

I smile, too.

"And your mom is doing well. The firm recently won a big case and they gave her a bonus for all the extra time she put in on it. She took me to Bakersfield last week to buy some new clothes and have lunch to celebrate."

My mom took Kelly shopping? And to lunch? It seems that while I may have left, Kelly's presence here hasn't waned at all. Quite the opposite. But shopping and lunch in Bakersfield used to be the thing my mom did with me, and I can't help the jealousy that wraps around my throat.

"Shopping, huh?" I ask, purposefully rummaging through the box in front of me, seeing none of it.

"We found some cute skirts."

As she says it, something becomes suddenly very clear to me. Kelly is mad at me for more than what happened with Sam before. She's mad at me for being here, mad at me for coming back to fill the spot as my parents' only daughter. My parents tell me during every phone call how much they miss me. Kelly must have seen an opportunity to have the family she'd always wanted and took it.

The betrayal stings. I never would have thought Kelly capable of such coldheartedness.

She pushes her box to the corner and grabs the next one—a simple act but all at once, she looks different to me, all perceived innocence gone. I wanted to forgive and forget the secrets she kept from me that summer, assuming she regretted them as much as I do mine. But she doesn't seem to regret them at all.

"So that's how it is now?" I ask. She furrows her brow in confusion. "Did you think I would stay in New York forever and you could just slip into my family like I was never there?"

The thing about having a friend with such fair skin is that I can watch her emotions color her face. Each shade of humiliation brightens her cheeks one degree at a time.

"You're not serious," she says. "It was just shopping. You never had a problem with me coming over to your house. Ever. Whether you were here or not. In fact, you nagged me to."

I did. When she was sick enough to miss school but we both knew her mom wasn't able to make her soup or check her temperature. For Thanksgiving dinners and Christmas mornings where Kelly had almost as many presents under the tree as I did.

"Of course I did, Kelly. I love you. My parents love you. I shared my parents with you because I wanted you to feel like you had a place where you would be taken care of the way you should have been. I wanted you to feel safe and loved."

"Oh, how generous of you," she retorts.

I ignore her snide remark. "This isn't the same and you know it. You don't want me here and that isn't fair. This is *my* home."

"You left it," she says, raising her voice. "And you never came back. You thought you'd find something better out there, and you did. Congratulations."

"You have no idea what you're talking about," I try to say, but she doesn't hear me as she charges on.

"What did you expect the rest of us to do? Sit around here waiting for you to grace us with your presence?"

"Don't be mad at me because your life hasn't turned out the way you wanted it to. That's not my fault."

"It's not my fault either," she snaps.

I've always had sympathy for Kelly's situation but using it as an excuse to stop living her life, to be angry at those who do pursue their goals…that I can't keep swallowing.

"It's a shitty situation nobody can do anything about but you don't have to take it out on me."

Kelly glares at me, so many layers of hurt evident in her eyes. She isn't mad at me about being stuck in Paso and we both know it.

"I'm sorry," I blurt out.

I rehearsed this conversation in my head a dozen times on the plane, and none of my speeches had started like that. But I wasn't prepared for how unsettling it would be to slip back into life here after being gone for so long. I wasn't prepared for how fresh Kelly's wounds would still be. There's no easing into this conversation.

"I should have told you that a lot sooner," I add.

My reasoning for not calling, not visiting, was easier to justify when I couldn't see the pain on her face. I should have tried harder. I should have done anything to show her how much our friendship means to me.

I let go of the box in my hands and move closer to her. She seems so small, crouched on the floor next to me, when in my eyes, she's always been larger than this life—larger than her mom makes her think she is, larger than this town… larger than me.

"Kelly, I'm so sorry. I made a lot of stupid decisions that summer. I've made a lot of stupid decisions in my life, mostly because I knew you were always there to help me fix them. Maybe I took advantage of that. I took for granted that you'd always forgive me for my…lapses in consideration."

A laugh bubbles up from her chest and I grab onto it like a life raft.

"Kelly," I say, my voice softening. "The biggest mistake I've ever made is allowing anything to get in the way of our friendship. And I didn't come back here just for my parents' planting party. I came back here for us. I want to be in your life again. I...I need you in my life again."

There's a long silence in which I hold my breath, waiting. Finally, Kelly sets aside the picture frame in her hand—a faded picture of the vineyard while it was being built—and stands.

"God," she spits, her voice echoing in this small space. "You are unbelievable. It's not that easy, Mallory."

"I know—"

"No, you don't know. You have no idea what it's been like for me these last ten years. You have no idea what's going on in my life."

I look away. She's right. I don't know anything about Kelly anymore, and to be honest, she knows little about who I've become. A decade can change a lot about a person. And that distance is my fault. I created this rift and allowed it to stay open.

"You can't—" She sighs, scrunching her eyes closed. It's an expression I'm intimately familiar with, having received it from her before, from my parents, from my teachers—that exasperation when I keep missing the point. "You can't just show up here and expect that we're all waiting around for you. You can't expect me to drop my responsibilities to deal with this."

To deal with me. Her words pierce straight through my heart because they confirm the beliefs that have haunted me since the day she said she was done with me, since the day the man who held my heart in his hands disappeared without a word. I don't know how to be who people need me to be, no matter how much I want to be. No matter how hard I try.

Tears sting my eyes. I blink them away before Kelly can see. It wouldn't be fair of me to expect her comfort.

Kelly clears her throat. "I need to make my mom lunch,"

73

she says. "I think you've got enough here. Tell your mom I'll be by tomorrow."

I nod, dejected.

Kelly hesitates a moment longer, then walks the long corridor out of the cellar. I start when the door falls shut. Leaning over, I pick up the picture Kelly had been holding, a glimpse into a past I never knew. They say history repeats itself and in this moment, it feels like they're right.

SEVEN

The following afternoon, I surprise myself by taking a nap, something I haven't done in years. I'm never relaxed enough during the day to nod off, but after another early-morning ride with Tyler and a little too much sun, I curl up on my bed like a cat and fall asleep before I realize what's happened.

When I wake up, I roll over and check the time on my phone. After 4:00 p.m. Several new messages from the office demand my attention, but my mind is too languid to formulate a response, so I set my phone back down and stretch my limbs in every direction, widening myself across the bed.

On the ceiling overhead is a poster of a horse. I placed it there the first night we moved in. It's small and cheap—the kind pulled out of a magazine, creases in the middle and the small tears from the staples. The edges have curled with age and it sags in the middle. I don't remember which magazine I pulled it from, I just remember it was the first thing I felt was truly mine after we left Chicago. All the furniture in this house was provided by the then owners—the dishes, the decorations, the laundry detergent smell. All I brought with me were my clothes, a few books from my previous school's summer reading list, and a magazine we'd picked up in a gas station on the long drive across the country. Dad had bribed me for support with the promise that there would be horses, and when I saw the poster in the magazine, I thought maybe I would learn to love life at a vineyard. Maybe it would come to feel like home. There was something about the way the mare's mane trailed behind her that looked like freedom. It looked like living.

And I did love it here. It suited my personality, this need to explore, to live with my bare feet on the ground and my head in the clouds. Dad has often said I was born with dirt under my nails and an allergy to fluorescent lighting. He said it fondly, taking pride in raising a daughter who shared his appreciation for connecting to the earth.

When was the last time I spent more time outside than it takes to walk to the subway? When was the last time I escaped to the ocean? When was the last time I even wanted to? When was the last time I was still long enough to ask myself these questions? Years, it must be.

Before I let myself run away with my thoughts, I drag myself out of bed.

As I'm getting ready for a local grape growers event, Mom calls to ask if I can pick up Kelly on my way. Mom had promised to do it but got stuck at work finishing up briefs.

I hesitate before I answer. My last conversation with Kelly didn't go like I'd hoped, and I'm sure she won't be thrilled by the change in plans. But ultimately I agree because the only way I'm going to convince Kelly she can trust me again is to be there for her, no matter how many times she pushes me away.

As a gesture of peace, I stop by a local boutique on my way to pick out a gift for Kelly's mom. As I scan the rows for something Shannon would like, I wonder if I'm a masochist. Naive or desperate. Kelly has made it clear she has no interest in hearing me out. Maybe she doesn't need me in her life anymore.

But these years without her have been the hardest and loneliest of my life. And if there's any chance she feels the same way, whether she wants to admit it right now or not, I can't give up on her. Not until I've given it my all. I owe us that much.

I make the assumption that Mom has let Kelly know to expect me, but when I arrive, Kelly isn't waiting outside for me. I sit in my car for a couple of minutes, in case her plan was to run out and meet me. She's never been comfortable having people in her house and even though I was the only person she ever let inside, she agreed to it rarely.

When several minutes pass with no sign of her, I cut the engine and grab the gift bag from the passenger seat. I step out of the car and approach slowly. My fist hangs in the air for several moments before I knock.

From inside, Kelly calls, "Come in."

I'm not sure what to expect when I step inside, what might have changed in the ten years since my last visit, but it looks almost exactly the same—a little two-bedroom single-wide paid for by Shannon's disability checks. The door opens to the kitchen, filled with mismatched dishes and decrepit appliances. The space is cramped but Kelly keeps it perfectly neat, making the best of their circumstances. I navigate the narrow dining area, following the ever-present sound of the TV buzzing in the living room.

As I round the corner, Kelly emerges from her bedroom, her fingers nimbly folding her hair into her trademark braid. She pauses when sees me. She was still anticipating Mom, who has apparently entered the ranks of the few people Kelly trusts with the secrets of her homelife.

"Mom had to work," I say.

"Oh. Okay. What's that?"

I motion to where I know Shannon will be sitting around the corner. Kelly purses her lips, unimpressed by my deed, and returns to bustling around. She wraps an elastic at the bottom of her braid and fills a cup with water at the kitchen sink.

"I just need a minute," she says.

"No rush."

"Mom, Mallory's here," Kelly says, leaving the kitchen. I inch my way into the room as Kelly delivers the water and rushes off to her bedroom. A Hallmark movie flashes a doe-eyed hero across the screen.

I invite myself into the living room and am relieved to find that Shannon looks about the same as I remember her, too. I thought she might look…sicker, but other than the oxygen tube running over her ears and into her nose, she still has good color in her cheeks, alertness in her eyes, and consistency in her weight, which admittedly has always been far past healthy. That's the reason Kelly has protected her mother and herself from mockery by keeping everyone away, locking everyone out of her life.

Except me. She used to trust me.

"Mallory," Shannon says, a smile lighting up her face.

"Hey, Shannon," I say. I lean over to give her a hug. I'm careful to avoid her oxygen tank and the tube she's tangled up in. When I get my arms around her, she squeezes me tighter than she ever has before.

"It has been a sad day without you here, Mallory Victoria," she says into my ear.

"I've missed you guys, too."

"Sit," Shannon says.

Shannon's hair is cut just above her shoulders and dyed red

where it must have once been a natural strawberry like Kelly's. Her fleshy cheeks have a rosy undertone, as well.

"This is for you." I hand the simple paper bag to her and her smile grows. She reaches in to remove the tissue paper and pulls out the terry cloth thong slippers.

"Oh, Mallory. You didn't have to do that."

"May I?" I ask.

Shannon hands me the slippers and I kneel to place them gently on her feet, one at a time. Her toenails are painted a bright red, no doubt Kelly's work. I sit back and admire the effect.

"Perfect," I say.

"Thank you," she says on a breath, taking my hand and squeezing it.

"How have you been feeling?" I ask her as I settle in next to her on the couch. Growing up, I used to sit with Shannon like this, waiting for Kelly to finish her homework or finish cooking Shannon dinner. I've always liked Kelly's mom. She has a dry humor that can bring tears to my eyes and a pride in Kelly that lights her up anytime Kelly walks into the room. I have to admit, though, that my feelings toward Shannon aren't entirely positive, knowing she's the reason Kelly has never left Paso, unable to follow her dreams or even to live.

"Kelly told you, did she?"

"Told me what?" I ask.

This surprises her—that Kelly has kept something from me.

"My mom mentioned she's been bringing meals over. She worries about you," I say. "And about Kelly."

Shannon wears a sad smile. "She's a good woman, your mom."

"She adores you, too. I know you're welcome over anytime," I say, though my invitation falls on deaf ears. I've invited Shannon over many times and she's never taken me up on it. She hasn't left the house in so long, I'm not sure she would be able to handle the stimulation, the sights and sounds, the busyness.

"Thank you," she says, "but I forgot how to pretend to be a normal human being about thirty years ago."

That's what I've always loved about Shannon—her honesty. She makes no excuses and blows no smoke. Forgetting how to pretend to be normal is one of her greatest accomplishments, in my opinion, and I wonder if I could take a page from her book.

"Look at you," she says. "You've grown up a lot."

"Have I?" I self-consciously smooth my hair. I dressed up for tonight, pulling out some of my "New York clothes," as Tyler has taken to calling them. I've dressed them down by keeping the formfitting knee-length black skirt and high-necked white blouse simple, with minimal accessories and ballet flats instead of heels.

"Everyone keeps saying that. I don't know. Maybe it's because the change was gradual for me and more drastic for everyone else."

"Maybe it's that fast-paced city life," she suggests.

I laugh. "Maybe."

"I always loved the city," Shannon says. "I lived in LA with my grandparents when I was a teenager."

That is, until she got pregnant with Kelly at seventeen and they disowned her. Kelly told me the story. It wasn't only her grandparents who disowned her. It was her entire family. That was when Shannon's depression started, as I understand it. Kelly's father walking out and leaving her a single mother without any support certainly didn't help either.

"My sister lives in that house now. I keep telling Kelly she should go down there. Bethany doesn't talk to me anymore but I know she'd be happy to have Kelly. She would never blame Kelly for my mistakes."

"Kelly was not a mistake," I say defensively, though I know that I don't have to tell Shannon that. That's not what she meant anyway. "That sounds like a good idea," I add more calmly.

I remember Kelly talking about her aunt Bethany. Bethany used to send Kelly birthday and Christmas cards. Kelly threw them away and gave the money to homeless men outside local bars. I don't tell Shannon that. I know it would upset her to know the depth of Kelly's loyalty to her.

"Kelly should have more family around her," Shannon says. "It's my fault she doesn't know them."

"I don't think she would agree with you. In fact, I know she wouldn't. Family is supposed to support you. Even when you make mistakes. Especially when you make mistakes."

Even if it means giving up your own happiness? a voice in my head asks. Is it right that Kelly should be Shannon's only support? Maybe not, but they're all each other has.

"You two have a special bond," I say. "You've always had each other to count on and that's what makes family, in my opinion. Not blood."

Shannon looks down at her hands.

"I'm sure you're right," she says. "Which is why I'm so grateful she has you. Your friendship has kept her going, Mallory. Even while you've been gone." She leans forward, frowning. "Don't let her fool you into thinking she's forgotten about you. She believed you would come back, and holding on to that belief kept her going when she didn't have much hope of anything else."

I shake my head. "I don't think—"

She holds up a hand to stop my denial. "She loves you, Mallory. She's proud of what you've done, but she's stubborn as an ox. No one knows that better than you."

I laugh, hot tears stinging my eyes. "Isn't that the truth."

Shannon sighs. "It's a family trait, I'm afraid. Which has its pros and cons." I'm not sure what she means. When I don't say anything, she goes on, "I'm not stupid. I know I'm tying her down here. I know she needs more than this."

I don't pretend to argue. It's not Shannon's intention to hold her daughter back. I know she loves Kelly more than anything else in this world. But even in the short time I've been back, I can see that Kelly's soul is dying, being stuck here. How could it not, taking care of her mom and working two dead-end jobs year after year after year? Kelly was always the dreamer. She could never be satisfied here.

Shannon sucks in a breath, the seriousness of the conversation raising her heart rate. She adjusts the oxygen in her nostrils. I place my hand on hers to calm her, but I can tell there's something else she needs to say.

"Mallory, I need you to promise me something."

I hope I can keep my promise, agreeing even before I know what Shannon will ask of me. Because for Kelly, what wouldn't I do?

"I need you to promise me that you'll talk Kelly into putting me into a nursing home."

"Wait, what?" I ask. Before the implications of this can sink in, she goes on, looking toward Kelly's bedroom door with urgency.

"I keep trying to tell her she's done enough for me but she won't hear it. She doesn't want me to be lonely, but she doesn't understand that it's lonelier for me to sit here and watch her wasting her life away. She is meant for so much more than this. She could go to LA. She could join a practice. She could do anything."

"I thought..." I think back to my conversations with Kelly, the way she's blamed her mother's condition for not leaving Paso. Did I misunderstand her? I don't think so. But why would Kelly blame her mother all this time when she's been free to go for years?

"She listens to you," Shannon says. "She might pretend like she doesn't, like she's got it all figured out, but she needs you to help her through this. I need your help."

"I would do anything for Kelly," I say. "I would do anything for you."

But would Kelly accept my help? Would she listen to me?

"Of course you would, honey," she says. "Of course you would."

Shannon narrows her eyes and I know there's more she wants to tell me, some wisdom she wants to impart, but before she can, Kelly reemerges from her bedroom. When Shannon and I hear her, we break apart.

"You ready?" Kelly asks me.

"Yep," I say, not quite meeting her gaze. I stand and reach out to touch Shannon's arm. "It was great to see you again," I tell her.

"You, too, Mallory. Tell your mom thanks for the casserole."

I give her a parting hug and she holds me longer than I expect her to. Her body is warm and soft and I melt into her affection.

"I will," I say, implying so much more with those two words than a polite gesture. "I promise."

I stand and notice Kelly watching us with suspicious eyes.

"Nice slippers," she says.

"She's worse off than she looks," Kelly says in the car on the way to the bar. She's been fidgeting in the passenger seat since we got in, almost as if she overheard my conversation with Shannon. Kelly is the kind of person who would come straight out about it if she had but her attitude is defensive, like she's ready to pounce at one wrong word.

"I enjoyed talking to her," I say, hoping this is innocuous enough.

"You didn't need to get her anything. She's fine. We're fine."

I sigh. "I know, Kel. I was just trying to do something nice."

During our childhood, I used to be able to do no wrong with Kelly. Our adoration of each other was bigger than any petty disagreement, any guy, any social misstep. Now I can do no right. Every conversation with her is a minefield.

Still, Shannon's words replay in my mind. Kelly is hard-headed, but she loves me. If the memory of our friendship kept her going during the hard times, as Shannon suggested, could my presence encourage her to take the leap into a new future?

"You know," I hedge, "maybe you could get some help with her. Have some time for yourself."

I flip on my blinker, turning onto the highway. Kelly snorts a bitter laugh at me.

"Like we could afford that."

"If you were able to get a job in your field..."

The more I let this LA idea ruminate, the more I think it could work. There would be nursing homes in the city, psychology practices. They could stay close, visit every day. Kelly could get an apartment within walking distance of wherever Shannon was living.

Maybe I could even find a marketing firm nearby...

"You know what, Mallory?" she says, turning toward me so she can make herself absolutely clear. "Don't come back here after all this time and act like you know anything about my life."

Her words cut, as she meant them to, but I'm not going to

let her keep throwing my leaving in my face. I only did what she wanted me to. She's being unfair.

"Maybe I would if you would stop shutting me out. I know I screwed up and I'm sorry, but you seem to be conveniently forgetting that you hid things from me, too. You lied to me all summer and acted like you were justified because you were upset. Because I hurt you. But you hurt me, too. You left me, too."

Kelly turns away from me, crossing her arms and looking out the window. It takes all my willpower not to pull over, to force her to face me, but Kelly is the kind of person who needs breathing room. She likes to think things through.

"I was doing you a favor," she says. "I was letting you go so I wouldn't hold you back."

"But why didn't you come?" I plead. "You didn't have to hold either one of us back. You've been telling everyone that it's your mom keeping you here, but that isn't true, is it? Your mom wants you to go. She wants you to live your life. She doesn't want to be a burden to you. She loves you."

"Stop," Kelly says, her tone bordering on hysteria. "I don't want to hear it. Don't you think I've told myself all of those things a million times since I was six years old and I was finally old enough to understand that we weren't a normal family? I've given her a million excuses, a million breaks, but the truth is, if she wanted to unburden me, she would get herself better. She would do whatever it took. She doesn't want to change. She doesn't care about me enough to get healthy, to have a life. So *I* could have a life."

With Kelly's psychology degree, I know she knows how depression and—based on my own assumptions—agoraphobia work. I know her emotions are getting the best of her, and for good reason. How much should a person give up their life for another? Especially when Shannon stopped seeking help for her condition a long time ago.

Still, I empathize with Kelly's mom. I understand how hard it can be to overcome the scars of the past. Even with the best of intentions, we can often get in our own way.

After a long moment, when some of the tension has dissipated, Kelly says, "Do you think that if I put her in a nursing home, I'm just going to stop worrying about her? Out of sight, out of mind? No matter where I go or what I do, waiting for her to die and leave me all alone will follow me everywhere."

I swallow hard, any response caught in my throat. I've always known Kelly has a hard time trusting people. I know she's spent a lot of her life feeling alone and like she has no one to lean on. But I had no idea that Kelly feared for her mom's life. Our parents are so young, the possibility hasn't become a reality for me yet, but my parents and Shannon are in vastly different circumstances.

I can't imagine how Kelly lives with this fear every day. It's no wonder she blames me for taking away the one other person in her life who she considered family.

"I never wanted to leave you, Kelly," I say softly, staring resolutely at the road ahead. "You made that decision for us."

"But you couldn't stay," she says, and the truth of it echoes between us long after we've fallen silent.

I reach for my wrist, the tattoos we share. We got them that summer, a promise to each other for the next stage of our lives. She held up to her end of the deal. She kept me focused. Her methods weren't how I imagined them the day the artist put them there in permanent ink, but her disownment was nonetheless effective. It was my role to push her, to bring out Kelly's courageous side, her sense of adventure. And I know just how to remind her.

As I take the off-ramp, I reach for the folded pink paper

inside my purse. This wasn't how I planned to give it to her—it deserves more ceremony than this—but it's my last-ditch attempt to remind her that she once believed in taking chances. She once believed in me.

I hold the paper out to her.

"What's this?" she asks.

"Take it."

She does and for a moment, she holds it like she doesn't know what to do with it. I'm surprised she doesn't recognize it immediately—it was her paper, her glittery purple pen. I wait patiently and finally she opens it up. I cast glances at her as she reads over it, trying to gauge her reaction.

I don't need to see it to know what's written there. I memorized it a long time ago.

Across the top, in Kelly's neat cursive, it reads *"Kelly and Mallory's Summer Bucket List."* Underneath she scrawled the year, which seems impossibly distant now.

Expressionless, she folds it back up and stares straight ahead. "You kept it?" she asks, her anger more forced. She doesn't want to let me off the hook, but the list is the symbol of who we used to be, the things we used to want, our shared sense of possibility.

We never got to finish the list, our summer cut short by hidden agendas and resentments.

I nod, a tentative smile pulling at my lips.

"I can't believe you still have it," she says. And if I'm not mistaken, there's a softness in her tone. A reminiscence.

"I've carried it around in my wallet," I tell her.

"No, you didn't," she says. "Seriously?"

I laugh. "I did. Everywhere."

"You haven't changed at all," she says. I can't tell if she means that as a compliment or an insult. It's true, I'm idealistic and often expect life to live up to my unrealistic fantasies. I'm also sentimental. The people in my life mean everything to me. Kelly's friendship has meant the most, even when I got caught up with Sam, caught up in a fantasy.

"You've never stopped being my best friend, Kelly."

I dare to say this while I don't have to meet her gaze, while she's wrapped up in the good memories we had from that summer.

She holds the list out to me. I push it back toward her.

"I'm staying until Sunday," I say.

"What? You want to do the bucket list?" she asks, incredulous.

"Why not? I promised you, didn't I? Let me prove to you that I can still keep my promises to you. I never meant to break them."

"Mallory, I—"

"I know I haven't been there for you since I left," I say, cutting her off, "and I'm so sorry for that. It's clear you've needed more support. If you'd let me, I'd really like to be here for you now."

Kelly frowns and chews at her bottom lip. Are those tears in her eyes?

"The thing is," Kelly says, "I don't know if our friendship is good for me. I don't know if it ever was."

"What?" I ask, breathless. How could she possibly mean that? We were everything to each other. All the plans we had for our future were the plans she made. We used to talk about raising our kids together.

So many memories of our friendship flash before my eyes—when I gave her my skirt, the first time she let me into her house, horseback riding through the vineyard thousands of times, laughing over family dinners. Was it all a lie?

"I don't understand," I say.

"I know," she says, a tear rolling down her cheek. I can

hardly see the road in front of me, but I can't stop driving. I need something else to focus on. "And that's my fault. I love you, Mallory, I do. But sometimes the reasons we love someone aren't healthy."

I don't believe there was anything unhealthy about our relationship. We were for each other what we needed to be. We filled the holes no one else could. The holes that have been emptied again with each other's absence. But what can I do? If Kelly doesn't want me in her life, I'm not sure how to convince her. If she really believes that, I don't know if I want to try.

But I have to ask, "Are you sure?"

Kelly places her hand over her eyes, her elbow against the window. The bucket list flutters to her lap. For the first time, she looks older to me.

"No," she says. "I'm not. But too much has happened between us and I don't know how to let it go."

In that moment, I can actually feel the sharp pain of my heart breaking. For her. For me. For us. And all I want to do is hug her. All I want is to save her, even if it's from me.

We arrive at The Drunken Pub, the favorite town bar, and the place is crawling with locals. Cars overflow the parking lot and down the street in both directions. Kelly and I have to park a quarter mile away and walk, getting greeted every few feet by people we've grown up with—other vineyard owners and laborers, small business owners, parents of the people we went to school with. Most of them are regular customers at Monet's Mug and stop to catch up with Kelly. Others, seeing me for the first time since I left, exclaim over how different I look and pepper me with questions about New York. I try to keep a smile on my face as I answer, try to swallow down the devastation I feel over this new picture of our friendship Kelly has painted, but my responses are distracted and half-hearted.

As we approach the front door, I wait for Kelly to join me so we can go in together. It would look unusual if we were out separately. It was once a rare occasion that either one of us was caught around town without the other. Then again, by now everyone is probably used to my absence. Kelly included. But she does seek me out, a sad concession of a smile tightening her face, and we duck inside, neither one of us looking at each other.

The lights are out and the open sign is off. My dad warned me with a mischievous grin that the details of the annual event are highly classified and to expect surprises. Kelly is obviously familiar with the ritual so I give her a far lead.

As the door creaks open, the sound of a hundred or more voices, country music, and clinking glasses overwhelms me. The bar is so packed that if the fire chief weren't sitting in the corner with three other men in uniform, the owner would surely receive a citation. Peanut shells crunch beneath our feet. Tossing them on the floor after eating from the baskets on every table is a tradition Joe Kennady has upheld since he moved here and bought the bar when I was a girl.

I spot Tyler. He's behind the bar, unruffled by the busy night or the amount of orders being yelled at him at once. It's unusual to see him cleaned up and dressed for indoors. He's without his customary ragged baseball cap, and instead of his usual run-down T-shirts, he has on a black collared polo shirt. The place is lit by dozens of lanterns tonight, but even in the dim lighting, the dark contrast to his light skin and auburn hair make his features brighter.

When he sees Kelly and me squeezing into a small opening at the bar, he moves around the other bartenders to come over to us, smiling and ignoring the line of people trying to get his attention.

"You made it," he says, leaning close so we can hear him.

His face is cleanly shaven and I catch a hint of his cologne, spicy and warm.

"Of course," I say. "I wouldn't miss it."

"Is this your first *ritual sacrifice*?" he asks us, deepening his voice on the last two words.

"It's mine," I say, rolling my eyes at the dramatics.

The Libations for Germination Party has been a tradition in Paso Robles since its inception when Joe moved to town, bought the old market that had been sitting empty for a year, and turned it into the one place in town where dusty, sun-burned farmers could get a good stiff drink that didn't come from a grape.

Every year on the night of the April full moon, the town gathers to put up their offering to the agricultural gods with the hope of bringing rain and a good season's crop. From what I understand, it's a farce—a play on the rituals farmers used to employ in pagan religions. My dad, being a vintner, has participated every year. I, however, have never been old enough to attend myself, and part of the tradition is that the details of the ceremony are kept secret. Mostly, it's an excuse for the townspeople to get together and drink.

"Well, I'd be honored to get you initiated," Tyler says as he pulls two shot glasses out from beneath the bar, flipping them right side up. He grabs a glass jug of something that's clear and doesn't sport a label. He expertly pours the liquid into each of our glasses.

"Oh, Lord," I say. "What in the world is that?"

"Gift from the Gods," Tyler says, waiting for us to try it. I hang back, still uncertain about what I'm getting myself into, but Kelly picks hers up and swallows some of it down, pull-ing a face.

"That's just as awful as always," she says in a nasal voice.

Feeling like I have something to prove to Kelly—though

I'm not sure what—I lift my glass to my nose. It stings my nostrils, making my eyes water. I cough and Tyler laughs.

"It's Joe's moonshine," he says. "Distills it himself just for this occasion."

"Is that legal?" I ask.

Tyler points to the sheriff sitting in the corner, sipping from his own shot glass.

"Technically, we're closed for business today," Tyler says. "What's a little moonshine between friends?"

"Is that why the sign was turned off?" I ask.

Tyler winks.

Someone squeezes in behind me, knocking me forward and spilling some of my drink onto the floor.

A loud chime echoes through the room and the crowd quiets. Joe, a muscular man in his late fifties with gray-black hair and a forearm tattoo of a mermaid, stands on top of the bar with an empty moonshine bottle and a wooden spoon.

Once the bar has fallen mostly silent, he begins in his booming voice, "Welcome to the eighteenth annual Libations for Germination!"

The crowd goes wild. I wish I could laugh and join in, hollering at the top of my lungs like everyone else, but the conversation with Kelly hangs heavy over me. My insides have melted into a pool at the bottom of my stomach. I venture a sip of my drink, praying for a tonic for this feeling. I choke on its harshness as it burns its way down.

"The reason we're here," Joe goes on, "is to, like our ancestors before us, perform a ceremonial ritual asking the gods to grace us with water, which we will turn into wine. Oh, yeah, and to celebrate this beautiful town of ours."

More cheering. I see Dad sneak in the back door, a shot of moonshine quickly finding its way into his hand. He pats a few men on the back and gets pulled into a conversation with another.

"What you're holding in your hands is a symbol," Joe announces. He holds his glass up and everyone in the room follows suit. With the light from the lanterns, they sparkle through the room like lighters at a concert. "Gift of the Gods is clear, like the rain, and like the tears of the men who have come and gone before us, angering the gods with their subpar wine."

Laughter ripples through the crowd and crinkles Kelly's eyes.

"We will drink this rain, taking it into ourselves to feed the crops during the long, hot summer."

"Hear, hear," the town responds, practiced at this presentation.

"We will drink these tears to wash them away, erasing the memories of any bad seasons before this."

"Hear, hear!"

This time Kelly and I join in quietly, infected by the energy of the room. I hear Dad's voice above the crowd. He catches my gaze and waves.

"We will drink to celebrate the prosperous season ahead!"

Joe says this last line with particular gusto and the crowd explodes. He lifts his glass a little higher, then swallows it down in one gulp.

I look around the room as everyone follows suit, and in that moment, the door opens and Sam slides into the already overcrowded bar. Everything about him is out of place, from the product in his hair to the shine of his dress shoes. He would look more at home in the tourist spots down the street.

He doesn't belong here.

That's why he catches my eye, I tell myself. Because of how very much he contrasts everyone else in the room with their jeans and muddy boots and old country demeanor. I don't know why I catch his eye—how or why I stand out to him—but his eyes land on me immediately, like I'm on his radar.

This celebration is for locals and he is not a local, but my dad spots him and folds him into his conversation without missing a beat. As he talks, Sam never takes his eyes off me.

I watch him, bringing the rest of the moonshine to my lips. I tilt it back in one swift movement.

Kelly follows my gaze and a cold expression settles on her face when her eyes lands on Sam.

I pull my attention away from both of them and tell Tyler, "I'm going to need another one of these."

EIGHT

I wasn't the only one who noticed Sam. The first time Kelly parked her run-down white Honda next to his sleek silver Porsche, she accosted me with questions. Who was he? What did he do? Where did he come from? How long was he staying? He was just as foreign to her as he was to me. People who drove cars like his never stayed longer than a week.

Her questions overwhelmed me. I felt oddly protective of Sam. Secretive. I didn't know a lot about Sam, but what I did know, he had measuredly given to me. After his first few weeks working with Dad, I knew his birthday—January 16, a determined and intelligent Capricorn—that he loved music and that he cherished his mother above everything else. I was beginning to paint a picture of who I thought he was and I didn't want anyone else's opinions to tarnish that.

Unfortunately, opinions came unbidden.

"He seems kind of full of himself," Tyler said to me on one of our morning rides.

"Who?" I asked, deflecting, though I had to admit there had been a few times I'd thought the same thing. That voice in my head—the one that reminded me that I came almost from nothing, and that he would never look twice at a simple girl like me—was quieter and easily drowned out by the voice that told me to move closer to him, to hang onto his every word, to hope against all hope.

"Mr. Sports Car. Who else?"

It wasn't just his car. The week before, I'd slipped one of his business cards out of his leather portfolio and he'd watched me, curious, as I examined it.

Samuel B. Ryder.

I'd always thought the use of a middle initial pointless and snooty—an attempt to sound royal or presidential. Of course, I didn't say that to him.

"What does it stand for?" I'd asked.

"Brendon." He'd smiled. "What about you?"

"Victoria. After my grandmother."

"Mallory Victoria Graham," he'd whispered, his lips elegantly forming each syllable. "You could be a duchess."

Sounding like royalty wasn't really a bad thing, I figured.

"He takes pride in himself and his work," I said in response to Tyler as we sat side by side with our toes in the pond. "What's so wrong with that?"

"Nothing. It's when you treat other people like you're better than them that it's a problem."

"He doesn't treat anyone like he's better than them."

Tyler raised an eyebrow skeptically. "Really? So you don't feel like you're a supporting actress on the Sam show?" he asked.

I didn't respond, nor did I meet his gaze.

"Exactly," he said, hearing the words I didn't want to say.

My feelings of inferiority when comparing myself to Sam

were a combination of so many things. Our age difference, his life experience, the impeccable looks he was born with. None of those traits were things he manufactured with the intent to make anyone feel lesser. They were what they were. Maybe he lived with a certainty that came from a privileged upbringing but I admired him for it. I hoped I could learn from him how to live with a similar outlook, a belief in myself that had so far eluded me.

Tyler wasn't the only one with reservations. As Kelly's initial curiosity wore off, she questioned me with more and more skepticism.

"So you're, like, his assistant?" she asked on a morning ride. We walked the horses through the grapevines. "I thought *you* hired *him*."

"My *dad* hired him."

"You, your dad, the vineyard. It's all the same. It just doesn't make sense to me that you're paying the guy and yet you're doing the grunt work."

I took a deep breath to temper my impatience. Neither Tyler nor Kelly had had a single conversation with Sam and yet they had so much to say about him. Even if I agreed with them, it wasn't like I could avoid Sam—we were tethered together by Dad for the rest of the summer, for better or worse.

"Dad asked me to. It's fine. It will save the vineyard money if we don't have to pay him for things like sorting through Dad's teetering stacks of paperwork and making trivial phone calls. But really, it's for my dad, not Sam."

It didn't help my case that I blushed every time I said his name.

Kelly watched me with narrowed eyes.

"Wow," she finally said. "I don't think you've ever actually liked a guy before."

I thought about denying it but I didn't want to lie to her.

Little did I know just how much lying I would be doing that summer. For now, I said nothing.

"Just don't forget what this summer is about, Mal. Don't waste it on a crush. It's not like anything serious can come from it. We're leaving."

I was quick to reassure her I knew and agreed, but when we left the horses in the stables and I met Sam in the kitchen to start work for the day, our conversation slipped from my mind as soon as he smiled at me.

"What are you working on?" I asked him when he returned to scribbling in his notebook, his pen scratching against the paper.

"An advertisement for a local paper. Well, localish. There aren't a lot of people in town to advertise to," he says. "Not people who don't already know about it."

I lifted one side of the newspaper scattered in front of him so I could see the title. He seemed to be studying other ads to model ours after.

"Dad told me what you're going to do with the old barn. A tasting room?"

Sam nodded.

The barn had been sitting empty since before we moved in, and as a girl, I'd always been afraid of it, making up stories during sleepovers with Kelly about how it was haunted. Whenever we'd walked past it on the way to the bus stop or to her house, we superstitiously walked in a wide circle around it.

But Dad had shown me Sam's mock-ups and they were breathtaking—the cute little wooden tables and the racks with glistening bottles of wine in every slot. A bar where Dad could open the bottles and pour the glasses, allow certain wines to breathe before serving them. In the back half of the barn, there would be an area for more cellar space, and a private party room that could hold twelve people. Glass doors would separate the private room from the lobby, keeping the open feel. My old stories seemed childish in comparison to Sam's vision. It was just a barn, and soon it would be something beautiful created by someone beautiful.

Sam dropped his pen and sat back, giving me his full attention. He overwhelmed me every time he did.

"It will be a chance for your dad to introduce people to his wines and to let them get to know him. Rich is a smart, passionate man and it's that passion that sells the wine, not the grapes."

It was disconcerting to hear my dad described with so much adoration or to try to see him from an outside perspective, but Sam was right—Dad's enthusiasm for good wine fingerprinted the skin of every grape that grew on this vineyard. That was something that couldn't be bottled.

He motioned me over to see his work. I hesitated but when he nodded his head again, I sat and scooted my chair closer to his, allowing a few inches between us. I sensed his proximity acutely.

"The culture here is so different from Washington."

I focused my attention on his clumsy sketch. In the foreground, he'd drawn a wine bottle with what looked like a logo on the label, but it was different from our current labels. In the background, there were squiggly lines that almost resembled grapevines from a high vantage point, like from the mountaintop where I rode Midnight most mornings. The big block text next to the wine bottle read "Taste the good life." The message was all there, but his drawing was the equivalent of stick figures.

I was so relieved to see he wasn't perfect at everything that I laughed.

"Hey, give me a break," he said, unembarrassed. "A graphic

designer will whip this up. I just need to give him the general idea."

"No, it's good," I said through giggles.

He stretched his long fingers across his chest, wounded. "You're going to hurt my fragile ego."

I thought, *I highly doubt that.*

"I like it," I said, though apparently not convincing enough, because he scoffed and pulled the sheet of paper away from me. "No, really," I said with a laugh, which I quickly stifled.

I reached for the drawing and he allowed me to pull it back over so I could study it closer.

"The wine bottle is great and the overhead shot of the vineyard would be beautiful. But what if, for the text, it was more like...*the perfect getaway*?"

"Hmm..." he said slowly, nodding, pondering.

"It just seems like most people who come to visit act like this place is like...heaven on earth or something. I mean, if you can't go to Paris."

Sam grinned. "Now there's a tagline. *When you can't go to Italy.*"

I laughed. "LA people would love that."

He nodded, his pen already back in his hand, scratching out his previous wording.

"You're pretty good at this, you know?" he said as he wrote down both of our ideas. "Have you done anything like this before?"

I moved away from him, embarrassed by his compliment. I shook my head. Truthfully, I'd taken a communications class my junior year and it was one of the only classes I'd excelled in without Kelly's help, but I didn't mention it for fear of reminding him that I was barely out of high school.

"You should consider it. Most people don't realize that the key to marketing is being able to put yourself in someone else's shoes. Namely, your ideal customer. You seem to get that naturally."

I shrugged, unsure how to answer. "It must help that you've met so many different kinds of people. On your travels," I clarified. He had mentioned frequent trips to Europe during our walks in the vineyard.

"Maybe. But I think you learn more about other people the more you learn about yourself. Growing up, I had a lot of time to think about my place in the world."

Sam's gaze grew distant—an expression I'd grown familiar with in observing him. Despite his charming smile, there was a sadness in him, just below the surface, and I'd never wanted to uncover anything so badly in my life.

"You were alone a lot?" I asked.

His attention snapped back to me, but he didn't answer. He stared right through me and his intensity unnerved me. I usually shied away from vulnerability but with him, I wanted to peel back my layers, hoping that in turn, he would peel back his.

"Maybe you're right," I said. "As an only child to two people who are always working, I spent a lot of time alone, too. Kelly comes over, but...her mom needs her."

Sam woke from his reverie and the muscles in his cheeks tightened to an almost smile. A pretend smile. Anger flared inside me as I thought about the prejudiced assumptions Tyler and Kelly cloaked him in.

"That must be it," Sam said. He picked up his pen again and started to scribble nonsensical designs in the corner of his page.

I didn't push it further.

NINE

"And now we make our sacrifice," Joe bellows before climbing down from the bar and disappearing into the crowd.

"Oh, Jesus. I need more alcohol," I tell Kelly. She shakes her head and points to the bathroom. I nod.

I lean over the bar to find Tyler. He's talking to someone at the other end so I have to wait for him. The crowd undulates, rearranging for things I can't see over their heads.

As Tyler gets closer, he must spot Sam, too, because his smile melts away and he raises an eyebrow at me.

"Another?" Tyler asks, eyeing my empty glass.

"Yes, please."

I pray Tyler won't say anything about Sam crashing the event. I don't want to talk about Sam, let alone find myself defending him. Thankfully Tyler just fills my glass.

I swallow half down immediately, honoring all the tears I cried for my own bad season, shuddering as the alcohol lights a fire down my esophagus.

"You're not letting him get to you, are you?" he asks, holding up my glass in question.

"No," I say unconvincingly. "It's not that. It's been a rough afternoon."

He sets the glass back down and tops it off. "What is it, then?" He rests his elbows on the bar, getting closer so we can hear each other over the noise.

"I spoke to Kelly's mom tonight," I say, lowering my voice even though he can barely hear me. "She seemed to be doing well, considering, but...she said something to me about Kelly."

Tyler furrows his brow.

I shouldn't care anymore. Kelly wants me to let it go and she's made it clear I have no sway on her decision, but I can't shake the feeling there's more she isn't telling me. And I'm not the only one who might be able to convince her to get out of her own way.

I lean in farther.

"She told me that she's been trying to get Kelly to go to LA for years."

"Really," he states, more than asks. "I always thought—"

"Me, too. And I know she's worried about Shannon's safety, but Shannon would be safer in a nursing home than by herself all day while Kelly's at work, right? She would have nurses and people to monitor her medications. It just doesn't add up."

Kelly doesn't owe me answers—not anymore—but it still hurts that she would keep the truth from me. I always thought I understood Kelly, but our relationship had clearly changed long before we fell apart.

Tyler shifts uncomfortably, preoccupying himself with a spot on the bar. "I couldn't say," he says. "It's not like we're close."

I'm surprised he would say that, considering Kelly works at the vineyard and makes his coffee at Monet's Mug most mornings. I always considered them friends, if not directly, then by proxy.

I study him, debating how much to push. "There's something you're not telling me," I say.

"I really don't know," he says more resolutely. "I mean, why are you still in New York?" he asks. "It was never your idea in the first place. And you said it yourself...you're not a city girl."

I look around at all the people who made up my world as I knew it before I left. Colombia wasn't my idea but I've always had a heart for adventure. I thought if I got out of this small town I would find something bigger, something better. But as they say, wherever you go, there you are. All the same things that kept me feeling stuck here, have me feeling stuck in New York, if I'm being honest with myself. I've forgotten altogether what I once hoped to find.

"Because of my parents," I finally admit. Someone knocks over a drink at the table behind me and everyone nearby scatters in uproar.

"Your parents?" Tyler asks, drawing my attention back to him.

"I know," I say. "It sounds backward. You'd think they'd want me to come home, and I'm sure part of them does want that. But they flew out for my graduation, and they were so proud. Not just proud, but shocked. Like they never really believed I could stick with something long enough to get a degree."

Tyler frowns. My voice grows louder over the crowd.

"Don't act surprised. I know what everyone thinks about me. I'm the careless one, the one with my head in the clouds. I'm always late and I can't make a plan to save my life, and you know what? You're all right. So I guess I just decided to stop leading the kind of life that lets down all the people I love."

"Mal—" Tyler starts.

"I saw it in their eyes, Tyler. For the first time, they really believed in me. I didn't want to give that up. So I did the responsible thing. I got a paid internship, which believe me, in marketing and in New York no less, is very hard to do. And I've just...stayed."

"I get it," he says. "I do. I mean, I want to do right by my uncle, too. What if I get to Montana and can't find any clients? What if I run out of money? Will I have to leave? Will I swallow my pride and ask him to support me? Will I get a job and then not have enough time to focus on building the horse ranch? It can seem like there are no right answers. Or at least like there are no answers that don't require a lot of sacrifice. But you know your parents love you no matter what, right?"

My shoulders slump. "Of course I know that. I've never doubted it for a second of my life." I twist the shot glass between my fingertips. "But love isn't the same as respect."

Tyler nods again, a deep understanding evident in the lines of his forehead.

"Did you see your dad?" Kelly asks, rejoining us. I guess we're back to being distantly polite.

Tyler busies himself behind the bar at her arrival and I take a sip of the moonshine, resolving to slow my alcohol intake.

"Do I want to?" I ask, wondering what further antics the night has brought on.

I look in the direction Kelly's pointing, where I see Dad standing next to four tables that have been pushed together in the center of the bar. He's surrounded by other vintners, who circle the tables, their shoes off and pant legs rolled up to their shins.

Joe silences the crowd again with his moonshine bottle and spoon. He raises his voice to explain the next part of the ceremony.

"In Greek, Celtic, Wiccan, and many other religious traditions, it was customary to offer something to the gods to ask for their favor. A gift, or an offering, if you will. Some called it…a sacrifice."

The crowd *oohs*, though most of them know what's coming. I raise my eyebrows at Kelly but she shakes her head, not giving anything away.

"Farmers offered up their best livestock in hopes that it would please the gods. And when that wasn't enough, they would offer up one of their own."

More ominous murmuring adds to the tension as we all wait for what Joe will say next.

"In a similar fashion, we offer up the best of Paso."

Joe looks around the room, enjoying his performance more than the rest of us, I think. Dad widens his eyes, like he doesn't know what's about to come next. But then Joe holds up two bowls—one overflowing with deep purple spheres, the other with yellow green.

"Grapes!" Joe shouts.

"I don't like where this is going," I say to no one in particular, but the glee on my dad's face warms me. He is so very loved in this town, by everyone. There isn't a single person in this room he hasn't helped, or who wouldn't give Dad the very shirt off their back. They respect his authenticity, his passion for viticulture, and for this town. And because he is always there for them, they are always there for him, no questions asked.

"Where do they get those grapes?" I ask Kelly. From here, I can tell they're wine grapes—not something that could be purchased at the store—but they look ripe, as if they'd been picked earlier today.

Kelly shrugs but the person behind me—a middle-aged woman I don't recognize—leans in to answer for her.

"Each of the vintners donates a bundle at the end of the previous season and Joe keeps them in his freezer all year."

I shake my head in amusement.

Joe picks up his monologue. "Each of the vintners who have chosen to participate in this sacrificial ritual will crush these grapes grown right here in Paso Robles as their offering to the gods, to ensure another great season."

The crowd cheers as the men surrounding the tables make their way to the chair, a makeshift ladder. Joe hoists the men onto the tables. It's quite precarious and some of the men are much older than my dad, but looking at them now, they could all be boys again as they bask in the attention and glory. When my dad climbs onto the table, I cheer especially loudly. Sam leans against the wall across the room, staring at me and clapping.

Once all the men are on the tables, Joe holds the bowls of grapes up high, eliciting another loud roar from the crowd, then he dumps them on the tables and the vintners—six of them—stomp wildly on the grapes, laughing, slipping around, and egging each other on. Other men surround the tables, offering the vintners hands to hold on to so they don't fall. The townspeople cheer them on as if it's a sporting event. The closest ones get sprayed with grape juice, squealing and laughing.

Side by side, Kelly and I clap and yell my dad's name over the din. When I look over at her, bitterness burns in my chest like acid. If we aren't friends, if we never were, what claim does she have on my family?

When the men are satisfied that every grape has been crushed, Joe bangs his wooden spoon on the moonshine bottle and yells, "Bring on the rain!"

After the official celebration, some of the crowd hangs around for another hour, finishing Joe's moonshine and chatting. As the night goes on, more of them trickle out. By ten o'clock, there are only about half of us left, which is still more than capacity.

I sit at the bar, stirring some fruity vodka concoction Tyler made me to reduce the alcohol content of my frequent refills. I haven't seen Sam since the grape smashing and Kelly got pulled into a game of pool. I alternate staring absentmindedly at my drink and watching Tyler walk up and down the bar, pouring moonshine for the other patrons.

"You look tired," Tyler says, suddenly in front of me again. "Why don't you head home?"

I nod toward Kelly. "She's having fun. I don't want to rush her."

He smiles warmly. "You're a good friend."

I snort. "Am I?" I ask.

The words fall out of my mouth, meant to be a rhetorical question, but I find I'd really like to know the answer. Especially when it comes to Tyler's opinion. I trust him to tell me the truth. For my first years in New York, I could blame my lack of friendships on the fast pace of the city and my focus on work. But the more time that passes, the more I've begun to feel like it's me. And Kelly has only confirmed my fears.

Tyler takes my drink and I hear it clink into the bussing bin. After a bit of searching, he pulls out a half-eaten sleeve of crackers and sets them where my drink was.

"I'm not drunk," I say as I peel the sleeve open farther. Though I'm not entirely sure I'm a good judge of my sobriety after three shots of moonshine and two cranberry vodkas.

"You are," he says, lifting my chin with a finger, affection warming his cheeks.

"Which?" I mutter. "A good friend? Or drunk?"

"Both," he says.

There's a clank of silverware on glass farther down the bar that draws our attention. I lean back and am surprised to see it's Dad. He hoists himself up onto a chair, then continues banging his fork against a mostly empty wineglass. Always wine.

"What is he up to now?" I ask Tyler, but Tyler only shrugs and shakes his head, as charmed by Dad as everyone else.

"Can I have everyone's attention, please?" Dad says, stumbling on his chair. As much as wine is a part of our everyday lives, I've hardly ever seen Dad drunk. I have the strong urge to rescue him before he hurts himself or says something ridiculous, but he's clearly having the time of his life. He has so much to celebrate.

"Before we leave here tonight," he says, "I just want to thank you all for being here and for supporting me all these years. I know twenty-one years ago when I showed up, I was some city slicker moving in on your territory. But far from trying to push me out, you all welcomed me and my family and taught me everything you knew."

He looks to the three other vintners who are still here and tips his glass to each of them in turn.

"The Wandering Vineyard wouldn't be the success it's become if it weren't for all of you, and I can't thank you enough for that. Because of your generosity, this old roughneck got to follow his dreams. Elizabeth couldn't make it tonight but I want to raise my glass to her, too, for being there for me for so many years of struggle. There were many years of wondering if we were going to be able to put food on the table."

Dad nods to me and at this, many faces turn in my direction. I put on a smile, but my cheeks warm in embarrassment at their attention.

"You know," he says, "it's because of that girl that I even had the courage to follow my dreams. You know what I mean, right? You go about your life, making money, making ends meet, and you don't think too much about what it all means or how quickly the days are passing by. But then we had Mallory and when I looked into her eyes for the first time, I finally knew what I was living for. And as she grew older, I wanted to do better for her. I realized the best thing I could ever do was to teach her to let her heart be her guide. It took me a while to realize I wasn't doing that myself, and that the best leading is done by example."

I know everyone must be looking at me by this point, and I'm not usually one to show my emotions, but I no longer care. Tears blur my vision and I grin stupidly at my father, whose pride has always given my own life meaning. He, my mom, and I have shared one hell of an adventure together, and sometimes it's hard to believe it's over. It's hard to swallow that we can't go back.

I feel Kelly's sudden presence behind me. The tears roll down my cheeks as I look up at her. My parents *and* Kelly. She has been my sister in every way but blood, and that doesn't just go away. It can't. There's a look in her eyes that says she knows it, too.

"And the best part of all," Dad goes on, "is that I know all the hard work and sacrifices were worth it. Because now my daughter is doing the same thing. She followed her heart to New York, got a degree from one of the best universities in the country, and is doing amazing work that she loves."

My smile falters. Is that what I'm doing?

As I look around the room, I see nothing but expressions of pride. *Small-town girl makes good.* I force congeniality through my tears.

"Mallory," Dad says, raising his glass to me directly, "I am so immensely proud to have raised such a smart, beautiful, kind, driven woman and you make me happier every day to be your father. In a few days, we'll be celebrating the success of the vineyard, which you also played a role in, but tonight, I want to celebrate you and all your accomplishments. So, to you, honey."

Everyone else in the bar raises their glasses and chants, "To Mallory."

Tyler appears in front of me with a water and the shot of moonshine he saved for himself. I've dreamed of moments like this as I sat alone in my cubicle, surrounded by people who know almost nothing about me. Now I'm surrounded by the people who are like family to me and, while technically everything Dad said about me is true, I feel like a fraud. I can't pinpoint why.

"To you," Tyler says softly. Genuinely.

I lift my water, looking around uncertainly. And when they all take a drink in honor of me, I drink, too, the ice-cold liquid getting stuck in my throat.

Kelly drives me home in my rental car. Not a fan of the moonshine, she stuck to water most of the night and didn't trust me to drive. She rolls down the windows, letting the dry heat whip through the car in an attempt to sober me up. It's too loud to speak over, and for that I'm thankful, because even though Kelly seemed softened by my dad's speech, I don't have words for the emotions coursing through me. I rest my spinning head on the window frame, watching the rolling hills climb and fall like whales swimming through the night.

At home the car door echoes across the vineyard when I slam it shut.

"Thanks for driving," I tell her through the open driver-side window.

"I'll bring it back tomorrow," she says. I nod and turn away.

"Hey, Mal," she says.

My heart stutters as she calls me by my nickname. I turn back to her.

"Don't think too much tonight, okay?" she says. She must have seen right through my reaction to all the unintentional lies my dad told tonight. She always could read me like a book. "Get some sleep. It will all look better in the morning."

I purse my lips, grateful for her thoughtfulness and also to be known so intimately by another human being. That is what I've missed in losing my friendship with Kelly. "I'll do my best."

She backs out of the parking lot and leaves me in the dark.

I see movement on the porch as I approach, wobbly on my feet. Thanks to Tyler's crackers and water, I'm no longer drunk, but a combination of the moonshine and my dad's words still has me tipsy, leaving me off-balance.

"Late night," Sam says as I reach the stairs. I can make out the shape of him but not much else with the porch light off—Mom must still be in her office, completely unaware of the outside world, as she tends to be when she works.

I didn't see Sam sneak out of the bar. I'd tried to keep my eyes from seeking him out and for once, I managed it.

"Not that late," I say. "I live in the city that never sleeps."

I reach the top of the stairs and stop, not ready to go to bed but not prepared to navigate another tricky conversation with Sam. Then again, the alcohol still in my veins may make it the perfect time to ask him how he could once so easily pretend to feel something for me. I'm discovering how exhausting pretending can be.

"Where's your dad?" he asks.

"Still living it up. He said he'd follow close behind me. What about you? You're just sitting out here by yourself in the dark?"

"It's a nice night," Sam says.

"Then why aren't you still out enjoying it?"

"I am out, and I am enjoying it."

My body feels like liquid, incapable of holding itself upright. The thought of getting myself up the stairs to my room right now is too much. I lower myself into the chair across from Sam to regain my equilibrium. Just for a minute, I promise myself.

"Had a little too much moonshine tonight, I take it?" Sam says with a chuckle. "That doesn't sound like the Mallory I know."

I snort a cynical laugh. "And what Mallory do you know?" I ask. I search the table for Sam's usual nightcap but find only a glass of water. Sam nudges it toward me but I wave it away. I lean my head back against the chair and close my eyes. "Since when don't you drink?"

Sam ignores the second question. "I thought I knew the Mallory who hates wine and used to be the one to nurse me back to health after a few too many drinks."

So he does remember. When I used to try to talk to him about our nights together on the mornings after, he blamed the alcohol for his fuzzy memory, evading my questions and my heartaches.

"Well, that just goes to show how little you know the Mallory in front of you."

"I think I'm getting to know her more," he says. "That was quite a speech your dad gave."

I lift my head to look at him. I still can't see enough to decipher his expression or the meaning behind his words.

"You were still there?" I ask.

"I struck up a conversation with a couple of the other vineyard owners in the back. They wanted to know more about the work I did for your dad. Apparently, your dad has a hidden agenda in inviting me back here."

I hear the smile in his voice. He adores my dad and I've seen very little make Sam happier than impressing him, which he does as easily as breathe.

"Dad gets emotional when he drinks," I say, writing off his affections for Sam and for me in one fell swoop. It's easier that way than to accept that Sam would ever have a reason to come back here, or worse yet, to stay.

"Maybe," Sam says. "But he was right. About you, I mean. It's not easy to do what you've done, Mallory. I think it's awesome that you went into marketing. You were always great at it. Most people don't stick with these things long enough to succeed. Most people don't have the guts to pursue their goals in the first place."

Sam's compliments fill me up with resentment. He always pushed me to strive for more, to set goals and achieve them, but he never told me how lonely success could be. And if he takes any credit for my success, for being the one to guide me in that direction, I hate him for it. Whether or not it's true.

"You did," I say.

"Which is how I know how hard it is. And what it takes to make it. I think what you've done is incredible."

I lean forward, my elbows on the table. After all these years, I still can't decide if his refusal to acknowledge the downsides of pursuing a career above all else is a pretense or a delusion. Frustration loosens my tongue. "But don't you ever feel like you just want to jump out of your own skin?" I ask, not expecting him to admit to anything. Sam wears his life choices like a well-cut suit—all confidence, no apologies.

But he mirrors my posture and the moonlight hits his face. It grazes the definition of his strong jaw, the slight curl of his hair, the length of his neck where his shirt has been unbuttoned and fallen open.

"Every day," he says.

I furrow my brow. "Then why don't you?"

His mouth quirks up on one side. "I'm here, aren't I?"

The quiet nights, the wistful days, the wine, the warm welcome from my parents. I get it. The vineyard lifestyle is the way I've lived most of my life, but I've learned how lucky

I am to have this place to call home. For most people, places like this are an escape from everyday life.

"But you'll go back."

"Yes," he agrees.

"Why?"

He thinks about it for a moment, then says, "Because what kind of life can you live without goals? Without hopes and dreams?"

There's that word again. *Dreams.* Something everyone seems to have but me.

"What's your dream?" I ask him.

He doesn't hesitate. "A five-thousand-square-foot house with an infinity pool that looks out to the ocean. A second house in Europe. France or Italy." He considers it. "Maybe Spain. A Bentley with a driver and if we're really going crazy, a private jet, or at least one I could charter."

A bitter laugh pours out of me.

"But *why*? For what purpose?" I ask before he can go on listing the most superficial dreams I've ever heard. Maybe he's relaxed and learned a few things in the years that have passed, but he hasn't changed. It's still all about the flash. The glitz and glamour.

Do you have a heart? I want to ask him. I know something stirs deep within him, in a place no one ever gets to see. It's what I tried so badly to uncover that summer. I wonder if there's a woman in the world who will ever get him to bare his truth, his soul.

"To say I could," he says with a shrug.

"No." I slam my hand down on the table. "That's bullshit."

"To prove I've made it," he jockeys.

"Made what?"

"Made it big. To prove that I'm successful."

"And what does that get you exactly?"

I can't help it. His responses infuriate me—I know they're just an act, a cover for something very real hiding beneath. No one wants success as badly as he does without a deeper insecurity. I know this because I feel it, too.

I expect him to evade the question, like he's done every time a conversation has gotten difficult between us. But he doesn't.

"Vindication," he says.

"With your dad," I assume.

"For one."

But he doesn't elaborate. I'm so surprised by his honesty, I forget to ask who else didn't believe in him, and why. How could anyone not see that Sam is a man who gets whatever he wants? I knew it from the moment I saw him—it just took me many months after he left to realize the implications. If he'd ever truly wanted me, we would have been together.

"After all this time, do you even remember what you're fighting for? Do you even remember who you are?" After a pause, a painful confession slips through my lips. "Because I don't."

Sam must not know how to take my admission because he doesn't respond. Finally, he says, "I remember you, Mallory. I could never forget you."

"Don't say that," I'm quick to counter. My head spins. "You don't get to say things like that. You left. You never called—not once. You gave me no reason to believe I meant anything to you and now you say this?"

There it is. Everything I've been holding back. Everything that has been sitting just below the surface. I tried to move on from the pain of his abandonment. I thought I had. But he changed me in a way I didn't fully understand until I came back here, and that isn't something I could just get over.

"I was an idiot," he says, but that's not enough. He altered the course of my life. No amount of words will ever be enough.

"You don't even know what you did," I say. "You have no idea what you leave in your wake in the single-minded pursuit of your goals. I sure as hell hope they're worth it."

I push myself out of my chair, fueled by adrenaline, to storm into the house but I lose my balance and trip over the leg of the chair. Hands reach out to steady me. Strong hands. Tender hands. Familiar hands.

"I don't know," he says, but I don't understand what he's trying to tell me. We never did seem to speak the same language.

"Let me go," I say, more a plea than an order, admitting that he has a hold on me in more ways than one.

He releases me.

I stand there, feeling like I should say something more, make him feel the hurt he caused me. But the look on my face must be enough. It must reflect all the loss and confusion and loneliness I've felt because he steps away from me. I turn away and go into the house.

TEN

"There you are," Dad said as I walked up the porch steps after checking another item off the Summer Bucket List with Kelly. I clasped my hands behind my back, hiding the evidence.

Dad and Sam were sitting at the table with steaks and glasses of a Wandering Vineyard Riesling. Dad knew where I'd gone, had given me nothing but a skeptical look when I'd told him, but I wasn't ready to get his opinion on it.

"You want some chicken?" Dad asked, already rising from his chair.

I nodded.

Once Dad had gone into the house, Sam asked, "What are you hiding back there?"

I blushed, unsure of how he might react but knowing I would tell him anyway. "I got my first tattoo."

"Ah," he said, drawing it out. "The old 'eighteen-year-old milestone.'"

Uneasiness tightened my stomach. I hated the implication that I was being young and stupid, or even worse, predictable. But his smile was encouraging.

I sat across from him.

"It's a friendship tattoo. Kelly and I are leaving for college in the fall and we know things will change. My dad has warned me plenty of times." I rolled my eyes. *Parents.* "We just wanted a reminder that no matter what happens, our friendship won't change. That we'll always be there for each other."

Sam nodded thoughtfully. "That's cool. I'm envious, actually. I never really had a friend I was that close to. No brothers or sisters."

"I'm pretty lucky," I agreed. "I don't know what I'd do without her."

Dad reemerged from the kitchen with a plate, another bottle of wine, and a declaration. "Tonight, Mallory Victoria, we celebrate."

"Celebrate what?" I asked.

"The start of the tasting room, of course." He placed the plate in front of me and lifted his glass in a toast. "The beginning of an exciting new chapter."

Sam clinked his glass to Dad's and I lifted the bottle up to theirs before setting it back down unceremoniously. Dad and Sam laughed at me.

But celebrate they did. Several hours later, I'd listened to entirely too many stories of my dad's childhood and watched him and Sam drink their way through three bottles of wine. At this rate, they weren't going to have any left to sell, I thought to myself, but I sat there anyway, watching Sam watch Dad.

He was fascinated by every word that rolled off my dad's tongue and Dad reveled in it. Mom and I had long since grown familiar with his stories but in Sam, he had an enthusiastic new audience. As I watched, I wondered if maybe Sam had finally found the friend he'd been looking for, or at least, someone who could be.

By ten o'clock, Dad had reached his limit and stood to collect the dishes. He didn't waver, but his chest was flushed and his eyelids drooped. I took the dishes from him.

"I've got it," I said. "You just make it up the stairs."

He waved my suggestion away but let me take the dishes. "I'm fine. Sam, are you going to stay?"

Like the last time Dad suggested it, my heart fluttered at the possibility and like last time, Sam shook his head.

"I shouldn't," Sam said, though he made no move to leave.

"Why not? You have somewhere to be?"

Sam pondered it, then shook his head.

"Stay," Dad said. "Elizabeth would be thrilled to have someone use the guest house."

Sam finally nodded. No one could deny my mom anything.

"Great," Dad said. "Mal?"

I'd stood there watching their conversation like a racquetball game, but I snapped my attention back to Dad then, my hands sweating.

"Will you make sure the guest house has towels and clean sheets?"

"Sure," I said.

Sam was going to be here all night. He would be sleeping just outside my window. I knew already I wouldn't sleep a wink.

Dad kissed my forehead. "Thanks, honey. I'm going to hit the hay. Night, Sam."

"Night, Richard."

I stood in stunned silence until Dad left. I heard each one of his footsteps fumbling up the stairs, and then the night fell into silence.

"I, uh… I'm going to just put the dishes inside and then I'll get you set up."

"I'll help you," Sam said, standing. He grabbed his plate and a couple of the empty wine bottles.

"You don't have to."

But when I headed inside, he followed me. The kitchen was dark, indicating Mom had already gone to bed. The dishes clinked as we placed them in the sink. Sam set the bottles carefully into the recycling bin so as not to disturb my parents and then he followed me back out. The soft breeze tickled my hair across my shoulders and cooled my hot skin.

"You know, this was the one place I didn't get a tour of before," Sam said behind me.

I swallowed hard and smiled at him over my shoulder. "I'll show you where everything is."

When we reached the end of the long gravel path, I fished the key off the doorjamb and wiggled it into the lock. Sam leaned against the other French door, watching me, a vacant smile on his face. I couldn't help giggling.

"What?" he asked me.

"You're kind of a lightweight." It wasn't that he and Dad hadn't drunk quite a few glasses of wine, but I was used to living in a town of vintners. They'd become mostly immune to the effects of the wine they drank so frequently.

"You're one to talk," he said, sliding in front of me to enter the guest house first. He fumbled in the dark but finally found the light switch.

"How would you know? You've never seen me drink," I retorted in good humor. He was teasing me, and it felt like our relationship had taken a step up from polite coworkers to friendly partners in crime. It felt good.

"Exactly," he said, slicing a single finger through the air as if he was making some profound point. I laughed more.

"The bathroom is there," I said to Sam, pointing to the small room to the left.

"Good." He disappeared into it, clattering sounds following closely after.

I shook my head and pulled the sheets off the bed. Mom had a cedar chest at the foot of the bed with clean linens so I went to work putting fresh ones on the bed and setting towels out for Sam.

When he reemerged from the bathroom, the bed was prepared for him, and he had removed his jacket, tie, and shoes. Tripping over the shoes, he placed the jacket over the back of one of the dining chairs, then collapsed onto the bed, his arms spread wide.

"If only your other clients could see you now," I joked. It hit me then that maybe they had. Maybe Sam was this friendly with all the people he worked with. Maybe he wasn't so relaxed with our family because he liked us, but because that was just who he was. I felt briefly jealous for my parents.

"Right," he said. "That would make my dad so proud, getting drunk with all my clients."

I didn't know what to say to that. I sensed there was so much he wasn't telling me on the topic, but I didn't feel like it was my place to ask.

"Do you?" I asked, all selfishness. "Get drunk with all your clients?"

Sam laughed. "God, no. Of course, I've never worked with a vineyard...or brewery...or whatever before."

It was convenience, not trust. My heart sank a little, but I reminded myself to keep my expectations in check. He was here on business. He wasn't here to be our friend. Or anything else.

"There's a towel next to your head," I said, and Sam turned into it, the thick white cotton enveloping his eyes. He grinned at his own bumbling and pushed it away. "There's a coffee maker in the kitchenette but I don't know how old the coffee is so you might just want to come into the house in the morning. I'll leave the back door open for you."

"'Kay," Sam said, his eyes drifting closed. His hands reached for his belt and my cheeks flushed.

"Oh, one more thing."

I went into the bathroom and pulled out the bottle of aspirin we kept in the medicine cabinet. I tapped out two and then poured Sam a glass of water from the sink in the kitchenette. I'd never helped ward off a hangover before—I was only going off what I'd seen in movies.

When I returned, Sam's belt was unbuckled but still looped through his pants. It seemed that was as far as he was going to get. I set the pills and water on the nightstand, then asked, "Need anything else?"

"Hands that work," he said.

"Sorry. We ran out of those last week."

As I turned to go, he reached out and grabbed my hand, sending an explosion of white light from my fingertips to my brain. His soft fingers wrapped around mine and he pulled me closer so he could get a good look at my tattoo. Being with him all night, I'd almost forgotten the aching soreness of it.

He sat up slightly and examined the arrow that was pointing straight at him. In that moment, I felt like my skin and the ink were betraying my secrets.

"What does it mean?" he asked me.

I hesitated, then I stepped a little closer to him. So close I could smell the sour perfume of the alcohol seeping from his pores. Somehow, far from being repellent, I found it alluring in its newness. Sam sat up straighter and I delicately adjusted our hands so I could wrap mine around his wrist. He followed my lead and wrapped his hand around mine.

"Her tattoo is here." I pointed to the spot just below his thumb. "It's a horse, running toward me."

"And your arrow points toward her."

"I keep her carefree," I said. "Like a horse."

"And she keeps you…?"

"Focused." A smile pulled at my lips. "Some people think I struggle with that."

Sam let out a deep laugh, and it covered my skin like sinking into warm water. He seemed soberer suddenly.

"I like it," he said.

"Kelly picked out the designs. You don't think it's stupid to get a tattoo at eighteen?"

Sam sighed and let our hands slide apart. I shivered and hid mine behind my back, feeling suddenly exposed. To bridge the silence, I handed him the pills and water and he swallowed them down obligingly.

When he set the glass down, he said, "I think you're brave. And I admire that."

Warm pleasure flooded into my limbs.

"Do you have any tattoos?" I asked.

"I missed the eighteen-year-old window."

"How old are you?" I asked, oddly fearful of his answer.

"Twenty-four."

Older, yes, but not unrealistically so.

He fumbled with his watch then, seemingly to break the tension but the wine liquefied his fingers. I reached for it before I realized how badly I wanted to touch his skin again, and unclasped the cool metal. I slid the watch off and set it on the nightstand.

"Thanks, Mal."

I was momentarily stunned by his use of my nickname. When I gained my composure, I forced myself toward the door.

"Hey, Mallory," he said, and I looked back.

He didn't say anything. He just stared at me like he was trying to tell me something with his eyes. *Say it*, I silently urged. But he didn't.

"Good night, Sam," I finally said and I pulled myself away from the guest house.

ELEVEN

I stand in front of the mirror in my room, squinting through my hangover, and tug on the bottom of my gray T-shirt— one I left behind in my closet when I went away for college. It still fits, mostly. Printed across the chest is a faded design of a horse and script that says Wild Horses. Even though Kelly and I hadn't been speaking to each other when I left for Columbia, I found it gift wrapped on the hood of my car the day before I moved.

I knew what she meant by it. She'd always told me I was like a wild horse and she feared Sam was taming me. At the time, I threw it in the back of my closet, angry with her and sure she wanted to be the one to do the taming.

My riding boots in the corner catch my eye in the mirror— the ones Sam used to tease me about. They're leather, the exact same shade of dark chocolate brown as Midnight, and rise to the knee. The toes are worn down and I remember how my heel would get stuck in the left boot where the material was

MIDNIGHT *at the* WANDERING VINEYARD

torn inside from pulling them on and off so many times. I wore them every day my senior year of high school—a present from my dad—but now they're covered in dust, untouched since the day Sam asked me if I'd ever thought of wearing something more fashionable. Because I knew what that meant in the same way all girls know what that means. They weren't good enough. I wasn't good enough.

I cross the room, lift them up with my fingertips, and blow the dust off them, wondering if they still fit. I sit on the bed and pull them on one at a time. They feel the same—worn in, comfortable, me. I smile and grab an old shirt out of my hamper to dust them off, then I walk around the room, admiring them in the full-length mirror. They feel as familiar as the rocking movement of Midnight at a gallop, as Mom's hugs.

But I can't bring myself to walk out of the room wearing them. They would attract too much attention and too many questions after all this time. I pull the boots off and set them back in the same spot, staring at them for a long moment before I head downstairs.

On the way down, my phone rings in my hand. It's Denise, no doubt calling about the contract she sent over late last night detailing my new job description and terms of employment. A standard agreement but the idea of reading through it makes me want to go back to bed.

I take a deep breath and answer anyway.

"You're calling to negotiate your salary," she says, ever presumptuous that if she hasn't gotten what she wants, the other party just hasn't seen it her way yet.

"You called me," I say with a laugh. "And you sent it over at nine last night. Midnight in New York."

"You must have been awake hours ago."

I sigh. "Actually, can you give me a few days with it? Things are pretty busy around here."

The stack of party decorations in the corner of the dining room is proof. I've spent every spare minute sorting through them and sneaking into the stables to spend time with Midnight.

"Busy?" she laughs. "What could possibly be keeping you busy? Is that why you haven't been responding to emails?"

I turn my head away even though she can't see me. I've tried to respond to emails, but the details of my coworkers' questions are fuzzy. That world seems so far away, as if it's someone else's life.

I know I'm pushing it. Denise expects me to start my new position on Monday, but I'm counting on the fact that she likes me enough to milk some extra time out of her. Denise has wanted this success for me since I first arrived at the firm and I have an unexpected affection toward her because of it. It's the opposite of how I felt last night, when Dad made his desire for me to keep working in New York clear, and I can't pinpoint the reason for my differing reactions. But even in my hungover state, I haven't lost sight of the fact that my dad's speech reiterated all my own arguments for why I took this route in the first place. It's the smart decision. It always has been.

"Mallory, I want to be ready to make the announcement when you get back," she says in a singsong voice.

I reach the bottom of the stairs and Sam is standing at the coffeepot like a monument, looking much more chipper than I feel. Oh, how the tables have turned.

I face away from him for some semblance of privacy.

"Mallory, you know what kills me more than the shoes I'm wearing?" Denise asks in her brazen tone.

"Waiting," I intone. I've heard this question three times a day, every day for the last year. "I will get on top of all that immediately," I say. "I promise."

"You're lucky I adore you," she says. I smile.

With nothing left to say, she hangs up. I let out a sigh of relief.

When I turn around, Sam is standing right behind me, looking freshly showered, with a cup of coffee in each hand.

Embarrassment prickles the skin on my arms, having been caught inebriated by Sam last night and being reprimanded by my boss this morning. So much for avoiding him—he's everywhere.

What are you doing? I want to ask. It's one thing to be here to support the vineyard and visit with my parents, but it seems like he's putting himself in my way and I can't think of a single reason he'd want to do that.

He hands me my coffee. Cream, no sugar.

"I'm sorry about last night," I say. "I don't normally drink like that. That was…embarrassing."

"Believe me, you don't know embarrassing. I've done worse. Much worse."

"I know," I mumble into my mug. I quickly shake my head. "I'm sorry."

"How did you sleep?" he asks, his voice morning-deep.

"Fine," I say. There's a long pause and Sam laughs.

"That's it?"

"What else is there?" I ask.

The truth is, I don't know how to talk to Sam. When he first arrived here, I was too starstruck to relax around him, and as the summer went on, I censored myself more than I would like to admit, always trying to say the right thing to get him to notice me, avoiding anything that would make him shut down.

"I talked to Tyler this morning," Sam says.

"Oh, really?" I can only imagine how that went.

"Your friends don't like me much," he says, stating the obvious. He can't be surprised.

I shrug, trying to be diplomatic. "They don't really know you."

It wasn't like Sam was here to hang out with us, though he

could have been a little friendlier with Kelly and Tyler. I told them bits and pieces about Sam, but even if I'd told them everything I discovered, they still wouldn't have known much because neither did I.

"I suppose not. Or maybe they think they know who I am," he muses. He's so casual about it, like he couldn't care less whether they liked him or not. He's so self-assured that nothing ruffles him.

"Are they wrong?" I ask.

A grin spreads from one corner of his mouth to the other, slowly, like honey down a spoon. And yet, in my hungover state, his games grate on my nerves.

"I guess that depends on what they think they know."

I'm exasperated by this conversation already, but I can't make myself walk away. There's this teenage girl inside me who wants validation that she wasn't crazy for thinking she had a shot with someone as gorgeous, smart, ambitious, educated, well-off, and cultured as Sam. There's this part of me that wants to prove to him that I knew him better than he thought I did...that I was no fool.

"Shall I?" I ask.

He smirks, putting his coffee on the island counter so he can give me his full attention.

"By all means."

I look him over, pretending to consider it. In reality, I've already put ample thought into who I believe Sam is.

"You put a lot of stock in how you appear to others," I say. I start off easy, with the obvious.

Sam tilts his head to the side, lips pursed in concession. "You and I both know, in business, appearance is everything."

"If there's a strong commodity to back it up," I retort.

"As there is," he assures me, the one thing I already know for sure. "Next."

"All you care about is money," I say.

He tilts his head side to side, contemplating. "I do like money. Who doesn't? But it isn't all I care about. It isn't even what I care about most. And really, it's what the money can do for me that I'm looking for. Nice car, nice clothes, travel, freedom."

"Do you really feel free?" I ask him. Is this the secret I've been missing all along? Because around the vineyard, money was the cause of so much stress, so many headaches, so many lost memories, it didn't seem worth it.

"I took a week off to come here. Last-minute notice. No boss to ask for permission. No bills to worry about when I get back home."

Thinking about my own apartment, his explanation doesn't sound half-bad. I don't know if I'd call it freedom—he still has to earn that money at some point, just like the rest of us—but I can certainly see how it would make life easier.

"Your fancy cars are compensating for something," I say, shooting him with the next one, admittedly below the belt in more ways than one.

He laughs and raises his eyebrows, all confidence.

"C'mon now."

My cheeks heat. Sam and I never went past kissing, but I have to concede, the times we were close to each other, I never got that impression.

To shake off my discomfort, I jump to the next one.

"You think your privilege makes you better than everybody else."

Sam's confident grin falls so quickly, I can almost hear it drop. His shoulders sink and for the first time ever, I can picture him as a little boy, innocent and openhearted. No facade, no armor.

"Is that what *you* think?" he asks.

My bravado wavers. I take a step back, putting distance between us. "We're talking about my friends," I say, but I can hear the lie in my voice. He stares at me with those eyes for a long few seconds.

"No," he finally says. "It's a common misconception when people are private."

He doesn't clarify whether this is a misconception he runs into personally, but I don't think he'd tell me if I asked, so I don't.

"And I don't like that word. I may have been born to a wealthy family, but I've made my own way."

I nod. I believe that.

"Next," he says, nothing in his demeanor still playful.

Suddenly, I don't want to play this game anymore. "I don't think—"

"Next," he pushes.

I clear my throat, my voice low when I say, "There's more to your relationship with your dad than you talk about."

This assumption is mine alone. I see the ripple of Sam's jaw as he clenches it. He's still for a long moment, then he grabs his mug and raises it in farewell. "I should find Rich," he says.

"Right," I say.

I feel a pang of guilt as he walks out the back door. Maybe I shouldn't have said anything, but he asked. I didn't expect him to take it so personally—didn't think he could. But as determined as I am to keep my distance, it has me wanting to know more than ever just who Sam really is and what's going on behind his eyes.

Later that morning, Kelly brings home my car and we take Dad's truck to pick up rental chairs for the party that is only a couple of days away. After making it clear that I should have no expectation of renewing our friendship, Kelly is more conversational but we stick to safe topics. We talk like I'm a customer at the coffee shop, catching up on small-town gossip.

Afterward, Kelly has to work so I drop her off, sticking around for a plain latte. As I watch her work, it's clear she has become a fixture in the community—everyone who comes in updates her on what's going on in their lives, even if it's been only hours since they came in last. And it's easy to see why.

Though I know she's in pain, she wears an easy smile and is present with everyone who walks through the door. It's a side of her I haven't seen before. A new side. She asks them questions as she steams milk and wipes down machines. They open up to her in those few minutes and appear lighter on the way out than when came in. If only she could see how much more she could help people. Maybe if she had the opportunity to serve people in a new way, a way that's closer to her heart.

When I get home, Sam's car is gone and Dad seems to have gone with him, so I decide to take Midnight for a ride before the heat becomes unbearable for either of us. As I pass by the stable office, though, Mom is sitting at the dilapidated computer when she would normally be at work. Her hair is pulled into a messy bun on the top of her head, the standing fan whipping loose tendrils around her face.

"Hey," I say, leaning against the door frame. She startles, then smiles when she sees me.

"Hey, love." Her eyelids are heavy with computer fatigue. I recognize it immediately as the nearly permanent state of my coworkers.

"What are you doing out here? Why aren't you at work?"

"I took the day off to finalize the guest list for the party. The caterer needs the final numbers and I want to make sure we'll have enough seating."

"No problem there," I say. "Kelly and I brought back enough chairs to fill a football stadium."

I slide into the office and plop down in the chair across from her. Holes have been rubbed into the chair's fabric and the vinyl bites into the backs of my legs now.

I used to sit cross-legged in this chair and line up my plastic ponies along the desk while Dad made phone calls and talked over my shoulder to the vineyard hands. For all my teen years, I couldn't wait to get out of this tiny wine town, but looking back now, those are the best memories of my life. Funny how time changes perception.

"Why are you handling the guest list?" I ask. "Can't Dad or Kelly do it?"

Mom shrugs. "Your dad never has the time or focus to be in the office and Kelly works a lot of hours at the coffee shop. She's been using any free time to sort through and collect all the event supplies."

"Couldn't you guys afford an office manager now?" I ask. I pluck the list off the desk and scan over it. I recognize many of the names. But there are a lot of new ones, too.

"Yes," she says hesitantly. "It's something we've been talking about lately."

"You don't have the time to go through the hiring process?"

"Actually...your dad wants me to do it. Full-time."

"He wants you to quit your job?"

She shrugs, not as excited by the prospect as I would expect her to be. I can't remember a time when Mom wasn't entirely involved in her work—evenings, weekends, holidays. Growing up, I would sometimes fantasize that we sold the vineyard, moved into a tiny house on one acre at the far end of our land, and spent all our time together, gardening and riding horses that didn't need stalls and survived solely on love. Nothing in our lifestyle would cost us any money because money was the only thing my parents ever argued about. Money, or the lack thereof, was what created the bags under their eyes, what kept them working at all hours of the day and night. It was all they ever seemed to think about. Often to the detriment of quality time together.

"I would have thought this is what you've always wanted," I say, reading the map of skepticism on her face.

She gives me a tired smile. "That's exactly what your dad keeps saying."

"Aren't you tired of working so much? Wouldn't you rather be home?" I set the guest list back on the desk and lean back in my chair.

"No," she says. The word comes out more like an apology than a denial.

"Oh," is all I can think to say.

Mom shuts off the computer screen and rests her elbows on the desk.

"The vineyard has been doing pretty well for a while, Mal." She picks up some stray papers from the desk and begins to file them. "It's not like we're sleeping on piles of money or anything, but I could have quit a couple of years ago."

"You don't want to quit?" I ask, still trying to understand. "I thought—"

"I can see why you and your dad would think that. When I first started working at the law firm, it was definitely for the money. It was for the money for a long time. I don't think we were ever very good at hiding how much we needed it," she says with a frown. "But over time…I really fell in love with what I do. I like helping families through their hard times. It feels like what I do means something."

"I'm sure it does," I say, though I've never really thought

about it. I don't know why I haven't. Maybe because she's never before said anything along these lines. But more likely because I've never thought of anyone being happy in an office atmosphere. I've spent so much time with Dad, Tyler, the vineyard hands, and the other vintners in town that working outside with one's own hands feels like the true normal.

Realizing this, I question my own motives for going into marketing. My parents may have encouraged my success but they never told me what it should look like. I'm the one who decided on the vision. If I believe no one could be happy in an office job, why have I been pursuing a career that could only ever end in a cubicle?

"I'm sure it does," I repeat.

Mom must see my internal debate because she laughs. She finishes filing the papers, stands, and comes around to sit on the desk. She takes my cheeks in her hands and smiles down at me.

"I know you and your dad could never really understand," she says. "You're both such hands-on people."

"Then why did you push me to go to college?" I ask. I'm not blaming her, but if she knew it wasn't the best fit for me, I'm surprised she would encourage that path.

"I wanted you to have options, baby. I didn't want you to ever struggle for money like we have."

If only she knew.

"I love my job, Mal. I love being here, too, and I could get swept up in taking care of the place and taking care of your dad, but I like having something that's just mine."

This is so much new information. I struggle to process it. I feel like I've been missing this giant piece of who my mother is.

At the mention of taking care of others, I think about Kelly.

"What's wrong with Shannon?" I ask. "Really?"

No one seems to want to reveal the depth of Shannon's illness, but if Mom has been regularly taking food to her and Kelly has opened her home to help, her health must be more dire than what everyone is letting on.

Mom frowns.

"Shannon had a quadruple bypass a few months ago," she says.

All the breath leaves my lungs. "What?" I ask.

"She had another heart attack at the end of last year and the doctors decided it would be best. It's been a hard recovery for her but she seems to be coming around."

I shake my head involuntarily as I imagine how hard that must have been for both of them.

"We've done as much as we've been able to," Mom says, placing her hand on mine to soothe me. It doesn't. Because I haven't done as much as I can and even if Kelly forgives me, I don't know how I'll forgive myself for that.

On Thursday morning, everyone at the vineyard is up early and crammed into the kitchen at five o'clock in the morning, waiting for the coffee to finish brewing. Mom and Kelly took the morning off work, and Dad had his four vineyard hands come in early. Tyler volunteered to help, as well as Sam, and there's a buzz of energy as we wait for the vines to arrive. Today we place the vines in preparation for the planting party on Saturday, when our guests will dig holes and lower them into their new homes. Once the truck pulls in, we'll have just a few hours to unload all the plants, and for six acres, there are a lot of them.

Sam came in this morning dressed in jeans and a designer T-shirt, which was surprising and kind of sweet, seeing him more relaxed and making an effort to fit into this lifestyle... as much as he ever could. I try not to look at his sleepy eyes, which are more vulnerable than usual and remind me of the ache I saw in them yesterday. He sits with Dad and the vineyard hands at the table, no doubt asking them a thousand questions about the planting process. Sam is insatiably curious.

I stand in the corner, taking it all in. I try to understand how at the office, I'm surrounded by twice as many people every day and all the talk sounds like empty noise. And yet here, with this little family we've made our own, the same noise sounds like love.

Knowing I will soon leave all this behind again, for who knows how long, weighs on my chest. I'm distracted from my worry when I notice Kelly and Tyler are speaking tensely in the corner, Tyler wearing a guilty and guarded expression, just like the one he wore the other night at the bar when I asked him about Kelly. Clearly there is more going on between them than either one is telling me. I don't have time to decide how I feel about that because just then the sound of a semi engine growls closer, calling us outside.

Quickly, we abandon our coffee mugs on the counter in a chaos of clattering ceramic and scraping chair legs to huddle on the back porch.

The morning is so hot we begin to sweat as Dad guides the semi around the stables, over to the freshly cleared land. The sun beats down on our skin like a punishment. When the engine shrieks and then falls silent, we hustle to the back of the truck where Dad hoists himself inside to examine his new babies.

He looks them over carefully and we hold our breath. When he gives his approving smile, we jump into action, grabbing the burlap-sack-wrapped vines one by one and head for the trellises.

"Two feet apart," Dad calls to us. "And don't forget to soak the bag."

Dad placed a horse trough filled with water at the edge of the new acres for just that purpose, which will hydrate the plants and keep them healthy while they wait to be planted.

As I break out into the field, bag dripping down my leg, Kelly trails behind me. Out of coincidence or habit, I don't know. Despite all the hurtful things she said the other day, I want to invite her to walk with me. But I'm still embarrassed. I'm angry. I'm hoping I misunderstood somehow.

Then she calls my name and my heart jumps stupidly. I sigh and slow down. I should know better than to ignore the warning signs that a relationship is doomed, but I can't help myself. I'm an idealist, an optimist, and even if I wanted to change that about myself, it's pretty clear I'm not very good at changing.

"Hey," Kelly says, breathing heavily with the weight of the vine. She's quiet, too, weary in a way that has nothing to do with the physical weight.

"Hey," I say.

We're walking shoulder to shoulder, but the thick silence between us conveys all the distance we've created with our thoughtless words. There's an invisible wall we can't seem to break through, no matter how much I claw at it with my bare hands.

"So listen," I say, "I know you don't want to talk about it, and you've made it clear that you don't want to patch up our friendship, but I can't leave here feeling like I didn't get to give you a real apology."

There's a hitch in Kelly's step but she recovers quickly. "It's really not necessary," she says and I can tell she means it. I guess, after the things she said on the way to the Libations party, we're even now.

"I just want to make sure the air is clear so we can really

put the past in the past. I don't want there to be any hard feelings between us."

"I was pretty hard on you," she says reluctantly. "It was hard for me to see past my own anger to try to understand your perspective."

Her response is gracious but the tension in her body proves that the anger is still there. "Maybe. But you were right about what you said the night of the tasting room party," I say. "I had become a different person. Because of Sam, sure, but also because of my insecurities. I didn't feel good enough for him and it made me question myself. I did things I wouldn't normally do because I thought if I could be a better version of myself, maybe he would notice me."

"Do you really want to be with someone you would have to change for?" she asks me, like she can't help herself. Whatever choices I make from here on out are none of her concern, but her psychology degree must be getting the best of her.

I stop and stare at Kelly, swallowing hard. "No," I say. "I don't."

Her gaze shifts to her feet and she lets out a slow exhale. I begin to walk again.

"I'm sorry about what I said the other night," she says, catching up again. "It wasn't fair. And it wasn't true. You know that, right?"

"I don't know, Kelly," I say, exhausted by the back-and-forth. "I feel like I don't know anything anymore. Not when it comes to you. I thought after all this time you would know that deep down, no matter how stupid I was, I loved you and I never meant to hurt you. I thought I would come back here and we could pick up where we left off. But it's clear things have changed. For both of us."

We reach the trellis where our vines will be planted and set them down, gauging the distance like Dad told us.

"Maybe things haven't changed as much as I wish they had," she says.

I place my hands on my hips and try to gather my patience.

"What is that supposed to mean?" I ask.

Kelly turns away, struggling to say whatever it is she's been trying to tell me. I give in and move closer to her, lowering my voice.

"Since when can't we say something to each other?" I beg. "Don't tell me we didn't used to share everything. Don't tell me we weren't there for each other, because you know that's a lie."

"I'm envious of you, Mallory," she finally says, bursting through the barriers in her heart. "I always have been and I hate that about myself. I hate you for coming back and bringing up everything I thought I'd put behind me."

"What are you talking about?" I ask, though the uneasiness in my stomach hints that I already know, that I've always known. I ignored the comments she made under her breath and the way she looked at my parents. To me, it was never a competition. I wanted her to have all the things I had.

"You're beautiful," she says, her voice wobbly. "You have a loving family, you'd do anything for anyone, and there's nothing you're afraid of. And that summer Sam was just another thing you had that I didn't."

"I—I didn't know you wanted a boyfriend," I stammer.

"I didn't. I mean… I just wanted someone to look at me the way he looked at you."

He didn't look at me, I want to say. Not the way I wished he would. At least not that I noticed.

"Now you've seen the world," she goes on. "You've gone out there and had the adventures you always wanted to have. And I've stayed here because I'm just a small-town girl who hasn't experienced anything. What kind of psychologist could

I even be? Who would want to take advice from me? I don't want to put myself out there to fail. I'm not that brave. I don't have the kind of courage you have."

"I think you do," I say. "I think you can do anything you want to do. I think you're beautiful and kind and smart, and you're the most determined person I've ever met. Which you'd know is saying something if you'd ever met my boss."

I laugh.

"And I've always loved you exactly as you are."

Kelly sighs. "That's exactly my point. Even when I'm awful to you, you're divinely forgiving. It doesn't even faze you."

I look down at my feet, toeing a clump of dirt there. It crumbles, and I stare at it helplessly. "It fazes me," I say.

Kelly nods, frowning. After a pause, she motions toward the truck and we walk again.

"Is this why you didn't come to New York?" I ask.

"Out of jealousy?" she says. "Not at all. I wanted to go with you. More than anything. I'm sure we would have grown in our own ways. I'm sure we would have figured it out. But I was so afraid that if I left here, I would never come back. And I couldn't do that to my mom. Our life may not be perfect, or great even, but it's ours. It's all I know. And she's my mom."

I nod. I understand exactly what she means. Once you start a life somewhere else—a job, an apartment, a circle of new friends and obligations—it feels impossible to go back. What you've left behind can become a past life so quickly.

"I spent a lot of nights mad at you for not being there," I say. "I missed you and the vision we had for what our life would be like in New York. It wasn't what we imagined, and I don't know if it would have been, even if you'd been there. Nothing is quite like you fantasize it will be, but it was easy to blame the problem on you. I felt so alone." My voice is unsteady. Because the feeling isn't as far away as I wish it was. "I cried myself to sleep so many nights."

Kelly brushes my hair over my shoulder, her hand landing on my back in the space over my heart. It's the first act of sympathy she's shown me, the first time she's taken any responsibility for her part in what happened that summer, and it takes all my strength not to dissolve into tears. But I've gotten good at pretending to be happy, and I draw on that experience.

"You didn't deserve to have to carry that guilt, Mallory."

I wish the burden was past tense. I wish the loneliness was past tense, too.

I nod, not sure what else to say.

"I accept your apology," she says quickly, before I have a chance to respond. I look to her expectantly. "I need to take responsibility for my own emotions. Stop blaming you and Sam and my mom and…" She trails off, glancing at the stables. "I wasn't the best friend to you either," she admits. "I changed our plans and I know I blindsided you. That wasn't fair. I told myself I was doing it for you, out of love, but that wasn't entirely true. And it was easier to be angry at you than take responsibility for my part in what happened that summer."

I breathe a sigh of relief, vindicated after all these years that it wasn't entirely my fault. I thought I could forgive and forget the way she abandoned me if only she would forgive me my sins, but her apology heals more than I can say. The air tastes suddenly crisper.

"So maybe we can be friends again," I ask hopefully.

Kelly's response is slow. "Maybe we can try. But I need some time. I need to work on me before I can work on my relationships with anyone else."

It's the most mature, selfless thing either one of us has said to each other in a long time. So even though it isn't what I wanted to hear, I nod, grateful for possibility.

"Someday is better than never," I say. "I can live with someday."

TWELVE

*T*hat evening, after all the vines are spread out along the trellises, their burlap sacks dotting the landscape like fireflies at
dusk, and after a long ride through my new stomping ground,
I find Sam on the back porch with two wineglasses and a
bottle of zin. His feet are kicked up as he watches the sunset
with the same rapt attention that most people reserve for action movies. Most people except my dad and me.

"Hey," he says, putting his feet down when he sees me.

"Hey," I say. I stop at the top of the porch steps.

"Looks like you got some sun today."

I reach up to press my fingertips to my forehead and it's
warm to the touch. A satisfied exhaustion from the work of
the day has softened my limbs and my mood. I welcome the
burn, evidence that I've communed with Mother Nature.
"Yeah. I'll have to put some aloe on it."

"Wine?" he asks, motioning to the glasses.

"That's okay. I don't want to intrude," I say, excusing myself to a cool shower.

As I pass, he shakes his head.

"Mallory," he says. "It's for you."

I stop and actually look at him. His gaze is probing, almost pleading. I don't understand this shift in him. I don't understand my feelings toward him now—not as resentful as I probably should be, not the wanting of before, but curious.

I nod, the way we left our last conversation thirsting for conclusion.

As I take my seat, Sam's demeanor turns more formal, more careful. He fills my glass and delicately passes it to me.

"You're drinking," I say. It's the first time I've seen him with wine since he's been here. "I was starting to think you'd given it up."

"Not entirely," he says. "I save it for special occasions now."

"Probably a good idea," I say, snarky out of habit more than true anger. Sam has been nothing but considerate of me since returning. I shake my head. "I'm sorry."

"No," he says. "You're right. You don't need to censor yourself. I was in a bad place the last time I was here. I made a lot of bad choices, things I'm ashamed to remember. And I wasn't…careful with you."

I mull over his word choice. *Careful.* Does he still remember me as a child who needed to be protected, who couldn't possibly know her own mind?

Sam said I shouldn't censor myself so I try being direct, something I was too infatuated to do before.

"Sam, I didn't need you to be careful with me. I needed you to be honest. If you weren't interested in me, you should have said so. At least then I would have stopped looking for any possibilities between us. I wouldn't have ruined things with Kelly and lost the closest friend I've ever had. Not that I blame you for that," I'm quick to say. "That was the result of my own actions."

Sam sets his wine on the table and leans back, crossing his ankle over his knee.

"When I was growing up," he says, "my parents were divorced for nine years. From the time I was seven to a few weeks after my sixteenth birthday, I had two houses, two families, two Thanksgiving dinners. I know a lot of parents divorce, but in the community I grew up in, people just didn't do that. I was at a private school with kids of politicians and other doctors and investment bankers. People who have images and reputations to uphold. I was the only kid I knew who was passed back and forth like a hockey puck. I spent half the week at my mom's, and the other half at my dad's. I got to the point where I just stopped unpacking my suitcase."

If I hadn't already set my glass on the table, I would have dropped it. Is this the same Sam? Willingly opening up about his life? Impossible. I listen with rapt attention, too afraid of breaking the spell on him to risk speaking.

"Don't get me wrong, they were two very nice homes and my shuttle was a Rolls-Royce. We had money. I got anything I asked for, and it was a pretty good life. I've never asked for anyone's sympathy."

"Money is no substitute for parents, though," I say.

Sam nods, giving a practiced half smile—the smile that says, *Thank you for your sympathy, but I'm fine.* And the *I'm trying to be fine* hidden underneath.

"My dad was a hard man to please before. That's why my parents got divorced. But after my mom moved out, he had no idea how to relate to me. He used to take me to work parties in his expensive cars to pick up women because he thought it would make my mom jealous. Unfortunately, it worked. I didn't mind it so much. His friends were nice to me and bought me food, and at least we were spending time together. One night, though, on the way home, I showed some interest in medicine and he sort of latched onto it. Finally something we could talk about. After that, his mind was made up. I didn't dare say anything otherwise for fear that he'd stop talking to me again. The man is the king of stonewalling. If he wants to, he can almost convince *you* that you don't exist. That's what he used to do to my mom when she pissed him off," he reluctantly murmurs.

He looks straight ahead, but he pauses, and I can sense he's waiting for my reaction. I don't know what to say. I'm caught off guard by his openness. I knew there was tension between him and his dad but I never imagined his childhood was so hostile.

"But…they're together now?" I ask.

"I think they just got tired of being alone. There isn't one thing they like about each other."

"That sounds hard," I say. "And sad. I'm sorry."

Sam turns his whole body toward me. I startle, straightening a little at the intensity with which he stares at me.

"He called me, Mallory. The day I left here. I did something he wouldn't approve of and I was sure he'd never talk to me again, but then he called me."

"Sam, you don't have to—" I don't know why I'm trying to stop him from explaining when that's all I've ever wanted from him. It's easier to be mad at him. It's easier to be around him if I continue to see him as impenetrable, self-centered, thoughtless.

"I've always felt bad about how I left here," he says. "I did know how you felt about me, and it wasn't fair of me to disappear like that."

"Right," I say distractedly, his apology practically straight out of the scripts I used to write in my head when I imagined having this conversation. In reality, all the punchy one-liners

I had planned escape me. They feel unnecessarily harsh in light of Sam's explanation.

Sam sighs and runs a hand through his hair. A few strands fall over his eyes, as disheveled as he is in his vulnerability.

"Listen," I say, moving toward him, "if that's why you came back here—"

"Maybe," he says. "I didn't want to come here for selfish reasons. I wanted to support your family. But I've never stopped thinking about you, Mal."

I swallow hard. Is it really me Sam has missed or the me I pretended to be? Either way, the longing in his eyes is all I ever wanted from him and even after all this time, it's hard to protect myself from it.

"I don't understand," I say. "You were so distant. You pushed me away at every turn."

"I was lost. I wasn't myself. I wish I had a chance to show you who I really am," he says. "That guy you were describing the other day... That's not me. I don't want you to see me that way."

"But I'm leaving," I say slowly. "I'm going back to New York as soon as the party is over."

As I look at him, open and real for the first time, I almost wish I had time to get to know him better. This is the most honest conversation Sam and I have ever had.

Sam nods, resigned, for once, to not getting everything he wants.

"I know," he says.

He reaches for the hand in my lap and takes it between both of his, holding it close to his mouth as if to kiss my knuckles. His skin is warm and soft and my body reacts to him in a way I never could control.

"I would do so many things differently," he whispers, and I wonder if he meant for me to hear it.

Me, too, I think, knowing all I've lost because of that summer.

Me, too, I want to say, tucking it away with all the other things I've wanted to tell Sam but didn't.

Saturday morning, the morning of the planting party, arrives and it's hard to believe the day is finally here. My visit has gone by in the blink of an eye, and as I stand out on the patio that final morning, drinking my coffee, it hits me all over again that Monday I will be back in New York, back in my cubicle, back to my studio apartment and my loneliness. No more trying it on to see if it fits.

This week didn't go at all like I hoped it would. I thought by the time the planting party came, I would feel reconnected to my home, to my family, to the life I held in my mind as my "real" life. I thought Kelly would have forgiven me, that we would have completed the Summer Bucket List, and we'd be planning our next adventure. Together.

In my most elaborate fantasies, I would be eighteen again and the world would be uncomplicated. My days would be filled with horseback riding, working outside in the fresh air, and laughing with the people I cared about and who cared about me. But everything is complicated. Everything has changed.

I wanted this trip to give me clarity and I have never been so clear: I can't go back.

Before our friends and neighbors start to arrive, I saddle up Midnight and ride her out to the pond, basking in the wind on my face, the pounding of her hooves against the dirt, the rhythm of her movement. Clouds have started to roll in and I wonder if the Libations for Germination Party has worked its magic.

Midnight and I stay out there for a long time, me using her mane as a pillow, while she stands guard, seeming to sense

I need protecting in this vulnerable moment. It's a goodbye unlike I've ever felt before and unlike with the land, or Paso Robles itself, which will live on forever, Midnight will continue to grow older with each year that passes. As tears roll down my cheeks, I hold her as if she is my child, as if she is my mother, as if she is my best friend. Because somehow, she is all of these things.

When we arrive back at the stables, Tyler is waiting for us.

"You ready for this?" he asks me.

"Ready as I'll ever be," I say.

As Tyler gets Midnight cleaned up, I help Mom set up tables on the porch filled with pastries, fruit, hard-boiled eggs, bacon, coffee, and an assortment of juices for our guests.

They start to trickle in around eight thirty: the elderly Italian couple who run the vineyard next door, a few of the local restaurant owners who stock and serve Dad's wines, my uncle who flew in from Chicago, with a friend of the family who picked him up in LA.

Dad also reached out to several of his favorite customers who keep up on the growth of the vineyard and like to be the first to taste and give feedback on any of Dad's new wines. Even some of Dad's suppliers have shown up to show their support, impressed by his never-ending enthusiasm for his work.

Altogether, there are about forty people milling around the property, eating off paper plates, and chatting in small groups. Many of them carry shovels they brought from home to supplement the few we use in the stables.

"Quite a turnout," Sam says, appearing next to me on the porch, where I've been overseeing the food and drinks. The rush has passed so it's just the two of us. I organize the plasticware to busy myself, unsure of how to act around Sam after his confession.

Last night, after he released my hand, we stood and melted

into a mournful embrace, both of us seeming to ache for what could have been in a different life. Our worlds are simply too far apart. They always were.

I keep the tone light.

"You can't be surprised," I say. "It is my dad after all."

Sam chuckles. "Not in the slightest."

He moves closer to me, our bodies inches from each other. The heat that flushes my skin isn't only from the balmy humidity.

"So you're flying out tomorrow?" he asks.

I nod.

"Are you feeling any better?"

I look up at him questioningly.

"You seemed sad when you came in from riding this morning." He must have seen me when I walked past the guest house. I thought I'd done a good job of washing my face in the pond. He's so different, this Sam who notices things about me.

"I'm going to miss this place," I say. "Everything. Everyone. But I'll be okay. Once I get back to work, I'll find my groove and it will be like I never left."

"Isn't that the problem?" he asks, nailing the question on the head. And for once, I feel like someone actually understands. Sam wants as much out of life as I do. It may look different—his desire for grandiosity and luxury as opposed to my wide-open spaces and forward movement—but at the heart of them both is an unfulfilled need for excitement. Is that what drew us to each other in the first place?

I dare to meet his eyes.

"It's not just this place," I admit. "It's all the things I've forgotten how to want."

Sam reaches for me and I don't move away from his hand as he brushes my hair from my shoulder.

He has that look in his eyes—the one from last night—and

I feel like I could melt into him all over again. It's good that I'm leaving. If I stayed any longer, things would get confusing.

"Don't lose that spark," he says. "Your hunger for life inspires people. It inspires me."

"We all have to grow up," I say, justifying the decisions I've made. "You're the one who taught me that." I say it without vitriol. It would have happened at some point and Sam only tried to warn me. Sure, we all want to live our dreams, the way my dad and Sam preach, but even when we do, the reality is different from the expectation.

"Maybe I was wrong," he says futilely.

"Have you found a way out?" I ask.

He purses his lips, not wanting to admit the truth out loud—that his money doesn't give him the freedom he's been searching for.

I spot Kelly walking across the parking lot and step away from Sam. Kelly sees me and with a cautious smile, waves. Squeezing Sam's shoulder reassuringly, I excuse myself to meet up with her, bringing a cup of coffee with me.

"It's not as good as you make it," I say when I hand it to her.

"I know," she says, her smile growing wider. "Thank you."

The light breeze sends her loose hair across her face and we both look up at the clouds, questioning them. Kelly isn't wearing her braid today. I feel looser, too, unwound.

"You're working on that tan," I say, referencing one of our bucket list items. We'd wanted to start our freshman year with tans worthy of calling ourselves Californians. Of course, Kelly, with her fair skin, always struggled to get any color that wasn't a shade of red. Turns out, all she needed was a day carrying grapevines.

Kelly laughs and touches her shoulder. "Maybe after today I'll go from translucent to ghost."

I laugh, my throat thick with emotion. It's only one moment, this inside joke between us, but it's the one I've waited a decade for.

Dad calls out over the crowd to get everyone's attention and beckons us through the stables. Kelly and I walk together to join them where people coo over the horses and the clean stables Tyler keeps. We gather in front of the new plot, and standing on a chair so he can see, Dad instructs us on how to dig a hole deep enough and wide enough for the roots, then how we should place the plant, sack and all, into it and cover it before moving on to the next one.

After a few cheesy wine puns, making everyone laugh, he sets us loose on the grounds while Mom stands guard with sunblock and sprays anyone who isn't sticky with it already.

Kelly and I glance at each other, wordlessly teaming up to share my shovel.

"So you're flying out tomorrow," Kelly says as we walk toward the far end of the new acreage.

"I am," I say. I glance sideways at her, wondering if this is idle chitchat or a leading question.

"How has New York been?" she asks. "Everything we hoped it would be?"

Leading, then.

I switch the shovel to my left hand, my right hand suddenly sweaty. It would be an innocent enough question from anyone else, but from Kelly, it's a question that doesn't have a right answer. If I tell her all the things I enjoy about New York, will she be more envious of me and rediscover her anger toward me? Of if I tell her just how difficult my days have been since I left, will she consider me ungrateful?

The truth is, no one knows how much I've struggled since I left—I made sure of it. Partly out of pride, but partly because I didn't want to let them down. When I made plans to attend Columbia University, I wanted more than anything to prove my family, Kelly, and myself wrong about my "whimsical" tendencies and how they might get in the way of my success. It was easier than I thought it would be because that free spirit slipped away from me before I got on my first flight.

"It's been good," I say noncommittally. "It's been fine. I mean, New York is everything they say it is. The energy, the culture, the people. Honestly, I spend most of my time at the office, so I don't get a chance to explore much."

I motion toward a spot along the back trellises where we can work undisturbed. Kelly leads the way.

"And Columbia?" she asks over her shoulder.

We find two plants next to each other and I pass the shovel to Kelly so she can dig first. As we work, trading off digging and planting, I start at the beginning, telling her about my classes. That was what she'd been most excited about—all the things we would learn and then share over imagined hours-long conversations in our dorm, each of us curled up in our beds, avocado face masks and wet nail polish. I tell her about the endless hours researching alone in my dorm room, the many, many essays I wrote, and the speeches I gave in front of my classmates. I even admit to throwing up in the hallway outside the classroom before giving my first speech, which makes her laugh.

I tell her about the few acquaintances I made and spent most weekends with—all the intellectual types who were averse to showering and who often talked about things that were over my head but who preferred coffee shops, wine, and good food to wild parties, binge-drinking, and getting buried under pizza boxes. How different my choices about who to spend my time with became between high school and college. But my college buddies were always there when I got stuck on an assignment, and never questioned me when I disappeared for days or weeks when I was too overwhelmed by the monotony of daily life to think straight anymore. They were exactly the kind of friends I needed then.

I leave that last part out.

Instead I tell her about the few events I attended and what the transition was like from college to my internship to having a full-time job.

"It all sounds very professional and important," she says, and I laugh. Truthfully, it *feels* professional and important. Which is why I feel so out of my element most of the time.

"It's mostly city versus country, I think."

"I think it's more," she says.

We work in silence for a while, the heat of the sun beading sweat down our backs. When we're done, we step back and look at our work approvingly.

"I want to come with you," she says, jarring me from my pensiveness.

"Wait, what?"

"I want to go back to New York with you," she repeats. There's so much hope in her expression it hurts. "I want to move to New York and get my master's at Columbia. I could still have the college experience I've always wanted. I could live close to you."

"But I thought you weren't sure if you wanted to be my friend anymore," I sputter. I'm not sure why I'm reminding her of this. "I mean, I want you to come, too."

My heart leaps at the idea of her moving into my tiny apartment, the two of us exploring the city together in a way I've never done. Both of us dating—with her there, in my imagination, I would have the strength to be vulnerable and put myself out there—and sharing heartbreaks and horror stories in the dark before falling asleep. Expanding our friend circle and attending events every weekend. It could be everything we hoped it would be and more.

With Kelly there, I think I could find a way to be truly happy in New York.

"I'm serious, Mallory," she urges.

"But, how?"

The shovel is abandoned now. Kelly shrugs and searches the air for answers. "I'll hire an in-home nurse for Mom," she says. "I can send money for food and medical bills. Anybody can make her meals. It doesn't have to be me."

I shift uncomfortably. "Would you be able to get a job making enough money while you're going to school, too? And still send money home?" It doesn't seem like the time to bring up the cost of living in New York, or the price of airfare.

"I'm sure I could get a job at a coffee shop," she says.

I can't help the skeptical purse of my lips. I want it to work as much as she does, but the idea seems off-the-cuff, which is unlike Kelly. Especially for such a big decision.

My tone soberer, I say, "You told me the other day that no matter where you went, you would never stop worrying about your mom."

"I'll call her every day. And visit as much as I can."

I sigh and I can see some of the excitement leaking from Kelly's posture.

"Maybe we can bring your mom with us?" I suggest but it's a half-hearted attempt. If Kelly can't afford a nursing home here, she certainly can't afford one there.

This seems to sink in and angry tears form in her eyes.

I take a step toward her. "Kelly, c'mon. You know I would love to have you, but nothing has changed. Your commitments have kept you in Paso for a reason. I'm not saying there isn't a solution, I just don't think this is it."

I see the ripple of muscle in Kelly's jaw at this real reminder. It's a delusion and we both know it.

"Mallory, I can't stay here," she pleads. "I can't keep living the same day over and over again. I can't survive one more day without any hope for a future. What if my mom lives another twenty years? What if I'm stuck here brewing coffee until I'm forty?"

Desperation makes her body rigid, like she's ready to jump out of her own skin to get away from this life. I pull her into a hug. She shivers against me, overwhelmed by her emotions. I would give anything to take her with me, to give her a chance at living out her dreams. But I'm afraid we both know that on Monday, she will crawl out of bed, make her mom breakfast, and clock in at Monet's Mug. Because that is her reality. And as I much as I want to, I can't save her from it.

After all the vines are planted, Dad and his employees stay out in the field to make sure the irrigation lines are giving them enough water to acclimate to their new home. Hopefully the rain will come down like it's threatening to. Everyone else goes home to clean up and prepare for the party tonight while Mom, Kelly, and Tyler decorate the stables for the evening. I take the opportunity to shower and pack.

When I'm dressed and everything is back in my suitcase, I sit on the bed and look around my room. There are so many memories here, every little detail a reflection of a part of my life. I have to admit there's nothing here that made me think the life I have now is where I would end up.

I remember a conversation I had with my dad once, back when Kelly finally convinced me to start applying for colleges. My dad had made a career of something for which he didn't go to school for, and my mom attended a technical college, so they never pushed me to attend a university. They were content to let me forge my own path and support me in whatever I decided. The only thing they didn't support was me not making a decision at all.

When I sat down with my dad in his office one day, torn over which classes I should register for when I had no idea what I wanted to do with my life, Dad set aside his work and shared his experience.

"Well, honey," he said, "most people don't know what they want to do at your age. There's nothing wrong with that. Look at me. I tried several different fields before I finally figured out that I could put all that wine I was drinking to good use. I was thirty-two by then."

"That's so depressing," I muttered. He laughed. At the time, thirty-two seemed so old, so very far away.

"What, being thirty-two, or taking that long to figure out what I wanted to be when I grew up?"

"Both."

He laughed again.

"Let me tell you a secret about being an adult," he said. "Maybe it will make it easier for you, maybe it won't. As kids—and yes, you are still a kid. You will be until at least thirty."

I scoffed, but he continued anyway.

"As kids, we have this idealized notion about life. We think we're going to avoid all the mistakes our parents made and fall into a job that fulfills us every day, meet the person of our dreams—"

"I do not want to meet anyone," I countered. Getting married and having kids one day were more social standards that didn't feel like they applied to me. This was before Sam.

"You will. And you're going to want everything to be perfect. But there is no perfect, Mal. Being an adult requires a lot of sacrifice. Sometimes you have to compromise. Sometimes you have to do the grunt work before you can accumulate the knowledge, experience, and qualifications to do what you really want to do. Sometimes life is hard, and that's okay."

"So what you're saying is, don't expect to be happy."

"What I'm saying is, don't expect to have it all figured out now. Or maybe ever. Hell, I don't have it all figured out. In fact, the older I get, the more I realize how little I know."

I flopped back in the chair, defeated. "If this is supposed to be a pep talk, you suck at it."

Dad sat back in his chair, too, grinning. He rubbed his chin in thought. "Okay, let me put it this way. Just take it one day at a time."

"Simple as that, huh?"

"Most of the time," he said.

So now, ten years after that talk, I take a deep breath, stand up, and put on my dress for the party.

As I'm curling my hair, Mom calls me from the kitchen. I find her downstairs, looking for something in the fridge, the zipper of her little black dress undone. When I come up behind her, she pulls her hair aside and I zip it for her.

"I thought the focus was supposed to be on Dad tonight," I say.

She gives me a wink and pulls me into a hug.

"I can't believe you're leaving already," she says into my ear. I breathe in the lavender scent of her perfume.

"We still have tonight," I say, though I know it's not enough. It's never enough. That's the thing about family—one minute you can't wait to get as far away from them as possible, the next you want to curl up in their arms and never leave.

"We wanted to have a special dinner with you before it got so busy."

"That's okay," I say. "It's been amazing just to be here. Just to hug you."

Dad comes down the stairs, freshly showered and adjusting the collar of his only suit, a crisp navy blue that never goes out of style. Very James Bond.

"Didn't I say you were grounded?" he says to me. "Mandatory house arrest."

Mom and I laugh because we know it's all just a joke. Dad wants me back in New York, "following my dreams." Somehow, having a dream has become its own suffocating expectation.

"Sorry, Dad. But I hope to visit more often. Maybe soon I'll even be able to afford an apartment you guys can stay in when you come visit."

I should tell my parents about the promotion. The contract is in my inbox. It doesn't get more official than that. But I don't want to see their excitement for me, thinking I'm getting what I've always wanted. I don't want to pretend I'm excited, too.

"We would love that," Mom says.

Dad comes over to smooth my hair and kiss the top of my head. "And now that the vineyard is doing so well, we should be able to afford to visit more often, too."

I bite my lip to keep my emotions from spilling over as I try to accept that I'll be lucky to see my parents two or three times a year for the foreseeable future. Before, I'd always assumed our distance would be temporary. There's no denying, though, that it has become our normal.

"We'll get to a show next time," I promise.

"Perfect," Mom says, her eyes watery, too.

I make them stand next to each other so I can snap a picture with my phone, like it's prom night. I catch Dad pulling at his tie and Mom looking at him with amused affection. I've managed to capture them exactly as they are, in this moment and in their life together.

Mom and Dad share a conspiring glance.

"What?" I ask.

"Well," Dad says, rummaging through a kitchen drawer,

"we didn't want to send you back to New York with nothing. We really appreciate you working so hard to cover your own school loans while things were tight here and we're really proud of your hard work. We've wanted to do something special for you for a long time and with the success of the last season and your mom's bonus, we're finally able to do it."

Mom squeezes Dad's arm.

"You guys didn't have to do anything," I say, embarrassed. It's me who owes them, not the other way around.

Dad pulls an envelope out of the drawer and sets it on the counter in front of me. Wary, I pick it up and lift the flap. Inside is a stack of hundred-dollar bills. Mouth agape, I thumb through it. It's two thousand dollars.

"You guys. I can't accept this. This is too much."

Mom pushes the envelope closer to me. "Don't be ridiculous. Of course you can."

"We want you to use it on your apartment. For furniture or dishes or decorations. Whatever you need."

A smile pulls at my lips but I'm too overwhelmed to find words.

"You can save it for when you get your new apartment if you want or you can use it when you get back. Either way, we just want to make sure you're comfortable and that you can make your place feel like your home."

Home. If only a couch could solve all my problems.

"Thank you," I say, overcome with emotions I'm afraid they misinterpret. I am grateful, but I would trade it for more time with them in a heartbeat.

Sam walks in the back door and sees the moment we're having. He holds up his hands in apology. "Sorry," he says. "I was going to grab those cheese platters."

"Of course," Mom says. "Thank you."

Sam goes around the other side of the island. I clear my

throat, getting myself together. I don't want to fall apart in front of my parents, let alone Sam. I slip the money back into the envelope and fold it up, getting it out of sight.

"Thank you," I say to Mom and Dad more earnestly. "Thank you so much for always supporting me and believing in me. I don't know how I got so lucky to have you as my parents, but I'm very grateful. It means a lot to me."

Everything is going to be okay. Like Dad said, if I take it one day at a time, one step at a time, I'll find a way to live this new life. This money will give me a fresh start, a chance to redesign my apartment and my life.

"I'm glad we can do this for you," Dad says, putting his hand on mine. "You've done more for this vineyard and for us than you know."

It feels like an apology for not always being there, for spending more time at their jobs than with me. But I understand now that it wasn't just about the money—their work is their passion, their purpose, their contribution to the world. And all they want is to know I've found mine.

With a quick nod, I accept.

"I love you guys," I say.

The three of us embrace. Over my parents' shoulders, I see Sam slip out the back door.

"We love you, too, Mallory," my dad says, and for the first time in a long time, I feel like I'm exactly where I'm supposed to be.

THIRTEEN

THEN

*F*or the few days after Sam spent the night for the first time, the energy between us became disconnected and broken. He suddenly had things for me to do that left me in the office all day, when before, he'd always kept me close in case he wanted to hash out an idea. And Sam was full of ideas. He needed to hear them out in the open air before he could decide whether they were any good or not.

That week, though, he didn't quite meet my eyes when he spoke to me and in those long, lonely hours in Dad's dusty, sweaty office, I questioned everything I'd done and said that night. I'd walked out of the guest house on a good note, I'd thought. Yet Sam had become distant and I didn't understand why. Maybe I'd fooled myself into thinking we'd become friends, or something like it.

I found solace in the time I spent with Kelly.

We took advantage of the late-summer nights and the loosened reins that were coming with adulthood to tackle items on our bucket list—sleeping outside under the stars, creating a time capsule that we buried under a tree at the top of our hill, being tourists in our town, the town we were leaving. We reminisced about high school like it was already a decade behind us and talked about the future like nothing but magic and fairy tales lay ahead.

Still, thoughts of Sam niggled at the back of my mind. Since Kelly didn't approve of my feelings for him, I kept them to myself, pretending he didn't mean anything to me. Rationally, I knew any attachment I formed to him was bound to end in heartbreak. I was leaving and so was he. It was easier to remember that when he wasn't around, but of course, I couldn't avoid him forever.

"Want to go for a ride with us this morning?" Dad asked over a breakfast of cold cereal.

"Do you have to ask?" I replied. I was so surprised to hear he was planning to take Rocket out, I didn't immediately catch the "us." Mom had left for the office as I was sitting down to eat. "Wait, who?"

"I invited Sam out."

"He said yes?" I couldn't picture Sam doing anything that led to the possibility of getting dirty. Did he own any clothes that didn't require dress shoes?

Dad nodded, milk dribbling down his chin.

I helped Tyler brush and saddle the horses while Dad checked on the grapes before Sam arrived. When I told Tyler our plans, he asked, "Can I hop on the back of Midnight with you?"

"Why?" I asked, though by his amused grin, I could guess.

"Because seeing Mr. Shiny Watch ride a horse is going to be hysterical."

I bumped my hip against his. "Lay off. He's probably ridden before. He's traveled all over the world, you know?"

"Wow. I'm so impressed," he said. "Just because you travel the world doesn't know you mean anything about life. Or people. Or yourself."

I stopped brushing Midnight's tail and looked at Tyler. "And what do you know about life?"

"I know it's about a lot more than how expensive my car is."

I happened to agree with Tyler, but I believed there was much more to Sam than that—he just held his cards closer to his chest.

"What's it about? The thing they call rodeo?" I asked, quoting Garth Brooks.

"I'm not a cowboy. I've never even seen a bull up close."

I laughed. I teased him, but for as much time as we spent together, I realized I didn't know anything about what Tyler's plans for the future were, or what he wanted out of life. Was working at our vineyard enough for him? Forever? Selfishly, I hoped it would be. I had to leave the vineyard, to go find myself, and it would make it a lot easier if I knew Tyler would always be there when I came back.

"Connection," he said in an uncharacteristically thoughtful response. But he said it quickly, like he'd been thinking about it a lot lately but didn't want to draw attention to it.

"Go on."

"Like with Midnight here." He patted her rump. "Or you. Friends. Family. The dirt beneath our feet. You can't tell me that guy is connected. Everything about him is perfectly tailored to put distance between him and everyone around him."

I couldn't argue with Tyler. I thought when Sam had spent the night, when he took off all his armor along with his shoes and jacket and belt. A little bit of honesty had slipped past his filter. Was that why he'd pulled away?

"What's it about for you?" he asked. It took me a moment to remember what we'd been talking about.

"Hell if I know."

He didn't laugh at my response, just continued to brush Midnight's hindquarters.

"What?" I urged.

"Air," he said.

"Air?"

"For you. Wind in your hair. Room to breathe. Blowing one way and then in the completely different direction." He laughed, seeming to picture something in his mind's eye. Or maybe at the truth of his words. My chest ached—with love or vulnerability—at being seen so clearly. Sometimes I wondered if Tyler knew me better than Kelly. Or maybe he just allowed me to be my completely flawed self more than I felt like I could with Kelly, who always pushed me to be better. I appreciated that aspect of our friendship, but sometimes it was exhausting.

Sam arrived then, taking my attention with him.

"So how do I do this?" he asked with a bashful grin.

I kept my pleasure in check at being the one to teach him how to put himself in the saddle. It took him more than a few tries to get the momentum to throw his leg over the other side and while at first I didn't know how he'd react to my physical guidance, when he didn't pull away from my touch, I used my hands to propel him in the right direction. His triumphant smile when he got it filled me with hope that a few awkward days wasn't a death sentence to our friendship. And as we rode through the vines that afternoon, Dad sharing stories from his childhood, Sam stole curious glances at me, like he was finally seeing a different side of me—a side that didn't have anything to do with my dad or the vineyard.

Dad and Sam started drinking earlier that day—eating,

talking, laughing, and sharing bottles of wine from the surrounding vineyards to assess the competition. For a few hours before dinner, Kelly came over and Sam's voice drifted up through my bedroom window while she and I took a reprieve from the heat and watched a movie on my bed. When she left to make dinner for her mom, though, I sat on the back porch step with a book; Sam and Dad's chatter in the background becoming my soundtrack of that summer.

When the sun finally set, Sam was mellow, dehydrated, and a little sunburned across the bridge of his nose. He took up Dad's offer to stay in the guest house without argument this time and Dad offered up my services once again to get Sam settled in. I ran upstairs to Mom's bathroom to get the aloe vera before I led Sam to the space he was quickly claiming as his own. He was more at ease this time, heading straight for the bathroom while I replaced the bedding I'd washed during his last overnight stay.

"I'm going to have to leave some glasses in here," he said with a laugh when he reemerged. "I can't throw away a pair of contacts every time I stay."

My skin flushed at the thought of him making it a regular occurrence. While I was still young, I knew it wasn't healthy—physically or emotionally—for Sam to drink past the driving limit often, but it also felt good to be needed. It felt good to be needed by Sam. It felt good to be alone with him, however fleeting.

"Do you drive back to the hotel blind?" I asked.

Sam shrugged and fell into the freshly made bed, his belt already off, his shirt untucked, his socks and shoes off. I filled a glass of water and left it on the nightstand with two aspirin.

"You might want to put some of this on your face," I said, handing over the aloe vera.

He furrowed his brow, then touched his nose and winced. "Damn."

I uncapped the tube and held it out for him to take. Instead, he closed his eyes and rested his head closer to the edge of the bed.

I couldn't swallow, couldn't breathe, as I squeezed some of the aloe onto my fingertips. I rubbed the gel between my hands to warm it, then slowly, delicately, I pressed my fingertips to the bridge of his nose. His skin was hot. He sighed.

I smoothed the gel over the rest of his nose and his cheeks, the shape of his face so unfamiliar. I covered his forehead, too, for good measure, and because I couldn't believe I'd been given permission to touch him so intimately. I hadn't realized until that moment how infrequently I'd ever felt the curves of another person's face.

When I finally pulled away, he murmured, "Thanks, kiddo."

The jolt of that one word after such a visceral moment woke me to reality like a bucket of cold water. *Kiddo?* Was that really how he saw me? Thankfully his eyes were still closed because tears prickled at the corners of mine.

"Welcome," I whispered.

I closed the aloe vera and placed it on the nightstand so he could apply more in the morning. It was time for me to leave. Sam didn't want me. He just needed someone to send his emails, make sure there was fresh soap in the shower, and stroke his ego when he had a new branding idea.

Then he tilted his head so he could look at me and his face was so beautiful my heart skipped a beat.

"Stay," he said. "Just for a few minutes."

I wanted to stay, but I knew I shouldn't. So far Sam had made the boundaries between our work relationship and our friendship pretty clear. Even at eighteen, and even as infatuated with Sam as I was, I intuited that those boundaries were better for my heart, whether I liked them or not. Sitting with Sam in the guest room would obliterate those boundaries. It would confuse my feelings for him with his feelings for me even more.

I pulled the chair from the corner over to his side of the bed, and I curled up in it, my feet tucked beneath me. Sam turned onto his side and folded his arm beneath his head, resting on his biceps.

"What do you want to talk about?" I asked him. I heard the defeat in my voice, but he didn't.

"You pick," he said, yawning.

There was something I'd been dying to know.

"You said at dinner the other night it was time for another adventure once you leave here?" We'd had a family dinner, Kelly included, which was as awkward as it sounded. But afterward, while everyone else cleared dishes, Sam had said something that piqued my interest. He said it when no one else would hear, to me alone.

"Yeah," he said, a smile pulling at the corners of his mouth. Every expression that crossed his face made my heart contract. I so badly wanted them to be for me.

"What did you have in mind?"

Sam rolled onto his back, his hands landing on his chest. "Climbing Colorado's fourteeners," he said on a dreamy breath.

This. This was what I'd been waiting for. A genuine disclosure of his deepest desires. Not fancy cars, not designer clothes, not perfectly coifed hair. A true calling of Sam's heart. Unfortunately, I didn't know what he was talking about. I hated to admit it but I needed to know more.

"Fourteeners?" I asked.

Sam laughed at his own clumsiness as he struggled to sit up.

"There are fifty-three mountains in Colorado that reach fourteen thousand feet above sea level," he said. "You have to get up at, like, three o'clock in the morning and climb thousands of feet to summit before the monsoons hit. The air is so thin at the top that some people bring oxygen with them so they don't get altitude sickness."

"That definitely sounds like an adventure," I said sarcastically, but I recognized that my own heart rate had sped up at the idea. The feel of my muscles working, the ground beneath my feet, the *air*.

"It's a little bit crazy," he said with a laugh, "but imagine the view at the top."

I could picture it immediately—Sam with his determined gait, his skin darkened by the Colorado sun, his curls dancing in the breeze, and nothing but trees for miles in any direction.

"It suits you," I said.

When I closed my eyes, I was there with him, my hair tracing the hollow of my neck as it got caught by the mountain wind, and Sam reaching his hand out to me. Just the two of us.

Wind in your hair, Tyler had said. *Room to breathe. Blowing one way and then in the completely different direction.*

I opened my eyes. Sam stared at me.

"What?" he asked. "You're smiling."

I shook my head. "It just seems…perfect."

Sam lay down closer to me this time and grabbed my hand, setting my nerves on fire. His thumb traced my tender tattoo like he was fascinated by its texture.

He yawned and his eyes fluttered shut.

"It will be," he murmured to himself. A few minutes later, when his hand slipped from mine, I ran my fingers over his forehead once more, wishing I could place a kiss there, that I was the woman in his life who could do things like that without a second thought. Then I crept out of the guest house.

The next morning, I woke him up with coffee and while at first, he seemed sheepish about the intimacy between us the night before, once he washed his face and put his clothes back together, he acted like himself again. As we drank coffee on the back porch, I tried to understand how he really saw me, the furtive glances, the emotions I felt between us. But which version of Sam was the true one: the Sam who was clear-minded yet guarded, or the Sam whose inhibitions had been swept away with a few glasses of wine?

FOURTEEN

NOW

I hear the music start as I'm putting on my makeup, and soon the parking lot is full again. From the bathroom window, I watch people with their glasses of wine, huddled in clumps. The sun has nearly set, and the string lights in the stables are on. It's a beautiful scene—a magical scene—and yet I find myself putting off going downstairs as long as possible. Once I join the party, that will be the beginning of the end of this visit and I'm not ready to say goodbye.

When I finally work up the courage, the party is in full swing. There are ten tables set up in the breezeway of the stables, five on each side with a space left open for dancing. Lights line the ceiling and each of the stalls. Rocket, entertained by all of the commotion, sticks his head out of his stall and nudges people passing by or nips at their hair. The mares, on the other hand, have retreated into their stalls to avoid the noise.

I sneak into Midnight's stall, where she's nestled against the far wall. The music drifts in, but it's muted.

"Hey, girl," I say. When she sees me, she reaches her nose out and I run my hand over the length of it, pulling her close to rest my face on hers. I've never been able to say the word *goodbye* to her. "I'm going to miss you so much," I whisper instead.

We stand that way for a long time, Midnight munching on hay, a humid breeze blowing through the stables. I close my eyes and memorize this moment, breathe it all in.

My body unclenches.

"There you are," Kelly says, coming into the stall. I turn to her. She looks lovely in a white summer dress, her hair loose and long with her bangs twisted and pulled back like a delicate crown. "People are asking for you," she says.

"I'm coming," I tell her. I kiss Midnight, and though she shows no signs of understanding the fact that I'm leaving, I sense a sadness in her, too—she's always mirrored my moods.

As I approach the stall door, Kelly puts herself in front of me.

"Before we go out there," she says, "I want to say I'm sorry about earlier. I got carried away."

I hold up my hands to stop her. "You don't have to apologize for anything. We'll find a way, okay? Whenever you're ready, I'd be happy to help you in any way I can."

"It was stupid—"

I place my hands on her shoulders and with resolution, I tell her, "We will."

Her shoulders relax. "Thank you," she says.

"C'mon," I say. "Let's go get some wine now that we're old enough to drink it."

Kelly laughs. "Let's do it."

For the next couple of hours, we eat, drink wine, and

dance. I pass Mom and Dad in an excited conversation with some friends of theirs from Chicago, people my parents call their best friends, but who I hardly know because of the distance between us. That's what distance does to relationships, it seems, but I vow to be optimistic.

I catch up with everyone else visiting from out of town and when they ask about my job, I try to inject as much enthusiasm into my responses as possible. *Act as if*, Sam once told me, and so I do. I act as if one day I will be proud of the accomplishments I've achieved, hoping one day soon I will be.

When the clouds finally open up and the rain comes down, we all break into cheers and refill our wineglasses, sure it's a sign from the gods of another great season. It's too bad so many of us won't be here to witness it.

At the thought of Sam, I look around the room, surprised to realize I haven't seen him all night.

"Who are you looking for?" Kelly asks.

I force my attention back to her. I don't respond, but I don't have to. She nods toward the office, where Sam is standing in the dark doorway. I can only see the outline of half his body, but when he sees me looking at him, he steps out into the light.

I look to Kelly. For permission? Or validation? I'm not sure. She nods again, so I stand shakily and move through the people toward him. He meets me in the middle of the room, the middle of the dance floor, and holds a hand out to me.

"Dance?" he asks.

"I didn't know you danced."

"Now you do."

Dancing seems like a risky act for someone who works so hard to appear perfect, but I allow him to pull me close, placing my hand on his shoulder. He slides his hand around my back, resting it on my hips. I'm stunned by the contact and how easily he shows it—here, in front of everyone. His cologne draws me nearer and I rest my chin on his shoulder, listening to the music, the rhythm of the rain on the roof, and his heartbeat.

"What time do you leave?" he asks.

"My flight leaves LAX at nine."

He nods.

"What about you?" I ask. "When do you head home?"

He shrugs. "Nothing is calling me home at the moment. Maybe I'll stay a few more days. Relax."

A giggle escapes my lips. "What, create some to-do lists? Restructure one of the local businesses for fun?"

He fails to suppress a grin. "Maybe you have some suggestions for me."

I consider it. "You could take a walk. Meandering through the vines could take you all day. Do you think you could manage being away from your phone for that long?"

"If I had good company," he says.

I don't think too deeply about his comment, whether he means me or if he's merely making a general statement. "I'm sure Tyler would take you out for a ride if you were so inclined."

Sam barks a laugh. "I'm sure Tyler would rather see me under a horse than on top of one."

I shrug, but I can't argue. My amusement at the prospect must be written all over my face.

The song changes—another slow song—and Sam rotates us on the dance floor, giving me a different vantage point. I can see Kelly talking to Mom, Mom with her hand on Kelly's back. Now that I know Shannon's situation, I'm glad for their connection. Kelly is going to need it.

"Well, maybe you can just do what you do best. Enjoy a cup of coffee on the porch at sunrise and a glass of wine at sunset. Maybe throw a book in there for good measure."

"That, I think I can handle," he says.

I pull my gaze away from Kelly and stare at the little curl at the nape of Sam's neck, begging myself not to reach up and touch it.

"Did you, um, ever hike those mountains in Colorado?" I finally ask. Realizing I had fallen for that particular delusion was the most humiliating moment of my life.

Sam clears his throat, decidedly not meeting my eyes.

"No," he says. His neck flushes. I imagine it's humiliating for him to admit he was deluding himself, too.

When he finally looks at me again, his expression is deeply apologetic. For the millionth time since I've known him, I wish I knew what he was thinking. Something powerful lies beyond those dark eyes, and I'm never going to know what it is. For a long moment, I'm afraid he might kiss me in front of all these people and leave me thinking about him—ever the one that got away—for the next decade. But he glances away.

"I hope you have a good life, Mallory. You're one of the few people who sees the world not as it is but as it could be. That's a special thing. Don't waste it."

It's the saddest goodbye I've ever heard, because it's the only one I've received knowing we'll never have a reason to see each other again.

It's the only goodbye Sam has ever given me.

The music shifts again, to something upbeat, but I'm reluctant to let the moment end. No man has ever affected my heart the way he does. The pressure of his body against mine, the skin of his neck, his cheek so close to mine—it's too sweet. But time won't stop no matter how much I will it to.

I take a step back and Sam's fingers slip from my waist.

"Don't give up until you reach your dreams, Sam," I say. "The real ones."

He smiles. "I won't if you won't."

He reaches his fingers out to me again but I turn away, back to Kelly. When I look back over my shoulder, Sam is gone.

The party shows no signs of stopping by the time I'm ready to head upstairs to get some sleep before my flight. Kelly, Tyler, and I huddle together underneath the overhang in front of the barn, hiding from the rain and the crisp night air to say our goodbyes.

"Call me," I tell Kelly, "whenever you're ready."

"I will," she says with tears in her eyes. I pray they're tears of hope, rather than despondence.

She pulls me into a tight hug and I squeeze her back. It's so different from the hug she gave me when I first arrived— soft, sad, but genuine.

"I love you," I whisper, and even though she doesn't say it back, it's enough that I've gotten to say everything I came here to say.

"God, I'm going to miss you," Tyler tells me, taking his turn pulling me into a hug. I'm enveloped by his strong arms and his salty scent. I feel a distinct ache at saying goodbye to him. If there's anyone here with whom I've left things unsaid, it's Tyler. But how do I begin to tell him that The Wandering Vineyard won't be the same without him? How do I tell him he's the only man who has ever made me feel accepted exactly as I am? How can I convey that I equate him with Midnight, with air, with that sense of freedom I so strive for?

"Go build your dream stables," is all I can say. "I want to come visit."

"You'd better," he says. "I mean it."

"So do I. I promise."

When I step back, we all stand there for a moment, none of us ready to face the inevitable. Kelly finally throws her hands up.

"I'm going to go home. I've done all I can do for this party."
Tyler and I laugh.

Kelly nods to Tyler, then walks off to the parking lot, ducking her head from the rain.

"I'm going to go, too," Tyler says, "but for less emotional reasons."

"Oh, yeah?" I ask. "For what reason?"

"I have something in my eye."

I smile and share a final hug with him before he disappears into the night, waving over his shoulder to me as he goes.

I stand there for a few minutes, taking it all in—the rain's promise of new growth, the proximity to all the people I love, the happy noise of success behind me. This perfect night that I wish could go on forever.

A light in the guest house catches my attention. I picture Sam in there, getting ready for bed. No doubt he came more prepared this time than the nights he half-heartedly and half-drunkenly slithered out of his clothes and fell into bed. I remember the electricity I felt on those nights, just being near him, the fire he set in my body.

I traipse across the gravel in my heels, the light rain dampening my hair, the pace of my heartbeat quickening. I'm not a girl anymore, not a *kiddo*. And if Sam and I both ended up back here at the same time, it can't be for no reason. I don't intend to leave here without proving to Sam that I was never as naive as he wanted to paint me. I was never as naive as I pretended to be.

I reach the guest house doorstep, take a deep breath, and knock.

When Sam opens the door, his expression reveals surprise. His dress shirt is off, revealing his undershirt and strong shoulders that I once laid my head on. His hair is fallen down and he looks like *my* Sam—the one only I ever got to see.

I step into his space, pressing my body against his, and with my hands on his cheeks, I pull his mouth to mine, showing Sam that when it came to him, I always knew exactly what I wanted.

He doesn't hesitate, not for a moment. He wraps his arms around me and pulls me closer, like he's been waiting for this moment for as long as I have. Our lips and tongues search each other hungrily, begging each other to fill all the pieces of ourselves that have been empty for so long.

"Why did you leave?" I ask against his mouth. My cheeks are wet and not because of the rain. "Why didn't you say goodbye?"

"I left because…" His breathing is heavy. "I was starting to feel too much for you."

"And you thought the best way to show that was to break my heart?" I ask, my voice reedy with emotion. Sam returned my feelings. It wasn't all in my head. "You made me feel crazy," I yell at him.

I push myself away from him, wrapping my arms around my body. Sam steps back, holding the door open to invite me in, but I can't cross the threshold. I can't be in there with him. Sam clears his throat and steps out onto the porch instead. The rain drizzles off the roof, making the space feel smaller.

"I know," he says softly. "I was…completely irresponsible with you."

All the anger I've been trying to hold back, trying to deny, boils to the surface.

"You were an asshole." The word is satisfying between my teeth.

Sam stands there with his hands at his sides, frozen like I'm a wild animal he's afraid to spook.

"I was. You're right. But I was also heartbroken, Mallory.

That's why I came here. My two-year engagement had just ended and I needed to get away from her. From everything."

His confession knocks the wind out of me. Yet another thing he hid from me. And even worse, I never suspected it. It made me feel better to think I'd mostly figured him out, but I didn't know anything and that realization makes me sick to my stomach. Who was it I was ready to run away with?

"Oh, so you do have a heart?" I retort.

"Ouch," he says, and the bruised look on his face finally shakes me out of my belligerence. I always thought of Sam as unshakable, but I've seen a different side of him this week.

"I'm sorry," I whisper. I take a step closer and let my hands fall.

Sam stares at me, and then, when I think I can't take the silence any longer, he lifts a thumb to my cheek and brushes my hair away from my face.

"I have a heart," he says, and as soon as he does, I know I shouldn't have come here. How can I let him go knowing I wasn't crazy? Knowing that if things had been different, there could have been a chance for us? That if things were different now, there still could be?

"Okay," I say, when what I'm really thinking is, *You've ruined me. No one will ever compare to you.* "Okay," I repeat, stepping away from him. Then I turn into the rain, leaving my heart in a puddle behind me.

I slog up to my room and slip out of my damp dress, methodically hanging it back up in my closet, where it will stay until I return again. I charge my cell phone, check my boarding pass and ID, and then I slip into bed, staring up at the ceiling.

Sam's final declaration to me echoes in my head. I got the answers I wanted, however feeble.

And yet his explanation only brought up more questions. A fiancée? Who? Did he love her? Was he really ready to commit to her? Was she as magazine perfect as him? Did he go back to her?

I listen as the party dies down and cars start and pull out of the parking lot. I replay our kiss, knowing Sam is just outside, knowing he's probably thinking of me, too. I force myself to stay in bed, to avoid making our parting worse. The light of the moon shifts from one side of my room to the other.

I don't know how much time has passed when my phone rings on the nightstand. Denise is already bringing me back into the fold. But when I pick it up, it's Kelly's name that flashes across the screen.

"Hey," I say quickly, sticky anxiety in my throat. "Are you okay?"

Her response is a sob and at first I worry she's having a harder time with my leaving than I thought. Or maybe she really can't forgive me and she wants me to know this good-bye will be our last. But when she can finally breathe enough to speak, what she says is much, much worse.

"I'm at the hospital," she gasps. "I think she's dead, Mal. I think my mom is dead."

FIFTEEN

I race to the hospital in the middle of the night, not sure what time it is or exactly where I'm going. All the lights in the house were off when I burst out the back door and ran to the parking lot.

The closest hospital is in Templeton, eight miles away, and the highway is dark and foreboding. Thankfully, the rain has stopped because I'm so anxious I can hardly see straight, the yellow lines blurring together. All I can think about is getting to Kelly as soon as possible and praying that what she said isn't true. It can't be true.

When I get into Templeton, I follow the lights to the only building open at this hour and park in front of the emergency room. I run to the first nurse I see and yell, "Shannon Grayer," at her breathlessly. She looks like she's about to ask my relation when the doors that separate the lobby from the exam rooms whoosh open and Kelly stands between them, crying and broken.

She collapses into my arms and I hold her there forever, tears stinging my eyes.

Eventually, one of the nurses leads us back to the room where Shannon is. I peek in through the windows. A white sheet is pulled up to her chin and her eyes are closed so peacefully she could be sleeping. But there are no doctors, no monitors beeping. Only empty, deathly silence.

I sit Kelly in one of the waiting room chairs and pull the nurse aside. She's about my age; her brown, curly hair is frizzy like she's been on shift for too many hours and her hair is begging for relief.

"What happened?" I ask her, knowing it will be a while before I can get anything comprehensible out of Kelly.

In a quiet voice, she says, "She had a heart attack at home. Her daughter brought her in and said she'd been complaining of chest pain and shortness of breath. Her records showed that she'd recently had a quadruple bypass and that she'd been suffering complications. We got her checked in and when the doctor came in to examine her, she had another heart attack. He tried to bring her back, and we got a rhythm a few times, but after the last time…"

Kelly must have called me in the middle of all that. That must have been why she was unsure. It horrifies me to think of her standing there, watching through the window as her mom slipped away in such a painful and terrifying way.

"What do we do now?" I ask.

"We'll need to take…her—" the body, I realize painfully "—to the morgue, and whoever is making the funeral arrangements can call homes in the morning. But if there's anyone who wants to come pay their respects, we can keep her in the room for a while longer."

I look at Kelly, her torso folded in on itself, her face in her hands.

"No," I say. "There's no one else."

"Then whenever she's ready," the nurse says. She places a

comforting hand on my shoulder, the only thing she seems
to know to do in this situation.

"Thank you," I say.

She nods and walks away.

I pause for a long moment, steeling myself to be the support Kelly needs right now. My time to grieve will be later.

"C'mon, Kel," I say, helping her up. "Let's go be with your
mom."

I pull two nearby chairs closer to the bed and for the
next couple of hours, we sit there, arms draped over Shannon while Kelly cries until she has no tears left. She doesn't
speak, doesn't open her eyes, just grasps the lingering presence of her mother's spirit. Though I want to fall apart,
too, I keep myself busy—getting Kelly drinks and tissues,
brushing her hair away from her face, collecting paperwork.
Kelly needs family to lean on and I'm now the only person
for the job.

Finally, when Kelly seems to have no energy left, I pull
her from Shannon's body, give a parting nod to the nurse. I
lead Kelly out to my car and pour her into the passenger seat.

By the time we reach the house, it's five o'clock in the
morning. For a brief moment, I realize I'm not going to make
my flight, but that's the least of my concerns. There's no fath-
omable way I'm going back to New York today.

I help Kelly up to my room, lay her down in my bed, and
cover her up. As depleted as she is, she's asleep before I can
sneak out of the room.

Dad is making coffee when I come downstairs. He's surprised
to see I'm still here, and it's when I have to repeat the words
myself—"Shannon died"—that I finally break down. He wraps
me in his arms and we cry for Shannon, cry for Kelly, and cry
for myself because I don't know how to watch Kelly suffer like
this, knowing there's nothing in the world I can do to fix it.

★ ★ ★

My mom takes charge of the cremation arrangements, refusing to let Kelly handle anything, which is for the best. The day after her mother's death, Kelly is fit to do nothing. She sits on the couch, face pink and swollen with a far-off stare, as we bring her coffee and tea and small amounts of food, all of which sit on the coffee table and turn cold.

When Tyler shows up to take care of the horses, I relay the news and he sits with her for a couple of hours while I muck the stalls, giving me a better way to release my anxious energy. After a tearful, sleepless night, it's a wonder I have energy at all.

While I'm out there, Sam hears the news and appears in front of Midnight's stall with a regretful expression. Though I'm covered in dust and hay, grief and desperation, he opens his arms to me and when he folds me in close to him, the embrace is unlike anything I've ever felt from him before. It's not about lust or expectations. There are no walls. It's pure selflessness and comfort.

On Tuesday, Mom takes Kelly to the crematorium to sign the final paperwork, and we decide to do a personal memorial service the following day, when the ashes will be returned to us. There's no one to fly in, no one in town who even knew Shannon. The only people who will attend are under my parents' roof.

As the reality of her death sinks in, that's what weighs on me the most. The times I spoke with Shannon, she was one of the wittiest and kindest women I ever met, and other than Kelly, me, and her family members who disowned her, no one else in the world will ever know that.

Kelly spends each night in my bed, still too overcome with grief to face returning to her own home. I drive over on Wednesday morning to pick out something black for Kelly to wear. Midmorning, the six of us gather on the patio, Kelly holding the unceremonious plastic bag of ashes she and my mother picked up from the funeral home.

I picture how we must look from overhead and imagine we resemble a murder of crows as we take off from the porch, through the vines, and up to the top of the hill. The path is longer and more arduous on foot, but today, that seems right. It's how we pay our respects for the hard road Shannon walked and the difficult journey Kelly has ahead of her.

We reach the top of the hill, where Kelly and I have shared so many heart-to-hearts, and look out on the property. When Kelly asked Dad if she could lay Shannon to rest here, where she would finally be able to see the world for the first time in twenty-plus years, he told her he'd be honored. Now, as we stand here, looking out at the great expanse, all of us seem to be seeing it in a different light, a mixture of sadness, fear, and uncertainty written on all our faces.

I've never lost anyone close to me before, and I discover there's something about death that forces you to think about how you're living your own life. When my own time comes, I wonder, will I feel like I've lived it to the fullest?

"Do you want to say something, sweetie?" my mom asks Kelly, running her hand over Kelly's limp hair. "You don't have to."

Kelly nods. "I want to," she says. Her skin is pale but she holds her chin high.

Mom gives her some space and we all wait in respectful silence for her final words for her mother.

Kelly clears her throat.

"Being my mother's daughter was a blessing and curse," Kelly begins in a soft voice. "After her parents and her sisters cut her out of their lives, she was so heartbroken that she couldn't bear to open her heart again. Not to anyone…except me. No one really knew her and I was left to take care of her on my own."

Kelly shifts uncomfortably and it ripples over the rest of us, looking down or away, but hearing every word.

"I grew up faster than anyone I know," Kelly says, "and had more responsibilities as a six-year-old than many people do as adults. I've felt the weight of holding someone's life in your hands. I've made so many sacrifices to take care of her because I didn't trust anyone to do it the way I would. And I loved her even as I watched her bury herself a little at a time."

I step closer to Kelly and lace my fingers through hers. Her voice begins to quaver as she continues.

"No one knew her like I did. No one saw how funny she was. Most days she would make me laugh until I cried, especially on the days when she knew I needed it most. I've never known anyone else who loved as deeply as she did. Which may have been the problem, but for her and me, it was what kept us going. It wasn't an easy life, but it was ours."

Kelly takes a shaky breath, but she lifts her chin higher, showing her never-ending strength.

"My mom may have taught me the hard way," she says, "but nevertheless, she did teach me how to be independent and how to take care of myself. At the end of the day, isn't that a parent's most important job?"

My parents nod knowingly. Dad reaches out to run a hand across her back and at this gesture, Kelly starts to dissolve.

"I will carry her with me," Kelly says, "every step of the way, for the rest of my life, and I hope that through me, she will get to see everything she couldn't see through her own eyes."

We all nod, praying for Kelly's wish to come true. I put my arm around her and she buries her face in my shoulder.

When Kelly doesn't move to speak again, Dad says a final prayer. Then each of us takes a turn reaching our hands into the bag of ashes and holding them out to the breeze. Even Sam takes a turn, Kelly nodding her approval. He watches me as he does, and though he doesn't know Kelly well, I know he's doing it for me. The ashes dance along the wind like dandelions, over the vines, through the trees, and back to the earth, where Shannon returns home. Ashes to ashes, dust to dust.

Afterward, we reconvene on the patio to offer Kelly more condolences. Mom more or less demands that Kelly return for every meal for the foreseeable future, even offering the guest house to her once Sam leaves, which Sam concedes immediately, promising to have his things packed within ten minutes.

Kelly waves it all off. "Thank you," she says. "But it's time for me to go home. I have a lot of things to figure out."

"I'll go with you," I tell her.

"I'll be okay," Kelly assures us. "I'm going to have to be alone sometime. Might as well get it over with."

"So… I'll call you, then?" I ask, unsteadied by this quick goodbye. My boss was all too accommodating about me staying for the services, even sending flowers. But I have responsibilities back in New York that I have to return to.

"Sure," Kelly says and squeezes my hand in parting.

"I'll take you home," Mom says. "And Rich and I will bring your car back from the hospital tomorrow."

We each give Kelly a hug in turn, and to my surprise, she even accepts one from Sam. When Mom and Kelly drive away, we all stand in silence, wondering how to return to normal life after a blow like this.

After Kelly leaves, I stick to the coping mechanism I know best: getting away as fast as possible. With Midnight, it's easier than in New York—to disappear, to be alone with my thoughts. The silence helps. It's becoming comfortable again. In the city, people are inescapable. There isn't an uninhabited square yard within a hundred miles of my apartment. But here, just on the other side of the stables, I can escape into a world where no one else exists, and so I do.

But no matter how fast Midnight runs or how far we go, it doesn't quite work the way it used to. I feel heavy in a way I've never felt before, in a way that not even Midnight or a strong breeze in my hair can revive. I'm not entirely sure what I'm upset about or who I'm upset for. There are no words to these feelings, just a numbness that fills me and weighs me down. And every time I think about getting back on a plane, I feel sick to my stomach.

I try to remind myself of why I need to be in New York. My vacation time is up, I have a promotion to accept, rent to pay. But in comparison to my reasons for staying, all of those things feel so meaningless, so inconsequential. I left Kelly when she needed me once before and I've never forgiven myself for that. I can't leave her this time. She needs someone. She needs me.

As soon as I get back to the stables, I pull out my cell phone and call Denise. I'm supposed to be at the office tomorrow morning, and spending the weekend catching up, so I suspect that she won't be happy with me, but when I tell her the situation, she's unexpectedly sympathetic.

"Mallory, contrary to popular belief, I am human," she says.

I laugh in spite of myself, and in spite of this awful situation.

"I really appreciate this," I tell her.

She tells me she has an account lined up for me and so I offer to work long-distance for another week and she agrees. She barks something at one of my coworkers and my email beeps with the client information before we've even hung up.

"See you soon," I say, but the line is already dead. I sigh and shove my phone back into my pocket.

A sound in the breezeway startles me. When I stick my head

out of Midnight's stall, Sam is standing there with his hands in his pockets, looking at me from under his brows.

"So," he says, "you're staying a little longer?"

"It looks that way," I say, resting my body and my head against the stall door frame.

The electric buzz that usually jumps between us is gone. Things have become too real around here, all charm gone. That's why it surprises me when Sam walks over to me, cups his hand around the back of my head and kisses me.

At first, I'm too conflicted to respond. Yes, we kissed on Saturday, but emotions were high and I was leaving. This kiss is different. It's a question I don't have an answer for.

But I allow myself to kiss him back. I allow myself this reprieve from the grief.

"I thought I was never going to get a chance with you," he says.

I shake my head.

"Sam, I…" I wait for the rest of that sentence to come, but it doesn't. Once again, I don't know what I want. Sam is the manifestation of every young girl's fantasy, and probably most grown women's, too. He's everything I've dreamed about since the moment I first laid eyes on him.

But I need to focus on Kelly. She's who I came here for, and that's more true now than when I first got here.

"I know why you're staying," he's quick to say, "and I don't want to distract you from that. But if you find yourself with a free hour, I'd love to just…talk to you." He leans in again and brushes his lips against mine, making it clear that more than talking would be welcome. And I can't help it—the spark returns.

When he pulls away, there's a hint of a triumphant smile there, though he tries to be a gentleman and hide it.

"You're not very good at not being distracting," I say.

He laughs.

"You know where to find me," he says and bows before turning and walking out of the stables.

After I watch him go, I grab the rake and wheelbarrow to muck Midnight's stall. Tyler keeps it so clean there's hardly any work to do, so I decide to clear out the old bedding and lay fresh shavings. I fill the wheelbarrow once, twice. The steady rhythm of shoveling and being so close to Midnight calms me, centers me. Sweat forms between my shoulder blades, on my upper lip, and I finally find that sense of peace I've been looking for all week.

"If only they would pay someone to do that," Tyler says behind me. I smile, not stopping my work.

"I like to do it," I say.

Tyler ambles into the stall and puts his hands on my shoulders. Next to my ear, he says, "You're the weirdest girl I've ever met, Mallory Victoria."

I laugh as he takes the shovel from me. I let him have it and sit cross-legged on the wooden bench in the corner of the stall. I watch him work, watch the way Midnight lovingly nibbles his shoulder. His sturdiness and steadiness is reassuring.

"Do you remember the weekend we spent in this stall?" I ask him. I lean back against the wall and close my eyes, recalling it.

"Of course," he says, and even though my eyes are closed, I can hear his grin. We can laugh about it now, but at the time, it was anything but funny.

I'd had Midnight for a year when she suddenly started limping. At first I didn't think anything of it, assuming it would get better in a couple of days, the way sprained ankles and bruises always do. But on the third day, I noticed a startling knot of swelling on the frog of her foot.

Dad called the vet immediately but by the time he got there,

Midnight was splayed out in her stall, showing signs of fever and dehydration.

When Tyler showed up for work that morning, he held my sobbing body in his arms as the vet drained the infection, fed Midnight antibiotics, and kept her on an IV for a few hours to get her fluid levels within the healthy range. After that, though, there was nothing else to do but wait. The vet left with promises to come back the next day, but Midnight was far from healed.

I couldn't leave her. My dad tried to physically take me back to the house to sleep that night but I refused. So instead, he brought the bench down from the porch for me to sleep on, and Tyler promised to stay with me, a prospect that would make most fathers' hackles go up if it was anyone but Tyler.

The bench has been here ever since, my anchor whenever I need grounding.

I raise my head and open my eyes.

"You brought over your air mattress for me to sleep on and you curled up on this stiff old bench," I say, smacking the wood.

Tyler shrugs. "I'm old-fashioned like that. Where I come from, the lady sleeps on the floor."

"And as Midnight got better, we played cards here until our eyes crossed."

"Wasn't much else to do," he clarifies.

"That's one of my favorite memories of this place," I say wistfully.

Tyler stops working and looks at me for a long time, a pensive smile on his face.

"Mine, too," he says.

We share another wordless exchange, and then he returns to shoveling.

"You ought to consider coming back, you know? Permanently," he clarifies.

I'm surprised to hear this from him, of all people. Tyler has always been the one who didn't have opinions on what I should do with my life, or if he did, he kept them to himself.

"Really?" I ask.

He shrugs but I can see that he's serious. "It just seems to me that a girl who actually likes shoveling horse shit couldn't possibly be happy in a big city."

I throw my head back and laugh.

Tyler rests the shovel against the side of the stall and comes to sit next to me on the bench. I scoot over to make room for him. My folded knee rests on his jeans. I lay my head on his shoulder.

"It's not only that," he says.

"What is it?"

"Your parents miss you, Mal. A lot. They would never say it to you, because they want you to be happy and they think you're happy in New York. But I know they're lonely. Things can get kind of monotonous out here on the outskirts of a small town when you don't have family to give it meaning."

"But...all kids move out," I say.

"Sure. But it's one thing to move across town. It's a whole other thing to move across the country. And you've seen them a handful of times in ten years."

"Have you been back to visit your mom?" I ask.

"That's different and you know it."

I nod. I do feel bad about visiting so infrequently. And I want to look at my future and say it will be different, but who's to say I won't get so caught up in one client after another, that too soon another ten years will have passed?

"It wasn't on purpose," I say, though I know it's a lame excuse.

"I'm not trying to make you feel bad," he says, placing his hand on my knee. "Life happens. No one blames you. And I wouldn't have said anything at all if I thought you were going back to a life that was important to you. But if you're not happy there, and they're not happy without you around, I think it's worth considering."

It's funny, the way Tyler can get through to me in a way no one else can. Coming from Kelly or my parents, or even Sam, the suggestion would have felt loaded with expectations. But from Tyler, it's simply a kindness because it comes from a deeper understanding of what really makes me happy. He knows how much my family means to me. And his motives are completely unselfish—he won't even be here.

"Yeah," I say. "Maybe you're right."

He pats my knee stiffly. "I hope I didn't overstep," he says.

"Ever the Southern gentleman," I say with a smirk.

"I'm not even from the South."

"Just your cowboy charm, then."

"Don't you dare buy me that hat."

I burst into laughter.

SIXTEEN

THEN

Sam and I were alone in the barn, with the blueprints from the contractors laid out on the floor in front of us. I sat cross-legged in the dirt while Sam squatted, allowing the dust to coat only the toes of his shoes. His long sleeves were rolled up to the elbows and I could see the hint of sweat pressing through the back of his shirt. He rubbed his index finger across his bottom lip, thinking, like he had been for the last fifteen minutes, as if the high temperatures were getting to his brain.

"You're going to have to get used to the California heat at some point," I teased. But even I was under its spell today, my mind lethargic, my skin itching for a cool breeze that could only be achieved in June atop Midnight's saddle.

Sam shook his head, coming out of his daze. "What?" he asked.

I laughed at his relentless commitment to his work. In the

month of having him at the vineyard, I'd hardly seen him drop his professional focus. Even when he and Dad were drinking into all hours of the night, the conversation usually stuck close to career ambitions and philosophies about life, which for them, centered around their work.

"No one wears long sleeves here in the summer," I said. "They hardly wear them in the winter. You're going to melt."

Sam stood and stretched. I caught the movement of his muscles under his shirt for the briefest moment before I averted my gaze.

"You're wearing riding boots," he countered.

I looked down at them. They were a birthday gift from my dad the year before—a prized possession. I wore them every day and while the leather had held up, they still showed signs of wear. The deep brown color was lighter at the toe, and there was a crease across the front of my ankle from squatting to clean Midnight's hooves.

"What's wrong with riding boots?" I asked.

He shrugged. "Did you go riding today?"

"No. But I might." I probably wouldn't. It was hard to take Midnight out after dark unless the moon was full. That wasn't the point.

"They're an expression of who you are, right?"

After a moment's thought, I nodded. I'd never thought of it that way, but I'm sure anyone who knew me would agree.

"How I dress is a reflection of who I am," he said.

I stood and wiped the dust off the back of my jean shorts. I tilted my head playfully. "I think who you are needs to loosen up a bit."

I made to reach for the hem of his shirt, to untuck it. I was drunk on the heat, more relaxed with Sam than I usually was. He moved away, laughing.

"Maybe you need to get more serious," he tossed back at

me. "Haven't you ever thought of wearing something a little more fashionable?"

I halted in my cavorting. His words struck a nerve. New York was one of the fashion capitals of the world and I often worried I wouldn't fit in there, that I couldn't be myself there—a simple farm-town girl. Mostly I pushed those thoughts to the back of my mind. I didn't have a choice. I was going with Kelly. I'd get through it.

But did Sam find me too simple, as well as too young? Were even my shoes more proof of my lack of culture and experience?

"You okay?" Sam asked.

The barn door creaked open, breaking the moment. Kelly barged in, her mouth set in a hard line.

"There you are," she said. "I've been waiting at the coffee shop for you for an hour."

I gasped. "Shit. I am so sorry, Kel. I completely lost track of time." I was supposed to meet her when she finished her shift.

She glanced at Sam, sure of the reason I'd forgotten about our date. At the beginning of the summer, she was worried I'd let work get in the way of our plans and I promised her it wouldn't. Neither of us had accounted for Sam.

"We can go now," I said, meeting her in the doorway.

She looked like she might call the whole thing off.

"Fine," she eventually said, exasperated.

I followed her out, shooting an apologetic look at Sam.

As we walked back to the parking lot, Kelly was silent, and even the crunch of the gravel beneath our feet sounded angry. I wanted to apologize again, but the more I ruminated on the situation, the more I felt justified in my actions. I was working after all, and never once had I been upset with Kelly when she got stuck at the coffee shop.

"You could have called the house," I said. "You could have hung out with us."

I spent so much time at the coffee shop during Kelly's shifts I was practically a fixture there. I didn't see any reason why Kelly couldn't do the same.

"I don't want to hang out with Sam, Mallory," she said over her shoulder. "I want to hang out with you."

I huffed at her response, trying to keep my cool. I knew this wasn't about me, or about being late. It was about Sam, and I was growing fed up with her unwarranted spite toward him. He had never been anything less than polite to her. And besides that, she could have tried harder to be kind toward him, if only for my sake.

"Maybe if you got a chance to know him, you wouldn't hate him so much," I said.

Kelly stopped walking and turned to me. Her eyes were wide.

"Mallory, for heaven's sake, this isn't about Sam." She looked off into the distance, her jaw set. "I don't want to talk about it yet but I just need you right now, okay?"

I resisted the urge to roll my eyes. It was always something. Was she worried about her fall schedule again? Most of the time, I could deal with her neuroses, her constant need for control. But I was beginning to feel like I was giving more than my fair share in our friendship. I was moving across the country for her. What else could she want? This was my last summer here, too, and despite what she seemed to think, I had my own ideas about how I wanted to spend it.

"Just please don't forget next time," she said.

I shrugged, not wanting to fight. "Fine," I said.

She exhaled, and after she calmed down, she nodded for me to walk beside her.

"C'mon," she said. And I did.

★ ★ ★

As June crept into July, the dry heat seemed to increase in correlation with my feelings for Sam. We spent most of every day together and staying overnight became Sam's Friday night routine. And because Dad and Sam's friendship continued to grow, he often stayed Saturday nights, too. Some weekends Sam would take a horseback ride with me, while others he would accompany Dad on a supply run to Bakersfield. I went with them whenever I could, attesting to Kelly that it was part of my job, though technically I wasn't getting paid for it. Kelly saw right through my excuses, of course, but as the tasting room construction neared completion, and along with it Sam's time here, I found myself caring less and less about what Kelly thought of my feelings for Sam. My subconscious longing to soak up every minute with him commanded my thoughts, words, and actions. It wasn't logical, it was pure instinct.

In Bakersfield, between pickups for hay, horse food, new wooden posts, and netting, we would have lunch or stop by a thrift store where I would help Sam pick out more suitable clothes for painting and horseback riding—T-shirts designed by companies instead of people, and classic Levis that fit him like sin. I found a pair of cute lace-up work boots that Dad bought me as an early birthday present, which became my new wardrobe staple, my riding boots inadvertently shoved to the back of my closet.

And at night, after Dad and Sam had their requisite glasses of wine—Dad resuming his customary single glass, and Sam more than making up for it—I walked Sam to the guest house and we talked until the early hours of the morning, my chair pulled close to his side of the bed.

We talked about who we were in high school—him, the debate team captain and the head of the school newspaper; me, the girl who spent too much time staring out the window and getting good grades only because Kelly would kick my chair to bring me back to reality. We shared our favorite movies, having none in common but promising to try at least one or two of each other's top three. And I made him tell me, in painstaking detail, about his mountaineering plans—where he would go, for how long, and what he wanted to see. In all the vivid pictures he painted, I imagined myself there. Just a daydream, I told myself, but anytime he touched me, my imagination became clearer.

It was mostly small talk but I felt like I was finally getting to know the real Sam—the Sam he kept to himself, hidden behind Italian wool and chrome. It was in the little details that he came to life, and as I uncovered them, I saw how they played out in our everyday interactions—the subtle movie quotes, the way I would sometimes catch him humming his favorite songs at sunset when he thought no one was listening, the smile he tried to hide whenever Dad complimented his work.

I tried not to notice that we never talked about his family, his homelife, or whether he had anyone waiting for him when he returned.

In the mornings, we sat in companionable silence on the porch with our coffees, sweetened with cream and sugar the way he liked it. He was always pensive in the morning and I respected his space, content to revel in his physical presence.

With the first week of August came an irrepressible heat, a buzz around the upcoming harvest, and the urgency to inaugurate the tasting room. It had come together almost overnight once the construction began. Concrete, windows, rooms, walls, doors, electrical, lighting. We watched the space transform before our eyes.

There was also the growing tension of what might happen with Sam before I left for Columbia in a few weeks, but thankfully, with the distraction of the upcoming events, I didn't have time to worry about it.

The busyness around the vineyard meant that the Summer Bucket List was put on the back burner. Kelly and I hadn't officially discussed it, but I had to reschedule our dates so often that eventually she stopped asking and I pretended not to notice. It was easier than having to see the look on her face when I told her I couldn't get away from the tasting room. But because we couldn't spend as much time on our own, she got over her resentment of Sam enough to spend more time at the vineyard with us, and I enjoyed that even more.

One night, we all gathered in the tasting room—Dad, Sam, Kelly, and me—to put on the first coat of paint. Sam and I had chosen a color called Old Map that was somewhere between gray and cream and added to the rustic look we were going for. Nineties country blared on the CD player and we all donned our ragged clothes as we took our rollers to the freshly textured walls.

Kelly and I sang along to every word, dancing as we worked, and I kept glancing at Sam, who managed to look even cuter in the clothes we'd gotten him at the thrift store than he did in his suits. Dad and Sam worked with a wineglass in their free hand and whenever Sam caught me looking at him, he grinned. Mom joined us late in the evening after work, not painting, but stealing a glass of wine and laughing as she judged which of us had more paint on ourselves than the wall. It was one of those perfect nights I knew I would always remember, even as it was happening.

We finished the final coat just before nine. Dad let us off the hook for cleaning up until the next morning and left me in charge of getting Kelly home. She'd had to leave her car at the coffee shop when it wouldn't start and Dad picked her up, promising to look at it in the morning.

After Dad followed Mom inside for the night, Sam crossed his paint-covered arms across his chest and said, "I'm starving. Is there anywhere we can get some food at this hour?"

Kelly had to get back to her mom and her bed for her early shift the next morning so we all piled in next to each other in the cab of Dad's truck. Sam next to me so Kelly could get out first. I tried not to look at him as I drove but I was overwhelmingly aware of the contact of his leg against mine. When Kelly got out of the truck in front of her house, her warning glance was clear. I knew she didn't trust me alone with Sam, but I'd already put it out of my mind by the time we made it back to the main road.

"So where are you taking me, Mallory Victoria?" Sam asked. He'd slid closer to the door once Kelly got out of the truck. But not all the way over.

"You'll see," I said.

I took Sam to a local Mexican dive that was popular for a quick lunch during high school and, I felt certain, was the opposite of the five-star cuisine and stuffy maître d's he was used to. His reaction confirmed my suspicions.

We sat on the patio, eating with our hands from the squeaky Styrofoam containers, hot sauce dripping from our chins, but I didn't taste a single bite. All my senses were focused on watching him, intoxicated by the way he came alive in this foreign environment and the way he looked at me for introducing him to it. I wasn't out on this limb on my own. I was sure of it.

"Should I take you to your hotel?" I asked when we finished.

Though I wanted Sam to stay—I always wanted him to stay—another part of me was curious about the life he led the rest of the week. Was he messy? Was he organized? Did he make the bed himself or let someone else do it?

"No. I'm going to need my car in the morning."

"Okay," I said, flushing with satisfaction.

Sam and I rode back to the house with the windows down. Sam found a Journey song on the radio and sang it off-key, both of us laughing the whole time. I watched him, the way he smiled, the way the wind blew his curls around his eyes, and I knew my heart never had a chance. Not with Sam. And I didn't care. I was willing to accept whatever consequences came, but what I couldn't accept was letting him leave in a few weeks, never knowing if we could have had something, even if only for a moment.

When we got to the vineyard, Sam challenged me to a race to the guest house, both of us laughing and sliding on the gravel all the way there. I slammed against the door first, panting for breath. Sam, having lost, staggered up next to me. Once I got the door open, he chased me inside, grabbed me around the waist, and fell back onto the bed with me in his arms.

I stiffened in shock—he'd never been so forward about touching me, always giving me a respectful amount of space. I didn't want to move and scare him back into politeness. I wanted his hands on me and more.

I gauged his expression. I could barely make out his features in the light of the moon coming in through the windows— we'd run right past the lights—but I could see his smile hadn't wavered.

He kicked off his shoes. When I didn't immediately do the same, he pulled my foot onto his lap and unlaced my boot, tossing it onto the floor. He held my gaze as he unlaced the second. When he fell back onto the bed, he rolled onto his side, his head propped on his hand.

Deciding he wasn't going to pull away from me, I stayed close to him.

"I forgot what it felt like to… I don't know, relax," he said with a laugh. "God, that's embarrassing to admit. That must sound insane."

I shook my head. I didn't know if he could see it.

"It's not crazy. I think that's how it is for most people."

"That's not how I want it to be for me."

"Then why don't you do it more often?"

Sam ran his hand across the blanket between us, his fingers long and smooth. "I guess I forgot how. Or maybe I didn't realize I wasn't. Does that make any sense?" he asked, laughing. "This is why I have to go to Colorado. Get away from everything."

As much as he talked about the mountains, and his goals for "bagging" them, the trip didn't sound relaxing. It sounded like running away. But what from, I still wasn't sure.

"I wish I could go," I said, and the moment the words were out of my mouth, I felt their truth. Not just because I wanted more time with Sam, but because I wanted to taste that kind of freedom. Maybe for most eighteen-year-olds going away for college was enough. But not for me. I needed to be outside. I needed to feel the sun on my eyelids, nature so close we became one.

Maybe I wanted to run away, too.

But I couldn't do that to Kelly. I couldn't abandon her plans.

"You can," he said.

I couldn't find the words to answer him, because all my focus was on the feel of his breath dancing across my cheeks, his mouth so close to mine. I knew exactly how to loosen him up, but I didn't know if I was brave enough to do it.

I'd never been the one to kiss a guy, always letting them make the first move. And it was *Sam*. He could kiss anyone, and I was no one. But I was known for jumping into things before thinking it through and I couldn't think of a reason to change now.

I leaned infinitesimally closer. Sam's breath stopped, but he didn't move away. I moved closer again, my heart beating so hard my entire body vibrated in anticipation. He was still. Finally, I leaned close enough that our noses brushed, and I could feel the warmth of his body so near to mine. Our breaths mingled together, and our lips tickled each other so softly.

I waited.

And then, gently, Sam pushed his lips to mine, completing the kiss and setting my soul on fire. His hand slid over my hip and pulled me closer. I wanted to put my fingers in his hair, but I was so nervous I didn't move. Instead, I reveled in the sensations of him and of knowing I wasn't alone in my feelings. The most beautiful man I'd ever seen was kissing me.

When he finally pulled away, he pressed his forehead to mine and let out a soft chuckle.

"Mallory Victoria," he said on a breath, "you are trouble."

The corners of my mouth tugged upward. "It's not the first time I've heard that."

But underneath my bravado, a sadness pooled in my gut, knowing I wouldn't share this experience with Kelly. We'd shared everything with each other until now, but I wouldn't allow her to take this moment from me. It was too fragile, too precious. The realization that our friendship was changing already was confusing and painful enough.

Thankfully, Sam kissed me again.

SEVENTEEN

NOW

On Thursday, Tyler and I walk the horses back to the stables after our morning run. It amazes me that after ten years away, I can so quickly fall back into my old routines. Yet after a week and a half away from New York, I'm starting to have a hard time picturing my life there. Waking up to Tyler and Midnight just feels right.

As Tyler and I brush the horses and chat about our plans for the day, a soft voice echoes across the breezeway. Kelly's voice. I intended to visit her today and tell her about my plans to stay but I'm glad she beat me to it. Her behavior since Shannon passed has been worrisome.

"Oh," she says when she sees me. "I wasn't expecting..." She trails off.

Me to stay. I fill in the blank. I try not to take offense at that. After all, I do have work obligations. But she's more important. Most people underestimate the necessity of good friends in life, and for a brief period in time, I was one of those people. I fell for the idea that being desired was more important than being loved. I learned quickly how wrong I was.

Kelly glances toward Tyler and he clears his throat, looking away. Maybe it wasn't me her expectations were centered on after all.

"Do you guys need a minute?" I ask her, unsure of how else to break the tension. "Or do you want to go for a ride?"

"Let's go for a ride," she says, pretending that's the reason she came over in the first place. As any good friend would do, I go along with it.

Tyler saddles up Tiramisu while I resaddle Midnight and ignore the awkward silence between them.

Once we're on the horses, I lead the way out into the vineyard at a walk. Kelly trails behind me like she always has.

The sun hits its midpoint in the sky as we make it to the top of the hill. We hide under the cover of trees, greedy for cooler temperatures. We bring the horses to a stop a few feet from the edge—Kelly on the right, me on the left, like a married couple shares their bed. This ride used to be our morning ritual before each school day. We never ran out of things to talk about—gossip, boys, our parents. More times than I can count, we held each other while we cried, curled up together in the dirt on this very spot.

"You stayed," she says over the birdsong in the trees around us.

I look at her, wishing she didn't sound so surprised. We left things between us open-ended, no rules or plans. But no matter how she feels about me, I'll always consider her a sister. A sister would do nothing less. But instead of saying all this, I simply nod.

"How are you doing?" I ask her, even though I know it's the most pointless question I could ask. But I have to ask because what else is there to say? It's impossible to convey my sympathy with words.

"I feel…uprooted," she says, tucking a lock of hair behind her ear. Her braid is back. "Without something to anchor me. I built my whole life around taking care of her, and just like that, she's gone. Last night, I wandered around the house like a tiger in a zoo for hours."

I'm more familiar with the feeling than I'd like to admit. That's how I walk through life—unsettled is my permanent state of being. Always searching for more, never quite feeling like I've found it.

"I'm sorry," I say. "I wish I could be that tether for you."

With remarkable clarity, she says, "No, you don't, Mallory. That's too much responsibility for anyone to carry."

I swallow hard, her declaration profound. At least to me. I, too, have built my life around what other people need. Or what I think they need. I'm coming to discover I'm not as in tune with those needs as I once believed I was. I'm not able to fulfill them like I wish I could either. It turns out people can only truly take care of themselves.

"Sam is still here," she says, speaking, no doubt, of the one I hoped would be my tether. "We haven't talked about him."

"No, we haven't."

The childish part of me hoped if I didn't draw attention to Sam, Kelly might not notice him, like covering your own eyes to play hide-and-seek.

"How have you been doing?" she asks. "With him here?"

I purse my lips to control my gratitude. I didn't realize how much I needed her to ask until she did.

"I'm sorry I didn't ask sooner."

"I didn't want to scratch at old wounds."

"You loved him," she says, the three words I never told anyone. But she saw it.

"I was stupid," I say. "I was blinded. And let's face it, I was young. It was the first time I'd ever felt that way about a guy and I didn't know what to do with it."

Kelly sighs, her body deflating. "I should have tried harder to understand."

"I didn't exactly give you all the info."

Kelly smirks. "I didn't exactly make it easy for you to talk to me."

I want to refute that, to make her feel better, but it's the truth. The pressure Kelly put on herself and our friendship to withstand the stress of growing up amplified her tendency to try to control the things that scared her. So instead, I allow the silence to stretch out.

"Are we talking about men for a reason?" I finally hedge, thinking of the obvious strain between Tyler and her. "Is there something you want to tell me?"

She shakes her head. "There's nothing to talk about. Nothing important."

"You know you can talk to me, right? Whenever you're ready?"

"I do," she says, meeting my eyes. "And same to you."

This is new, this opening I've been waiting for. Did my decision to stay change things in her mind?

"I want to tell you everything now," I say. "About what happened that summer. If you'll let me. If you're up for it."

Kelly shrugs. "Maybe it doesn't matter anymore. Maybe it does. I don't know."

"I have to be honest with you," I say. "You told me to call you when I was the Mallory you used to know. I don't think I am. I don't think I have been since that summer, and I probably never will be again."

"Well, I'm certainly not the girl I used to be. I don't think any of us are. Isn't that the point of growing up?"

My feelings on the subject are mixed. I always thought the point of growing up was to become more myself, but over the years I feel like I've grown further away from the woman I thought I would be. People keep telling me it's called maturity, but it feels more like a straitjacket.

Kelly shifts on Tiramisu and reaches into her back pocket. She pulls out the sheet of lined pink paper, folded twice, and holds it out to me. I take it in my fingers, the familiar texture of it like the smell of Mom's cooking, the words of a favorite song.

"I've missed you every day, Mallory," she says, bringing tears to my eyes. When she looks at me, there are tears in her eyes, too. I reach for her hand and to my relief, she allows me to take it.

"I've missed you, too," I say, barely above a whisper.

"And I could use a distraction." She nods toward the paper.

"You want to do the bucket list?" I ask.

"If you want to. For as long as you're here." I smile, thinking of the possibilities. I may not be able to bring her mom back, and I may not be able to be Kelly's anchor. But, it seems, she's allowing me to be her friend. And that, I'm equipped to do. "What's first on the list?" I ask.

"I feel like we should update this bucket list," I say to Kelly that night as we sit behind the stables, out of view of the house, with a pack of cigarettes and a bottle of butterscotch schnapps on the dusty ground between us. Kelly pulls her lawn chair closer to mine, framing the evidence of our rebellion. At least, it would have been rebellious...when were teenagers.

"No," Kelly urges. "Reliving it like we would have back then is the whole point."

"Yes, but..." I pick up the pack of cigarettes—a brand I've never heard of. "I don't feel as adventurous as I did ten years ago. Not this kind of adventurous."

"That's because we're not young and stupid anymore. Well, not *that* young."

Still, getting a little drunk and stupid might be the shortest distance to distracting Kelly from her grief, and for getting her to open up about what's going on with Tyler. I'm not going to let it go that easily.

Kelly sits back in her chair and crosses her legs, her worn jeans bunching up at the crease where her thighs meet her hips. Her deep green T-shirt brings out the color of her eyes.

"But with all the added experience between us, butterscotch schnapps was the best we could come up with?" I ask. I peel open the cigarette packaging and slide one out with the tips of my fingers. I hold it like it's made of glass, not sure how much pressure will crush it.

"I don't know," Kelly says. She picks up the bottle and examines it in the sunlight. She also listened to my dad all the times he taught us how to properly drink, though I'm not sure this is what he had in mind. It glows like liquid amber, shooting color in every direction. "I just asked the guy behind the counter at the liquor store. He told me chicks apparently dig this."

"The funny part is," I say, "I think my dad would be less mad about me smoking a cigarette than about me drinking alcohol that's made from something other than grapes."

"You're probably right." Kelly leans forward and pulls a cigarette out of the pack, then places it between her lips. She holds the lighter up and flicks it a few times with her thumb until the flame finally holds.

"What are you two up to?" a male voice asks from behind me. Kelly and I both jump, the cigarettes falling to the ground. Kelly hides the lighter behind her back like we really are teenagers. Tyler stares down at us, his arms crossed, amusement pulling at the corner of his mouth.

I giggle. "Oh, you know, getting hammered."

Kelly plucks the cigarettes out of the dirt and brushes them off. "Want a drink?" she asks, though her focus is more on the cigarettes than him, not a real invitation.

"As much as I'd love to witness whatever trouble you two are going to get yourselves into, I have to get to work."

"You're better off. I assure you," I tell him. "I get all emotional when I drink… Start professing my love to everyone. Sometimes inanimate objects."

"I remember. Better you than the rednecks I serve every night."

"Call in sick," I say. Kelly hands me my cigarette and returns to trying to ignite the lighter.

"Big plans, Mal. Big plans. You okay?" he asks Kelly, leaving plenty of distance between them.

"Sure," Kelly says, slinging the lid of the lighter open and closed.

"I'm here for you," he says, but his body language says he's only offering to be polite. "I'll see you ladies tomorrow."

Kelly snorts and gives him a tight-lipped smile. I listen to his footsteps disappear through the stables.

"What was that about?" I ask when he's out of earshot.

Kelly sighs. "Smoke first?" she asks, leaning forward, lighter out.

I place my lips around the cigarette as she places the flame to the end. With my eyebrows furrowed reluctantly, I breathe in like I've seen in movies. The first puff of smoke fills my mouth like hot ash and I choke on it, pushing it out my nose and mouth.

"Eww," I say, my voice reedy as I hold my breath in an attempt to avoid inhaling any more of it.

"My turn."

"My reaction didn't deter you at all?"

She puts her cigarette in her mouth. I hold mine out to her

and she leans in to light hers. She closes her eyes against the burn of the smoke and coughs, too, though not as much. We sit back in our chairs, both of us taking short, intermittent drags and watching each other's reactions.

"So. Are *you* dating anyone?" she asks.

I make a face. "Straight to the hard stuff, huh?"

"Have we ever beat around the bush?" she asks.

I flick the ash off the end of my cigarette to disguise the fact that I'm not smoking it. Kelly takes another drag and it goes down smoother, with just a hiccup of a cough.

She's right, and I'm thankful for a positive reference to our past, rather than just the negative ones.

"Not at the moment," I say. "I've dated a couple of people. Nothing serious."

I breeze over the subject because it's embarrassing and because they were mostly attempts to be a "normal college student" and to forget Sam. The two short relationships failed on both accounts.

"Really?" she asks, incredulous. "You were supposed to come home with sweeping love stories so I could live vicariously through you."

She makes a joke of it, but it's obviously too soon for both of us because neither of us smile. I clear my throat and move on.

"What about you?" I ask. I try to imagine Kelly in a relationship and it's impossible. It's not that any man wouldn't be lucky to catch her attention, it's that Kelly has always been too shy to date. She used the reliable and understandable excuse of taking care of her mother.

"Kyle McGraw," she says. I balk.

"Wait, wasn't that Kyle's mom you were talking to at the Libations party?" There was something about the way they interacted that was more familiar than a barista-customer relationship. I should have realized.

"Yeah," she says, her cheeks darkening.

From what I remember from our junior year, Kyle was tall, handsome, and fascinating to our classmates with his stories of working on his grandparents' farm each summer. He would come back every year with bigger biceps and an air of maturity gained by reuniting with his long-distance girlfriend. Kelly had a crush on him back then but nothing ever came of it because of Kyle's unfailing loyalty. In that way, Kyle and Kelly were perfectly suited for each other.

"For two years," she says. Kelly inhales deeply from her cigarette and blows it out slowly, her lips pursed into a tight circle.

"Two years? And I knew nothing about it?"

She shrugs. Of course, the only person who would have told me would have been Mom and I had long since stopped asking about Kelly. It was too painful to realize that my parents were more in the know about her life than I was.

"How did it happen?" I ask.

"How else? He came into the coffee shop a lot and one day, he finally asked me out. No sweeping love story."

"That's all?" I ask. This jaded Kelly is hard to swallow. "You were crazy about him."

A hesitant grin creeps across her face. That's more like it.

"Okay, I was thrilled. I was crazy about him. For the entire time we dated he gave me butterflies. He had this sturdiness about him. Not just physically but mentally and emotionally. Like not even a tornado could pick him up. I felt safe with him. I knew he would never hurt me, and he didn't. He made me feel loved and taken care of."

"Loved?" I ask.

Kelly nods. "He wanted to marry me. Move away. Start a family in Wyoming."

"Married?"

She laughs again. "Is it really that hard to believe? Yeah,

I guess so." She answers her own question. "To be honest, when I look back on those years, it feels like they happened to someone else."

"Is that why you aren't together anymore? Because he wanted to leave?"

"His heart has always been in Wyoming, hasn't it? I couldn't blame him."

I bring the cigarette to my mouth but just the scent of it turns my stomach, so I fake it, not wanting to break the moment. I want Kelly to keep talking. I want her to tell me everything.

"And Tyler?" I ask. "What's going on there?"

Tyler was the other person Kelly had a crush on during our teen years, but we hardly ever talked about it. Truthfully, I avoided the subject, worried about how it would change our dynamic if they ever did date. I hoped my silence would discourage the notion, and it seemed to have worked. Besides, he was too old for her anyway.

Kelly doesn't answer right away and I'm surprised to find my palms sweaty, eager for her response.

"We dated," she finally says. "For a couple of months at the end of last year. Nothing came of it."

I nod, but inside, my thoughts are spinning. I shouldn't feel as bothered as I do that my friends dated. It wasn't exactly behind my back and they're both consenting adults now. I shouldn't feel as relieved as I do that things didn't work out, but I'm ashamed to admit that I am.

"Did you guys…?" My cheeks warm. Kelly and I never got to the point of talking about sex and I avoided the conversation with college friends and coworkers, uncomfortable with the vulnerability of it. But in this instance, I'm painfully curious.

Kelly purses her lips. "No." She flicks ash at the ground. I sense a bitterness about the topic. "Did you sleep with Sam? Before?"

"No," I say a little too emphatically. "No. It wasn't really like that."

It could have been like that. I would have given Sam anything. Everything.

"What was it like?" she asks.

"It was…exciting. And sexy. And unexpected."

"Unexpected?"

"C'mon. Neither one of us ever really believed I'd ever fall in love. And a guy like him? Liking me back?"

"Like him? Mal, please. No one is out of your league. But I've never really understood why you weren't interested in guys," she says.

"I guess I thought," I say, "that if I didn't have any attachments I could just live. Go where I wanted, do what I wanted. In a way, I was already doing that. I was too busy looking in front of me to notice anyone standing beside me."

Kelly nibbles at her lip the way she does when she's thinking. "You do know the problem with that theory, right?"

"What?" I ask.

"You can't live without relationships. They come with challenges, sure, but what does anything mean if there's no one there to experience it with you? When you die—" she swallows hard "—who will carry your memories for you?"

I don't know what to say to that. So much for distraction.

I take another puff of my cigarette and press my lips together to keep from coughing, but nature takes over and the smoke climbs back up my throat and bursts out of my mouth against my will. I clutch my chest as I hack the last of it out of my lungs.

"Okay, I'm done," I say.

Kelly bursts into laughter. "Aww, Mal. You're so pure," she teases.

I drop the cigarette on the ground and stamp it out with my boot. Kelly watches the whole thing with the hint of a grin. I lean back in my chair, trying to compose myself. She watches me and I watch her as a curtain of seriousness falls over her face.

"It's because of him, isn't it?" she asks. "The reason you haven't dated anyone. I saw the way you've been looking at each other since you got back."

I don't answer her because I don't have to. We both already know. I've tried to avoid him, tried to deny that my feelings for him have never fully gone away, but Sam is undeniable. Still, I think if I said it out loud, the black hole inside me that he left behind would open up and eat me alive.

"Tell me what happened, Mallory," she says.

EIGHTEEN

I sit at the dining room table on Friday morning, coffee and notebook in front of me, sweet early sunlight pouring in through the blinds behind me. It almost counteracts my dry mouth and the dull ache at the back of my head. I don't usually drink so much or so often. Alcohol has dulled the sharp edges of coming home, but makes them even sharper come morning.

As perfect as the setting is for creativity, it doesn't stop me from raking my hands through my hair as I try to come up with the right words to describe the floral company I have been tasked to write brochure copy for. I force myself to sit up straighter and try to imagine one of the bouquets from their website on the table in front of me. I search for the feel of their petals on my fingertips and their pungent scent in my nostrils, but instead I remember the feel of Sam's lips and the scent of his cologne.

It jars me from my vision and I try to erase him from my mind. When a sound comes from behind me, I jump, expecting to have conjured him. But it's Mom, dressed in her business casual attire, her hair still damp from the shower.

"Morning, love," she sings. She breezes over to the coffeepot and pours herself a cup. "Do you want breakfast?" she asks, bringing the mug to her lips.

I toss my pen to the table and sigh. "No, thanks."

"Tough morning?"

"Just trying to come up with something for work."

Mom comes around the island to look over my shoulder at the blank notebook.

"Off to a great start, I see," she says. "What are you working on?"

"The florist who hired the firm wants a brochure to send out to larger companies about their high-end bouquets and delivery service. For hotel lobbies and things like that."

"They didn't send you a sample to draw inspiration from?" She waves her hand toward the empty table.

"I'm kind of known around the office as the one with the overactive imagination."

She laughs. "Well, they have you pegged."

Mom drums her fingernails on her coffee mug.

"Hmm…if only we knew someone in marketing…"

"Not helping."

"Okay. You know what you need? A break. You've hardly left the property for almost two weeks. It's no wonder you've lost your inspiration. C'mon."

Mom sets her mug on the island and grabs her keys, heading for the back door. I jump up, surprised by the sudden shift.

"Wait. Where are we going?"

"Bakersfield."

"Don't you have to work?" I ask, stumbling out the back door behind her.

"Are you coming or not?"

Bakersfield is where Mom and I have always taken our mother-daughter shopping trips that I've treasured and missed since being gone.

"I'm coming," I say quickly and pull the door closed behind me.

On the two-hour drive, Mom calls in to work to take a personal day and I admire how easily she asks for what she wants. In many ways, Mom is the most conventional one in the family, but she's still not afraid to play hooky.

For the rest of the drive, she asks me questions about every detail of my life in New York, wanting to know about each one of my coworkers, where my favorite place is to eat lunch, who I hang out with and where their parents live. I normally hate what I used to think of as hovering from my parents, but after what Tyler told me about how lonely they are without me, I welcome the opportunity to include my mom in my everyday life.

Mom and I go straight to our favorite used clothing boutique. She's convinced the colors and textures of the fabric will inspire me.

"This has flowers on it," Mom says, holding up a polyester blouse with shoulder pads. I look up from the rack where I'm swiping through shirts, not really looking at any of them but enjoying the screech of the metal hangers. The repetitive rhythm makes me feel like I'm accomplishing something.

"You're not suggesting I wear that," I say. "That looks like something Grandma Patti would wear."

Mom laughs. She's teasing me. She did this when I was a teenager and highly embarrassable.

"And that's an unnatural shade of orange so it's not even good inspiration for the brochure."

"I'll put it in the cart," she says with a grin, but I watch her slip it back onto the rack. "You know, you don't seem too anxious to get back to work."

I pull out another top that looks like it fell right out of the '60s, trying to capture the lighthearted mood from the moment before, but it's gone.

"I think I'm just having a hard time connecting to it, being away from the office."

"I didn't mean the project," she says.

"Oh." My fingers slip from the sleeve of a shirt. "Well, I'm just trying to be here for Kelly."

"Mmm-hmm." Mom analyzes me, one eye on the clothes she's thumbing through, one on me. "But you enjoy your work, right?"

"I do," I say. "I enjoy being creative and it's a challenge to come up with new marketing angles that haven't been done a thousand times already."

"But?" she hedges.

"But?"

There's a hitch in my laugh as I rack my brain for ways to reroute the conversation. My mom is the last person I want to admit my unhappiness to, for many reasons. First, because she was the one who pushed me to go to Columbia even when it turned out Kelly would be staying. The last thing I want her to think is that I'm not grateful. Second, because she's so proud of what I've accomplished at the firm.

"Come here, Mallory Victoria," Mom says.

I hang up the shirt in my hand and hesitantly circle around the rack. Mom meets me halfway. She eyes the salesclerk before speaking, as if the teenage boy behind the counter would be interested in my existential crisis.

I suddenly feel much younger, like I'm about to be on the receiving end of a parental lecture.

"Is this your paralegal face?" I mock-whisper to her to try to defuse the tension. Her expression is somber.

"Tell me you're not staying in New York just to make your father and me happy," she says.

"I…" The rest of the thought gets caught in my throat.

A frown overtakes her features—a look so rare from her that it slices through the fibers of my heart. She tucks my loose bangs behind my ear. In a burdened whisper, she says, "I don't know why you would ever think your dad and I wouldn't be proud of you no matter what you did. Or where you did it."

I sigh. "You guys have been so excited about all the things I've accomplished since I've been there—"

"We've been excited because we thought you were excited. We thought maybe you'd finally found something that made you happy."

"I was happy here," I say, hurt by her words. Did I give her the impression I wasn't?

"Maybe *happy* isn't the right word," she says. She nibbles at her lip as she thinks it over. "Mallory, there's more to happiness… no, fulfillment…than being content to move from one task to the next without any direction. Yes, that may be enjoyable in the moment, and there's a lot to be said for that, but one day you'll look back at your life, and I think you're going to want it to add up to something. Maybe it's hard to understand how important that is now, but when you get to be my age, you're going to want to believe your life has meant something. That it *means* something."

Once again, my mom surprises me. It's a speech I might expect from my dad, but Mom has dreams for her career, too? All this time, I thought she only did it for the money, but I can see how much fulfillment—to use her word—she could get from seeing broken families pieced back together in new ways. I know from listening to her talk to Dad over the years that her opinion is highly regarded at her firm, and that is fulfilling in its own way, I'm sure.

"Maybe I'm just not wired like that," I suggest. I have no doubt that what my mom is saying is true, but I've never been able to understand how people stick to anything long enough for it to add up to something bigger. I've never been able to do it myself.

"Honey, everyone is wired like that. It's human nature. It's sort of like falling in love. If you've never experienced it, it's hard to know what it feels like. But once you do..." She gets a faraway look in her eye.

"Can you please not think about Dad like that in my presence?"

Mom laughs and I try to turn back to our futile search for inspiration, but she catches my wrist.

"Mallory, that's all I want for you. I know that's what your dad wants for you, too." She says it so simply, so matter-of-fact, that I wonder how I could have so greatly misunderstood their intentions.

"I do, too," I say.

"Good," she says. "Now, are you sure you don't like those shoulder pads?"

When Mom and I get home that afternoon, Dad cuts out of work early to take Mom out on a date. I teased Mom at the thrift store about how in love they are, but I actually find it admirable for thirty years of marriage. I don't often think about marriage, but if and when it happens for me, I hope I share that kind of unending adoration with the man I end up with. I guess Dad was right—I am idealistic.

That evening, Sam wanders into the kitchen to find dinner while I'm already foraging, hopelessly clueless without Mom's home cooking.

"It's quiet in here," he notes.

I peek out from behind the fridge door. Sam's eyes are red and his hair is mussed in the way it tends to be after he's been engrossed in work all day. When he gets in the zone, the house could burn down around him and he wouldn't notice.

"My parents went out on a *date*." I whisper the last word, like it's illicit. Sam laughs.

"They're very lucky," he says, and I know he doesn't just mean today.

"Yeah, yeah. What have you been working on so intently today?"

"Those guys I was talking to at the bar the other night, Chuck and Aaron... They're interested in doing some business restructuring. I told them I'd put together proposals."

I lean against the counter. "Would you really stick around longer?" I ask.

"Maybe," he says. "A lot of it I could do remotely. Besides, what else am I going to do all day? Like you said, I don't know how to relax."

"You said that," I remind him. He nods, conceding. "Is this the excuse you're giving my parents for extending your stay?"

It still hard to believe I'm the real reason, and that he's been completely straightforward about it. This time I'm the one who's unsure.

"Your parents love me," he says. "I don't need an excuse."

I roll my eyes. "And don't you know it."

He winks.

"Have you eaten at all today?"

His shrug is long and unapologetic. *You know how I get.*

"Well, I can't cook so you're stuck with..." I glance over at the contents of the fridge. "Leftover spaghetti or a sandwich."

"Didn't I see..."

Sam reaches around me and comes out with the cheese and salami Dad keeps on hand for wine tastings.

"We're not supposed to eat that," I say.

"I'll buy more tomorrow," he counters.

"Is there a single rule you don't feel you're above?"

I'm not entirely sure if I'm flirting with him or still taking out the frustrations of my eighteen-year-old self. Either way, he seems to be enjoying it.

"I will not build a campfire if there is a no-campfire sign. That is where I draw the line."

"When have you ever camped?"

We stare each other down and I try to keep my stony composure, but a giggle escapes me and yet again, he's won.

"Come eat with me," he says, nodding toward the back porch.

I consider it. Are we friends now? Have I forgiven him? Do I trust myself to make good choices when he's around?

"I'm bringing wine," I decide.

I peruse Dad's house stash to find the white that pairs perfectly with peppered salami and meet Sam at the porch table. He unwraps our dinner while I pour two glasses.

"I haven't seen Kelly today," he says as he slivers the first slices of cheese off the block with a paring knife. "I'm not keeping you, am I?"

"That's considerate of you to ask, but no. She's been working."

"Good." He smiles.

For the next couple of hours, Sam and I sit on the back porch, eating and chatting. Now that he's opened the door to his family life, his upbringing, his extended family, and his childhood adventures around the globe, conversation comes easily. I ask him probing questions about Europe, Asia, and South America. He answers with hysterical stories about bathroom blunders, foreign foods, and simple requests lost in translation that got his family kicked out of some places and almost arrested in others.

After my first glass of wine, I'm laughing so hard that my cheeks ache. I notice that Sam's glass has gone untouched.

"Are you in some kind of program?" I ask, realizing my potential faux pas.

Sam is taken aback. "No. I'm just trying to be respectful."

It's a sweet but unnecessary gesture. "I'm a grown woman, Sam. I can handle it."

I scoot his glass toward him.

He hesitates, then raises it to me. We finish the bottle by the time the sun goes down.

"You know what I missed the most from my first visit?" Sam asks as I twist my empty glass between my fingers. The food is gone, as is the wine, and we no longer have any reason to stay here, but neither one of us seems to be in a rush to leave.

"What's that?" I ask. There are so many things to miss from the vineyard that I've begun to crave them preemptively.

"I missed talking to you in the guest house."

His answer is unexpected. I've missed it, too, and at his admission, I feel a pang in my stomach to return to one of those moments. There are times like that throughout life, I've noticed, where you don't know it will be the last time until it's over. And by then, it's too late to ever go back.

But here we are, and it pains me to admit how badly I want it.

"Will you walk me?" he asks.

I remember my rule. About not being alone in the guest house with Sam again. And then, like all the other times, I ignore that voice in my gut telling me to protect myself.

"Sure."

Our movements are stilted. Do we clean up from dinner

first? How close do we walk to each other? Is he leading or am I? In the end, we leave the dishes—I'll be back in a few minutes—and walk side by side, a few inches apart but not touching, though every cell in my body is reaching out to him. By the way he keeps glancing over at me, I can tell he's battling his own emotions.

He opens the door for me when we arrive and I enter the domain that he has made his own over the last couple of weeks. His paperwork is scattered over the dining room table. His suits hang from the window curtain rod for lack of a closet. The bed is tidy but made in a way that is not my typical fold, throwing the organization of the room slightly off.

"You've sure made yourself at home," I note.

The coffeepot is out on the counter and well used.

"You said the carafe was broken."

There's a mischievous smile behind his nonchalance.

"Want some?" he asks.

I shake my head. He really will go to any length to get what he wants. It makes me more cautious, being alone with him.

"No, thanks."

I wander around the room, pretending to look things over but really keeping space between us.

"Want to sit?" he asks.

I glance to the table, where papers are piled on its surface and on the chairs.

"Here."

He motions toward the bed and then pointedly pulls over the wicker chair I used to sit in. He places it next to the bed for himself. Against my better judgment, I sit on the comforter, my hands in my lap. Sam settles into the chair, unbuttoning his sleeves and rolling them up.

"So how much longer are you going to stay?" I ask.

"I don't have a plan. What about you?" he asks. "Must be hard to leave Kelly right now."

"I'm supposed to be in the office next week."

"Supposed to be?" he asks.

I've never been accused of wearing my heart on my sleeve but it seems everyone can see my unhappiness. I'm not as good at keeping my feelings to myself as I thought. Between my conversation with my mom, my looming return date, and now this, the pressure to have all the answers is starting to feel constricting. I stand up and pace the room. Sam leans back in his chair.

"It's funny you should ask. My mom said something to me today. I know she was trying to help, but I feel like it made everything more complicated."

"What did she say?" he asks.

"That they—she and my dad—don't have any expectations of me or what I do with my life."

His one-note laugh is skeptical if not resentful. "Wow, that is complicated."

"I know it sounds like a blessing, and it is. Except I've some-how built my entire life around those expectations without realizing it and now that they're not there, I feel more lost than ever."

His only response is the purse of his lips, and it finally hits me who I'm talking to. I'm sure Sam would have given any-thing to have parents who supported him in following his own goals, and here I am lamenting it.

"Shit. I'm sorry."

"No, don't apologize," he says, waving it off. "Parental ex-pectations are a heavy thing, even if they're implicit. Look at me. I'm still stuck in Seattle, a short drive from my parents. Still, essentially, working for my dad."

"But the expectations on you are real. The expectations I've felt buried under are all my own. I just didn't realize it."

"Why do you think that is?" he asks. When I don't stop pacing, he reaches out and takes my hand, gently pulling me toward him until I'm standing between his knees. I consciously slow my breath.

"I just wanted them to see me a certain way, you know? I wanted everyone to see me a certain way."

"What way is that?"

I search for the right word. Who is it I see in my mind's eye when I picture the best version of myself? Or, at least, the most acceptable version?

"Capable? Dependable? Worthy," I say, my voice hitching on the last word. I shake my head at myself. "And here I've been so judgmental about Kelly's choices. Did you know her mom told her to put her in a nursing home and move to LA? All this time she's been convincing herself that she's been stuck here when the door was open the whole time. And now I realize I may be doing it on the other side of the country, but I'm still drawing a cage around myself in chalk."

"Mallory," he admonishes. "You are all of those things."

"Maybe," I say. "But I'm the one who has to believe it."

I collapse back onto the bed and cover my face with my hands.

Sam laughs. A full, head-back chuckle.

"You're laughing at me?" I whine, but in truth, I'm glad to lighten the air. The pressure has become too much. While I've learned that my parents don't have the expectations I thought they did, they aren't the only people I have commitments to anymore. There's Kelly and her grief, my boss, my landlord. If I sign the contract Denise sent me, I'll be committed to New York for two more years.

Sam leans forward, resting his elbows on his knees. "If you erased the lines," he asks, "what would you do?"

"I don't know," I mumble into my palms. "What is wrong with me?"

"Hey, at least you're questioning it. Most people go through life never once asking themselves if the life they're leading is the one they want."

I try to imagine what my life will look like if I continue down this road and I can't. But when I look for off-ramps, my mental image is just as blurry. I didn't know it at the time, but when everything fell apart with Kelly and Sam, I stopped listening to that voice inside me that used to lead me from one happy moment to the next without thought of the consequences. The voice of my heart. And because I stopped listening, it stopped speaking.

"Okay," Sam says. "I'm going to tell you something and I don't know how you're going to take it, but I think you need to hear it."

"Okay…"

I sit up and Sam scoots closer until our knees are touching. His intensity shakes me.

"Mallory," he says, "you aren't like any person I've ever met before. You're brave, and exciting, and you have the purest heart. I didn't know it when I left, but I know it now."

I look away, embarrassed by his compliments. "Yeah, well, that's the problem."

"No," he says. He places his finger to my chin, turning my face back to his. "That's the solution. Do you remember that wild, funny, happy…woman?"

He clears his throat. That summer, he never missed the chance to remind me of how much younger I was. He made me feel like anything but a woman.

I nod. I do remember her. But she seems so far away—my past as blurry as my future.

"She's the one you ask," he says.

I awaken the next morning to the sputter of a coffeepot as it begins to brew. My eyelids fly open and my gaze darts around the room. Soft light dances across the white comforter that I have pulled up to my chin. Sam emerges from the bathroom, his wet hair dripping on his bare shoulders, soaking through his white undershirt. He wears his slacks but no shoes, and somehow it's the sight of his bare feet that makes this moment too personal.

"Morning," he says.

"Morning," I whisper.

"How did you sleep?" He pours a cup of coffee in the kitchenette.

"I…don't know… Where did you sleep?"

After opening and closing the fridge door, Sam comes back to the bedroom and places the mug in my hand, his fingertips gripping it around the lip. "On the floor," he says.

"Oh, God. I'm sorry."

"It was better than the chair."

"Did I…pass out?" I ask, horrified.

Sam laughs. "I wouldn't exactly call it that."

I thought back to the night before. I was lying down after Sam shared his little piece of advice, and I wasn't that drunk. I was, however, overwhelmed by our conversation and haven't been sleeping well since Shannon died.

"I wasn't drunk," I assure him.

"It would take more than three-quarters of a bottle to put a vintner's daughter under the table."

"Half," I correct him.

"Eh," he says, his smile teasing.

I groan and take the first sip of my coffee. It warms me down to my toes. "What time is it?" I ask.

Sam sits in the chair and pulls his socks on. "Eight."

"Shit. I'm supposed to be meeting Kelly." I climb out from under the covers, ungracefully holding my coffee aloft.

Sam catches me by the elbows and steadies me, putting us face-to-face once I'm on my feet. The squareness of his jaw makes me want to put my teeth there.

"Um...thanks," I say.

"See you later?"

I nod and escape before I further embarrass myself, taking my coffee with me.

An hour later, I stumble into the local thrift store fifteen minutes late and apologetic. Kelly is already on the hunt and doesn't seem to notice my tardiness but the guilt eats at me anyway. I promised myself I wouldn't be distracted by Sam.

"I'm so sorry," I say, breathless as I approach. "I, uh, drank a little too much last night and had a hard time getting out of bed."

It's the truth, I tell myself. I've learned my lesson about lying to Kelly. But I don't think Kelly would feel the need to hear all the sordid details. Grown woman should have *some* dignity.

"Can I pull this off?" she asks me, holding a black Pink Floyd T-shirt to her chest, rainbow emblazoned across her left breast.

"Um..." I'm not sure if she's serious so I remain noncommittal. This is the unspoken vow of shopping with girlfriends—wait for them to take the lead.

"That's a no," she says and sticks it back on the rack. "Please tell me you haven't resorted to drinking alone on a Friday night."

I busy myself with shifting through the other T-shirts, contemplating how much to say.

"No. Actually, I was with Sam."

"I want to try this on," she says in return, pulling a dress off the rack.

"Oh. Okay."

Kelly holds up the dress to Joan, the grumpy, middle-aged woman who owns the store, and nods toward the dressing room. Joan, wearing her permanent frown, waves her in.

Kelly closes herself into the tiny stall and I crumple onto the stool across from the door to talk to Kelly through the slats in the door.

"You're mad," I conclude.

There's a long pause in which I watch Kelly's feet step out of her jeans, and then the hanger disappears from where it was hooked to the top of the door.

"I'm not mad," she says.

"It's fine if you are. I know I'm older now. I should know better with him."

"I'm just surprised, that's all."

"Yeah," I say. "You and me both."

For some reason, Tyler pops into my head and I wonder if he would be as gracious. There are so many logical reasons to go back to New York and pretend I never ran into Sam again—that I never met him at all—but last night proved that logic escapes me when it comes to Sam.

"After what he did to you, I don't know you could trust him again."

I sigh and bury my face in my hands. "I don't," I mumble.

"Am I missing something?"

The door swings open and Kelly stands in the doorway.

"Oh."

I straighten in surprise, taking in the lines of her long legs, revealed in plentitude beneath the hemline of the little black dress she's wearing. It hugs her like a second skin. I don't know if this is how she dresses now but I've never seen her wear anything so sexy. For as long as I've known her, she's been a jeans and T-shirts girl, like me.

"Wow," is all I can manage to say. "It's…different."

"That's exactly what I was going for," she says, though her stance is awkward, like she doesn't know where to put her hands.

She doesn't explain, just shuts herself into the dressing room.

It takes me a moment to recover. When I remember where our conversation left off, I stand and pace in front of her door.

"I feel like I'm right back where I was before with him," I say. "I feel like I'm having amnesia or something, forgetting how much he hurt me. I feel like I'm going to make all the same stupid decisions I did before."

The door opens, Kelly in her jeans and bra. "That's a lot of feelings," she says. I stop in front of her, exasperated with myself for allowing myself to get this worked up over Sam again.

"Why aren't you mad at me for even thinking these things?"

Kelly pulls her shirt over her head and frowns. She leans against the door frame.

"I understand the way people can keep a hold on your heart. Believe me. But that's not the point. The point is, what are your expectations this time around? Of him? Of whatever might happen between the two of you?"

"None," I say. "I'm going back to New York. Nothing can happen."

"Would you want something to happen if it could?"

"Are you really asking me that?"

"Why not?"

"Because what's the point in even going down that line of thought?"

Kelly drapes her dress over her arm and pulls me to the stools to sit. I keep waiting for her anger to flare up. The last time Sam was here, she could hardly stand to be in the same room with him. But now, she's eerily calm, which is more nerve-racking.

"Because there's clearly something between you still," she says. "It was always there. Of course he was interested in you. If he hadn't been, do you think I would have been so upset? He wouldn't have dragged you along like he did and it would have fizzled out before the grapes turned yellow."

She takes a deep breath, as if fortifying herself for what she will say next. She takes my hand in hers.

"But you, Mallory, are magnetic. Ever since you first came here, you've drawn people to you. Everyone, really. Including me. You don't even realize how easily life happens for you, because it's so natural."

I can't quite meet her gaze. I'm not entirely sure if I should feel grateful for the compliment or ashamed of my good fortune. To me, life doesn't feel easy. There have been many people along the way who have been resentful of traits and skills I don't realize I have. And in comparison to the struggles Kelly has had to overcome, I have lived a charmed life. What right do I have to want more?

"You and Sam have that in common," she adds. When I frown, she laughs. "In a good way. I can see why you're drawn to each other."

I never would have put myself in the same class as Sam but there must be something that has brought him back to me. There must be a reason we're attracted to each other.

"If you're trying to figure out what you really want, how can you do that if you write off possibilities before you've given them a chance?"

"Sam isn't a real possibility."

Kelly raises her eyebrows. "He is if you want him to be. If we can learn anything from my mom's death, it's that. The truth is, my mom could have walked out of that house any-time she wanted to. She wasn't stuck there. She chose to live most of her life within those four walls. And I didn't realize it, but I've been making that same choice. Because that's all I've ever known. But once you step out that door, Mal..." Kelly shakes her head. "The possibilities are endless."

I look down at our hands and I'm shaking. There was some-thing about Sam being off-limits, merely by being so far out of my league, that made wanting him safer. Deep down, I knew he would never feel about me the way I felt about him. But the idea of actually having him? I've never been more terri-fied in my life. I pull my hand away and clench it between my thighs to make it stop.

"I can't believe you of all people are encouraging this," I say.

"A true friend would never hold you back," she says sadly. "Would never make you feel bad for being who you are, or the journey you have to go on to explore your boundaries."

"Are you shrinking me?" I ask. She laughs. It suits her.

Kelly shrugs and holds her dress up. "I'm saying you shouldn't be afraid of possibilities."

NINETEEN

*T*he day following our first kiss was the first time I began to realize that all those silent mornings after might not be entirely motivated by Sam's hangovers. It was Saturday and my parents had left for Bakersfield. I waited for Sam on the back porch, reliving the night before and the tingle of his mouth on mine. I watched the guest house door, waiting for him to stumble out sleepy and rumpled. Our coffees grew cold.

When an hour had passed with no sign of him, I took our mugs back into the kitchen, dumped them in the sink, and refilled them before I ventured out to the guest house. I knocked softly and let myself in, but the bed was empty. The bathroom door was open and I didn't have to peek inside to know he was gone. The energy in the room was still.

I walked out to the parking lot, and Sam's car was still there. Confused, I kept walking. There was only one other place he could be.

A truck was parked in front of the tasting room. I recognized it as belonging to part of the construction crew. I stood there for a long moment, debating whether or not to go inside. We wouldn't have the privacy I hoped for so I could assess whether or not it was going to be another week of exile in the office, but I had coffee in my hands and I wanted to see him. I wanted to know the night before hadn't been a dream.

Balancing both mugs in one hand, I pulled open the new door—made from reclaimed wood that had been neglected inside the barn for decades now, wrought iron hardware, and hand-forged iron that curled its way through the tempered glass, letting light in to brighten up the room. It swung easily.

When I entered the room, Sam and the foreman, Gene, both looked over their shoulders. Sam was put together as usual, all signs of the night before erased.

Gene was used to me popping in and out of their conversations so he gave me nothing more than a small wave before resuming his monologue about chandelier lighting and wiring diagrams.

I smiled at Sam and held out his coffee. He took it, giving me a terse almost smile, before engrossing himself in conversation again, swiftly closing me off like I wasn't even there.

I stood stunned for a moment. It wasn't as if I'd expected Sam to take me into a romantic embrace and kiss me like in a black-and-white movie, but I thought we'd reached a new level in our friendship. Relationship. Whatever it was. I thought, with his kiss, he'd finally admitted to me that we had something more than a casual working relationship and playful banter. I thought it had meant something.

Overwhelmed by my confusion—wanting to be strong, but wanting Sam more—I was frozen, my feet fixed to the new ceramic tiles, pretending to listen to Gene's every word and hoping Sam would give me a sign—a single look, a touch, his body swaying ever so slightly in my direction. But he gave no indication he was even aware of my presence in the room. I felt like a fool.

Gene left half an hour later and Sam and I stood in silence for a long time, each of us waiting for the other to speak. Finally, he said, "Listen, I'm sorry if I did or said anything stupid last night. I don't always remember everything that happens when I drink. It's kind of embarrassing."

A soft chuckle escaped his lips but there was nothing funny about it. The bottom of my stomach dropped out and my heart plummeted into it.

"Oh," was all I had the courage to say.

He bowed a little goodbye and left me swimming in my humiliation and heartache.

Over the next week, we returned to polite work conversation when we were together, but mostly, we were not together. It took me twice as long to do anything he asked of me because I spent so much time analyzing everything, wondering if I'd somehow misinterpreted that night. I didn't have much experience with men, but I assumed kissing was pretty straightforward. More than anything, though, I feared losing our late-night conversations, his laugh, the tingling behind my belly button whenever he was near me.

Kelly pushed to do the next item on our bucket list but I was too distracted to commit to anything so we perused the local thrift stores instead, Kelly insisting that we would need new clothes for college. She loaded me down with jeans and simple print T-shirts I would normally pull on and strut around the store for her approval, but under the harsh dressing room light, everything looked so worn, so plain. Not fitting for the woman who would hold Sam's attention.

"Nothing?" Kelly asked when I emerged from the dressing

room and piled everything back into her arms. I gave an in-different shrug.

I hardly noticed that Kelly hadn't tried on anything.

Later, when Kelly was working, I borrowed my dad's keys and drove back to the thrift store alone. I scanned through the items again, looking for slacks that would collect every granule of dust on the vineyard and knit tops that would catch on the splintered wood but that made me look like a woman, not a girl.

The following Friday, I eagerly anticipated Dad's usual in-vitation for Sam to stay for dinner and wine. Unlike the last time Sam pulled away from me, his cold front didn't pass that week. He was as distant as ever as we stood around the new serving bar in the tasting room, discussing its progress.

"Do you still have reservations at Grey Mountain for to-night?" Dad asked Sam.

My ears perked up. Sam had plans?

"Yep," Sam said. "Meet you there at six?"

"Actually, Elizabeth is getting off work early today and she wanted to have a date night."

Sam held up his hands. "Enough said. We can do it next week."

"Actually, I think it's a great idea to check them out. Get a feel for how they present wine. They've got impressive rat-ings, so they're doing something right. Besides, even if I went, I probably wouldn't recognize what those things were," Dad said with a laugh.

"Sure, sure," Sam said. "I can check it out on my own."

"Why don't you take Mallory?" Dad suggested. I whipped around to face them. "Or did you have plans, Mal? She's got great taste. Gets that from her mother."

I looked to Sam to gauge his interest in having me. As much as I wanted to spend time with him again, to get past this awkward patch, I didn't want him to feel forced, like Dad was saddling him with his little sister at prom. He looked at me—really looked at me—for the first time all week. It wasn't exactly an invitation, but it was enough.

"I'm not busy," I said.

"Perfect," Dad said. "We'll catch up tomorrow and you can let me know what you guys think." With that, Dad swept out of the room, leaving muddy footprints behind him.

"We're going to have to ban him from his own tasting room," I said, grabbing the broom. Sam laughed, a salve to my soul.

"Pick you up at five forty-five?" he asked. I nodded, devil-may-care. As soon as his car disappeared into a cloud of dust, I dropped the broom and ran to the house.

Grey Mountain Vineyards was one of the most recognized names in Paso Robles wine. Their tasting room was top tier, which was why none of us had ever been there in all the time we'd circled around each other at wine shows and Best of Paso Robles lists. While Dad prided himself on his small-town, homegrown approach to wine, Grey Mountain was *glamorous*. There was no other word for it. They offered dinner and an evening tour through their vines, which were meticulously strung with lights for twenty-five acres. They were booked for weeks in advance.

I learned all this from the article that had been written about them in *Food & Wine*.

When I heard the sound of Sam's tires crunching on the gravel, I gave myself one last look in the mirror, took a deep breath, and forced myself to glide down the stairs, rather than bound.

Sam met me at the steps of the back porch. He looked as breathtaking as ever. He'd put on a jacket for the occasion but left the top two buttons of his shirt undone, revealing the smooth, tanned skin over his collarbone.

"You look…very nice," he said. He seemed to choke on the words. I'd worn a lace cap-sleeved summer dress I'd been saving for a special occasion that fell just above the knees and was soft white. I'd knotted my hair up into a messy bun and wore the only heels I owned.

Sam's eyes told a different story than his mouth. He wanted to say more and I wanted to reassure him that my parents had already left, that we were alone, but he cast his gaze downward and held out his arm. I almost didn't take it, to prove the point that I was no one's burden, but to touch him… I slipped my fingers over the crook in his elbow and tottered in my heels over the uneven ground to his car.

Sam drove us through the windy dirt back roads that led out of our vineyard and into Grey Mountain Vineyards at the north end of town.

As we parked in the parking lot, a nervous sweat stung my underarms like needles. I looked at the others emerging from their cars. The people who would be sharing our dinner table were dressed in suits and designer evening wear. Looking down at the outfit I'd so meticulously coordinated and had been so proud of, I'd never felt more like the child Sam thought I was.

Embarrassment welled up in my throat and I contemplated asking him to take me home but then he was opening the door for me and offering me his hand. I forced myself to take a deep breath and slipped my hand into his.

Dinner passed by in a haze of panic. All twenty guests for the evening were seated at a large farm table in the middle of the tasting-room-slash-barrel-room, Sam directly across from me. I sat on the hard wooden chair in constant worry that I would say the wrong thing, use the wrong fork, or

JAMIE RAINTREE

drop a single morsel of food on my white dress and have to strategically hide it for the rest of the night. Worse, when the sommelier began to pour the wine, I had to admit to being underage, shame warming my cheeks so fiercely I thought they might catch fire.

Sam's stilted moves proved he was just as uncomfortable, probably wondering how other people would feel about him bringing someone who wasn't even old enough to drink to a wine tasting. I was grateful when he struck up a conversation about business with the man sitting next to him so I didn't have to try to join the conversation. Instead, I sat quietly, watching him and how stiff his spine was, how overly polite his conversation. His laugh didn't have that ring I was used to and it made me sad that he would ever dull it for anyone.

After dinner, I was grateful to disappear into the darkness of the vines. Sam offered his arm again and once we'd fallen away from the crowd, straggling at the back of the line, his shoulders relaxed.

"So?" he asked me. "What did you think?"

He was a couple of glasses of wine in and, apparently, talking to me again. The correlation didn't go unnoticed.

"It was…" I decided to be honest. "Snobby."

To my surprise and the surprise of the woman a dozen feet in front of us, Sam laughed, loud and unbridled. The laugh I knew and loved. "Your dad was right to send you," he said.

"Didn't you find it uncomfortable?" I asked in a whisper, aware of people close by. "You seemed uncomfortable."

Sam drilled me with his eyes, maybe shocked I'd seen through his act. After another moment of walking, he softened. "My dad would have loved it," he mumbled.

I didn't know what to say. He always avoided elaborating on his relationship with his dad.

It took us another forty-five minutes to walk the rest of the vineyard and when we were done, Sam bought a bottle of red and a bottle of white to take to Dad. When he parked back at home, Sam turned off the car and we sat there. My feet ached but I refused to reveal my lack of experience in heels by taking off my shoes.

"Are you going to stay?" I asked.

"I don't think I should," he said.

I nodded, expecting his answer. I wasn't brave enough to ask him why. "Will you let me show you something before you go?"

We looked at each other across the small space, both of us questioning, doubting, worrying...and wanting.

"Sure."

We got out of the car and Sam followed close behind me. His presence prickled the hairs on the back of my neck. At the porch, I said, "Wait here." Sam narrowed his eyes but nodded. I walked into the house, but was so worried he would leave that as soon as I closed the door behind me, I mercifully slipped off my heels and ran upstairs to change.

He was still waiting when I returned in cotton shorts and a plain white T-shirt. He looked me over.

"What are you up to?" he asked. I blushed but didn't answer.

Midnight snorted when I entered the breezeway.

"Hey, girl," I called.

I unlatched the door to her stall and saddled her quickly in the breezeway, lit by the moonlight. "C'mon," I said.

Sam sighed but, gripping my thigh for support, pulled himself up and slipped into the saddle behind me.

I led Midnight out behind the stalls, onto the trail Sam hadn't yet traveled. This trail was mine, one I kept for myself when I wanted to be alone. Tyler was the only person I regularly shared it with. Sam was hushed behind me, waiting to see what I had in store.

Once Midnight was sufficiently warmed up, I said, "Hold on tight," and with a wicked grin he couldn't see, I gave Midnight a nudge with my heel, a little click of my tongue, and she took off. Sam's hands slipped around my waist.

We rode into the night with nothing but the *bah-da-bum-bah-da-bum* of Midnight's hooves on the dirt and the wind in our hair to accompany us. I didn't have to tell Midnight where to go. She led us through the desert landscape of the back acres, through dry bushes, over the hills, kicking up a trail of dust behind us. Sam held me tighter and tighter and maybe I should have pulled Midnight back a bit, but I couldn't. I was addicted to the feeling of lightness, like if Midnight just kept running, my feet would never have to touch the ground.

She was forced to stop when she reached the pond, skidding to a sideways stop and prancing to show her excitement.

"You okay?" I asked over my shoulder. My voice echoed in the fresh silence.

"Yeah," he said. He sat back, releasing me.

I slid off Midnight's back and landed with a thud on the sand that surrounded the pond. The water glittered in the moonlight, equally magical and eerie. But it was not knowing what was beneath the surface that made it exciting.

Sam not-so-gracefully slid off next to me, gripping Midnight in a bear hug until his feet touched the ground. Midnight sauntered down the shoreline, drinking from the water, and I kicked off my boots to stick my bare toes into the water. Warm. I stepped in farther, the water reaching my knees, and looked back at Sam. He watched me from dry land.

"You're going to have to take those shoes off," I said with a laugh.

He was unusually quiet, not used to not being in control. But he obligingly took off his shoes and rolled up his pant legs, then he waded into the water until he reached me. The water lapped at the bunched-up cloth and I laughed.

"What exactly do you have in mind?" he asked. He was out of his comfort zone, and he liked it.

I slid my hands under the lapels of his jacket and shook it off him, tossing it back to the sand. I waited for him to wince away from me, but he didn't. I held out my hand and he slipped his into it, and together, we moved in farther until the hem of my shorts was soaked and stuck to my thighs.

"What?" he urged, like a dare. So I did it—I yanked hard on his hand and we plunged into the water, which was so close to the temperature of the night air, I almost didn't feel it.

We both came up laughing and gasping for air. He shook his curls out, sprinkling the pond and me with droplets of moisture.

"I can't believe you just did that," he said with a laugh.

"What are you going to do about it?" I splashed him.

He lunged for my wrist and pulled me to him. His hands guided my legs around his waist until we were closer than I'd ever been with a man in my whole life. With his face a mere inch from mine and the strength of his body holding me up, I felt like my chest would crack open.

And then he looked into my eyes like he couldn't believe me either, couldn't believe this moment. He kissed me, holding nothing back. We stayed out there, kissing, wrapped up in each other, like we were the only two people in the world.

We rode Midnight back to the house, both of us soaking wet aside from his jacket, which he wrapped over my shoulders. My parents still weren't home after we put Midnight back in her stall so we sneaked into the guest house, where Sam stripped down to his boxer briefs and undershirt, and we toweled ourselves off as best we could. I wanted dry clothes more than almost anything, but not more than this moment with him, which I feared would be broken by any hint of reality.

So we both curled up in bed, damp and happy. I felt gratified. I'd broken past Sam's barriers, proven to him and myself that our first kiss wasn't an anomaly, wasn't a mistake, wasn't just driven by alcohol. I'd proven I wouldn't be ignored or brushed aside. And no matter what Sam said, his actions told me he wanted me, too. I only hoped it wasn't just for the summer.

He wrapped my body around his again, and we kissed more, his hands exploring the shape of my body, until we both fell asleep.

TWENTY

NOW

I sit at the dining room table that afternoon with my mom's laptop, feeling no more inspired than the day before. After annoying myself by arrhythmically tapping my pen on the table for several minutes, I open a new internet browser tab to search for boarding stables in upstate New York. Just out of curiosity. How long would it take to get there? How much would it cost? Do taxis drive out that far? Would my new salary cover it? I follow one link after another into the abyss.

"Horse yoga?" Sam reads over my shoulder sometime later.

I start and slam the laptop shut. When I look sheepishly up at him, he gives me a half grin, entertained by me as usual. It reminds me so much of the way he used to look at me that I forget about the possibilities of the future and focus on the possibilities of now. After all, it was Sam's suggestion to find the old Mallory. Since he was the last person to see her, with him is the most logical place to look.

"Do you want to go horseback riding?" I ask him.

"Sure," he says.

"Really?"

Sam laughs. "Yeah."

While Sam changes into jeans, I saddle up Tiramisu for him, Tyler being the only one who can handle Rocket's devilishness. Sam appears in actual boots, making me laugh.

"Did you buy those just for your visit?" I ask him. I picture him in the store, uncomfortable but determined. It's adorable. The boots are excessively shiny, but so is everything else he owns.

He slips his hands into his front pockets. "I came prepared for anything."

I smile, softening. "Good."

I throw my leg over Midnight and cluck my tongue at her. I take it easy as we set out on the trail. A benevolent breeze cools our skin and billowing clouds cross over the sun occasionally, casting uneven shadows over the vines. It's the kind of day I could disappear into like camouflage.

"So," I say, "you don't have anyone missing you back at home, do you?" If we're going to entertain the idea of spending time together, I have to know I'm not being led on again. I'd like to trust the Sam I've seen since returning but I thought I could believe what I felt for him the last time.

Sam has settled into the saddle, more comfortable than before.

"You mean a girlfriend?" he asks. "You think I'd kiss you if I had a girlfriend?" He sighs. "Don't answer that. No, I don't. I've dated a few people. One serious. Nothing that was likely to work out."

So neither one of us has had much luck in the dating department. I'd like to think that means something—that I've had as much of an effect on Sam as he's had on me—but likely it just means that, as Kelly said, we're more similar than I thought.

"They weren't likely to work out," I say, "and you dated them anyway? That doesn't sound like you."

"What do you mean?" he asks.

"In work, all your choices are so purposeful."

Sam purses his lips, contemplating like he hadn't thought of it that way before.

"I suppose you're right. I've never been very solid in my personal life. You know. You try things out. You hope they'll work. Most of the time they don't."

"But you thought it would work out with your fiancée?"

It's time the two of us had everything out on the table.

When Sam doesn't answer right away, I look back at him. His gaze is out across the hills, over the trees, hundreds of miles from here.

"Too soon?" I ask.

"No," he says. He meets my eyes. "It's been a long time since I've thought about her actually. She's the daughter of one of my father's friends. He's a doctor, too. They lived in Olympia, which is a couple of hours away, but they'd visit for events or if they were in town for business. Our families took a cruise to Alaska together once."

It's hard to imagine Sam's life in Washington. The water. The green landscape. The passports and yachts and five-star dinners.

"So you grew up together?"

"Yes and no," he says. "We saw each other so infrequently that I hardly remember her before we were sixteen."

It's no mystery what caught his attention at that point.

I pull Midnight back so Sam and I are riding next to each other. Midnight nudges Tiramisu and they prod at each other like toddlers, playing in the sun. Sam and I laugh, and I tug Midnight's face away.

"Did you date as teenagers?" I ask him.

"No," he says. "There was a kiss. On that cruise. But otherwise, the two-hour drive just didn't make sense. And I was too caught up in my own life with school, my parents fighting, and my own friends to think of her that way."

"When did it change?" I ask.

He exhales, the weight of remembering heavy. "She came to my college graduation party. It was just me and a few friends. My dad refused to attend the ceremony so my mom didn't either. She walked on eggshells with him after they got back together. But she must have told Hannah because she Hannah showed up."

Hannah. I latch onto her name, as if it's significant. As if it tells me everything about their relationship, everything I need to know about what Sam wants in a woman.

"It really meant something to me that she was there," he goes on. "My family didn't support my career in business the way I wished they would. I don't blame my mom but I couldn't be caught up in their games anymore. With Hannah there… Well, she was like family. But that night, something changed between us."

We ride in silence for a few minutes as I process this. He still speaks about her with a reverence, the way I find myself talking about him. Maybe no one entirely gets over their first love.

"What happened?" I ask.

"We were together for two years," he says. "We moved in together, supported each other in starting our careers. And even though my dad didn't approve of my work, we formed a sort of truce over his approval of my relationship with her. After two years, getting engaged felt like the right step. But the minute I put that ring on her finger, I wanted to call my dad and that's when I realized how far down the wrong path I'd gotten. I didn't want to call him because I was excited to share the happy news, but because I wanted his approval. It hit me then that it wasn't Hannah I was in a relationship with. Not really."

I nod. "That must have been really hard for you," I say.

Sam considers it, passing the reins between his hands. Another cloud consumes the sun, dropping the temperature. A chill runs down my spine.

"I thought he would cut me out of his life when I broke it off with her, which I shouldn't have let sway my decisions. But I did. I thought I had broken free from him when I chose business school over med school," he says. "But at the first hint of praise from him, I fell right back into old patterns."

"No one could blame you."

"Hannah does. She hates me. Thankfully it didn't ruin the friendship between our parents. She's married to someone else now. Just had her second kid."

"Wow," I say. I know a lot of people are married with kids before thirty but I don't personally know anyone who is. We're all still too focused on our careers. But that could have just as easily been Sam. He could be a father by now. I could have never met him. "Do you ever regret your decision?"

"I used to," he says. "There was a lot to love about her. She was kind and great with my family. She never questioned me. Always let me follow whatever whim I got into my head and went along with it."

"But?" I ask. I hang on to that *but*.

"That's not what I wanted for the rest of my life. I don't think it was what I needed. It was too easy."

I laugh. Only Sam would say something like that.

"Isn't easy good?" I ask. "Isn't that what people strive for?"

Sam chuckles softly, seemingly at himself. "I guess I've always liked a challenge."

Is that what I am to him? A challenge to overcome? Someone his father wouldn't approve of, who he could have all to himself?

I urge Midnight a little farther ahead, hoping he won't see the places I'm still rubbed raw.

"What about you?" he asks. "Anything serious?"

"Don't change the subject," I say. "How old are you now?"

I hear the smile in his voice when he says, "We're pulling the age card out again, are we?"

"You started it."

Sam pulls Tiramisu's lead to draw her closer to me until our knees are rubbing side by side.

"Thirty-four," he says. "Not exactly an old man."

"Isn't it about time to start thinking about settling down, though? Wouldn't it be better to find something easy?"

In essence, not me. Not someone who still has so many untapped desires bubbling under the surface, so many things still to figure out.

"Which answer would you rather hear?" he asks me, his voice low.

"My opinion is irrelevant," I say, my gaze on Midnight's saddle, but the words are laced with wanting. I've always wanted my words to matter to Sam.

"Don't ever write off your opinion, Mallory," he says.

I don't know if he means specifically about his love life or in general, but either way, my stomach flutters. That's the thing with Sam. He's always been able to either make me feel like the most important person in the world, or like I don't exist. But never in between.

"The truth, Sam," I say. "I've only ever wanted the truth. No matter how painful it might be to hear."

Sam nods solemnly. "We're both a little too old to play games, aren't we?"

"Right," I breathe. As much as I've castigated him for not

being open with me, I can't deny how much I've struggled to be straightforward with him. I never said out loud how much I cared about him. I never asked in words how he felt about me. I was too afraid of what his response would be to either confession.

He holds his hand out to me and I stare at it, knowing exactly what he's asking of me. I look to his eyes, which are relaxed, easy; where we go from here is entirely up to me.

I take a shaky breath and then I take his hand. Maybe we don't need words after all.

On Sunday morning, I wake up to Kelly in my bed. Some locals threw a back-road bonfire last night and Kelly had invited me to go with her, but it was mostly people we went to school with, who are the one thing I don't miss about leaving Paso. Besides, I really needed to get some work done on the brochure.

Kelly came over last night to get ready. She wore the dress she'd gotten from the thrift store and somehow it looked even shorter than before. I didn't mention my concern over her change in behavior or her seeming lack of emotional processing of her mother's death. She could be doing it on her own, in the many hours she spends alone in their house. But the dress she wore implied she wasn't, along with her real motive for attending the party—Kyle was in town and she was lonely.

Kelly is sprawled out next to me in her little black dress, her heels dropped off the side of the bed like they came off sometime during the night. She drools on my pillow and the bedroom window is open, a dry breeze wafting through the room. I can't imagine the reason for that and decide I don't want to know.

I nudge Kelly until she stirs. "Morning, sunshine."

She groans a response.

"Plans didn't work out as you hoped?" I ask, stifling my laughter.

She groans again.

After I drag Kelly out of my bed, offering her a towel to wash her face and a spare toothbrush to clean up, I decide we should check off the next item on our bucket list. Kelly, hungover and smelling like smoke, disagrees but once she raids my closet for activewear, she meets me on the porch. Sweat has beaded at the back of my neck and underneath my sports bra while I waited, as well as between my skin and the backpack I have tightly strapped on.

I hand Kelly a water bottle and a hat.

"What's this?" she asks.

"You're going to need to stay hydrated. And the hat is to keep the sun off your face."

Kelly pulls the hat on over her braid and, after a few failed attempts to find a comfortable place for the water bottle, clips it to her waistband.

"I don't know if I like the sound of this. Or the look of that backpack. Just how long are we going to be gone?"

"Hey, you already agreed to it. It's on the list."

"Then I agreed to it ten years ago."

"Just like I agreed to smoking," I say. "You said the list is sacred, and damn it, we're going to treat it that way." It's surprisingly fun to have the tables turned, me being the responsible one.

"You are way too perky this morning," she complains, squinting through her headache.

I start in the direction of the stables.

Kelly reluctantly follows me to my favorite trail, which is less private since Tyler started running trail rides through the property again. If we had more time I would have researched a better trail nearby for a hike, but for today, this is adventure enough. I've rarely placed my feet directly on it and it's stunning, to see it from this angle, eight feet lower. It feels new all over again.

Kelly is less enchanted.

"I never would have chosen this voluntarily," she says, already panting.

"And yet, you wrote it on there. The thing is entirely in your handwriting."

Between breaths, she says, "You can be very persuasive."

I laugh. "Nothing better for a hangover than to sweat it out," I say. "Besides, we've been hiking for all of five minutes. I hiked for an entire week once and it was the best week of my life."

"There's something wrong with you," she says, but I find her snark humorous.

"It can't be that surprising to you," I say. "You know about that time I tried to run away, right?"

It was shortly after we moved to the vineyard but before I met Kelly. I was angry at my dad for uprooting our lives, as any seven-year-old would be, and I decided that if Dad was unwilling to return to Chicago, I would go myself. I packed my rolling suitcase, walked out the back door, and planned to hoof it across the five states between here and there. I never made it off the grounds, as many acres as the vineyard covers. I got lost among the vines, but that didn't stop me from walking until my legs finally gave out. My parents assumed I kept walking to try to find my way back to the house, but Kelly knows the truth—I walked to see what else I might discover. The fact that I had nothing to eat, nowhere to sleep, and that my parents might be worried sick never crossed my mind.

"I remember," she says. "Your parents have retold the story a thousand times."

We both laugh because to my parents, that story is the epitome of what it was like to raise their roaming daughter—

the result of having parents who always made me feel loved and safe, I suppose. That night when Dad found me, instead of being angry at me, he fished my blanket out of my suitcase, spread it out on the ground, and we lay on it together, staring up at the stars in the twilight sky. He didn't once ask me if I wanted to go back, only getting up once I was tired enough that I suggested it myself.

"I guess I never got over my tendency to drift," I admit.

"You made it through college," she says encouragingly. "I have to admit, there were times I had my doubts."

I might be offended by the comment if it were coming from anyone but Kelly, but she is my mirror. There's no hiding from her honesty, and while it can be uncomfortable at times—frustrating, even—that's what I count on her for. That's why I need her in my life.

I sigh. "There were times I had my doubts, too. That's why I had to...take some breaks here and there."

"Hiking," she says.

"Hiking. The North Country Trail. It goes south from the New York–Pennsylvania border and wraps around the Great Lakes. I made it sixty-six miles. I only had a week off work and I wasn't used to carrying the heavy pack."

"Only," Kelly deadpans. She doesn't know about the plans Sam and I discussed and I'm too embarrassed to admit them, that I fell for his smooth talk. There are some things we don't even tell our closest friends. Some shame we carry alone.

"I could have walked on to the end," I say. "I could have never come back."

Kelly and I hike the rest of the way to the pond, evading piles of horse manure, and to my satisfaction, as we set our stuff down on the sandy shore, Kelly looks flushed but gratified.

I open the backpack and pull out the blanket I shoved into

the bottom, spreading it out for us to sit on. I also pull out the sparkling waters, mixed berries, and protein bars I got from the store last night.

"Look at this," Kelly says, impressed.

We sit next to each other and sip from our waters as we watch the sun glinting across the water.

"So why this bucket list goal?" Kelly asks me. "Why today?"

I open the container of berries and offer her one. She takes a raspberry.

"I thought you might want to get away," I say. "It seemed like you wanted to escape last night."

"You have no idea."

"Do I have anything to worry about?" I ask. The scent of nicotine still covers her skin, something I never would have thought Kelly capable of. Everyone responds differently to death but this behavior deviates so drastically from the careful choices Kelly has always made. I would hate to see her get into trouble.

"I want to be different," she says, staring out at the water. "I can't be the same."

I nod. I know exactly what she means.

"I know it's soon," I say, "but have you thought about what you want to do?"

Kelly takes one of the protein bars and opens it as she ponders the question.

"You know, for as much time as I spent during our teen years planning the future, I don't think I ever really let myself believe the day would come."

I take a slow breath. I have to remind myself I've forgiven Kelly for lying to me.

"And the day I seriously thought about it..." The day she asked me if she could go with me, I realize.

"Kelly, you can't feel guilty about that," I say, moving closer to her. Tears form in her eyes and her bottom lip puffs out like a child's.

"I was going to leave her when she needed me the most," she says.

"You couldn't have known that. You couldn't have known what would happen."

She wipes roughly at her eyes. I rub her back in a sad attempt to soothe her.

"She wanted you to go," I add.

"Go where?" she asks bitterly. "Those plans were fantasies. And even now, when I try to picture a future without my mom in it, without that piece of shit house we live in, outside this small town, it's like it doesn't compute. Like I'm too afraid to hope for anything because I know I can't have it."

"But you can," I'm quick to say. "Maybe you don't have to go far. Your mom said you have family in LA. There are a lot of career opportunities in LA."

Maybe I could go to LA, too. I could find a job there, and I'd be close enough to home to visit more often. I'd be trading one city for another but for Kelly, it might be worth it.

"I don't know," Kelly says. "Maybe. I have no idea how much it would cost to make the move." After a pause: "Shit. Without Mom's disability checks coming in, I might not even be able to afford to stay. I hadn't even thought of that."

Kelly buries her face in her hands. I wrap my arm around her shoulders.

"Don't worry about that right now," I say. "Whatever you decide to do, we'll figure it out."

She rubs her hands down her face and takes a deep breath, then picks through the berries, her expression stiff.

"I finally have the freedom I've always wanted," she muses. "So why do I feel so guilty?"

★ ★ ★

Tyler pulls into the parking lot just as Kelly is leaving. I give a final wave to Kelly as Tyler hops out of his truck, swinging his keys around his index finger. He wears a day's worth of strawberry stubble and the way he meanders in my direction in his fitted jeans and white T-shirt, he looks more cowboy than ever. I attempt to make a joke, but the words don't reach my lips.

"What are you up to?" he asks.

"Showering, probably," I say, motioning to my sweaty hiking clothes. "Unless you want to take a ride."

"I have some time," he says.

But when I turn toward the stables, Tyler grabs my hand and pulls me in the direction of his truck instead.

"Hey! What are you doing?"

"I have a better idea," is his only response. He hops in and I get in on the passenger side.

"Where are you taking me, cowboy?" I ask.

"You'll see."

He fires up the engine and bolts down the dirt road, bouncing us all over the dusty cab, a grin from ear to ear. I grip the handle above the door, shaking my head at his antics but laughing nonetheless.

On the main road, the ride levels out and Tyler turns south, away from the heart of the town, leaving me even more puzzled. But I trust Tyler so I relax and let him take me wherever he wants to go.

"Oh," he says. "I have something for you."

Tyler leans across me to open the glove box. He reaches inside and pulls out a plastic toy horse. He's sheepish when he hands it to me.

"I came across this and thought you might like it."

I laugh. It's such a random gift when Tyler and I have never been ones to exchange gifts in the first place. It reminds me of the toy horses I used to play with in my dad's office. And as I look it over, I realize the markings are almost exactly the same as Midnight's. Tyler acts nonchalant, trying to pass it off as an aloof gesture, but I can tell he put some thought into it.

"This is really thoughtful," I say.

"I thought you could put it on your desk or something."

I squeeze his arm. "Thank you."

Tyler clears his throat. "You're welcome." He reaches over again and closes the glove box.

After a short drive out of town, Tyler makes a left turn down a long driveway with an overhead sign that reads West Wind Farms. The property expands for acres in every direction, but instead of grapevines, it's mostly grass, the occasional tree, and, as the name implies, the breeze that brings it all to life. Ahead there are several log-cabin-looking buildings—a house and a couple of others that must be barns or some kind of storage.

"What's this?" I ask him.

"You'll see," he says.

Three dogs surround us as we approach the buildings. I hold my breath as Tyler navigates them, but they move around the car intuitively, used to farm life. Tyler pulls into a lot and shuts off the engine.

"My friend owns the place," Tyler says. "His name is Mick. Do you know him?"

I shake my head. I used to think I knew everyone in this town, but Kelly and Tyler have proven that the only way to truly know everyone is to make them drinks.

"He comes into the bar from time to time and we became friends. He lets me hang out here pretty much whenever I want. Which is often," he says with a laugh.

"The anticipation is killing me."

We get out of the truck and the dogs attack us with their

noses. They trail along behind us as we approach what I can now see are the stables. There are a couple of horses saddled up and tied out front. One woman, adorned in riding gear, sits atop one of them while someone stands next to her, grips the reins and talks to her about something that looks very serious. Another couple leans against the barn chatting, and when they spot us, the man smiles and uses his whole arm to wave at Tyler.

"C'mon," Tyler says, taking my hand and pulling me toward them.

The man has young features but the lines of his face prove him to be in his early to midforties. His blond hair is cleanly cut and his face is smooth. His body is unusually athletic for someone who runs a horse ranch.

The woman, a silky brunette, is of similar age and put together, her clothes impeccably clean.

"Mallory, this is Mick," Tyler says, introducing us. Mick's rough hand grabs mine tightly. He introduces his wife, Diane.

"What's going on, man?" Mick asks Tyler as he crosses his arms over his chest and leans back on his heels. "Want me to have Wesley saddle up a horse for you?"

"No, thanks. Just wanted to show Mal around, if that's okay with you."

"No problem."

Tyler thanks him and leads me inside.

"So what are we doing here?" I ask Tyler, awed as I take in my surroundings.

These aren't just stables—they are horse mansions, with the cleanest, most ornate stalls I've ever seen. The barn is almost twice as tall as ours and nothing but the finest woods have been used, which have been sanded and polished to the point of artwork. They stretch on for more than three times the length of our barn.

"What is this place?" I ask.

"It's a boarding facility and riding school," Tyler says.

He approaches one of the stalls and a large, healthy bay pokes her head out and stretches her nose to Tyler. Her hair is shiny in the way that only horses fed the highest quality food and supplements can be. She must be a show horse.

"This is Athena," Tyler says. "I don't want you to get jealous or anything, but she has a crush on me."

I narrow my eyes at him and reach out to the mare. She lips my hand, searching for treats, and despite coming up empty, must decide I'm okay, because she allows me to run my hand along her nose.

"Hi, Athena," I coo. "Are you leading our poor Tyler on?"

"Hey," Tyler says, making me laugh. "Do you want to see the rest?"

"Of course," I say.

Tyler takes me to the food room and we collect a bucket of carrots. He introduces me to the rest of the horses, telling me a little about each of them as if they are his closest friends and instead of this being eccentric, I find it endearing. Midnight loves me with the kind of unconditionality that makes her my best friend so I understand his connection to them.

Afterward, he takes me into the tack room, which looks more like a showroom, everything clean and gleaming, like it's never been used. He lets me peek into the office, which is just as pristine. It could be the set of a movie.

Finally, we end up at the riding ring, where the woman we saw on the horse when we came is cantering the beautiful gray mare. The man stands in the center of the ring, calling out directions to her. Tyler and I cross our arms over the top bar and watch them for a while. The way the horse's mane blows in the wind and the graceful way her hooves stab into the dirt over and over again—I could watch them all day.

"So what's the deal?" I finally ask him.

"I just wanted to share this with you," he says. He turns toward me, resting his foot on the bottom bar, his elbow on the top. "I know it's a far-fetched dream and I know I have a lot of work to do, but this is what I envision for my uncle's farm. I hope one day it will be mine."

"Wow," I say, a little taken aback. Tyler has always seemed like a simple man to me. The kind of guy who finds beauty in an everyday kind of existence, which is part of his charm. "You've never told me you had all these big plans."

"Well—" he shrugs "—ten years ago I didn't know what I wanted. Hell, last year I didn't know what I wanted. But I think I'm finally hitting that age where I've figured out enough of what I don't want that I can narrow down what I do want. And I've decided I want this."

The excitement in his blue eyes brightens his whole face. It's infectious.

"I think it's perfect for you," I say. "I can't imagine a better fit, actually."

He seems to really take in my approval, his chest expanding ever so slightly. "Thank you."

"So is that what it takes?" I ask. "Age? Life experience? Failing a few times before you finally figure out what you want?"

"Pretty much. I also think that sometimes someone on the outside, who knows you really well but isn't swayed by emotions or other people's opinions, might be able to offer some guidance."

"Someone like you?" I ask.

"Sometimes I think I know you better than you know yourself." There's a gleam in his eye.

"Oh, really? Go on, then. What do I want?"

Tyler nods toward the people in the ring, not specifying which role he imagines for me.

"This?" I ask.

I look around, but I have a hard time allowing myself to think of what it could be like to spend all day every day with horses. Speaking with people who are as enthusiastic about them as I am and as excited to learn. The slower pace, the outdoors. I don't dare to see it as a real possibility because if it's not a real possibility, I don't want to get my hopes up.

"I know you have your job in New York, but before you go, I wanted to show you another option. And I wanted to tell you that once I get established, you'll always have a place wherever I am."

I open my mouth, but no words come out. It's the kindest thing anyone has ever offered me, and, I think maybe Tyler is right—maybe he does know me better than I know myself. But what I want and what makes sense aren't always the same thing. No matter what my mom says, I still have commitments in New York. I can't just walk away from it all. That's not the kind of person I am. It's not the kind of person I want to be. I know that much.

"Thank you," I say.

"You're welcome," he says. He puts an arm around my shoulders and I fold into him, finding comfort in his warmth and familiarity. We stand there for a long time, watching the woman and her horse, and dreaming.

TWENTY-ONE

On Monday morning, the aroma of freshly brewed coffee wakes me, strong and immediate. I sit up in bed, looking for its source. On the nightstand, a mug goads me, coaxing me into the day and to the one who made it. I take a sip—still hot—and trace its path back down the stairs, where Sam is waiting for me in jeans, a smile on his face.

"Let's go for a ride," he says, the magic words.

"Okay."

We both ride Midnight this time—me commanding the reins, Sam's arms wrapped around me. I don't hold back, riling Midnight up like an excited puppy as we gallop down the path to the pond. The sun pours gold over the land and over us, filling me with contentment. This time, I'm in control. This time, Sam has to trust me. And he seems to.

When we reach the pond, I hop off Midnight to help Sam down. The moment his feet touch the ground, he wraps his hand around the small of my back and pulls me into a kiss.

I melt into him.

I melt into the moment.

When he pulls away, I ask, "What was that for?"

"You're still in there," he says, searching my eyes for the woman we're, apparently, both looking for.

"Why are things different this time?" I ask him. A cool breeze floats off the pond, sweeping between us and around us, like it could sweep us away.

"I'm done caring what people think," he says. "My dad. Your dad. My standing in the business world."

"I'm not your fix, Sam," I say, no matter how badly I may want to be. I can't fill the holes in his life any more than he can fill the holes in mine. "I have to go back to New York."

"What if," he says, "for today, we don't have any goals?"

"I think," I say, running my hands over his back and marveling at how free I feel to do so, "nothing has ever sounded better."

And so for the rest of the day, we forget about everything else. We forget about everyone else. He takes me to the hole-in-the-wall Mexican restaurant I introduced him to the last time he was here, where I showed him that food didn't need to be Michelin rated to be delicious.

I take him around town. My version of town. We start with my high school—the only high school in town, Home of the Bearcats stamped in big maroon letters across the front. The fence keeps us out front, only because I don't want to risk Sam tearing his expensive jeans. Not that it's ever kept me, or any of the rest of the student body—past or present—out on the weekends. I settle for telling him stories about the trouble I used to get Kelly into by cheating off her tests, convincing her to ditch last period, and taunting our classmates at track practice after school.

We visit a family friend's olive farm, which from a distance could be mistaken for a vineyard. Sam and I stroll through the trees, our fingers intertwined, admiring the flowers and their woody and dusty scent.

Then we sneak onto another winery's property and race their remote-controlled sailboats across the koi pond between tours. We laugh as we run out after being spotted. The owners are friends of my dad's but I don't tell Sam that.

By the time we return to the vineyard in the late afternoon, I'm so intoxicated with a sense of abandon, with this town I love, and with Sam that it seems nothing could bring me back to reality. But as we pull into the parking lot, a red BMW is parked next to Dad's truck, ostentatiously screaming for our attention.

"Who could that be?" I ask, more to myself than Sam.

Sam laughs.

"So he did decide to come."

"You know the owner of this car?" I ask.

"Come on. I'll introduce you."

We find Sam's friend in the kitchen being grilled by Dad. I recognize him as Sam's friend immediately because he has the same polished look, same *GQ* style, same brand of watch glinting from his wrist. He's taller, though, and lankier, his hair lighter, his eyes blue. And while most women might consider him attractive, he's missing that indescribable magnetic quality that Sam emits.

The men light up when they spot each other and shake hands, pulling each other into a one-armed hug. They exchange *how are you*s and the usual niceties. I don't miss the newcomer's comment on Sam's attire, but Sam laughs it off.

"You've already met Rich," Sam says. "Let me introduce you to his daughter. This is Mallory. Mallory, this is Todd. We went to business school together and he's driving through for a meeting in Los Angeles."

Dad raises his eyebrows at me, smiling, clearly having already accepted this stranger from Washington. I take Todd's hand, wary of him and the world he represents—the side of Sam that everyone else sees on a day-to-day basis, away from the vineyard life. The real Sam? Or the side of himself Sam is trying to escape from?

"Very nice to meet you," he says in a clear, throaty voice.

"You, too," I say.

"I'm sorry I don't have longer to spend in this beautiful place. I can see why Sam doesn't want to come back."

We all laugh, though mine is strained and merely to be polite.

"At least with the short time you'll be here, you get to see the best part," Sam says, smiling at me.

"Dinner?" Todd suggests.

"That would be great," Sam says. He looks to Dad and me. "Would you guys like to join us?"

Dad begs out, having promised to eat with Mom.

"You probably want to spend time with your parents while you can," Sam says, but Dad waves us off.

"Go," he says. "Have fun."

Not wanting the perfect day with Sam to end, I agree. Todd suggests the swanky Italian restaurant that is listed on every "must see" guide written about Paso Robles, which is where he must have heard about it. Despite living here, I've only been once because one plate costs as much as it takes to feed our entire family and vineyard hands at home.

I run upstairs to change. Despite owning plenty of appropriate clothing, nothing feels quite right. I finally end up in a pair of black slacks, a white sleeveless silk top, and a pair of black pumps. I feel more like my New York self than I have in almost two weeks but the pants don't fit quite like I remember and the top seems too low cut all of a sudden. I tug it up as much as I can, swipe some eye shadow over my lids, and meet the guys out in the parking lot, where I attempt to look graceful while every rock threatens to knock me off-kilter.

Todd is kind enough to take the back seat in Sam's car but Sam spends the entire time chatting over his shoulder, asking Todd questions about his business, which turns out to be marketing, as well. Todd owns a firm similar to the one where I work, but more grassroots and seemingly with a more West Coast culture. As he tells Sam about his firm's success, he talks about the employee fitness plan and locally grown catered lunches he's added to his business model recently. When Sam shares that I'm in marketing as well, and the name of my firm, Todd looks me over with an impressed nod. If I'm not mistaken, his view of me shifts from small-town vintner's daughter to someone who holds her own with him and Sam. I must admit that the recognition isn't unpleasant.

When we arrive at the restaurant, though, Sam and Todd are drawn to one another like magnets and I end up trailing behind them, a third wheel. The tenuous progress Sam and I made today seems to reverse with every passing minute.

We're seated quickly where I'm left to lose myself in the menu and the astronomical numbers listed next to each item. I order a small salad, making the excuse that I'm not very hungry, though Sam doesn't buy it. He quietly offers to pay, which only makes the moment more awkward. He gives me an apologetic frown, knowing I'm not comfortable in this kind of environment.

But that's as much comfort as he provides for the rest of dinner while he and Todd chat about the latest social media conference, books by self-proclaimed wealth gurus, and client-building strategies they've been experimenting with. And even though this is also my line of work, their perspective is so different—I have nothing to contribute to the conversation. Like before, I feel like a kid sitting at the adult table.

If this is the kind of people Sam spends his time with, it's no wonder his sole focus has been on how quickly he can get ahead and what the features of his future yacht will be.

Once we've finished our main courses and are waiting for dessert, which I opt out of, along with a sixteen-dollar glass of wine, Sam excuses himself to the bathroom and I'm left alone with Todd.

He smiles at me with his zest for life and self-importance.

"So how do you know Sam?" he asks. I find this an odd question, considering he came to the vineyard. Did Sam not mention why he was here? Or that he'd come before? These two are apparently close—went to business school together, share clients, regularly meet for drinks. Has he not mentioned me at all?

I align my fork next to my empty salad plate.

"He did some consulting work for my dad at the vineyard ten years ago."

"Ten years ago. Wow." Todd sits back in his chair. "That must have been right out of business school."

"Pretty close, from what I understand."

He nods, clearly unsure what to say next, and I don't do much to help, content to kill the time until I can return home and try to forget this night, try to forget how Sam has just shy of ignored me the entire evening.

"Did Sam tell you about the new project we're working on?" he asks.

I shake my head. Todd leans forward again, excited to have a topic that will ease the tension until Sam returns.

"Sam and I have been working on a business model where we can combine our skills and our companies. As you know, Sam has more of an in-house approach to creating success for his clients, whereas I focus more externally, creating campaigns to bring customers to my clients."

He motions to me here, recognizing that our work is similar.

"Up until now, individually, we've been working with smaller businesses, doing pretty well, I'd say, and sharing clients from time to time. But with the plan we're creating, we hope to work together, offering a well-rounded approach to pitch to large corporations, which would take both our businesses to a whole new level."

I'm surprised Sam hasn't mentioned this prospect to me, but based on his goals, not at all surprised he started this initiative. At least, what his goals used to be. I'd like to hope our conversations and his time at the vineyard, where he feels so at ease, may have shifted his perspective a little.

"That sounds great," I say, mostly because his eyebrows seem to be demanding a response. "Really smart."

Todd laughs. "Of course it's smart. Sam came up with the idea. The man's a genius, as I'm sure you've noticed."

I nod, grateful for once to share my high opinion of Sam with someone else who really gets it.

"That he is," I say.

"His call was perfect timing. I was headed down here for a meeting anyway. I'd told him all about the fitness machine company I'd be pitching and how worried I was about landing it. It's the biggest pitch I've ever done, straight to the board of directors, and while I feel confident in my work, I didn't think they'd trust such a small operation to help them reach the level of exposure they're hoping for.

"And then one day last week, out of the blue, Sam calls me up says, what if we pitch them together?"

I sit up straighter, suddenly interested. "He called you about this last week?" I ask.

Todd nods. "First thing Monday morning. He's the only person I've ever known who actually likes Mondays," he says with a laugh.

That was the day after Shannon's death. Two days after the party where Sam and I said our goodbyes with a promise that we would chase our real dreams. A week after he admitted that most of his pursuits for success were fueled by his desire to prove something to his dad.

Is that what he's really been working on in the guest house all week?

I guess our time together hasn't meant as much to him as I thought it did.

"And he's going with you to the pitch?"

"Tomorrow."

I struggle to swallow.

"Wow. That's...exciting."

Todd misses the skepticism in my voice or chooses to ignore it. He strikes me as the kind of guy who ignores anything he doesn't want to hear. But maybe that's my cynical side speaking.

Sam returns to the table then, a hopeful smile on his face at seeing Todd and I getting acquainted.

"Well, good luck with that," I say to both of them. I thought things between us were different. I thought Sam was different. But no matter what Sam might say to me, his actions prove that this is the kind of life he wants. The ten-dollars-for-a-side-salad kind of life.

Sam furrows his brow. "Good luck with what?"

Sam and I don't get the opportunity to speak on the way home since Todd does all the talking. And once Todd brings up their new business idea, Sam grows quiet, answering Todd with nods and reluctant hums. I encourage Sam to accompany Todd back to his hotel so they can prepare for their meeting. Sam must have thought I would never notice his absence since

Tuesday is Kelly's day off and we would naturally be spending it together.

Alone in the kitchen, I heat up leftover tuna casserole from my parents' dinner and cry. I thought I was older and wiser. Too old and too wise to fall for Sam's illusions. But it isn't even Sam I'm angry with, it's myself. For getting dressed up and allowing myself to be dragged into an environment that made me feel out of place, less than enough. I'm mad at myself for betraying my own authenticity for a man, or to try to impress anyone.

I'm still feeling emotionally hung over the next morning bleary-eyed, a cup of coffee in hand, when I get a text from Kelly.

Heading to LA for the morning. Will text when I get back.

It's just the getaway I need.

Swing by here first, I respond.

By the time she pulls into the parking lot, I'm outside waiting for her with two travel mugs of coffee and a bag of chips I scrounged from the pantry.

She rolls down the window and asks, "What exactly are you doing?"

"I'm coming with you. I'm not letting you go to LA alone."

"You do know you're voluntarily signing up for the probable scenario of ending up stranded on the side of I-5?"

"Let's take the rental," I say. "Might as well get my money's worth."

Once we've switched cars, Kelly behind the wheel, she asks, "What are the chips for?"

"It's not a road trip without junk food."

We take turns choosing radio stations as we pass from one small town to the next. I toe my shoes off, kick my feet onto the dash, and rest my head against the seat as the sun rises over my shoulder.

Kelly explains the reason for the trip. She hasn't been able to get anyone from Social Security on the phone to find out if there are any more of her mom's disability checks coming. Without that money, she won't be able to afford the mortgage on her house so she has to explore different options for supplementing her meager income or find a new place of her own.

She's working awfully hard to stay in a place she tells me she never wanted to be in the first place. But who am I to say she should give up the one thing she has left when she's already lost so much?

So I nod and encourage her in the way that best friends do because I know support is what she needs right now, not a critic.

But after a sweaty trip into the city and two hours in line at the Social Security office, Kelly discovers they can't tell her anything without a death certificate and paperwork proving that Kelly is the next of kin on Shannon's estate.

I had long since escaped the snaking, coughing crowd and only listen to Kelly's account of the news once she's returned to the parking lot and climbed onto the hood of the car to sit next to me. We face the busy street and watch the traffic pass for a few minutes, blowing exhaust-filled heat into our faces.

She reaches into her purse and pulls out a pack of cigarettes, putting one in her mouth and fishing out a lighter. She lights it and takes that first inhale like she's been smoking for years.

I watch all of this with my mouth agape. This is the girl I've always known to be careful, thoughtful, never stepping out of line.

"Don't look at me like that," she says. "My mom is dead and I'm homeless."

I consciously close my mouth, unsure of whether this is

one of those times a best friend intervenes or if it's one of the times she looks the other way.

"What am I going to do, Mal?" Kelly asks. She's smoked the cigarette halfway down.

I squint at her through the sunlight and sweat.

"What do you want to do?" I ask.

"Coming down here was completely pointless."

It could be her chance to explore the area. I know Shannon hoped Kelly would move here and create opportunities for herself. She encouraged me to give Kelly a nudge in the right direction. But while I may have once had Kelly's ear on matters like these, she's made it clear since I've been back that her decisions are entirely her own.

"Hey, at least we got to do our road trip," I say. "Officially."

Kelly snorts. "I wouldn't exactly call this a road trip."

I watch the cars fly by again. I feel helpless to guide Kelly in figuring out the next direction of her life when I can't figure out the direction of my own.

"I have an idea," I say, hopping off the hood. Kelly starts from my sudden movement. "Give me the keys."

She raises an eyebrow but hands them over.

She doesn't ask questions as I get us back on the I-5 and head toward downtown. She leans the seat back, blasts the air-conditioning, and closes her eyes, not sitting up again until we're engulfed by high-rises, honking, and foot traffic. I almost feel like I'm back in New York City, even though it would be sacrilege for me to say so to any New Yorker.

"This is a one-way," she says, turning the radio down.

I ignore her, searching the buildings for what I'm looking for. Downtown was the only area I could think to find it.

"Aha," I gasp when I catch sight of the tacky neon sign. I cut someone off to snag a parking space that is only half-vacated. Kelly doesn't notice my maneuver. As if in a trance, she gets

out of the car, never taking her eyes off the tops of the buildings. I dodge traffic to join her on the sidewalk.

"I've never been downtown before," Kelly says.

"Really?"

When I think about it, the only time I visited before was
with my mom on a work errand to pick up paperwork for the
law office. I hadn't thought much of it then—the city's buzz,
the sense of being dwarfed by the buildings—but there's something familiar and almost comforting about it now.

"Do you have any change?" I ask.

We feed the meter from her purse and I coach her to hold
it tighter as we pass a sketchy-looking alley. When we stop
at the storefront with a sign advertising tarot card readings,
Kelly laughs.

"I thought I was going to get out of this one."

"You put it on the list."

She groans. "I'm too old to fall for this stuff now."

"We're both looking for guidance on what to do next,
right?" I ask. She looks skeptical. "It'll be fun. Come on."

I drag her into the shop and a bell rings over the door. The
small lobby is dank. It smells of incense and the musty curtains that hang over the front windows. There's no one at the
small front desk so before Kelly changes her mind, I ring the
bell that sits on top.

Almost immediately, a squat older woman bustles out from
behind the curtains that lead to a back room. Her face is round
and kind but there's an intensity in her eyes that unnerves me.

"Well, let's go," she says breathlessly in a Russian accent
before she turns back and hobbles down a narrow hallway.
Kelly and I share a glance but follow.

The psychic turns into a small room that is sparse compared
to the ornate decorations of the lobby, like she either ran out of
money to finish the job or only used the expected trappings to

draw people in. There are potted plants on the floor and small tables around the room. Candles give the space a dim glow.

I motion for Kelly to take the chair at the small circular table in the center of the room while the old woman drags a chair over for me. I sit to the side, giving Kelly the focus.

"You're in love, no?" the woman says to the room. I look to Kelly and shrug.

"I...don't think I'd call it that," Kelly says.

"Of course you are," the woman responds as she falls into her chair. "Young girls like you, always in love."

As the woman shuffles a stack of cards in front of her, Kelly rolls her eyes but I smile in encouragement.

"You are sisters, no?"

"Yes," I say.

"I read for your relationship?" The woman waggles a stumpy finger between the two of us.

"No, just her," I say. Kelly tries to argue, but I repeat, "Just her."

"You have a question?" the woman asks.

Several expressions pass over Kelly's face, slowly, each one evolving from the next: sheepishness as she glances at me out of the corner of her eye, then shame, then resolution.

"I do. Yeah," she says. "What does my mom want me to do with my life?"

My throat tightens and I reach for her hand.

"She leave us recently," the woman says, nodding her head. I'm not sure if intuition tells her that or she gains that insight from Kelly's face, but she shuffles and begins to lay the cards out in a shape I don't understand, nodding to herself.

Kelly squeezes my hand as she waits for the verdict, suddenly much more believing.

"Wheel of Fortune." The woman points to the card with a circle in the middle that looks like a clock or a compass.

"Change. A big change comes to your life now. Eight of Cups. A choice. You must decide… Will you hold tightly to what you have known or will you take a risk? You have been playing it safe, not listening to your heart when it calls you."

I bite my lip, struck by the accuracy, and the way this stranger is saying all the things I've been wanting to—trying to—say to Kelly.

"You are called now to be brave," the woman goes on. "Stop worrying about what you think others want for you. Do what you want to do. Allow yourself to be pulled in the right direction."

Kelly tilts her head toward her lap.

"What if I don't know what I want?" she says in a small voice. I squeeze her hand.

The woman lays out another card.

"You know," she says. "You don't listen to what is all around you. Listen." The woman points her finger violently at her own head. "Your mind is wrapped up in choices but there is no choice. Your heart has the answer and is only waiting for you to catch up."

She sweeps the cards back into a pile with one swift movement and shuffles again. She lays the cards out in another formation.

"There is a man," the woman says. "He has admired you for a long time."

"Kyle," Kelly says, her voice rough with what I realize is tears. It's hard to see her face behind her hair, which is loose today. "If he admires me so much, why did he reject me the other night?"

"No. Nine of Wands. He feels hurt. He keeps his feelings to himself."

"We dated a few years ago. It's not exactly a secret."

The woman shakes her head, squinting her eyes closed. She's quiet for a few seconds—listening or *seeing* or egging us on.

"He's been watching you since you were a girl. He doesn't feel worthy of you. He wants to tell you, but he feels it's too late."

Kelly looks to me but I come up short. We didn't hang out with many guys in high school but we knew them all. I don't recall anyone acting shy around Kelly who didn't come out with their feelings eventually.

"I don't think so," Kelly says more soberly, her walls creeping back up. She almost believed. She wanted to.

"He would do anything for you. He's in love with you," the woman goes on. "And when you see him in a new light, you may find that you love him, too."

There's a long silence in which Kelly stares at the woman, blank faced. Then a high-pitched laugh pierces the room. The tarot reader and I both start in shock. My eyes widen at Kelly, who, under usual circumstances, wouldn't offend a nun. It continues to roll out of her in waves until tears form in her eyes, leaving me speechless to apologize on her behalf when the tarot reader's face hardens.

"I can't believe I almost fell for that," Kelly says between gasps.

"Kelly," I chide. I pull out my wallet and fish out the money we owe the woman, plus a hefty tip.

"You're good," Kelly goes on. "Well done. You even played off my dead mother. Hey, if you're going to play, you might as well go all in, right?"

The woman, in a seeming act of revenge, pulls another card and slaps it onto the table. Knight of Swords is written across the bottom in an old-fashioned font, and the card depicts a horse. Its mane blowing in the wind. Its expression determined. It's the look in the horse's eyes that draws me in and I lean closer. I almost miss the violent intentions of the man atop him.

"You ride horses, no?" the woman asks.

Kelly suddenly stops laughing. "Not… No," Kelly stutters. "Not really."

"Your spirit is free but you are chained down by your own fears."

Kelly slowly reaches for the tattoo on her wrist, running her thumb across its lines pensively.

"You try to ride away, and you make it far, but it is never far enough. You cannot outrun yourself."

Kelly looks to me, her eyes probing, questioning. *Why is she looking at me?* I hold my breath, shaking my head, my mind refusing to follow Kelly's train of thought.

"It's for you," she says, her brow furrowed like she's not sure how to feel about that.

I shake my head again, but as I think about everything the woman has said in the reading, connections form and answers rise to the top like a magic eight ball.

The woman looks directly at me now, her voice more gentle.

"Shannon asks that you lead by example," she says.

Kelly and I reach for each other's hands at the mention of her mother's name. The woman's ice-blue eyes bore straight into mine.

"She says you are the true leader. When you are brave, you make others brave around you. She asks you to lead her daughter to the path that is waiting for her."

A hush sucks the air from the room. Then Kelly bursts into tears.

TWENTY-TWO

THEN.

The morning I woke up next to Sam was the best and most confusing morning of my life. His dark curls danced across the pillowcase. The tension he usually wore on his face had been rubbed away. To see him in his sleep, relaxed and defenseless, I saw the Sam I knew he kept hidden from everyone else. And yet, he'd let me see this side of him. He'd trusted me.

But too quickly, the memories of the way Sam usually reacted to our evenings together washed over me and I found myself antsy to escape before he woke up and remembered how close we'd been, before he regretted it and pulled away.

And while my parents didn't usually hover too closely over me, I didn't know how they'd react to me spending the night with a man—an employee, no less—regardless of how innocent it had been. I slipped away while he was sleeping.

Later that day, Kelly, Tyler, and I went on a ride together. As they talked, I nodded in all the right places, laughed when they laughed, but my mind was on the night before as I tried to decipher this new feeling shooting through my veins—gratitude and pining wrapped up into one emotion that seemed to have leaped off the cliff of "crush" and into something that hadn't quite landed on love. I liked it.

"Mallory," Kelly snapped at me.

We were already back at the stables, brushing the sweaty horses. I blinked out of my reverie and stared at her. I didn't remember arriving here, could hardly recall the ride.

"Seriously, what is going on with you?" she asked, her voice uncharacteristically tight.

"Sorry. Friday. Hot springs. Got it," I said, catching up with the conversation.

"No," Kelly said, tossing her brush to the ground. "You're not skating over this again. You've been distracted, even more forgetful than usual, and distant for weeks. What is going on with you? Actually, don't answer that. I think we all know exactly what is going on."

I was paying attention now, defensiveness tightening every muscle in my body. This was about Sam. Again. She had been resentful of any moment I spent with him all summer and I didn't understand why. She would have me all to herself at Columbia—at least as far as she knew. Sam and I hadn't talked any more about hiking, but after our night together, my hope had returned.

"And what is that?" I asked.

"Oh, please. Don't pretend we don't all know what is going on here. You're in love with a guy who is only going to use you, and that's if you're lucky enough to get his attention in the first place."

I gasped, physically struck by her words. Kelly had certainly always been open about her opinions, and I didn't always agree with them, but she had never used her words as a weapon before. When I glanced at Tyler, I could see that he was shocked, too.

"That was really mean, Kel. And not true."

I *had* caught Sam's attention and the fact that my best friend didn't believe it—didn't believe I was worthy of him—stung like nothing I'd ever felt before.

Kelly scoffed, picking the brush back up and disappearing into the tack room to replace it. When she came back out, she was a little more composed. "I don't understand what you think is going to happen with him."

I didn't know what I expected to happen with Sam either, and if I did, I certainly wouldn't have shared it with Kelly in that moment. Not with the level of disdain in her voice.

"You don't even know him," I said instead.

"I don't want to know him! I want to spend my time being with the people that mean something to me. People I'm going to know longer than a few weeks. Although, frankly, I'm starting to wonder. If one good-looking guy can make you forget about all the plans we had for this summer, maybe college will make you forget about me completely."

"Maybe I don't want to go to New York," I said, finally admitting it because this was about more than Sam. The more I thought about spending another four years in stuffy classrooms to get a degree I felt certain I would never use, the more Columbia looked like a prison.

"Yes, you do," she said in a low voice.

"How do you know what I want?" I shrieked. "I don't even know what I want."

And having people constantly tell me what they thought I should want was exhausting.

"That's exactly my point," she spit back. "And as long as you keep trying to be what you think *he* wants, you're never going to figure it out."

"But I'm supposed to listen to you?"

"I know you better than he does," she said. "I know you better than anyone."

She exhaled heavily, like knowing me so deeply was a weight she carried. She looked tired. Pale. She'd grown weary over the course of the summer and I'd only now noticed, proving everything she was saying was true.

But my defensiveness got the best of me.

"Funny," I said, "considering how little you understand yourself."

I regretted the words as soon as they came out of my mouth—a gun at a knife fight. There were so many heartbreaks from Kelly's childhood that led her to try to control life with a white-knuckle death grip. For our entire friendship, I'd known that about her and had given her a wide berth when she got too tightly wound. I forgave her character flaws the way she forgave mine. That's what made our relationship work.

And now I'd thrown it all in her face. All those years of her trusting me with the parts of herself that scared her, and I'd used it against her.

"Kelly, I'm so sorry," I said, tears pricking the corners of my eyes. Maybe Kelly was right. Maybe I was turning into someone else. The real Mallory would never purposely hurt someone she loved.

"Don't bother apologizing," she said, her voice icy. "Clearly you do know what you want."

Kelly stalked toward the parking lot.

I stood there, huffing for air, my blood pulsing through my body with such ferocity that I swayed with its rhythm. Tyler's arms wove around me from behind and I broke down, collapsing into him.

TWENTY-THREE

NOW

*K*elly falls asleep on the way home, emotionally exhausted and, I'm sure, avoiding me. She wouldn't let me comfort her as we left the tarot reader, wouldn't speak to me as I navigated us back to the freeway. On the long drive home, I replayed everything the cards said, wondering at what point they began to come up for me. Was the reading mine from the very beginning?

When we get to my house, I try again to talk to her about what happened but she can't seem to find words as she moves from the rental car to her own. She vaguely says she'll call and backs up without looking at me. I hug myself as she drives away, feeling emotionally raw and confused. Is she angry at me about what the cards said or for taking her there in the first place? Either way, I wish I could apologize, to get back to where we were before.

I traipse up the porch steps, where Dad and Sam are sitting with the remnants of dinner and an open bottle of wine. I stop and stare at Sam, his expression uncertain after the way we left each other the night before. I couldn't help but feel lied to even though Sam has made no commitments to me. In fact, we both specifically agreed to take it one day at a time. But what's the point of this experiment if he's already making plans to go back to his old life? What's the point if I'm still planning to go back to mine?

When you see him in a new light…

I remember what the psychic said. Could I accept Sam for who he is, blind ambition and all? Could I be a part of his life without losing myself? Would that make the difference?

Sam clears his throat and excuses himself from the table.

"Do you want to go for a walk?" Sam asks. I look to my dad. Does he sense what's going on here? Does Sam care? Do I?

He's in love with you…

"Sure," I say.

He places his hand on my back and guides me out into the vines. The angle of the sun casts long shadows of the grapevine canopies along the dry ground between the rows. The temperature has started to cool but I can still feel the dried salt on my skin where my back was pressed against the car seat. Sam shoves his hands into his pockets and looks over his shoulder, back to where my dad is watching us, and I feel the sting of betrayal once more. So he does care.

"Are you okay?" he whispers. "What happened?"

I run my hand through my hair. "I don't even know. I feel like I don't know anything anymore."

"Where have you been all day?"

"With Kelly," I say. "It doesn't matter. Do you ever feel like no matter what you do, it's wrong?"

Sam raises an eyebrow at me.

"Never mind."

"No, come here." Sam wraps an arm around my shoulders

and pulls me close. I bury my nose into his chest, the cotton of his shirt soft and comforting.

"What, we're far enough away now?" I ask.

"Don't do that," he says. "I'm trying not to be disrespectful."

I look up at him, our faces inches apart. "To who?" Worried that I've screwed things up with Kelly again, I hardly feel strong, but I'm too exhausted for bullshit. I'm tired of feeling jerked around.

Sam glances at my lips and I can tell he wants to kiss me. I turn my face away before he can.

"You still don't trust me," he surmises.

I break free from his grasp, walking away farther into the vines.

"Why should I? From the moment we first met, it's been all about you, Sam. What you want, what you don't want. What you need, what you can get away with. Have you given one single thought to what I might want or need?"

I'm yelling at the vines, too angry to ask these questions to his face.

"No," Sam says.

I stop walking.

"You're right," he says to my back. "I didn't consider your feelings the last time I was here. I wasn't expecting you. I wasn't expecting how you would make me feel. I probably haven't considered your feelings as much as I should this time either—"

I cut him off with a glare.

"I'm trying," he says, his voice softer. "I really am. But it's something I need to learn. My parents weren't role models in that department. And Hannah… Well, I wasn't at my best with her."

He comes closer to me, but keeps a cautious distance.

"I want you in my life, Mal," he says slowly. "You make

me better. At least, you make me want to try. If I fail completely, well, you can't be blamed for that."

I can't help it—I laugh. Sam smiles and wipes the tears forming beneath my eyes with his thumbs, his touch gentle and exhilarating. Every time.

"Do you remember that song we danced to?" he asks. "At the opening of the tasting room?"

Of course I remember. For better or worse, every moment with Sam has been etched into my mind. It's no wonder no man has ever been able to compare to him. Anywhere they might go, Sam has already traveled and claimed. On the one hand, I can't imagine how anything long-term with Sam could ever work. Sam is a man of excitement, of adventure. Nothing keeps his attention for long. On the other, I don't know how I cannot try.

That's the reason for my tears, despite the way the day went with Kelly. I know what Kelly is going through isn't really about me. But if Sam really does love me and I'm hopeless without him, how can I get on a plane in two days and pretend none of this ever happened?

"'Leather and Lace,'" I say. "By Stevie Nicks."

He nods. He remembers, too, despite the way he tried to play it off in the days after our night together. Our summer together meant something to him, too.

He holds his hand out to me. After a moment's hesitation, I slip mine into it. He pulls me close and wraps his hand around my waist, as if we're dancing again. I resist the urge to rest my head on his chest or give in too easily. I've fallen into his trap too many times.

"That song reminds me of us," he says. "Of what we could be."

He begins to sway me to the rhythm in our heads, there in the middle of the vineyard, with the last rays of daylight dancing over us, in this private world created by the acres of grapes that surround us.

He sings the words off-key. I laugh at this perfect man who can do anything but hold a tune. I'm always grateful to see the cracks in his flawless facade.

"You're terrible," I say. "You shouldn't do that ever again."

But I could stand here with him like this forever. Luckily, Sam grins and keeps singing.

"You give me something, Mallory," he says when he finishes the chorus.

"My leather? It's the saddles, isn't it? They're not the most comfortable in the world, but they do keep you strapped to a moving horse—"

"Hope," he says, cutting off my sarcasm. "Inspiration. You make me want to see the world through your eyes and it makes me feel alive."

I'm speechless. I've spent so many years trying to change, to be more stable, reliable, and understanding of the expectations of the modern world. I thought that was what everyone wanted from me.

"Are you sure it's not the leather?" I ask.

"Mallory, listen to me. Up until now, I didn't think about giving you anything in return, and I apologize for that. Maybe I felt like I didn't have anything to give—"

I shake my head. How could he not see the way he lights me up? He's the one who makes me feel alive.

"There's something I can give you now," he says.

"What do you mean?"

Sam stops dancing. "Todd likes you."

"He does?" After the way I ignored him the entire night? I could laugh, but I don't.

"He thinks you're smart and apparently your firm has quite

a reputation in the industry. He thinks you could bring a lot to growing his firm. He's very interested in hearing your ideas."

"Wait, what?" I say, dropping our hands.

"The meeting today went well, Mal. Really well. We need to make some updates to the proposal but if things go the way I hope, we could close this deal next week. This is huge. For both of our businesses. We're going to need help."

"So you're offering me a job?"

"Not me, no. But Todd is, if you want it."

"In Washington."

"I know you're having a hard time trying to decide what to do next. Maybe a change of scenery would be just what you need. I promise, it's not as rainy as they make it out to be. And there have to be more horses there than in New York City. Heck, if you like it there, I'm sure we could find a way to get Midnight shipped out."

I only half hear what he's saying, but from what I do hear, it's clear he's already thought this through. "I'm confused. You're saying you want me to come live in Seattle? By you?"

"Well…yeah."

"You want…? Wait, what do you want?"

Sam laughs and takes my hands in his. "I want to see what could happen."

"That's a big commitment to make just to see what could happen—moving to the other side of the country."

"The only way to ever see what could happen is to commit, right?"

He's doing it again—that charming-smile-gets-anything-he-wants thing.

This time, though, he wants me. Real and in public. And that changes everything.

"But? I thought you didn't want all that anymore. I thought that was why you were here."

He wraps his hand around the back of his neck. "I don't know," he says. "Business calls to me. It's not all about the money. It excites me, these kinds of deals. The possibilities. The challenge. The risk. Maybe I need to do it differently, but I don't think I could give it up altogether. I don't think I want to."

As he says it, something in him shifts, like he's finally accepting this himself. Something in me shifts, too—the way I see him. My aversion to his corporate lifestyle has never been about the work or even necessarily about the extravagance. It was because it never seemed like a conscious choice. His choice, rather than an excuse to show up his father. But somehow, in the midst of doing what he thought he had to do to get out from under his dad's thumb, he found his passion. He found himself.

I step forward and kiss him.

"I'll think about it," I say.

Sam smiles against my lips. "Okay."

The next morning, I wake up to several missed calls from Denise. A feeling of dread washes over me and my mind starts generating justifications to give her for not being back in the office yet, not calling, not having sent over that brochure copy I promised. Denise and I didn't discuss an exact date for my return, but I should have known that when Denise said a week, she meant seven days, not the loose five-to-ten-day range we use around the vineyard, which is subject to change based on the weather.

Not wanting to hear the disappointment in her voice, I send her a text.

I'm so sorry. Things are still a mess here and I hate to leave before all the arrangements are settled. Can you ever forgive me?

I try for playful, pulling the friend card.
The response comes back immediately.

I'll deduct a pair of designer heels from your next paycheck.

I laugh and relief washes over me. With a deep breath, I reply.

Is there any way you can spare me for a few more days?

The next response takes longer.

I'm starting to question your commitment to this job, Mallory.

My stomach sinks. As much as I've questioned whether New York is where I belong, deep down, I've always pictured myself returning. Settling back into my apartment, maybe getting a bigger one with my promotion. Eventually running into a man on Fifth Avenue who would make me forget about Sam. Mostly.

I know it's a lot to ask, and I wouldn't if it wasn't important.

I watch her chat bubble grow and shrink several times.

Send me the first draft of the florist brochure today.

Thank you! You really are the best boss ever!

She doesn't respond, though I don't expect her to. I breathe a sigh of relief and tramp down the stairs to get Mom's laptop to finish—start—the brochure copy.

Dad is in the kitchen, pouring himself a second cup of coffee and finishing the scrambled eggs Mom must have made him before she left.

"Well, good morning," he says, his mouth full. "You're looking better today."

I bite my lip, realizing how shell-shocked I must have looked the night before after Kelly left, but also what he may or may not have seen between Sam and me. If he did see us hugging, kissing, he shows no sign of it.

"Thanks," I say. "I think."

"Hey," he says. "I was just about to head out for my morning walk-through. Want to join me?"

I make a noncommittal noise, glancing toward Mom's office, but then I acknowledge how little time I've spent with my dad since I've been home. The brochure can wait one more hour.

"Yeah," I say. "I'd like that."

The weather has grown steadily warmer over the couple of weeks I've been here and the moment I step off the back porch, I wish I'd grabbed a hat. But the travel mug of coffee Dad offers will suffice. I walk alongside him into the vines.

For a while, we walk silently and I watch Dad inspect the grapes, checking for signs of mold or insects. He pulls a few bunches of young grapes that aren't flourishing to keep them from interfering with the health of the rest of the vine. He places them into a small plastic bucket that clips to his belt.

I reach out and touch the leaves, feel their texture between my fingertips. Their vitality, their color. Humans are designed to connect with nature, to be inspired by it. Who wouldn't want to bring a little piece of it with them when they spend most of their day inside an office? And no doubt the florist is as meticulous and dedicated to caring for their flowers as Dad is with his vines. Finally, the brochure concept clicks.

"I can't help but notice you're still here," Dad says, pulling my attention back to him. He smirks at me through his weatherworn squint.

"Well, you're just full of flattery this morning," I say.

He laughs.

"Yeah, I guess I am. My boss gave me another few days. I just don't feel like I can leave Kelly right now."

Or Sam. He's given me a lot to think about. I don't know how I'll make such a big decision in only a few days.

"That's very thoughtful of you. Must be hard for her."

I nod. I hoped she would have called by now, but she hasn't. I want to reach out to her, but I know she needs her space.

"Harder than I think she's letting on," I say.

Dad frowns and reaches his hand out to rub his calloused hand over my hair.

"I can't imagine you being without parents at your age. I would never want that for you. I know you're an adult and you can take care of yourself, but no matter how little I talk to my parents, there's relief in knowing they're there. And let me tell you, a person never gets so old that they don't need their parents."

He hooks his elbow around my neck and pulls me in close so he can rub his knuckle into the top of my head, making me squeal.

"Dad," I complain, smoothing my hair, but I believe everything he's telling me. I don't want to know a world where Dad isn't endlessly walking rows of grapevines and Mom isn't dishing out life advice alongside chicken Parmesan. I don't know what Kelly's traditions with Shannon were—and maybe Kelly is only discovering them now that they're gone—but she must be missing them. We've been good at staying distracted but we can't evade the grief forever. That sick feeling in my stomach returns.

"How do you do it, Dad?" I ask. "How do you have so

many strong relationships?" He makes it look so easy, navigating the intricacies of marriage, friendships, and managing his employees.

Dad looks taken aback but proud. "What do you mean?" he asks.

"Watching you the other night at the Libations party... People around here really love you. You've done so much for all of them and yet you still keep up with everything at the vineyard. And even though we're far apart, you're never more than a phone call away. How do you do it all?"

I've never in my life seen my dad blush. Until now. He reaches for another cluster of shriveled grapes and drops them in the bucket.

"Life is just about priorities, honey," he says. "And they change as you get older. When I was your age, my priority was work, too. You remember. Although I'm sure you and your mom would argue that work is still my priority, and it is. But I wouldn't hesitate to drop everything if you or your mom or anyone of our friends needed me, and I hope you know that."

I think about it and come to the conclusion that, yes, I do know that. I struggle to ask for help, especially from my parents. I want to prove to them and to myself that I can handle things on my own. But I do know that if I ever released the hold on my pride, they would both be there in a heartbeat.

"There are a few things I've learned about relationships in my life," he goes on. "Would you like to hear them?"

I laugh. Dad has always been careful about giving me advice based on my fierce independent streak.

"Yes," I say. "Please."

He smiles.

"Well, the first thing I think it's important to do is let go of expectations. I've seen a lot of my good friends divorce because they had unrealistic expectations of their spouses. But this is true in friendships, too. Take what people give you and let that be enough. Because people usually give all they're capable of giving, the way they're capable of giving it, and expecting more than that is just setting the relationship up to fail."

I nod pensively. I think about Sam and the expectations I've had of him to give up his career, not understanding that Sam's work is an important part of who he is. It's what makes him *him*. And I wouldn't want him any other way.

On the other hand, I think about the offer he made me— moving to Washington, not with him but near him. What are his expectations of me? Is he trying me on to see if I fit in his world? And if I don't, where does that leave me? Nothing about his life will change, but I'll have given up my job, my apartment, the promotion I've worked so hard for.

"Okay," I say. "What else?"

Dad grins, getting a kick of out me asking for advice for once.

"Don't be afraid to ask for help," he says.

"Did you come up with this one specifically for me?"

He chuckles. "No comment. Actually, most people struggle with this. Especially when we lived in the city. People these days value independence so much that we've become disconnected from each other. We think we can do it alone. But you come to a town like this where we have to support one another to be successful. To survive, even. Asking for help strengthens relationships. It lets people know you appreciate their place in your life. And gives them permission to ask for help in return. We need more support than we realize, or sometimes want to admit."

I wish Kelly would ask for more help. I wish I had more to offer. Then again, I haven't asked for her help since I've been home, let alone all the years I've been gone, quietly lonely and craving being surrounded by my people. I could have hopped on a plane. I could have made it work. I should have.

I stop walking. Noticing, Dad stops, too. He sticks his shears in his utility belt and places his hands on my arms, steadying me.

"And?" I ask. "The last one?"

He rubs his thumb along my jaw.

"Lastly," he says, "relationships are the most important thing. It can take a while to figure that out, but if there's anything I've learned from talking to people older than me, we all get there eventually. At a point in everyone's life, after all the titles have been earned and the money has been made, we look around and realize none of those things have given us the happiness we've been searching for. But when you're surrounded by the right people, a ten-minute conversation, walking through a vineyard with someone you love, can mean everything."

I want to laugh and cry at the same time.

"That's all it takes to make you happy, huh?"

I've tried so hard to be a better daughter for them, a better person. So much so that I've missed these moments with them…these little moments that end up being the most important ones.

Dad frowns at my tears. He pulls me into his arms and I melt against his chest, squeezing him close.

"Mal, if you're happy, we're happy. That's all a parent ever wants. That's all we want for you," he says. "Wherever that might take you."

"I just wish I knew where that was," I say, my voice watery.

Dad tilts my chin up, looking me in the eyes.

"You always have a place here, baby girl. No matter how old you get, you're always our daughter and this is always your home."

TWENTY-FOUR

THEN

As the summer drew to a close, all the things I'd been avoiding came to a head. Kelly and I never talked about our fight and the cutting things we threw at each other so casually. Maybe we both felt stung and sorry in equal measure and figured that canceled everything out. This was how we finished our last summer at home: in denial.

We shopped for the dorm supplies, and I pretended I hadn't said anything about not wanting to attend Columbia, even though the question haunted me every waking moment. Kelly left most of the decor choices to me as her unspoken apology. Mine was to check off a couple more items from our sorely neglected Summer Bucket List. Every time she pulled it out and I saw how many items we had to finish, acidic guilt coated my tongue.

I escaped on the back of Midnight, tracing trails of hoofprints up and down every acre of The Wandering Vineyard property—places I'd never traversed before in the search of freedom and answers. I found none.

Sam and I planned a party to introduce the tasting room to the Paso Robles wine community. We spent many nights working late, designing it down to the last detail, wanting it to be perfect for Dad, for us, and for all the work we'd put into creating a new vision for the vineyard.

Many nights we worked at the little table in the guest house, poring over guest lists and wine lists and catering orders—Sam often lubricating the task with a glass or two, whether my dad joined us or not...and oftentimes he didn't.

When we reached the point where our eyes were crossing and we couldn't plan anymore, Sam would crawl into bed, I would curl up in the chair in the corner of the room, and we would talk about our views on life, love, and the future.

They often differed—he was more of a pusher, a big dreamer, while I had a simpler view on life, preferring to go with the flow. But the passion with which we discussed our ideas stimulated us and bonded us in a way that agreeing on everything never could have.

The one thing we did agree on was the necessity of adventure and we elaborated on our vision of weeks in the mountains, being led only by the pull of the wind and our whims. The call to that lifestyle pulsed through my veins and I could see in Sam's eyes that it did for him, too.

We amused each other and challenged each other, and sometimes, we kissed each other. But it wasn't about the kissing or the way our bodies molded against each other, our senses heightened by the enticing secrets we shared. It was about finding someone who truly understood the other, or at least wanted to try. In that way, we were exactly the same and every moment of it was exhilarating.

I grew used to Sam's hot-and-cold behavior and stopped

taking it personally. He got over it quicker, taking only the day to withdraw, opening up by nightfall so we could start our dance all over again. Kelly was wrong about him, but I knew she would never admit it.

That's why, as the party drew closer, my internal debate about whether or not to invite Kelly grew more heated. I couldn't believe I'd kept it a secret from her for so long already, baffling myself when she asked me what I'd done that day and I glossed over the details, avoiding any hint of the biggest celebration we'd ever had on the property.

The truth was, I wanted Sam and myself to go to the party together. *Together* together. After spending every evening with each other for three weeks, I thought it was time we came out of hiding, whatever we decided to do afterward. Our summer had become the most important thing that had ever happened to me. It opened me up in places I didn't know existed. I wanted that to mean something. I needed it to. And if Kelly was at the party, I would feel her judgmental eyes on me with every move I made. She didn't even try to understand, didn't want to. I wouldn't let her steal this summer from me and with it, everything I'd discovered about myself.

So I did the unthinkable: I didn't invite her.

It was easier to keep the secret than I thought it would be. She worked at the coffee shop and heard about everything that happened in our little town, so I was fully prepared to give up the cause if she asked about the party. But she didn't. Our conversations had become so polite anyway, that offering up no more information than was solicited was our new norm.

On the day of the party, the vineyard was abuzz with visitors, and Kelly was working a double shift. A few fellow winemakers wouldn't make it to the party but stopped by to wish us luck, weaving around caterers, suppliers, Sam, and me. There was a restless excitement between us as we strung lights around the trees, assembled tables, and lined up our wine selections for the night. Their new labels with Sam's logo design glinted silver under the recessed lighting above the bar. Everything we'd created together would be put on display tonight, and while the party was about Dad and the vineyard, it was clear we were both reveling in the display of our success.

As the sun began to descend in the sky, we dusted our hands off and called our work done. Sam's grin was filled with relief as we went our separate ways in front of the porch steps.

I glided down the stairs an hour later in a dress I'd bought for the occasion—a little black dress that clung to my curves and tied at the back of my neck. My mom was in the kitchen, attempting to raise the back zipper of her dress and put her shoe on at the same time.

"Let me help you," I said with a laugh. I took charge of the zipper while she worked her foot into her heel and responded to a work email on her BlackBerry. When she finished, she smoothed her dress and turned to me.

"Mallory Victoria," she said, almost breathlessly, running her hands over my shoulders. "You are a woman."

I blushed. I'd been wanting someone to acknowledge that fact all summer, and now that the time had come, I didn't know what to say.

"Thanks," I mumbled.

Everything was perfect. More than a hundred people showed up, including most of the local vintners, restaurant owners, and wine sellers from every city in a hundred-mile radius. Even the local news appeared to capture the event.

The DJ we hired played Frank Sinatra and other swanky jazz music to set the tone, and the lights we'd strung from the trees lit up the dirt parking lot turned dance floor in front of the tasting room. Some danced, some huddled in groups and talked wine. Dad spent the night where he felt most comfortable—behind the bar, serving wine samples hand over fist and entertaining guests with stories of how the tasting room came to be, Sam the willing butt of all his jokes.

He was so far away, showing no indication I'd crossed his mind.

My vision for the night evaporated slowly, leaving me feeling empty.

Mom circled the perimeter of the party and every time she caught my eye, I could see the question there. It asked, *Where is Kelly?* I asked myself the same question with exponential frequency as the night wore on and the distance between Sam and me grew more palpable.

But finally, as the food ran out and the DJ started to loosen up with his song choices, Sam caught my eye across the crowd. He looked more handsome than ever in a perfectly cut suit and pale pink tie, his hair long and his skin glowing from his summer under the vineyard sun. He nodded toward the makeshift dance floor and every inch of my skin flushed.

I met Sam in the middle of the dusty patch of ground that had been packed down by the shoes of our visitors. The film crew had long since left, and the crowd had begun to thin but there were enough people left that we could disappear into them. Sam put his hands on my hips but left a respectable amount of distance between us. His touch was becoming familiar but never normal. I cautiously wrapped my fingers around the back of his neck and fell recklessly into his smile.

"Fit for a duchess, Mallory Victoria," he said, looking me over. I tilted my head down so he wouldn't see me blush.

"It's been a good night," I said.

"It has. Even better than I expected. Every one of the wine sellers who showed up left their cards for your dad. They want him to call on Monday to discuss terms."

I gasped, barely controlling my urge to hug him in gratitude and pride. The success of this tasting room wasn't just about the vineyard—it was about my parents not having to work so hard, not having to worry about money, being able to take care of themselves when I was gone, wherever I might go.

"That's amazing," I whispered. "You have no idea how much this means to my parents. To me." There was an unguarded intimacy when I said, "Thank you, Sam. For everything you've done for the vineyard and…everything you've done for me."

It was a risk. Sam had the tendency to pull away when I got too close, and we were out in the open for everyone to see. Maybe that was what gave me the courage to say it. We were holding each other, however innocently, where my parents could see. Where anyone could see.

"Thank you," he returned. "You've done so much to help me this summer. I really couldn't have done this without you."

"That wasn't what I meant," I mumbled.

Sam looked away, suddenly antsy in my arms. But he didn't pull away. He leaned closer to my ear.

"Thank you, too," he whispered. Nothing more than that, but in his eyes, I saw everything I needed to see.

Someone tapped on my shoulder and I turned to see who it was. There, her eyes swollen and red, her work apron still tied around her front, stood Kelly.

I froze, so overcome with panic I couldn't move, couldn't speak. There was nothing I could say that would erase the clear sense of betrayal on her face anyway.

TWENTY-FIVE

NOW

After the talk with my dad, I lock myself in my mom's office and I get to work on the brochure copy. I find that once I close out the distractions, the words come easily. I fall into the zone I've become comfortable with and am known for around the office.

And as I work, inspiration from the grapevine fresh in my mind, a thought creeps in: I didn't choose this work for my parents, for Kelly, or for Sam. I chose this work because marketing has always come naturally to me, and because I enjoy it. I'm good at finding the right words to convey a message, and when I do, it's the most satisfied and fulfilled I feel these days. It would be unfair of me to blame anyone else for the choices I've made—unfair for them and for me. My decisions are what have gotten me a coveted position at a top marketing firm. I earned that all on my own. Now the question is, what am I going to do about it?

After a couple of hours, my brain is fried and I need a break. I stretch and hunt through the kitchen to find something to eat. I steal some of the cheese Sam restocked the day before and walk barefoot onto the porch to get some fresh air. The warm breeze calms my nerves and draws me back into the present.

Maybe moving to Washington could be like this. I could work normal hours, breaking up the time with walks by the shore and smoothies from the in-house organic juice bar. Maybe I'd have my own office with a view. Maybe what I've struggled with in New York isn't my job, but the lack of anything else. The lack of nature, the lack of friendships and relationships.

If I moved to Washington with Sam, it could be different. I would have a similar title, but I would also have the Pacific Ocean. I would have forest and rain, a whole new world to explore. I would be closer to home when I wanted to visit. And if Sam is serious about transporting Midnight and boarding her nearby, I would have my horse. I wouldn't have Kelly, or Tyler, or my parents, but I could make new friends. They would never be able to fill the space my family does, but they could be a new kind of relationship. An adult one.

Most important, I would have Sam, the one person I've wanted more than anything else in my life. The possibility of it still doesn't seem real, but as I look to the guest house, in the light of day I realize things have changed. Sam isn't a fantasy anymore. He isn't a figment of my imagination, the holes in my knowledge of him filled with hopeful musings. All I wanted that summer was to know Sam, and for the first time I feel like I do. I feel like I'm looking at him and our potential future with clear eyes.

A car pulls into the parking lot and I notice it's Mom's black SUV. I check the watch on my wrist. Only 2:00 p.m.

I already find her early arrival odd before Dad sprints past me from the stable office. My stomach twists. I'm drawn down the steps toward them, the rocks biting my feet. I don't care. Something is wrong. I know it.

Mom steps out of the car and is immediately engulfed in Dad's embrace. From this angle, it looks like she's been crying, which I've hardly ever seen my mom do. Elizabeth Graham is an eternal optimist. An it-will-all-work-out-the-way-it's-supposed-to person. The only time I remember seeing her cry was when her grandmother died.

I speed up.

When I reach them, gasping for breath, I ask, "What's wrong?"

Mom looks at me and her face crumples. She reaches out to me and Dad releases her, a mournful frown on his face. Mom pulls me into the hug and squeezes me so tightly my ribs ache.

"What's going on?" I demand. After Kelly's middle-of-the-night call, I expect the worst.

"I'm getting laid off," Mom says. She pulls away to wipe at her face.

So it is the worst. For Mom, at least, it is, as I've recently discovered. She's worked for her bosses for the last fifteen years. She's been loyal and invested in their clients. She lives and breathes her work. It's what gives her purpose.

Once she's composed herself, she explains.

"They told me today that they're closing the office. Jerry has decided to retire, so Chris is going to work from home and have his wife do paperwork. Paperwork!" She scoffs. "As if all I do around there is take messages and type up memos."

I look to Dad for how to react. Mom must have told him everything on the phone because this isn't news to him. I'm at a loss for what to say.

"They better give you a damn good severance package after

all you've done for them," he says, his nostrils flaring. My dad is a very even-tempered man, until someone upsets my mom.

"I'm not being fair," Mom says, sniffling. "They value me and what I do. They always have. I'm sure Chris is afraid he won't be able to afford me without Jerry there to bring in more clients. It's just a shock. We just closed the biggest case the firm has ever taken on. I thought we were growing, not downsizing."

"All the same," Dad says, clearing his throat.

"How much longer do you have there?" I ask.

"About a month. We need to get everything organized and packed up. Shut the office down."

"What will you do after that?"

"I have no idea," she says, her voice hollow.

We walk back to the house together. Sam approaches with concerned eyes. Knowing Mom and Dad will want to have some space to process, I grab Sam by the elbow and lead him back to the guest house while Dad takes Mom inside.

"What's going on?" Sam asks as soon as I close the door behind me. I lean against it and watch him as he kicks off his shoes.

"Mom lost her job."

His eyebrows lift in the same blank shock I must have worn when I heard.

"I'm sorry," he says. "I don't know how this is possible."

"I think that's pretty much the consensus right now," I say, pushing myself off the door. I pace the small space, itching to ride. I empathize with what Mom must be feeling. Lost, confused, aimless. I hate that this is happening to her. She gives so much of herself to take care of people.

Sam's hand around my wrist stops me. "Is there anything I can do to help?" he asks.

"What, you're going to give us all jobs?" I ask bitingly.

He doesn't respond, waiting for my frustration to pass. I sigh.

"I'm sorry. I just keep feeling like things can't get any worse and then—"

"Come here."

Sam pulls me toward the bed. He sits next to me, placing his palm up on his knee, an invitation.

I kiss him instead, soft and tentative at first, but once I'm sure he isn't going to pull away, I push into him. My lips, my body. He wraps his hands around my back, gripping his fingertips into my shirt, my skin. Without breaking contact, I climb into his lap, my mind going numb of all thoughts, my senses taking over. I keep pulling him closer, running my hands through his hair. I wrap myself tighter to him, as if I could swallow him down, like the satisfying burn of cheap wine in the pit of my belly.

"Whoa," he says, pulling away. He pries my arms loose from his neck. "Are you okay?"

"No," I breathe. "I'm not."

I've barely started to picture a possible life in Washington. I need to know that if I give up everything to move there and accept this job, it won't be taken away just as easily.

Sam leans forward and rests his forehead against my collarbone. The tenderness and submission of the gesture stuns me. "I'm making things worse," he says. "I'm pushing you with this crazy plan of moving to Washington."

"No," I say, though I'm not sure he's wrong. Is the idea of moving to Washington crazy?

"I should go home," he says, sitting up again. "Give you some space to sort things out."

"I want you to stay," I tell him.

"You do?" he asks, looking up at me. And there's not an ounce of conceit in his demeanor. He's defenseless and hopeful and, if I'm not mistaken, a little fearful. The possibility that I have the power to break Sam's heart dawns on me.

"I want you, Sam," I say softly. "I've always wanted you. You're the only thing I've ever known I've wanted, beyond all doubt. You're the only thing I've ever wanted just for me."

It's a relief to say the words. I've held them inside me for so long, knowing that if I said them aloud to anyone, no one would understand.

But Sam understands. Finally.

His eyes take in every inch of my face.

"I want you, too," he says.

"Let's go out tonight," Sam says, driving back to Paso. I sit in the passenger seat of his car with my shoes off and my feet on the dash, which he's assured me is fine with him.

As we weave out of the mountains of the Coast Ranges, our little adventure for the day, the pink light fades on the other side of my eyelids and with my other senses, I take in the feel of Sam in the seat next to me, the smell of the trees, the wind whipping through my hair.

Sam wraps his warm fingers around mine to pull my attention back to him. I look to him.

"We should go out tonight," he repeats.

Or we could keep driving, I think.

We could take this highway to the next and end up in Washington or wherever we wanted. We could never look back. We could skip making any hard decisions and just go.

But I recognize that urge for what it is, as well as this day trip I suggested. It's my tendency to wander, to try to find myself through movement. But I cannot get lost. I must face these choices and make the right one this time.

"Sure," I say with a smile. Sam's face glows blue in the light of the dash, and he's still breathtaking.

"What do you want to do?" he asks.

My mind goes to Kelly and how she hasn't called since we got back from Los Angeles.

"I don't know," I say.

When we get back to the house, plans still undecided, Sam and I split off to change. I enter the kitchen and Kelly is sitting at the dining room table alone. She watches her fingers as she picks at her cuticle. She looks better, a little more color in her cheeks than when I saw her last.

I close the door and let the stillness settle.

"Where are Mom and Dad?" I ask.

"In the living room," she says. "We finished dinner half an hour ago."

"Oh," I say. "I'm sorry I missed it. I didn't realize you were here."

"That's okay." Kelly sighs and pushes herself out of her chair. She leans against the counter across from me and crosses her arms protectively. She stares at the toe of her shoe, which she jiggles back and forth. "I got a phone call today," she says.

"From who?"

"The bank."

"The bank," I repeat.

"Turns out," she says, "my mom has been stashing money away for the last ten years."

I stand up straighter.

"What do you mean?"

Kelly drops her arms, lowers her shield. "Her disability checks were the one thing she always took care of. She had it set up to automatically deposit into our account. Apparently, some of it was automatically deposited into a savings account I knew nothing about."

I raise my eyebrows. "Well, how much money is in there?"

"Ten thousand dollars."

"Ten thousand dollars?" I shout.

Kelly laughs, nods.

"That's...unbelievable."

"I know. I don't know whether to be mad at her or grateful. We certainly could have used the money all these years. But that hundred dollars a month probably wouldn't have made enough difference anyway."

"It could certainly make a difference now. Do you think it will be enough to save the house?"

She nods, her eyes bright.

We stand there for a moment, stunned by the news. I don't know if she's going to say anything about what happened the other day. She seems to have realized she doesn't need to. If she was upset that the message from her mother seemed to be for me, this money proves that Kelly is the one Shannon always believed in.

That's if we decide to believe any of it at all.

"We should celebrate," I say.

"Celebrate how?"

"I don't know... Something spontaneous."

It's another item on our bucket list—the one I urged Kelly to add.

"Let's get dressed up and see where the night takes us."

Kelly laughs. "Okay."

I remember Sam is waiting for me. I bite my lip.

"What?" Kelly asks.

"Sam asked me out on a date tonight."

She raises her eyebrows. "A date?"

"I'll tell him I can't," I say, grabbing for the door handle. "You're more important. He'll understand."

"Mal." Kelly reaches out to stop me. She frowns. "You are just as important."

"But Sam—"

"Makes you happy," she says. "And you make me happy."

Our relationship really is different. I have to keep reminding myself. "What are you saying?" I ask.

"Bring him with us. Then everyone's happy."

"Are you sure?" I ask.

Kelly motions for me to go upstairs and change.

"I'm sure," she says.

The night takes us to The Drunken Pub. It's the perfect first stop for the night. Kelly drives, and seeing Sam sitting in the back of a five-hundred-dollar car in a suit that probably costs four times as much is heartwarming. He's getting used to our little country life and it looks good on him. When we arrive, I make a big show of adjusting his shirt and brushing him off, to which he laughs and nudges me away. Kelly catches the exchange and gives me a happy grin.

It makes me blush, her seeing me like this. This side of me still so new and raw that I'm struggling to accept it myself. I feel naked with my joy on display, but I'm done hiding from myself. I take Sam's hand and he smiles.

The bar is as packed and noisy as expected, half the town crammed inside. At The Drunken Pub, every night is Friday night.

I spot Tyler behind the bar and in spite of my resolution, my hand slips from Sam's.

"I'll grab us a table," Kelly says over the noise.

"I'll get drinks," I respond.

One of the vineyard owners waves Sam down. Sam nods his exit and, ever polite, weaves through the crowd to catch up with him.

"Well, hello there," Tyler says when I reach the bar, leaning over it to hear him. "What's a nice young lady like you doing at a bar on a Wednesday night?"

I nod toward Kelly and they exchange a wave.

"What can I get ya?" he asks.

"Chicken wings," I say. "Two orders."

"Nothing to drink?"

"We're trying to behave."

"You got it."

My *thanks* is interrupted by a loud screech that fills the room. Silence falls and all the TVs go black. I glance around, looking for the source of the noise. Three loud taps echo over the speaker system and then, into a microphone someone says, "Welcome to karaoke night at The Drunken Pub!"

The room explodes with cheers and clapping. I can't believe my luck. I grin and make my way back to Kelly, slamming my palms onto the table where she's sitting.

"Oh, you wanted spontaneous," I say.

Her eyes melt closed in surrender but her grin gives her away.

Kelly, Sam, and I huddle over the wings and the song list, giving each other comical suggestions and laughing as we imagine each other standing in front of a room full of people belting out Britney Spears lyrics. Joe, the owner, sets the tone for the evening with Rod Stewart's "Da Ya Think I'm Sexy?". Kelly and I grab onto each other as we try to stifle our giggling.

Danny and Bobby, the local jokesters, do a delightfully colorful rendition of Blake Shelton's "Some Beach." Sam shocks us by encouraging them with whistles and backup lyrics, his suit jacket slung over the back of his seat and an extra button of his shirt undone to cool himself. I fail to keep my eyes away from those extra inches of skin. Hours pass and, woozy from heat and laughter, I almost forget none of us have had a sip of alcohol. We're having too much fun just being in each other's company.

We forget all about our other pursuits for the night, too en-

JAMIE RAINTREE

thralled by watching our favorite community members shedding their inhibitions.

Finally, Kelly's name is called. I drum the table and whoop as she makes her way to the dark corner next to the karaoke machine, covering half her face with her hand the entire way. I call out louder when the opening piano notes ring out and Kelly tentatively sings the first lines of "Before He Cheats" by Carrie Underwood. The crowd goes wild, knowing what's coming, and the further she gets into the song, the more Kelly loses herself in it.

I wonder if the song choice is a coincidence and what exactly happened with Kyle the other night, but I doubt I'll ever know. There are things about this new Kelly that I'll never get to see and that's okay. There are things about me she'll never fully understand either. We're not kids anymore. We've matured in the last ten years and I'm realizing my relationships have to mature, too.

Sam whoops when Kelly moves into the hook. I look over at him, softened and enchanted by this man I'll probably never fully understand either. The question is whether our relationship is mature enough now to withstand that. Catching me looking, he slides his hand to my thigh underneath the table, weaving his fingers into mine.

The moment is broken when Kelly falls back into her chair, breathless and glowing.

"I can't believe I just did that," she says.

"I can't either," I laugh. "Who are you and what have you done with my best friend?"

My name is called out and my stomach flips over. I give Sam and Kelly a final wary glance and make my way to the microphone.

"Ready?" the MC asks. I take a breath and give a swift nod.

The snare drum hits and then the piano begins, slowing the

pace with a song I've always loved: "I Can't Make You Love Me" by Bonnie Raitt. My body melts into the familiar beat and I relax a little, closing my eyes to forget about everyone staring at me. This is my bucket list item and I'm going to get the most out of it. I'm learning to be spontaneous again. I'm learning to trust myself again.

As I sing the first line about turning down the lights, I acknowledge that I've had the lights turned down on my life. It's been easier that way, hiding in the dark. Focusing on Kelly, being distracted by Sam, avoiding my boss so I wouldn't have to look inside myself and be honest about what I want. As long as I don't have the answers, I don't have to make any decisions and I can live in this space of in-between where I don't commit to the wrong path. In doing so, I haven't committed to the right one either. I'm afraid of disappointing anyone but I've been disappointing myself and that's the biggest betrayal.

I sing about turning down the voices inside my head so I can hold on to the hope that I can have what I want without hurting anyone, without leaving anyone behind. So I can allow myself to fall—in love and out of this false sense of safety. Life isn't safe. Things will break. They will fall apart. Nothing is guaranteed.

And when I sing the chorus, I wonder if it's myself I'm singing to. I've been waiting for someone to come along who would love me—as a girlfriend, as a friend—but there are so many things I don't love about myself. I'm so afraid of making a single mistake. Could I find a way to love myself in spite of them, the way I used to? Could I be brave once again?

When I sing about closing my eyes, mine are wide-open and I catch sight of Sam watching me. I'm transported back to our last summer together. So many times I tried to convince myself that Sam felt something more for me, but then the morning would come and he would be a completely different person. I should have been strong enough to let him go, to accept that he could never feel about me the way I felt about him. But I was too young to recognize a losing battle.

The look in his eyes now, the way he seems to remember it, too—regret it, even—I wonder, if I do take the chance, will I always be waiting for morning? Will I always wonder when he'll disappear again?

If I follow his path, disappearing into my love for Sam, will I ever learn to love myself?

Movement from behind the bar catches my attention. Tyler's jaw is tight as I finish the last few lines, his entire body pointed toward our table. Toward Sam.

When the final note of the song dies out, the bar sounds resume and shatter the moment. No one seems to notice the effect the song has had on my heart. I shove the microphone into the MC's hand and make my way back to the table, people clapping and patting me on the back the entire way.

I sit down next to Sam. Kelly has gone off to socialize. I spot her in a dark corner with someone we went to high school with, smoking a cigarette.

Sam places his hand on the small of my back.

"I didn't know you could sing," he says. I put on a smile, suddenly uneasy. "I'm feeling kind of tired. Want to get out of here?"

I glance back at Kelly with a frown. "I think that would be best."

"Have a good night," Sam tells Kelly as he gets out of the car. I hold the door for him so he can climb out of the back seat. None of us seems to be disappointed in ending the night early, having gotten as much adventure as we could handle.

"You, too," Kelly says, putting the car in Reverse.

Before she can leave, I walk around to the other side and lean into Kelly's open window. I give her a kiss on the cheek and say into her ear, "Thanks for being open." When she furrows her brow questioningly, I nod toward Sam.

She doesn't say anything, but gives me a knowing smile.

I step back, and Sam and I wait for her to pull down the drive before he holds a hand out to me. I take it.

"Thanks for letting Kelly come tonight," I say. My words all but disappear into the quiet.

"I'm glad to finally get to know her better," he says. "I'm glad she's finally been willing to get to know me."

"Me, too," I say.

We reach the bottom of the porch and I stop to say good-night. Inside, all the lights are off though it's not even midnight. My parents are already in bed but I'm far from sleep, too restless to sit alone in my room, debating whether or not it's time to pack my bags, and where I should take them to.

My eyes and Sam's meet, both of us thinking the same thing. Ending the night at the guest house is our tradition. Without a word, I intertwine my fingers in his and allow him to guide me.

The door is already unlocked. Sam holds it open for me and I walk into the cool space. It's so dark with the porch light off that I can't find the light switch as I fumble for it. When the door closes, I can see nothing but I feel Sam's hands on my hips. He pulls me away from the switch and presses me against the wall next to the door, pushing himself against me. My other senses are heightened, and I feel his breath on my face like a fiery energy, sparking and crackling over my skin.

There's a long pause where both of us knows what's about to happen and neither one of us seems to believe it. I've compared every man I've ever met, ever dated, ever slept with to Sam with only daydreams to compare it to. So many nights I've thought about having his hands on my hips, in my hair.

And now I'm in the guest house with Sam again, in the middle of the night, and this time, I'm not a girl. Neither one of us is questioning how we feel about each other. There's absolutely nothing between us, not even Sam's walls.

His lips meet mine, strong and certain. I place my hands against his chest and run them up over his shoulders, the way I've longed to do so many times, touching him like I was never brave enough to do before. His hands curl around my back, cradling me in his arms and brushing his lips against mine until I'm weak, hardly able to comprehend that this breathtaking man wants to be with me.

Just as quickly, he pulls away and disappears into the darkness.

I wait, trembling, searching. A moment later, light peeks into the room as Sam pulls aside just enough of the curtain to allow moonlight to spill over the white bedding. Then he comes and takes me by the hand, guiding me into its glow.

Standing before him, I wait for him to kiss me again. He gazes into my eyes, speaking to me without words. He's never been good at telling me how he feels but in my heart, I know. I let my eyes communicate to him the three words I still can't quite bring myself to say. We draw the moment out. We've both waited too long to allow this night to be over too quickly.

With my hands shaking, I reach up and unbutton Sam's shirt, one at a time. I untuck it and then reach beneath, running my hands over his bare stomach, his taut skin. He pulls my shirt over my head, his thumbs tracing the curves of my body as he does, and then drops the shirt to the floor. His expression is more serious than I've ever seen it, and I wonder if he's fantasized about this, too.

He comes closer to me, wrapping his arms around me to unhook my bra. He pulls it away until only my sensitive skin is pressed against his warm body. I look up at him and the hunger in his eyes tells me there's no more waiting.

We both stop running.

TWENTY-SIX

THEN

*K*elly walked out of the party, into the thickness of night, and I raced after her.

The music faded into the background, the crunching of our shoes on the gravel and our heavy breathing replacing it. I didn't know where to begin.

"Did you really think I wasn't going to find out?" she spat out over her shoulder.

"I didn't—" I started to say, though I didn't know how I planned to finish the sentence. She didn't wait to find out.

"I mean, really? In a town as small as this? And you had a news crew here, for God's sake. Do you have any idea how insulting that is?"

I could hardly keep up with her angry flight toward her car. I panted in exhaustion, and in pain from the damn heels.

"You found out about it on the news?"

She stopped then, and I nearly slammed into her.

"No," she said, her eyes glowing as she glared at me. "Mallory, I practically live at the vineyard. I've known about it the whole time."

Her words were a punch to the gut and I found myself too breathless to respond. She had been testing our friendship and I'd failed.

"You were so careful not to mention it," she went on. "I was too blown away that you could actually betray me so completely to confront you about it, but I held on to a very little amount of faith that you would get your head out of your ass before the actual day of the party. All the way up to the time it was supposed to start, I waited for your call. I had Jeff on standby to take over my shift so I could be here."

She choked over the words, embarrassed by the vulnerability of them. She covered her face and wobbled like she would fall over.

I reached to catch her fragile body in my arms, shame washing over me like a hurricane. I had done this to the person I loved. "I'm so sorry," I cried into hair as she sobbed against my shoulder.

For a long few minutes, neither of us could catch our breaths enough to speak. Then, finally, Kelly stood tall and looked me in the eyes like she was about to say the most important thing she'd ever said in her life. And she did.

"My mom is in the hospital, Mallory."

"What?" I choked out.

"I got a call but it wasn't from you, it was from the EMTs who picked her up off the floor…" She could barely get the words out, and I realized why she was so distraught. "I've been calling you for hours but you couldn't answer because you were too busy in his arms. I've been trying to tell you all summer how much worse she's gotten but you're so caught up in your own world that you can't see anything else."

She started walking again, leaving me dazed and dizzy with questions.

"Is she okay?" I called after her.

"I hope he's worth it," she called back.

"Can I come with you?" I tripped over my own feet as I stumbled after her. She turned on me.

"It's too late for that, Mallory," she cried. "You don't get it. It's not just that you weren't there when I needed you most. It's that your family is my family, too. At least I thought they were, and you know how much that has meant to me. You know how much I've needed that. This place, with you, is the only place I've ever felt safe. Or loved the way someone is supposed to be loved. And you cut me out on the most important night of your lives."

I covered my mouth to stop the sob rising in my throat. Tears spilled onto my cheeks.

"I don't even recognize you anymore." She motioned to my outfit, the meticulously smoothed style of my hair, the extra makeup, the heels.

I felt assaulted by her words, mostly because they were true. They broke me in a way I couldn't fully comprehend in that moment. All I knew was that I felt an overwhelming sense of not being enough. No matter how dressed up and put together I was, Sam still couldn't show his affection for me in public. No matter how much I tried to be who Kelly needed me to be, my own selfishness got in the way at every turn. And no matter how much I tried to follow my own heart, it always led me away from the people I loved. This summer I'd made the wrong decision at every turn.

"These were our last few weeks together," Kelly said, "and you gave them away to someone you don't even know and probably never will. And you and I will never be these people again. We'll never be who we are to each other right now. If time wasn't already going to make that true, you just guaranteed it."

"What do you mean, our last few weeks together?" I asked.

A car drove by, the headlights flashing in our faces. Kelly's was shiny with tears, distorted almost beyond recognition with anger, and hurt, and grief.

"Come on, Mallory," she said. "I was never going to Columbia and we both know it. I can't leave my mom here alone. She can't even cook a meal for herself."

"But you—"

"I knew you wouldn't go if you didn't think I was going with you."

"I wouldn't," I was quick to say. "I don't want to."

"You have to, Mallory," she cries at me. "You have so much potential, it's sickening. You can't spend the rest of your life in this small town for me. Not for me, and sure as hell not for *him*. I won't let you. You have the chance to make something of yourself. It would be selfish of you to throw it away when I…"

She looked away, hiding more tears. I tried to go to her but she stepped farther away.

"That isn't fair," I hissed. "This is your dream."

"Yeah, well, I guess you're not the only one who lives in an imaginary world."

She walked away then, the broken pieces of my heart in her hands.

"But hey," she said as she unlocked her car, "once you get settled in New York, call me if you ever find the Mallory I used to know."

I stood, my mind reeling, as she got in and sped past me, like we'd never known each other. Like we never would again.

When the dust cloud disappeared behind her, I went into the house, ran up to my room, and cried into my pillow. I sobbed until my muscles ached, Kelly's words playing over and over again in my head. In one moment, my entire future had shifted and it would never be the same. It couldn't be.

Once I calmed down, I did the first thing I could think of: I went to Sam. If Kelly wasn't going to Columbia, I was going hiking with Sam. And never in my life had I wanted to escape so badly. I needed to not feel the pain ripping at my insides. I needed to know I hadn't thrown away my friendship with Kelly for nothing.

There was a soft light emanating from the French doors of the guest house and a shadow moving inside.

I banged on the door, my breathing rapid and my heart pounding. Everything rode on the moment when I would ask Sam to be honest with me, when I would ask him to love me. I'd avoided the question all summer but now that I'd decided, I couldn't hold it back any longer.

The door cracked open, and Sam appeared in the cautious space. His dress shirt was unbuttoned and hanging open, revealing his undershirt. His feet were bare and his hair messy and I could picture coming home to this vision every night for the rest of my life.

"Is everything okay?" he asked, his face pinched in concern.

"No," I gasped, no longer able to hide my true feelings, my pain, my desire.

"Things didn't go well with Kelly?" he asked.

I shook my head and waited for him to move aside to let me in.

But he didn't.

There was an awkward pause between us.

"Can I come in?" I asked.

He had always been the one to invite me inside at night, sometimes just shy of begging me to join him, but this time, the door stayed firmly between us and he looked down at his feet, unable to face me.

"I don't think that's a good idea," he said.

All the air was pulled from my lungs. "Why not?"

"Mallory..." he beseeched me. "You know this could never happen. I live in Washington. I work for your dad. And you're young. You have so much life ahead of you. I don't want to hold you back from that."

My chest constricted, and my vision swam. My last possibility was disintegrating before my eyes.

"But what about hiking?" I asked, my voice feeble. I sounded pathetic, I knew, but I was desperate. If I didn't have Kelly and I didn't have Sam, I had nothing.

Sam's eyes softened, sympathy in them.

"I never said we would go *together*," he stated, as unaffected as ever. "But you should go. You've spent your whole life on this vineyard and there's so much more out there."

I ran through every conversation we'd ever had in my head. Had I really made it all up?

No, I may have been naive but I wasn't stupid. He may not have said we'd go hiking together but it was implied in every conversation, every touch, every kiss. And I'd believed him.

"Screw you," I said, my anger erasing all my efforts to be the perfect woman for him. I didn't care anymore. I couldn't even remember why I'd wanted him in the first place. He was arrogant and condescending and a hypocrite. "You've been all over the world and you can't see a good thing when it's standing right in front of you."

I stormed off, never looking back. I held back my tears as I stumbled up the dark stairs and barely made it back into my bed before I cried myself to sleep.

When I woke up the next day, Sam was gone.

TWENTY-SEVEN

NOW

I wake up the next morning with Sam's arm draped over me. His body is wrapped around mine, his chest against my back, his chin tucked into my shoulder. With my eyes still closed, I recall the night before.

The depth of his kisses.

His soul reaching out to mine.

The sheen of sweat between our bodies.

There wasn't a single drop of alcohol to blame it on. It was just the two us and everything we ever wanted from each other.

I open my eyes and marvel at his strong, smooth forearm, the details of his hand, each of his fingernails. I trace them with my lips, using all of my senses to take in every inch of this body I thought I'd never get to touch.

When my mouth reaches his palm, Sam stirs.

"Good morning," I say softly.

"Indeed it is," he says.

I roll over to face him and curl myself into him, placing my ear against his chest. I'm all too aware of my nakedness. It's still new to me, being close to a man. I'm not used to revealing myself.

Sam twists his legs into mine to pulls me closer. He kisses the top of my head.

"Last night was perfect," he says. "This is perfect."

I agree.

We don't rush the morning after, breaking the pattern of emotional turbulence and second-guessing. Sam seems to sense I could use the reassurance and he holds me close, running his fingers over the peaks and valleys of my body.

Eventually, I lock myself in the bathroom and, embarrassed, pee in the house that feels much smaller all of a sudden. I dress in my clothes from last night and we share a cup of coffee at the dining table, not wanting to go outside or open the doors on this fragile moment. We talk about our work and our plans for the day and we savor this time for as long as possible.

But when I see him eyeing his stacks of paperwork, I know we both have to get back to real life. We have to trust that what we've shared *is* real life, not a caught-up-in-the-moment thing. He walks me to the door and I give him a long, final kiss.

"You'll be here later?" I ask him, fingering the collar of his shirt.

"Mallory." He grabs my fidgety hand. "I'll be here," he says, and I believe him.

Thankfully, no one sees me leave the guest house and I'm grateful not to be spotted doing the walk of shame. I don't want anything to break the spell I'm under. This night means so much more than a one-night stand or the fulfillment of

Sam's and my long-held desires. No one else can understand that the way we do.

After my shower, as I'm drying my hair, I hear a car pull into the parking lot. I pull back the curtains to see if it's Kelly. It isn't and I don't think much of the unfamiliar car—we're used to customers, suppliers, and employees coming and going.

A few minutes later, though, as I'm getting dressed, I hear Mom's laughter and my curiosity draws me to discover who our guest is. I pull my shoes on and go outside.

As I draw close, I overhear Mom's conversation with a woman who looks to be in her midthirties, with silky, stick-straight brown hair and a wide stance. She holds a little blonde girl on her hip—three or four years old, maybe. Her mother struggles to wrangle the many layers of the white skirt she's wearing, but the woman hardly notices her own battle, as caught up as she is in her conversation with my mom. I keep a respectful distance.

"Did your dining room table come in?" my mom asks her.

"It did!" the woman says. "Do you want to see a picture?"

"Of course!"

She sets her daughter on the ground to pull her cell out of her back pocket. She and Mom lean over it to inspect the picture while the little girl meanders over to me with a curious grin. She's the only one who seems to have noticed my presence. I give her a small smile, letting her know it's okay to approach.

"Your hair is pretty," she says in her elfin voice.

"Thank you," I say, trying not to laugh. "I like your dress."

"It's a princess dress," she declares.

"I can see that."

"Oh, Aubrey," the woman says. "Don't bother the nice lady."

Mom sees me standing there and reaches for me.

"Actually, this is perfect," she says. "Now you can meet my daughter."

She motions me over. Aubrey runs to my mom and leaps at her. Mom catches her and swings her around, finally landing Aubrey on her hip like it's a well-rehearsed routine. We must have had a similar routine when I was that age but I don't remember it.

"Aubrey," Mom says, "this is my daughter, Mallory."

"She's too grown-up to be a daughter," Aubrey says.

We all laugh.

"Even daughters grow up, believe it or not."

"Hi. I'm Chelsea," the woman says. She reaches for my hand and I shake it. "I feel like I know you already. Your mom talks about you so much."

"She does?" I ask.

She must see the wariness in my expression because she clarifies.

"I'm a client of your mom's," she says. "Well, not your mom's but the office. I've just spent more time with her than the lawyers I pay hundreds of dollars an hour."

She laughs and Mom shrugs apologetically.

"Worth every penny," Chelsea assures, pinching her daughter's cheek. Being that my mom is in divorce and family law, I can imagine how Mom helped Chelsea. Judging by her naked ring finger and her smile, it seems things went her way.

"Her case is the big one we just closed," Mom tells me and I nod.

Unexpectedly, tears begin filling Chelsea's eyes and she waves at her face in an attempt to dry them. Mom frowns and reaches out for her.

"I'm sorry," Chelsea says. "I promised myself I wasn't going to do this. You've seen me cry too many times already."

"Hey," Mom says gently, running her hand over Chelsea's shoulder. "What have I said?"

"Never apologize for my feelings," Chelsea says. "I know. I just… I don't want this visit to be about me."

Chelsea opens her car door and leans in for something. Mom purses her lips at me in sympathy and bewilderment.

I can go, I mouth, but Mom shakes her head.

Chelsea turns back and hands Mom a box wrapped in green paper with large shiny polka dots and a bow.

"What's this?" Mom asks. She lowers Aubrey to the ground and Aubrey immediately latches herself onto her mother's leg.

"I heard about what happened at the office and I was shocked," Chelsea says. "After two years of seeing you every week, I was actually sad to think I wouldn't get to come into the office anymore, as crazy as that sounds. And now, with the office closed, I can't even drop by to say hi. But I wanted to give you a gift even before I knew. Just to show my gratitude for all you've done to make sure I get to be the one to raise my little girl."

Mom exhales loudly and I think she's going to cry, too. She unwraps the gift and I take the paper from her hands. When she lifts the lid on the box, she peers inside and gasps. I lean forward to catch a glimpse of it but I can't make it out. I take the lid from her and Mom draws the statuette out of the brown paper it's wrapped in. She holds it up so we can all admire it.

It's a figure of a woman in a blue skirt, sitting with her ankles crossed. Standing in the space between her knees is a girl about Aubrey's age, with flowing brown hair to match her mother's and a pink dress. The mother's ear is close to the little girl's heart, both of them with their eyes closed. They wear peaceful smiles as if time has stopped just for them and there is nowhere else in the world they would rather be but next to each other.

"I know how much your daughter means to you," Chelsea says, smiling at me. "And I wanted to make sure you never forgot how grateful I am for what you've done for our family."

Chelsea runs her hand over Aubrey's hair and there's no mistaking the unending love she feels for her daughter. I recognize it in the way my mom looks at me.

Mom can't contain herself any longer. Tears slide down her cheeks and she reaches for Chelsea, wrapping her in a hug. I hear Mom whisper, "Thank you," in her ear and in that moment, I fully understand what Mom was talking about when she said that one day I would want to feel like my work had meant something.

No client at my firm has ever looked at me like that. I've never spent more time with a client than a perfunctory meeting to get the most necessary information about their business. And before now, as passionate as I am about everything else in my life, I've never even thought to get to know them better.

Because as good as I may be at creating marketing campaigns and writing brochure copy, that's not where my heart is. And as long as my heart isn't in it, my work will never mean more to me than a title on a business card.

My mom turns to me with watery eyes and rosy cheeks, and she pulls me into a hug.

"Being your mom is the best job I've ever had," she says and I allow myself to feel every word of it, every emotion of it. I feel her heart pressed against mine, and that long, aching sense of loneliness I haven't been able to shake inexplicably drifts away.

This is what Kelly meant by needing relationships. It's not just about parents or boyfriends or friends. It's about giving a little bit of myself to everyone I meet and allowing them to give a little bit of themselves in return. Chelsea and my mom may never see each other again, but they've made an impact on each other's lives that they'll never forget. If I create those kinds of connections, I'll never be lonely a day in my life.

After Chelsea leaves, Mom and I walk back to the house together.

"Can you help me with something?" I ask her, fumbling with the wrapping paper. She laughs and takes it from me.

"Of course," she says. "Anything. What do you need?"

When I tell Mom my plan, she knows exactly who to call. I get on the phone with the woman, a client of the firm's, and as I tell her what I want to do, she shares her story with me and cries and agrees immediately. We make plans to meet in an hour.

Before I head out the door, Mom stops me and looks at me. She doesn't say anything, just stares at me with glistening pride in her eyes.

"I love you, too," I say, laughing through my discomfort.

No matter how old I get, I'll always be their child. And while it can be awkward at times to be seen through those eyes, there's also a steadiness in it.

"Okay, I have to go," I say, laughing again.

"Fine," she says, releasing me. "Go. Have fun. I love you."

"Thank you," I call to her as I bound out the back door.

When I arrive on Kelly's doorstep, she's surprised to see me. She must have just gotten home from work because she smells like dark roast and sugar. Her braid is limp, loose strands falling around her face.

"What's up?" she asks. "Did we have plans?"

"We do now," I tell her.

"I don't suppose you're going to tell me what these plans are?"

I grin and shake my head.

"You do know we already crossed the spontaneous item off our bucket list, right?" she asks. "We crossed them all off."

"This isn't spontaneous," I tell her.

"Oh, now I'm even more worried," she says, laughing. She nods me inside and disappears into the house. "I'll change."

"Wear something comfortable," I call after her as I close the door behind me.

I step inside hesitantly. The house has always been dim, having very few windows, but it's even darker without Shannon's presence here. It's even more still without the buzz of her favorite shows in the background. I've been very aware of Shannon's passing, but being back in her space makes it more real, and the sadness washes over me anew.

As I round the corner into the living room, I gasp. The room is empty. The white couch where Shannon used to sit is gone, as is the TV across from it. End tables, bookshelves, chairs—all gone. All that's left are the distinct outlines in the carpet where the furniture sat, scraps of paper and sunflower-seed shells and staples littering the floor.

When I look to Kelly for explanation, she's leaning against her bedroom door frame, dressed in yoga pants, her arms crossed. Her expression is blank.

"What happened?" I asked.

"Donated it," she says simply. "I couldn't keep walking past it. This house will never be the same without her here. No point in keeping all those reminders. I haven't gone in her room yet," she adds, nodding across the living room to the opposite door.

I step toward her and she pushes off the door frame, meeting me in the middle of the room. We wrap our arms around each other and Kelly dissolves into sobs that rack her body. She squeezes me tightly and I hold her closer, leaving tears on her shoulder too.

"Is it ever going to get easier?" she asks me.

"I don't know," I whisper. "I don't know."

Kelly lets me go to grab tissues from the bathroom. When she returns, we dry our tears and look around the room, both of us remembering Shannon and this life she lived. It may not have been a big life, but she made an imprint on Kelly's life, and mine. My parents, too, having shared her daughter with us, and entrusting her to us when she left. Every impact makes a ripple. We never know how far it will reach.

"There's someone I want you to meet," I say.

Kelly nods, wiping her nose. "I'm ready," she says.

I wait for Kelly in my rental car while she locks up, and then we head toward the highway. To shake off the somber mood, I roll down the windows and turn up some country music. Kelly sticks her head out the window, letting the wind revive her, and we sing along to every word of "Cowboy Take Me Away."

"There's something different about you today," she says over the music.

I shake my head, but can't help my involuntary smile.

"Uh-huh," she says, knowing the exact reason why, as only a best friend could.

We turn off the freeway into downtown, home to our city's many festivals, hot springs, and historic sites. This area, at least, hasn't changed much. So many of my childhood memories have been made here, running through grass and vendor booths, dancing to live music.

"Where are you taking me?" Kelly asks.

"You'll see," I say.

I park on the south side of Downtown City Park and cut the engine. Kelly turns to me.

"You're making me nervous," she says.

"It's going to be great. I promise," I say. I nod her forward and we both get out of the car.

The sun has started to set and a cool breeze rustles through the trees. Kelly walks alongside me and I spot the woman we're here to meet underneath the gazebo.

As we approach, Kelly whispers, "Do you know this woman?"

Anna must be one of the few people Kelly doesn't serve coffee to.

"We're about to," I say, just as mom's client spots us and smiles nervously.

Kelly and I step into the gazebo and I reach out to take the woman's hand. She's in her late forties, with a puff of wavy brown hair and kind chocolate eyes.

"You must be Anna," I say. "I'm Mallory. And this is Kelly. The one I was telling you about."

Kelly and Anna shake hands, both of them standoffish.

"I'm sorry," Kelly says. "Mal has been keeping me out of the loop. I'm not really sure what we're doing here."

I pull the bucket list out of my back pocket and hold it out to Kelly. She looks at it in confusion, grabbing for her own back pocket, where she's been carrying the list since I gave it to her.

"I thought…"

"Take it," I say.

"But we finished it."

She takes the pink paper and unfolds it, reading the item I added to the list while she was locking her front door. It's the only thing on the list in my handwriting with a big unchecked box next to it.

"'Help someone in need.'"

She looks up questioningly, at me and then at Anna.

"Is there something I can help you with?" Kelly asks, no further explanation needed. Because that's Kelly's heart. All she ever wants to do is to help others. That's why a degree in psychology has been her life goal.

Anna smiles, tears filling her eyes, and nods.

We sit on a bench nearby and Anna explains how she recently went through a divorce. She tells Kelly that she was married for seven years to a man who was overly critical. It started with small things—the way she folded his shirts or the meals she prepared. Over time, his criticism escalated to bigger things, like the way she talked and how she acted around their friends. Their biggest point of contention, however, was Anna's weight, which had gone up in direct proportion to how often her husband's cutting comments increased her stress and anxiety levels. And the bigger Anna got, the more he verbally and emotionally abused her.

"I looked in the mirror one day," she tells us, "and I didn't recognize myself. Not only because of the weight, but because I had lost my will to keep living."

Anna's voice catches. Kelly's face is red, too, Anna's story hitting close to home. But she doesn't cry. She gathers her strength to be there for someone else in a way she's never been able to do for herself. It's what she's been missing since Shannon's death, and what neither of us had realized until now is not Kelly's weakness, but her biggest strength. Taking care of her mom kept her in Paso not only because Shannon needed her, but also because Kelly needed to be of service. It feeds her the way riding feeds me. It gives her life meaning.

"That realization terrified me," Anna says. "I knew right then that if I didn't leave, I would give up completely. On life, and on myself. That's when I met Elizabeth. She was such a friend to me through the divorce proceedings, but since everything was finalized, I've been feeling a little lost. I was so grateful to hear from her and Mallory today."

I smile encouragingly. Kelly nods.

"What can I do to help?" Kelly asks, her voice concerned but calm.

"Anna's been looking for a walking partner," I tell Kelly. "She wants to get healthy again. For herself, and for her baby."

Kelly's eyes widen, and for the first time, I see the crack in her professional demeanor. She looks to me, then to Anna. Anna nods and places her hand on her belly.

"Five months," Anna says. "And before she gets here, I'd really like to find myself again. I want to be good mom to my daughter. I want to be healthy for her."

This is too much for Kelly—the one thing she always wanted from her own mom. Her tears spill over.

"I'm sorry," Kelly says, trying to keep it together. "My mom…"

Kelly covers her eyes and we give her space to gather herself. I put my hand on her back, holding her up so she can hold up Anna. When her breathing steadies, she wipes her eyes and asks, "When do you want to start?"

"Whenever you're ready," Anna says.

"How about now?" I suggest, motioning to the park.

Kelly laughs. "You really did think of everything, didn't you?"

"I promised you we'd finish the bucket list," I say. Quietly, I add, "I wanted you to know, you don't have to leave to live your dream. There are people who could use your help here. If that's what you want."

Kelly smiles and squeezes my knee in a gesture of thanks. *I love you*, she mouths and my heart overflows.

Kelly turns back to Anna and asks, "Are you up for it?"

"If you're willing," Anna says with a laugh, acknowledging the unusual circumstances of their meeting.

"Absolutely," Kelly says. "I would be honored."

"How often will we get to do this when you come to Washington?" Sam asks me in bed late that afternoon. My head rests on his arm, my nose grazing the side of his neck, the hint of cologne making my heart skip a beat.

"That depends on how often you behave yourself," I say, as if I would ever deny him.

"Damn," he says. "That's never going to work."

I laugh and scoot up so that we're face-to-face. His brown eyes sparkle at me. The wall air-conditioning unit kicks on with its monotone hum but it does little to dry the sweat wherever our skin meets. We hardly notice.

"You really want that? For me to move to Washington?" I ask casually, as if I haven't been thinking about it in every spare moment. Since talking with Kelly and Anna, I haven't been able to stop asking myself where my dream lives.

"Of course I do."

"What if things don't work out between us?" I ask.

"What if they do?" He kisses me playfully.

I allow it for a moment, this naive optimism, but then I pull back. Sam and I have a long history of not being on the same page, and I can't uproot my entire life under any misconceptions.

"Sam, I need you to be serious for a minute. It's not like you're asking me to move in. You're not making any commitment to me here. I'd be stupid to jump into this with my eyes closed."

Sam's smile falters. "I know."

"I know moving in together would be a big leap. I'm not even ready for that. But if I moved to Washington, it would be for you. There's nothing else for me there. You have to know that."

"That's not true," he says. "You'll have a job."

"I won't have my parents. I won't have Kelly. If I were to leave New York, why wouldn't I come back here?"

Sam traces his finger along the side of my face, brushing my hair behind my ear.

"You wouldn't have a job," he says and I know he's right, though his tone is regretful. This town isn't big enough to sustain a marketing firm, or much else that isn't related to tourism or wine. "I've already told Todd how amazing you are. Believe me, the job is yours."

I'm less certain about taking a job I haven't interviewed for and know almost nothing about. But marketing is marketing, I suppose. And Todd must have an idea of how competitive he would need to be to convince me to move.

"What if it isn't right for me?" I ask.

"You're going to love it there," he says. "I promise. Imagine it. We could go out to dinner every night. Walk along the bay. Do that hike we talked about. Go to the theater."

"You like the theater?" I ask. But it's Sam. "Of course you like the theater."

"Go to the farmers market on Saturdays," he says, ignoring my teasing. "Whatever we want. Whenever we want."

I exhale, trying to imagine it. Sam could show me how he lives, share his passions, let me into his world. That was all I ever wanted from him, to get just a peek behind the facade, and now he's offering to show me everything.

"We could look into shipping Midnight out. Boarding her somewhere close. Somewhere you could ride her whenever you want."

He's saying all the right things, but something in my gut is still unsure.

"What if I don't want the job?" I ask. I don't know how Sam will take the idea or how much of what he finds attractive about me is attached to me living a similar lifestyle to his. But if I'm going to leave New York, I could get out of marketing, try something new.

"Then we'll find you a job at another firm."

Sam shrugs, unfazed. In his mind, there are no obstacles, only challenges to be overcome.

"No. I mean…what if I don't want to do marketing anymore? At all?"

"Oh." Sam pauses. "I thought you liked your job."

"I do. But I don't think it's what I want to do forever."

"Well, what do you want to do?"

"I don't know," I say.

Sam traces his finger along my collarbone while my words hang in the air between us. I search his face for signs of what he's thinking, frustrated with myself for, yet again, hoping for Sam's approval.

"What if," he says, then stops. "What if you do move in?"

It's an offer he doesn't want to make. His hesitation proves that. It's the offer of a man who doesn't want to lose me and I can't discredit the sacrifice he's willing to make just to have me close to him but I don't want to be anyone's charity case, especially not his.

"And do what?" I ask.

"Whatever you want. You could take the time to figure it out without any pressure."

"And you would support me?" I ask, incredulous. The proposition is unrealistic. We are not that kind of people. There's nothing traditional about us.

"I could," he says. He pushes his pelvis closer. "We could do *this* whenever we want."

I push him back. I can't fall into his charm. I won't.

"You'll be busy," I argue.

"I'll make time," he says emphatically. "I want to. I told you. I want a different kind of life. I want you to be a part of it."

And it sounds like a great life. But it doesn't sound like my life.

"Are you just asking me to come with you so you can change?" I ask, mumbling against his collarbone, almost hoping he doesn't hear me. I want to ignore all the warning bells going off in my head. I want to be the girl who has her happily-ever-after with the notoriously un-gettable prince.

Sam leans away so I can't hide in him.

"Mallory. I want the kind of future we could have together."

I force myself to be brave, to look into his eyes.

"But do you want me?" I ask. "Do you understand the difference?"

I need to know that if reality doesn't live up to his fantasy, I'm not going to be left broken and alone again. I can't put myself in the position to give up myself to be who he wants me to be. That carefree eighteen-year-old girl he's been searching for is still part of me, but she's not everything I am.

Sam opens his mouth but he can't seem to find the words. I can tell he wants to give me the answer I'm hoping for but he doesn't know what that is. It hurts me to see him so uncertain.

"What do you know about me, Sam?" I ask.

"Who are we, but what we make of ourselves?" he asks.

I snort a laugh. "That's a big philosophical question that means absolutely nothing."

Sam rubs his hand over his forehead, leaving a red mark above his eyebrows. "I don't know what you're asking."

I sit up, pulling the sheet over my chest.

"Come here," he says, trying to pull me closer, but I don't let him.

"Tell me one thing about me that doesn't have to do with marketing or vineyards or horses," I say. Those are interests anyone could pick up from a twenty-minute conversation

343

with me. If I'm going to be with someone, I want it to be the person who knows what scares me, the way I like to be held, just how important my family is to me.

Sam's irises flit around as he racks his brain, but he won't find anything there. Sam has never asked me about my ideas, my thoughts, my preferences. Any conversation we've had has revolved around him. I only realize it now. I used to be okay with that but not anymore. Not for the rest of my life.

I get out of bed, leaving the sheet, no longer embarrassed by whatever imperfections Sam might see. I was never going to fit into his perfect life and we both know it.

"I don't know what you want me to say," Sam says as I pull on my pants.

"I don't want you to say anything," I say. I button my pants and then stop, sighing. "You can't help who you are, Sam."

He doesn't argue the point. He's worked hard to discover that for himself.

"And I can't help who I am," I add. "Whoever that might be. I don't know. But what I do know is that you can't love me until I figure it out."

"Come with me," he urges, moving across the bed toward me. He reaches out for me, but I step back, grabbing my shirt. My body still wants to go to him. I think it always will. "We'll figure it out together."

"No," I say. "We won't. Because if I go with you, I'll become the woman you want. I won't be able to help it. I'll lose myself in you, and maybe I'll be just happy enough with that. But a piece of me will always be missing. There will be an ache of wondering that will never go away. You wouldn't be happy either. You don't want half of me."

Sam drops his hand to the bed.

I pull my shirt over my head, then I lower to my knees

beside him. I place my palm against Sam's chest and feel his heartbeat beneath his skin. His hand covers mine.

"I want to go with you," I say. "And there's a good chance I'll regret this for the rest of my life. But a lot of people, you included, have been telling me to follow my heart. And I think that's what this is."

"You're making a mistake," he says, his stare obstinate and surprised. This time, he won't get what he wants and he doesn't know how to handle it.

"Maybe," I say. "But it's my mistake to make."

His hair falls over his forehead as he lowers his head. He nods.

"I love you, Sam," I whisper. "I have from the moment I first saw you."

I haven't figured out much in my life, but I do know what love feels like. I've been blessed to be surrounded by love my entire life.

Sam looks up at me, but he doesn't say it back. I don't expect him to. The fortune-teller was wrong about that. Sam still isn't ready to love. I hope, for his sake, that one day he will be.

"Go live that life you're picturing," I say. "It sounds amazing."

When my fingers slip through Sam's, a piece of my heart stays with him. I grab my shoes and before I leave, I look back at him. He gives me a small smile that tears at my insides.

When I close the door behind me, I can't imagine how I was strong enough to get on this side of it, but I know I can't go back. I clutch my chest to hold myself together and will myself to take another step forward. When I do, I look up, and Tyler is standing on the path, his jaw and fists clenched, his gaze boring straight through me.

"Wow," is all he says as he tosses the bucket in his hand. I startle as it clatters to the ground.

TWENTY-EIGHT

*W*hen Tyler shows up to feed the horses the following morning, I'm in the stables waiting for him. I spent most of my last night here trying to decide if I was angry with him for his reaction, for storming off. I finally decided I wasn't. I'm not mad at him. He's one of my best friends because he cares. Because he isn't afraid to tell me when I'm being stupid. I know he only wants me to be happy.

He comes in whistling, making me smile. Nothing ever rattles Tyler for long. I admire that about him. When he sees me leaning against a saddle stand in the tack room, though, he stops, unsure, like I am, of where we stand.

"I'm sorry," I say, cutting right to the chase. I'm not waiting a decade this time to let my friends know how much they mean to me.

He flips his keys over into his palm and shoves them into his pocket.

"You don't have to apologize," Tyler says, though his tone says otherwise. "You don't owe me anything."

"Actually, I do," I say, pushing myself to standing. "I owe you a lot. You're the only person who has ever supported me without any expectations of your own."

Tyler lets out a dry laugh. "If that were true, I probably wouldn't be so pissed right now."

I shrug, giving him that. If Tyler has had expectations of me, though, they've always been aligned with the ones I have for myself. That's probably why I never felt pressured by them.

"Last week, you said you knew me better than I knew myself," I say, stepping closer to him.

He rolls his eyes, maybe sheepish over his presumptuousness, maybe doubting whether he still believes it after yesterday.

"What do you know about me?" I ask him.

"I don't want to play games, Mal."

"C'mon," I say. "Humor me."

Tyler sighs, wandering over to the halters. He inspects them instead of me. Then again, there's a lot of me to be found in this room.

He sighs again.

"I know you hate mice," he says, giving in. "You're like an elephant. If you even hear the squeak of a chair, you're climbing up the closest thing you can find."

It's such an unexpected answer, I laugh. But it's true.

There was a time, I remember, when Tyler was the closest thing to me. He ran me out of the house, piggyback, until Dad caught the offending chew toy Dad's best friends had left behind from their visit with their incredibly yappy Yorkie.

"Okay," I say. "What else?"

Tyler turns to lean against the saddle stand on the other side of the room. His smile, though reserved, has returned.

"I know you have terrible taste in headwear," he says.

I narrow my eyes and point a determined finger at him. "It's happening. Prepare yourself."

Tyler's eyes light up with humor, and a little bit of the weight lifts from my heart. Maybe he'll forgive me for not knowing myself the way I should and making mistakes with Sam all over again. Maybe he'll forgive me for not taking his advice the first time.

"I know that you would do anything for someone you care about," he says more seriously.

I hum a tone of agreement. "That's been my problem all along, hasn't it?"

"I don't see it that way," he says. "It's a rare trait and I think it's something to be treasured."

"But it's gotten me so far off track."

"That's part of the journey. Usually the best part."

Only Tyler could make me feel better when it's him that I've hurt.

"Sometimes it leads you to bad choices," I say.

But no matter what happens, I don't regret being with Sam. I can't. Now I know what we could have had. Now I know for sure that it wouldn't have worked.

I also know that I can fall in love and that heartbreak doesn't have to be the end of my story.

"I shouldn't have reacted like that," Tyler says. "I know how much he means to you. I know what you've gone through. It's only natural."

Even though he's trying to be supportive, I can see it pains him.

"I wish I could tell you it turned out differently than it did last time," I say. "Well, this time we did say goodbye."

Tyler frowns and slowly closes the small space between us. He takes my hand and briefly, I observe how different it is from Sam's. Tyler and I have never touched each other this way before and I'm surprised at how at home it feels—not electric, but right.

"I'm sorry, Mal."

I'm sorry, too, but I don't feel as sad as I thought I would. I know I made the right decision, for once.

He lets go of my hand and it feels empty without him.

"So what now?" he asks.

"I can't go back to New York," I say.

He nods, like he expected this. He does know me. "Your parents will be glad to have you back."

I shake my head. "I don't think I can stay here either."

At this, he raises an eyebrow.

"I love this place," I say. "It will always be my home. But it's my dad's dream. Not mine."

"So what is your dream?"

I shrug. "I guess I'll have to figure that out."

"You know," Tyler says, pulling a halter off a hook and tossing it to me, "the offer to come visit me in Montana still stands."

I sit on my bed and stare at my riding boots. The brown leather. The worn toe. The symbol that used to represent who I was—simple, reliable, warm. I let something someone once said to me make me forget who I was. I let him make me feel like I wasn't enough. I tried to be who I thought he wanted me to be and in the process, I lost everything.

Then again, I chose that. I was the one who stepped out of those shoes and walked away.

I grab the boots from the corner and, one at a time, pull them onto my socked feet. I place them side by side, touching, and examine them. They feel like me—a little foreign, the leather a little tight, but still me.

"They look good on you," Kelly says from the doorway. I look up at her. "I thought you got rid of those. I can't believe they're still in one piece."

"Tell that to my toe," I say, wiggling it against the thinned leather. She smiles.

"It's nice to see you wearing them again."

"Thanks. I guess, no matter how hard I try, I'll always be riding boots," I say. "And Sam will always be dress shoes."

"Tyler told me," she says. "I'm sorry. How are you feeling?"

"Directionless. But that's always been where I'm happiest."

Kelly comes into the room. Her hair is loose today and she's wearing black again. I'm finding my way back to who I once was and Kelly is finding someone new entirely.

"You must be going somewhere," she says. "You're packed."

I look to the suitcase in the corner. It's overflowing, the clothes I've taken from my dresser—the ones I feel more comfortable in—stacked on top of my work clothes.

"New York?" she asks.

"For now," I say. "I have to go buy an inordinate amount of expensive shoes to try to bribe my boss into not hating me."

"I'm sure she'll forgive you."

Kelly leans over to look at the framed pictures lining my dresser, most of them of the two of us.

"For leaving?" I say. "Not likely."

Kelly straightens. "You're quitting?"

I nod.

"Wow." She pauses, soaking that in. "What are you going to do?"

I get up and go to my suitcase, reorganizing my clothes so I can get the zipper closed. "First, I'll need to pack up my apartment. And see if I can break my lease."

Kelly organizes the printed emails from my office into a neat pile and hands them to me. "What if you sublet it?" she asks.

"Maybe," I say. "But trying to find someone would probably be a pain in the ass."

"Maybe not," she says. "Actually, I think I know someone who might be interested."

"Really?" I zip the paperwork into the top pocket and turn to her. "Who?"

A grin spreads across her face.

"No way," I gasp. "You're going to New York?"

She nods, laughing.

"I'm going to sell the house," she says. "I won't get much for it, but between that and the money Mom left me, I should be able to supplement my barista income."

I want to go to her, to wrap my arms around her and tell her how excited and proud I am. But I'm too overcome with emotions. It's even more than her mom hoped for her. It's her dream come true and exactly what she deserves.

"I'm so happy for you," I say.

"Thank you," she says. "And thank you for introducing me to Anna. Spending time with her yesterday…it reminded me how much I love listening to people, and supporting them. I called Jasmine. Do you remember her from school? She had a baby six months ago and she said she'd love to walk with Anna. I think they'll make a great match."

"Perfect," I say.

Kelly sits next to me on the floor.

"That fortune-teller was right about at least one thing," she says. "You do inspire me to be more."

She takes my wrist and grasps it so our tattoos are facing each other. I trace her horse with my fingertip, its mane blowing wildly.

"I've been missing your focus," I say. "I need it."

"You have it. No matter where you go or what you decide to do, I'm always here for you."

"I don't think you need me to push you toward adventure anymore," I say. "You're doing pretty great on your own."

She laughs. "I always need you, Mal."

I smile, hoping that's true.

"Where will you go after New York?" she asks.

I clear my throat. "I'm going with Tyler to Montana," I say with feigned nonchalance. "We're going to meet there in a month."

"Oh," she says. "I did not see that coming."

I stand and resume packing.

"Yeah, me neither. He's going to be starting a horse ranch with his uncle and he's going to need some help getting it up and running. Tyler feels like he has enough saved to get started and I'll contribute as much as I can. I don't know how long I'll stay, but with everything I know about managing the vineyard, I should be able to help a little."

From my nightstand, I pick up the plastic toy horse Tyler gave me.

"You know he's in love with you, right?" she asks.

"It's not like that," I say.

The skin on my chest flushes. I study the horse intently. Somewhere deep inside me, she's putting words to a feeling I've always known was true but wasn't ready to hear. I still don't know if I am.

"It is for him." She crosses the room and takes the horse from my hands so I have to look at her. "That's why things never went anywhere with him and me," she says. "We went out for months and even though you'd been gone for years, all he could talk about...was you."

The words of the fortune-teller come back to me.

He's been watching you since you were a girl. He doesn't feel worthy of you. He wants to tell you, but he feels it's too late.

"I'm sorry," I say. It's another thing Kelly wanted that I took for granted. I never meant to come between them. I would have stepped aside if I'd known I was in the way.

Kelly shakes her head. "Don't apologize, Mallory. He was never mine."

"I don't know what's going to happen," I say, fumbling through my words. "That's the point. I need, for a little while, to not have a plan."

"I think he'll wait as long as you need," she says, handing me back the horse. "He's been waiting a long time already."

Sam leaves early the next morning. He sends his final good-byes through my dad, which I'm grateful for. We've already said everything there is to say to each other. He's headed to LA, where he'll close that deal and check all his goals off his list. He'll live a picture-perfect life, and I truly hope he finds a woman who fits in next to him.

After breakfast, I take Midnight for a ride. I soak in every moment of it. I promise her, as much as myself, that I will be back soon. No matter where my whimsical heart takes me, I will always find my way back home.

The morning breeze is cool as I load my suitcase into the back of the rental car. I close the trunk and take a moment to appreciate the view. I've always loved this vineyard, for many reasons. It's where I grew up, and where my parents are, yes. But it's also where I've learned so much about life. Memories have been made on every inch of these many acres. Most of them happy. All of them meaningful.

The crunch of gravel alerts me to the arrival of my farewell party. Dad holds Mom's hand, Kelly tucked in next to them. Tyler trails a few steps behind.

Dad hugs me first and I rest my head on his shoulder, like I've done millions of times.

"I love you, Dad," I say, my voice watery. "Damn it. We're just getting started and I'm already crying."

I pull away and wipe at my tears. Dad places a hand on one of my cheeks, a kiss on the other.

"I love you, sweetie. Let me know if you need any help packing up your apartment. I'm sure the grapes can live without me for a couple of days."

"The question is whether you can live without the grapes," I say, and he grins.

Mom is next. "I hate saying goodbye," she says, pulling me into a hug.

"It won't be for long. Montana is much closer than New York. You're going to get tired of me, I swear."

"Not possible," she says.

I pull the envelope of cash out of my back pocket and hold it out to her in the privacy between us so Dad won't see.

"Take this," I tell her. "Use it to hold you guys over until you figure out what you're going to do."

She pushes the money back toward me. "Honey, no. That's yours. You take that and use it for your new life. That's why we gave it to you."

"But—"

"I'll find another job," she assures me.

I smile, sliding the money back into my pocket.

When Mom steps away, Tyler is standing behind her with a timid grin. I suddenly don't know how to look at him.

"One month," I say, trying to be the way I've always been with Tyler. I know we'll find our old rhythm when we get to Montana but the shift in our relationship is still too fresh. He seems to sense it, too.

"I'll send you pictures when I get there. Just in case you think about changing your mind."

"Not a chance," I say.

"Well…" He does an awkward bob of his head, then gives me a quick pat on the back.

Kelly comes up to me and places her hands on my shoulders. Together, we exhale deeply, finding our peace in each other. Kelly always has been and always will be my other half.

"Thank you," she says.

"For what?"

"For not forgetting us. For not giving up on me."

"That's what friends are for," I say.

"Sisters," she says. "That's what sisters are for."

I pull her to me and hold her tighter than I ever have. When I step back, I can hardly look at her. We're going to be on opposite sides of the country, but this time, our love will never be too far away.

"Let me know when you sell the house," I say.

"I will," she says. She squeezes my hand one last time, then lets me go.

When I look up, I see so much love in the eyes of the people who have seen me at my best and my worst and have loved me anyway. Whoever I might be. I give them a final wave, get into the car, and set off to find out.

★ ★ ★ ★ ★

ACKNOWLEDGMENTS

Always, I have to thank my family first and foremost. To my amazing husband, thank you for keeping our real life running so I can live in my fantasy worlds. I'm grateful every day that you support my art in every way possible, especially the late-night kitchen brainstorming sessions. You are seriously the best. My girls—you are my joy and my inspiration. Also, my biggest fans and best publicists. Thank you for being proud of Mommy.

Thank you to my amazing agent, Claire Anderson-Wheeler, who breathes life into the less developed parts of my stories. They are so much better for it.

To my editor, Allison Carroll—thank you for always believing in me and making me feel capable. I couldn't ask for a better supporter. A big thanks to the entire Graydon House/ Harlequin team, as well. Thank you for being excited about my stories and championing them every step of the way.

Many thanks to Shawna for brainstorming so much of this story with me over these many, many years, and for constantly asking to read it. You've been waiting a long time for this one—I hope you love it!

Deborah, thank you for suggesting the setting that finally brought this book together. It blossomed into something so much bigger than I imagined, and I couldn't be happier. Let's go visit!

Thank you to James and Peggy for always being willing to lend a hand. I could not live my dream without you guys, and I'm endlessly thankful for your support.

Dad, thank you for making my childhood an adventure and for forcing my books on everyone you meet. If I'm successful, it will be your doing.

To my writers' group—there are just no words to express how much you all mean to me and how much you keep me going. I hope Wednesdays will be ours for decades to come.

Last, but not least, I want to say a huge thanks to all my sisters—the one I grew up with (I love you, Sarah!), and the ones I've adopted for myself. Aimie, Alyson, Amanda, Amy, Bubble, Deborah, Eleanore, Erika, Gina, Riki, Selena, Shawna, and Victoria—you make my life whole. You make me the best version of myself. I love you.

MIDNIGHT AT THE WANDERING VINEYARD

JAMIE RAINTREE

Reader's Guide

GRAYDON
HOUSE

1. What was your favorite bucket-list item Mallory and Kelly completed? If you had a summer bucket list, what would be on it?

2. What did you think of The Wandering Vineyard? Have you ever visited a vineyard? What was the experience like?

3. Did you connect with Mallory's free-spirited nature? Why or why not?

4. How did you feel about Mallory and Kelly's friendship? What are your thoughts on how their friendship evolved?

5. Do you think it was fair of Kelly to hold a grudge against Mallory for the choices she made in the past? Do you think it was right for Mallory to be so willing to forgive Kelly's secrets that summer?

6. Do you find adult friendships to be different than childhood friendships? In what ways?

7. How do you feel about the way Sam interacted with Mallory, both in the past and present? Was Mallory truly

duped by Sam in the past or was she willfully ignorant of his signals that he wasn't ready for a relationship?

8. Do you have any sympathy for Sam, either in the past or the present? Why or why not?

9. What do you think of Mallory's ultimate decision not to pursue a relationship with Sam? Do you think she made the right choice?

10. What do you think Mallory will do next? Do you think she'll open up to a relationship with Tyler?

11. What wine would/did you pair with reading *Midnight at the Wandering Vineyard*?